Lou in the
Limelight

BY KRISTIN HUNTER

The Soul Brothers and Sister Lou
Guests in the Promised Land
Boss Cat

God Bless the Child
The Landlord
The Survivors
The Lakestown Rebellion

Lou in the Limelight

A SEQUEL TO *THE SOUL BROTHERS AND SISTER LOU*

BY
KRISTIN HUNTER

Charles Scribner's Sons

NEW YORK

For all the young people
who wanted to know
what happened next.

CHAPTER 1

"Come on, Lou. Let's try it one more time. Just one more time for me, baby," Marty Ross coaxed, purring into her ear.

Louretta tried to swallow and found she couldn't. "May I have a glass of water, please?" It came out as a cross between a croak and a whisper. Her voice had cracked on the last cut of their all-day recording session. Now she had no voice at all.

"Let's move it along. Move it, move it!" urged Fred Marcus, the vice-president of Jewel Records, pacing the floor of the studio and banging his palm with his fist. With his silver hair, gray eyes, and silver suit, he looked like newly minted money. Which was, apparently, all he ever thought about. "You know what those musicians are costing us by the hour? A hundred twenty-five apiece, and you've been here since eight this morning."

It was now four in the afternoon, eight hours and seven cuts later.

"Let me handle my artists, Marcus. I have to give this little girl everything she needs. She's worth it."

"I'll believe it when I see it on the charts, Marty."

"You," Marty told him, "have all the tender loving feelings of a snapping turtle."

Feeling, as he often said himself, was the main ingredient of Marty's personality. He responded emotionally to the soulful quality of The Soul Brothers and Sister Lou's music. His feelings had made him decide against his better judgment to represent a group of unknown singers. He shared their sufferings and felt their sorrows. He cried a lot for the plight of poor people, black people, and humanity in general. "I can't help it," he would say when he cried. "I'm just a very feeling person."

Usually, though, Marty was smiling, as he was now, trotting across the studio to bring Lou a glass of liquid and two of the tiny licorice throat lozenges. The smile put a dimple in each of his apple cheeks. He had a pink cherub's face, an Afro curlier than any of theirs, and a special talent: the ability to cheer up every member of the group and make each of them feel like the most important person in the world—to Marty Ross.

His hands, like his eyes, were moist. "Put these in your mouth, dear. That's right, under the tongue. Tired? Let me rub your neck." Marty's fingers were like fat pink sausages. He couldn't play any instrument, but he gave great neck rubs.

"The session was fabulous, Lou. Every cut was a winner except that last one. Just run through it one more time, and we can wrap it up."

The neck rub was relaxing. She could also feel his warm breath on her neck. Smell it, too. He chewed spearmint, a flavor Lou disliked. "I don't think I can do it, Marty."

"Shhhh. Don't talk. Rest your voice a minute. Let me spray your throat." She opened her mouth and let him squirt her tonsils with the awful-tasting anesthetic. "Sure you can do it, Lou. You're the toughest little trouper I've ever seen, and I've seen plenty. I think you ought to take one of these for energy."

She looked suspiciously at the green pill he held out to her. Marty was a walking medicine cabinet; every pocket of his suits seemed filled with pills, sprays, lozenges, and capsules.

"What is it?"

"Just a vitamin, dear."

"Oh." She tried to swallow the pill with a sip of the orange juice Marty had brought her instead of water, but choked on it and splattered it on his snowy white shirt. "What's in this orange juice, Marty?"

"More vitamins," Marty muttered, frowning and dabbing at his shirt. He was fastidiously clean, often changing shirts three times a day. "Now look what you've done."

"It's *gin!*" Lou announced to the world. "I thought I could trust you, Marty."

"Shhhh. Don't tell everybody everything I do for you. Don't give away my trade secrets, hmmmm? Of course you can trust me. It's a proven fact orange juice contains more vitamins than water. And the gin will help relax your throat."

Lou ventured another sip. "It tastes worse than the spray."

"It's an acquired taste; you'll learn to like it. A little relaxation never hurt anybody. Trust me. I look after you better than your own mother."

All of Momma's stern rules and warnings came to Lou's mind at once. She held out the glass. "I asked for plain water, and that's all I want."

"Oh, all right," Marty said, still angrily inspecting his shirt. "I try to help, and this is my thanks. You don't need my help anyway. Whoever heard of a weak *black* girl?"

That did it. Lou tossed the rest of her drink against Marty's chest and watched it splash, spread, and soak in. The pink softness of his face hardened into porcelain; faint cracks appeared around his eyes and mouth, making him look, suddenly, like an old, ugly doll. "Drop the temperament, kiddo," he said. "You're not a star yet. One more performance like that, and you never will be."

Oh, yes, I will, Lou thought defiantly. She was very, very good, and she knew it, even though this fast-paced, exhausting recording session had caused her to falter and doubt herself. Her voice, stronger than most adults', had a range of over three octaves, and she was normally in complete command of its expressiveness and power. She could command an audience, too, thrilling it to excitement or stunning it into silence.

"You were going to change that shirt anyway," Lou said in a voice that anger had restored to normal.

Marty turned his back and said to the lean, restless Jewel Records executive, "All right, Marcus, she's ready. As ready as she'll ever be." Without looking back, he strode off and left her alone in front of the mike. Since this cut was to be a solo, the wall of warmth around her that was usually provided by Frank, David, and Ulysses was missing. With Marty gone, too, she felt the vast chill of the studio and her small loneliness in it like a person flung into outer space.

Love thump thump
Oh love thumpa thump
Oh careless love
Thumpa thump thump thump

went the instruments in a rhumba rhythm. The song had been chosen mainly because it was so old that no royalties had to be paid for it.

Twang twang brrrittt

went the electric guitar, a scary outer-space sound, far more complicated than Blind Eddie Bell's simple acoustic guitar accompaniments at their rehearsals.

"Once I wore my apron low,
Once I wore my apron low"

The rhythm track—piano, drums, electric bass, and guitar—rumbled and rippled at $125 an hour apiece. The recording company was advancing the money to pay them, but it would have to be paid back out of The Soul Brothers and Sister Lou's earnings.

"You followed me through rain and snow."

High in his glass enclosure, the sound-mixer listened through his earphones and twiddled his dials. Next to him, the recording engineer gave the sharp hand signal that meant "cut." Lou, numb with fatigue, had no idea whether she had sung badly or well.

But then she saw the producer raise his hand, thumb and forefinger joined in a circle, to the sound-mixer, who returned the signal. And Marty appeared in a fresh white shirt, beaming and applauding.

He was pleased! He wasn't angry anymore. Lou felt a rush of relief and elation. For all Marty's faults, and she was beginning to suspect that he had many, his enthusiasm was the only force that had kept them going all year through the long hours of hard rehearsals and poorly paid or free appearances to get them "exposure," when they wanted to be having fun like all the other teenagers. His encouragement had allowed her to withstand Momma's disapproval of "Devil music" and her late hours and her teachers' complaints about the many classes she'd missed. She'd just had a taste of how she felt without Marty's support. Small, helpless, and lost.

"You did it, kids! You did it! A solid gold winner!" Marty exclaimed, bouncing and glowing. Lou felt like embracing him, but his wife Gloria, a silent blonde whose primary function seemed to be supplying him with freshly laundered shirts, might not like that. Instead, The Soul Brothers and Sister Lou embraced one another. Wide, jovial Ulysses wrapped her in a bear hug. Tall, gangly David tried to kiss Lou's cheek, missed it by at least a foot, and smacked Frank's instead. The shorter boy made a face. "You must be gettin' desperate, Hoss. Keep your jibs off me. I don't want to catch the ugly disease." But it was all in fun for that brief, glorious moment.

Big Mouth Carrington, the disc jockey who had started all this with his constant plays of their single, "Lament for Jethro," floated up to them like a helium-filled balloon and shook each of their hands. "Congratulations, Miss Hawkins; congratulations, young men," he said in the soft, polite voice that contrasted so sharply with his glib on-the-air patter. "I heard the whole session. I think you've got a winner here. I just hope you can keep your heads on straight from now on. This is a crazy business. I wish you good sense. I'd wish you good luck, but I don't think you need it."

"Maybe so, maybe not," the record executive said. "It all depends. If we get enough air plays—"

"Mr. Marcus," Big Mouth interrupted gently, "they're already getting plenty of air plays. I've seen to that."

"I mean *national* air plays, Carrington. Your little local show helps, no doubt about it, but let's be realistic."

Offended, Big Mouth wheeled and moved away with incredible speed for such a huge man. Marcus ran to catch him, but the disc jockey was gone. "Omigod, what a goof," he exclaimed. "Lester," he said to one of his assistants, "send him a letter of apology. No, a telegram, and a dozen of those Texas steaks, and a gift certificate to that new French restaurant. What's it called? *Truffes?* Dinner for two. He'll eat both."

"Mr. Marcus, I don't think Big Mouth would like that," Lou said.

"Why not? There's nothing he likes better than food."

"But he played our record for nothing. He played it because he liked it. If you send him gifts, he might feel insulted."

"That just shows how much you have to learn, young lady. Show her the receipts for the steaks we already sent Carrington, will you, Lester?"

The evidence was placed in front of her eyes. Three bills, each for a dozen steaks shipped from a ranch in Texas to Mr. Roy Carrington, each for a hundred dollars.

"Of course, Mr. Ross advanced us half the money. I must say, he has a great deal of faith in you young people."

"See how many things I do for you?" Marty asked rhetorically. "Half of them you don't even know about. No wonder I get no appreciation."

Lou's head was spinning with confusion and exhaustion. She was grateful for the shabby, familiar form of Blind Eddie Bell, tapping his way toward them.

"How'd you like the session, Eddie?" Mr. Marcus asked.

"Fine, except for that last arrangement," said the old musician who had taught the group everything they knew.

"What was wrong with it?" Marcus demanded.

"It wasn't respectful. 'Careless Love' is a sad old, serious ballad. That Spanish jump arrangement wasn't fitting. People ought to respect old things."

"You're behind the times, old man," Marty said rudely. "Young kids buy records, and they want stuff they can dance to."

"I don't care what they want, it was wrong. *Sinful* wrong," Eddie said. "And those fancy new wired-up instruments, they took away from the singing."

"I wish he'd shut up. Who invited him here, anyway?" Marty muttered.

"Why don't you speak to the arranger, Eddie?" Marcus said genially. "I'm sure he'll appreciate your suggestions." He put an arm around Blind Eddie's shoulders and turned him toward the empty bandstand. "Go ahead. He's right over there with the musicians."

Lou watched, appalled, as her old friend started off confidently toward the bandstand, paused uncertainly when he reached it, and began tapping his white cane in ever-widening circles, trying to find the arranger who had never been there and the musicians who were no longer there. The photographer had already taken their place and was setting up his equipment.

Marcus and Marty did not even try to hold back their laughter. It bounced across the studio and came back to them.

"Eddie's right," Frank said, with a fierce look at the white men. "People ought to respect old things." He loped quickly to the old man's side, talked to him softly, and led him back to the dressing rooms.

"Wasn't Eddie one of your first stars?" Louretta asked Marcus.

"That's ancient history. In this business, we have to move with the times and think young." *Respect old things and old people,* Lou thought. It was something she had been taught all her life. She said nothing, but raised her eyes and stared long and pointedly at his gray, thinning hair.

Marty, clapping his hands briskly, broke up the silence. "All right, gang, it's time to change for the cover shot. Be dressed and back out here in ten"—he glanced at his watch—"no, make it five minutes. Move it, now! On the double!"

Like an energetic sheepdog, he herded them toward the dressing rooms.

"What's the rush?" Ulysses complained. "Why must everything be done in such a hurry?"

"We only have the studio for today," Marty explained as he bounced along beside them, three steps to their one. "We're supposed to be out by five o'clock. We stay any longer, we run into overtime. And the overhead on this place is a monster."

"Why? They don't heat it," Lou commented. Her sore throat had returned, and she was beginning to suspect a cold coming on. "They don't clean it, either."

"So take a hot shower. But hurry it up. Remember, the photographer gets paid by the hour too."

Lou stubbornly continued to take her time walking toward the dressing room. Marty doubled around behind her and gave her a smack on the rear. "I said, speed it up, Miss!"

She looked at him in shocked anger and fled into the women's dressing room before tears could overwhelm her. She took a long, luxurious shower—the first private one of her life. At the school gym, the girls used open showers, and at home, her family only had an old-fashioned showerless tub.

As she reluctantly reached to turn off the water she heard a frantic banging on the door and then Marty's voice. "Lou! Lou! Move it on out of there! You're holding up the shot. Everybody else is in place!"

Shining with wetness, her hair a wild damp tangle, she opened the door partway with nothing between her and Marty but a large towel. Behind Marty, the tall photographer raised his camera and started snapping. She slammed the door, but not before he had clicked his shutter several times.

Lou got into her dress quickly. She didn't like this clingy, skimpy dress, but Marty had picked it out for her to match the satin jumpsuits the fellows would pose in. It was ready-made, which saved money, even though it was too small. Marty never stopped reminding them of the need to cut corners and of how much money he was risking on them on the chance that their future earnings would more than repay him.

"I want those pictures," she told the photographer when she came out in the shiny purple dress and the matching purple high-heeled shoes. A makeup artist pushed her roughly onto a stool and quickly teased her hair into a ten-inch bush, brushed her face with powder, pasted extra eyelashes on top of her already thick ones, and put more purple on her lids and lips.

"What pictures, dolly? I don't have any pictures. And I won't have any unless you get into the pose," the photographer said.

"Don't worry, I'll take care of this guy," Marty said. "Go smile for the birdie."

Too weary to argue, Lou took his word and got into the position chalked for her on the floor—lying on her side, one hand propping up her chin, one hip arched until the wrap skirt fell away to reveal most of a thigh. Behind her, in a lime overall, Frank struck the same pose facing the opposite direction. David and Ulysses, in red and blue overalls, knelt at either end, hands on one another's shoulders.

"You guys on the ends, get your heads level," the photographer ordered. "The tall one's head is too high."

They tried to make the adjustment and lost their balance, making the entire pyramid collapse.

"What are we, singers or acrobats?" David wanted to know.

"You're performers," Marty said sternly. "You do it all, and you do it on schedule."

Wearily, they rearranged themselves in the awkward pose.

"That's the ticket," the photographer approved. "Show the pearlies, girlie. Smile! This is your big day."

Lou gave him a stretched grin that would look natural only on a jack-o-lantern. But the photographer seemed satisfied. He snapped at least two dozen pictures while the floodlights burned her eyes and her eyes burned anger at the camera. Then the room went suddenly dark and blue and orange spots danced before her.

"Done," the photographer pronounced.

"One minute to five," Marty declared, herding them to the door. "We just made it. Meet me at the old Tiara Theater tomorrow morning at eight."

"But tomorrow's Sunday!" Lou protested.

"When else can we rehearse? Every other day's a school day. I must be out of my mind, working with school kids.—Oh, yeah, before I forget." He pulled a roll of documents from his inside coat pocket and passed them out. "Take these home and get a parent to sign them."

"My mother says I need a lawyer," David said.

"So does my father," Frank added.

"Tell them," Marty countered, stepping into his long pink car, "that I *am* a lawyer."

Marty drove off, leaving The Soul Brothers and Sister Lou to walk home through the shabby streets they'd grown up in. Walking along the Avenue with its many faceless, boarded-up buildings, they paused, by habit, at the old storefront church that Lou's brother William had turned into a printing shop. At Lou's urging, William had let them use part of the building for a clubhouse where they held dances and published a newspaper and practiced singing at the old piano the church had left behind. One of their dances had ended in tragedy, though—a police raid and the fatal shooting of their friend Jethro Jackson. The clubhouse had never been as attractive to them after that. But the song they'd written about Jethro's life and death had become a hit record and led to their frantic new life as budding professional singers. Jethro had left a hollow space in the group that Lou had filled, but no one could ever really replace him. It had been two years since Jethro's funeral, but they still missed him.

The November wind blew trash along the sidewalk and chilled them through their thin coats. They started walking homeward again.

"Did you guys believe Marty when he said he was a lawyer?" asked David, the youngest of the foursome.

"Why not?" Ulysses said. "He's a promoter and an accountant. I guess he can be a lawyer, too."

"He's a doctor, too, don't forget," Lou said. "He has a cure for everything."

"And he passes out the cures. Which makes him a druggist, too," Frank said.

"He told me today he was a mother," Lou added.

"Now *that,*" Frank said, "is something you can believe."

CHAPTER 2

Momma grabbed Louretta the instant she walked into the house, dragged her to the kitchen, and scrubbed her face roughly with a dishrag. Not even a washcloth—a sour, filthy dishrag and the old-fashioned brown lye soap Momma bought God only knew where. Throughout this humiliating procedure Louretta's mother kept up a stream of angry accusations:

"You don't look like my child. You look like a streetwalker. For all I know, you *are* a streetwalker. Never know what time you're coming home, and when you do, you strut in here looking like a harlot of Babylon!"

"Bubb—" The dishrag stopped Louretta's explanation. Not that Momma would have understood anyway. Not that she would have even listened.

Since Lou's singing had begun to take up most of her time, Momma's initial pride in her accomplishments had soured to disapproval. She wanted Lou in school every day, and she wanted her at home all the rest of the time to help with the house and the younger children. She'd let Lou's older sister Arneatha sail off to California again as lightly as a balloon—but then, Arneatha had always been flighty anyway. Lou and William, the eldest, were supposed to be the serious, dependable ones. Lou suspected that Momma didn't want either of them to become independent because she wanted to keep them both at home to help her—forever.

"Shut your fresh mouth before I use some Brillo on it! You've got enough paint on you to cover a wall. And false eyelashes too!" Momma ripped them off with an ungentle hand. "What's wrong with the ones the good Lord gave you?"

It was so unfair. But Lou was determined not to cry. She tightened her jaw. "I'm not a little girl anymore, Momma."

"Do I have to put you cross my knee to prove who's big around here and who isn't?"

"No ma'am," Louretta said with automatic respect.

"I don't care if it is your birthday! I won't have you running the streets all hours of the day and night and looking like a tramp and never telling anybody when you'll be home."

Louretta needed no dishrag to silence her now. She'd forgotten her own birthday!

Momma knew it. "So busy running with the Devil and singing his music you forgot your own birthday, didn't you? Well, some other people remembered. Look there!"

Momma turned Lou with a rough push so she could look at the kitchen table. It was littered with crumbs and other items: a small stack of cards and packages, some crumpled party favors, soggy paper plates with melted ice cream, and about a third of a cake with part of an inscription still on it:

—etta
Sweet 16

Disappointment probably .accounted for at least part of Momma's anger. She'd gone to all of this trouble, and Lou hadn't even shown up. But, like the remains of any party, these were depressing and pathetic. Worse, they were all wrong: it had been an eight year old's birthday party, not a sixteen year old's.

"I *hate* birthdays!" she screamed, her eyes filling with hot, angry tears.

"You *what?* Well, if that's all the thanks I get you can be sure I'll never have another party for you, Miss. I baked that cake for you myself. Tried to keep your brothers and sisters from eating it before you got here. Now I'm glad they did."

"I'm sorry, Momma," Louretta said, the storm spent, contriteness setting in. "But why didn't you tell me?"

"It was a *surprise!*" Momma's rage was far from over.

"Oh."

"The whole family was here, and a few of your friends, too. That young lady teacher who thinks so much of you, and that boy you like so much—Calvin. I don't think either of them will be back any time soon. I had to tell them, 'That girl's gotten so womanish, I never know when she'll be home. I'm not even sure she lives here anymore.'"

Louretta was not exactly sorry she'd missed Miss Hodges. She didn't want to have to explain her many school absences to the kind English teacher. How could she say that school was dull compared to the excitement of cutting a record album? That would be an insult to Miss Hodges's standards.

Calvin was a different matter—someone she *did* want to see. The way he had of looking mean when he was being sweet, and of disappearing when he even suspected his feelings were about to be hurt—everything about him was very difficult, but very special. His feelings had surely been hurt today. Momma was probably right—he wouldn't be back for a long time, if ever. He was a gifted artist, with all the temperament that was supposed to go along with it. So much temperament that keeping Calvin around would be like having a tiger in the house. And yet, Lou wanted him around. Oh, when she thought about it, *how* she wanted him around. She hadn't had time to think about it much lately, though.

"You didn't have to tell them that, Momma," she said.

"Well, it's the truth, ain't it? You weren't here yesterday, or the day before. Bet you don't even know what day that was, either."

Louretta strained her memory through the hectic blur of rehearsals and recording sessions. "Day before yesterday . . . I know I had the day off from school," she began hesitantly. "Was it a holiday?"

"According to your teacher, you've had a lot of days off from school lately. Yes, of course Thursday was a holiday, fool! *Thanksgiving!* You weren't even here to thank the Lord for your blessings."

14 Come to think of it, Thanksgiving had been on everyone's mind at school—except Louretta's. She had been too busy rehearsing to remember it. Besides, she was beginning to question a lot of things. Like why her family insisted on observing all the national holidays. Why they had cookouts in the park on Memorial Day (in memory of what?) and firecrackers on Independence Day (celebrating independence from what?). And why did they commemorate Thanksgiving? Poor and black as they were, what did they have to be so thankful for?

"Why do we make such a big deal out of Thanksgiving, Momma?" she questioned. "We didn't come over on the *Mayflower.* We came over on slave ships."

Momma reacted with instantaneous fury. "You talk like a Communist. Come back here and let me scrub the rest of that mess off your face."

Louretta retreated. "I can wash my own face, thank you." Lately her mother needed to be reminded of things like that.

"Well, make sure you get all that mess off!" Momma shouted as Louretta moved away. "Throw that hussy dress in the trash, and come back down here in something decent.

"You used to be so smart and serious," her mother continued sadly. "You were the one I expected the most out of. Now you're so mixed up you don't even know when Thanksgiving is or *why* it is. I give up on you, Louretta. I'm gonna turn you over to the Lord and let Him handle you from now on."

Good, Louretta thought as she climbed upstairs. Let the Lord listen to her mother's angry lectures for a while. She didn't want to hear any more of them. She was angry, humiliated, frustrated, sad—feeling just about every negative emotion anybody could name. She was exhausted. Plus she was sure now she felt a cold coming on.

Having to wait nearly an hour for her little brothers Andrew, Gordon, and Randolph to get out of the bathroom, and then having to clean up the mess they had left before she could use it, tripled Louretta's frustration. When she started her bath running and went for her robe and came back to find her eight-year-old twin sisters, Bernice and Clarice, waiting outside with their towels, she simply shoved them aside, went on in, and locked the door.

Saturday night is still N.N.B.N. in this house, she thought. National Negro Bath Night. Old-fashioned and dumb. Like everything else around here. Including Thanksgiving dinners, and the old-fashioned tub with no shower, and the flaking, bulging plaster bathroom ceiling, and ice-cream-and-cake birthday parties. After the boys' baths (*why* couldn't some of them bathe on other nights?) there was no hot water. She had hoped for a long hot soak to dissolve her anger, but had to settle for a quick cold soap-and-rinse instead.

And there was no toothpaste.

Someday, she promised herself, I'll have *cases* of toothpaste. Cartons of fine perfumed soap. Piles of thick new towels. And a bathroom all my own to use whenever I feel like it. There was no law against bathing on Sundays, Mondays, Tuesdays, Wednesdays, Thursdays, or Fridays, but there was no way to convince Momma of that.

No way, either, to convince Momma that she had been working throughout the long weekend to gain things like those for herself and her family. That the makeup and the tight dress were her work clothes, just as her brother William's coveralls and printer's apron were his. She sighed. She had known all along her mother would never see it that way, so she always scrubbed her face and changed before coming home. Until today and that mad rush from the studio that left her no time.

She was determined to go on with her singing. She would just have to find ways of slipping in and out so Momma couldn't prevent her. It wasn't going to be easy.

Doesn't she know sixteen is old enough to have parties at night?

She sneezed.

The words of a song were taking shape in her mind as she rubbed herself dry. "One more minute!" she yelled in response to bangings on the bathroom door. She finished drying herself hastily and ran past Bernice and Clarice to her room to write the song down.

The room was chilly. She sneezed again, jumped into bed, pulled up the covers, and began writing furiously. It was an angry song, and it came quickly.

But not quickly enough.

Lou had a room to herself now that her older sister Arneatha had left home again, but it didn't really afford her much privacy. Someone knocked shave-and-a haircut, two-bits on her door. She knew who it was. The rest of the family didn't even have the consideration to knock. She put her notebook under the covers and called hoarsely, "Come in!"

"How de do, Sister Lou?" Her big brother William was haggard with fatigue. He needed a shave, too, and his shoulders sagged with the weight of responsibility for the entire household: Momma, Louretta, her five younger sisters and brothers; Clarice, Bernice, Gordon, Andrew, and Randolph, and their niece Cora Lee, the baby Lou's older sister Arneatha had left behind.

"Caught a chill, Brother Bill," Lou replied truthfully, clutching her old chenille bathrobe tightly around her throat. He's only twenty-three, she observed, and he looks *old.* There were even some gray hairs in his neat natural. The usual warmth of their rhymed banter was swallowed up by the chill of the room.

"Well, now," William said, dragging both his feet instead of the usual one, "maybe you overdo, Sister Lou."

"I was just thinking the same thing about you."

"Don't worry 'bout old Bill, he ain't over the hill," he rhymed. "I'm a grown man. I can take it. But you're still a little girl."

Rage lent her voice power. "Not you *too,* William! I know Momma will always think I'm a child. But I could always count on you to take me seriously."

"You still can," he said, sliding into the chair beside her bed with a deep sigh that sounded like he hurt from the inside out. "You're my best girl."

"I shouldn't be," she replied with a frank look that made William's eyes widen, then look away in embarrassment.

"What went wrong between you and Shirley?"

He shrugged. "Water under the bridge . . ."

"Who sent it under the bridge?" she pushed, though she knew it was none of her business. "You, Shirley, or Momma?"

He made a grimace of impatience, then closed his face so tightly it was like a concave stone. Cheeks sunken in as if he needed dentures.

"I'm sorry, William. Please don't go all far away on me like that. Please come back and be with me. I promise I won't bug you about your personal stuff anymore. I know you're the oldest, but you always used to listen to me like I was a person, not a child. I need you to listen to me that way now. I have to talk to somebody, and you're the only one who can understand."

"Sounds like a long, serious discussion," he observed. She didn't realize she had been gripping her brother's hand tightly enough to leave nail marks on it until he withdrew it and reached into the paper bag at his feet for a can of beer.

"Got another one?"

William looked at her with raised eyebrows.

"It's my birthday."

"Okay."

It tasted bitter, but not as bad as the lingering nastiness of that dishrag. The second swallow of her first beer didn't taste as bad as the first. And it got rid of the dishrag taste for good.

"Momma thinks I'm doing bad things and getting into trouble. With boys, I guess, like Arneatha did. Is that what you think, too?"

William shook his head. "I know you, Sister Lou. You've never been a player. You've always been serious."

"Thanks, William. I came home tonight with makeup on, and Momma scrubbed my face with a *dishrag.* She even called me a prostitute. I never even got a chance to tell her I'd been working."

"Working?" His forehead was furrowed with puzzlement.

"Yes, working, the same thing you do all the time—sorting mail all day and printing all night. No wonder we never get a chance to talk anymore. And Momma was so mad at me for missing my birthday party, I never even got a chance to tell her we cut our first long-playing album today. Now I don't even want to tell her."

William clinked his can against hers. "Well, all right! All roo! Congratulations, Sister Lou!"

"We spent the whole day cutting the album. And then they shot the picture for the album cover. That's why I came home in a tight dress and makeup. I didn't have time to change."

"I'm sorry Momma didn't understand."

"She never will, Brother Bill. I don't care, as long as *somebody* does."

"Well *I* do, Sister Lou. Guess it was a lot more exciting birthday than ice cream and cake with the folks in the kitchen, uh?"

She nodded.

"Guess you would rather have had a blue-light cellar party anyway, right?"

She laughed. William did understand. Boys and girls danced under dim lights to celebrate birthdays at *her* age.

"Except Momma would be afraid you'd be down there doin' the slow drag or the belly-rub or the grind-in-a-corner."

"Except I was working so hard I forgot what day it was."

"See what I mean? Serious worker. No player. I know you, Sister Lou." His own face turned serious as he turned the empty can in his hands. "I sure don't want to spoil your big day, Lou. And believe me, I wish you and the guys all kinds of success with the album.

"But I know a few things about show business, things you maybe haven't had a chance to find out yet. It isn't all glamorous, the way it looks from the outside. It's hard work. Guess you're finding that out already. But there's more to it than that. It's a rough way to make a living. Can be dangerous sometimes. Look—I know you're excited and happy about it now, and I'm happy for you, but I can't help wanting my little sister to be safe. Even though I know how much you want to be a star."

"I don't care that much about being a *star!*" she said vehemently, then corrected herself. "All right, maybe I do want that a little, but the main thing I want is to make some money and help out around here. William, you called yourself 'old' a few minutes ago. And you know what? You *look* old! You're only twenty-three, but you look twice that old. I think it's because you have to take care of the whole family."

"Girl singers get old before twenty-three, most of them," William said somberly. "Laura told me today she's worried about you not keeping up in school. Half the time, she says, you aren't even there."

"'Laura?' Hmmmmm." Louretta said significantly on hearing him call her favorite English teacher by her first name.

"Signifying is bad as prying—"

"And both are worse than dying," Lou finished. "Broke my promise, didn't I? I'm sorry. You don't have to tell me anything. But *if* she's your new girl friend, I think it's great."

"We're just good friends, Lou," he said. "We've decided to leave it like that for a while, okay? She understands about my responsibilities."

"So do I. I want to help you with the responsibilities. That's why I'm working so hard. So the kids can have a break, and so you can have whatever you want—Laura, or a full-time print shop, or just a chance to rest."

"I could never enjoy it if it happened because my little sister's life was ruined," he told her.

"It's *my* life, and it's what I want to do with it!" she exclaimed. "You better start living your life too, William!" Her angry song lyrics were running through her mind. "Momma doesn't know what's best for either one of us. She only knows about her own life. I don't *want* to be safe. I want to take my big chance even if I fail. How will I know unless I try? I want to be a singer because singing is the best thing I do. And Marty says this album has very good prospects because 'Lament for Jethro' is moving way up on the charts, and we have a head start in the business, too, because it's our own song, not somebody else's. And I almost forgot, I need you to sign some papers for him."

"What papers? Who's Marty?"

"Our manager, Marty Ross. You met him once, I think."

William sighed. "I don't remember. I think I'd better meet this guy again and check him out before I sign anything. I wish I hadn't been too busy lately to keep an eye on you, little Lou."

"I'm not little," she protested. "I'm just short. Maybe that's why everybody around here treats me like a child."

"I didn't mean it that way, Lou. But you'll always be my little sister, and I'll always feel I ought to look out for you. That's why I want to meet your Marty. And I want you to meet Lucas, this fellow I work with. He's one hell of a piano player, talented as they come. He limps like I do. Maybe that's why we got to be buddies; I don't know. But he didn't have polio. He got shot in the knees.

"It was a mob shooting, Lou. Big-time criminals control a lot of the music business, from jukeboxes at the bottom to record companies at the top. Lucas didn't understand that. He refused to do something they asked him to do, so they shot him to teach him a lesson. Shot his knees, not his hands, so he could go on working for them.

"Lucas used to be a professional musician. But he hasn't touched a piano since, except once in a while when he's relaxing around his friends. He figures he's lucky just to be alive sitting on a stool and sorting mail. Lou, if I thought you were a child, would I tell you a story like that?"

"No," she was forced to admit.

"Still want to go on with your singing career?"

"Yes!" she cried. "It's my only chance! Your only chance too, William. Yours and Laura's and Gordon's and Andrew's and Clarice's and Bernice's and Randolph's and Cora Lee's too, if you could only see it. The little royalties I get from that record aren't enough to help this big family."

"I haven't used your checks for the family. I've saved them for you," he told her. "And there's always more than one chance in a person's life. If you were older, you'd know that."

"Maybe so. But this is my best chance, and I want to take it. I don't care about being safe," she said, though she was shivering under her covers, and not entirely from the cold. Something told her she didn't want to give William a chance to check Marty out.

"Please sign these contracts for me now, William. I need them right away."

William read carefully for ten minutes while she sat in tense silence, then rubbed his eyes, skimmed the last few pages, and signed. "Promise me you'll be careful, will you, Lou?"

"Sure I will, Brother Bill."

"And if anything ever seems like it's even getting *ready* to go wrong, give me a holler. Promise?"

"Sure I will, Brother Bill."

She fell into a heavy sleep as soon as he left her room. She didn't really wake up later when Momma came in and started talking to her. Something about special church services in the morning, an all-day revival with a famous visiting evangelist. Something about how she planned to take Lou there to receive the Holy Spirit and let the congregation pray her away from the Devil and his ways. Lou heard it and agreed to go without ever really waking up. Which didn't make it a real promise.

Before the house began to stir in the morning, Lou was dressed in her rehearsal tights and leotard and carrying her shoes in her hand to avoid making noise on her way out to the Tiara Theater.

CHAPTER

3

"I'm sittin . . .
On top
Of the world . . ."

Singing, then humming it, *dah dee dah, dah dee dah, dah dah,* Lou dipped the long-handled silver spoon into the frothy topping of the mountainous fudge sundae she'd ordered for breakfast. Disappointed—it wasn't real whipped cream, but that tasteless, insubstantial stuff that came out of a pressurized can—she dug under the foam to get to the good part underneath.

Louretta had to sneak her sweets. Marty didn't want her to have any, especially chocolate. Not on account of her figure—she was, if anything, too thin—but because of her skin. A complexion like a pepperoni pizza was the usual result of eating one or any of her other favorite foods. But she needed them as antidotes to the nasty things like snails and mushrooms she was forced to eat at lunches with Marty and his friends. Lou had never had a silver spoon in her mouth before, she certainly hadn't been born with one there, and she was going to *enjoy* this sundae.

Wonderful Room Service. Pick up a phone and get whatever you wanted—even if it wasn't real whipped cream; even if, now that she looked at it, the spoon wasn't real silver. For a brief moment she thought nostalgically of herself and Momma whipping up real cream to go with the gingerbread they had baked together. New York's hotels couldn't equal that. But then she remembered her mouthful of dishrag, and decided that nothing at home would ever taste good again.

It had all happened so fast. Lou thought back to that Sunday morning two weeks ago, when she had sneaked out of the house so early she had to wait an hour outside the theater before Marty arrived to open the door. His wife Gloria was with him, stepping out of their long peach-colored car with stacks of cardboard boxes and a fortune in gold bracelets on her arms.

The boxes, as it turned out, were full of food. Their rehearsal began with a celebration in the dark, dusty theater that still stank of the sweaty bodies that had packed it for the Saturday afternoon double feature.

Ulysses found a door to lay across two stage carpenters' sawhorses, and Gloria spread a paper tablecloth over it for the feast over which Marty presided, bubbling as enthusiastically as the champagne he poured for each of them.

"Here's to you, kids," he said, raising his plastic glass. "I want you to get used to champagne for breakfast, because you're on your way now. I can see it already. Sister Lou and the Soul Brothers in bright lights on Broadway! Cheers."

"The name of the group," Frank said, "is The Soul Brothers and Sister Lou."

"Sure it is. Sure. We can worry about the billing later. The point is, you kids are headed for Broadway! So celebrate!"

"Broadway?"

"Do you mean it?"

"Are you serious?"

"Well, not exactly. The Linden Theater is off Broadway. But all the best acts get started there and move on to bigger and better things. I called a friend of mine last night, and he booked you right away. He's going to see that some very important people are in the audience. He loved your record. Everyone's going to love your record. And I love you! I'd hug you all if I could reach you!"

Marty's eyes were wet with emotion. Frank, who was seated nearest him, edged his chair away. "How could your friend have heard our record so soon?" he asked.

"I played it for him over the phone, of course."

"The whole album?" Lou wondered, thinking about the

24 phone bill.

"Of course, of course! And then I sent him a tape by messenger. Can't waste time in this business. Time is of the essence." Marty punctuated one of his favorite sayings by looking at his watch. "Which reminds me. We rehearse today and every night from now on. You'll only get to do two numbers and maybe an encore, but I want you to have a whole repertoire ready. I've already lined up some club work for you in the Villege. —Say, look at these beautiful kids, Gloria! Do I know winners when I see them, or don't I? Huh? There's nothing but gold and diamonds in their future. Starting today, they're on a gold brick road to the Great White Way!"

Gloria did not reply, only jingled her gold bracelets, gave him one of her eloquent raised-eyebrow looks and went on opening boxes and laying out paper plates and trays of food. Louretta had a feeling that Gloria had lived through many of Marty's bubbles of enthusiasm and seen more than one of them burst. She was beginning to appreciate this taciturn woman whose phrases were as clipped as her husband's were long-winded; whose common sense and irony were a perfect balance to his optimism and expansiveness.

"What's that pink stuff?" Ulysses asked.

"Lox," said Gloria, who never used more than one word if she could help it.

"Smoked salmon," Marty explained.

"And the brown stuff?" David asked.

"Pastrami."

"Spiced beef, you'll like it," Marty said.

"What's the gray stuff?" Frank wanted to know.

"Gefiltefish."

"Filet of carp," said Marty.

"Yeccchhhh. I don't eat that," David said, making a revolted face.

"What's the black stuff?" asked Louretta.

"Caviar."

"Sturgeon eggs."

"I don't eat *that,*" she said, and covered her mouth, gagging.

"Yes, you do. All of you are going to develop sophisticated tastes immediately. Where you're going, they don't serve grits and gravy."

"What kind of food is this, anyway?" Louretta wanted to know.

"Jewish," said Gloria.

"Are you Jewish, Marty?"

"That's for me to know and you to guess. It could be short for Martin Rosenberg, *nu?* Or for Martino Rossini, *mi faccio chiaro? Or* for Martinez Rosario Rodriguez. *Quien sabe?* It's a useful name. I know a few words in all three languages. I can deal with all the people I have to in this business and make like I'm their long-lost cousin. With this hair of mine, I can even pass for a soul brother."

"Never," Frank told him. "No way."

"Eat," Gloria said.

"By the way," Marty said, "this isn't Jewish food anymore. It's *New York* food, and you might as well get used to it. New Yorkers, especially show people, eat deli morning, noon, and night. You can get it any time, you can send out for it, it comes fast, it's nourishing, and it saves time. Have a pickle. All of it tastes better with a pickle." Marty poured more champagne all around.

Louretta took a pickle. David was choking on the smoked fish; Frank, gagging on the caviar. Ulysses, however, had made himself a fine-looking sandwich of pastrami, cream cheese, and coleslaw on dark bread. Sleek and wide as a whale, he would always find the most pleasureable way of maintaining his 250-pound frame.

"A toast," Marty said. "To your success in the Big Apple."

Lou had a brief twinge of guilt. It was Sunday, after all. She was supposed to be taking communion in church, and instead she was drinking wine in a theater. Knowing what Momma would say about it, she decided to follow the Devil as far as he would take her. She drained her plastic goblet and held it out for a refill.

"Anybody besides me want to drink to my birthday?"

"Sure," David said. "I'd rather have a cherry soda, though."

"How old are you?" Marty asked.

"Sweet sixteen. Was. Yesterday. Forgot because I was working all day."

"You're not sweet," he said. "But I'm glad you're sixteen. Happy birthday. That means we can forget about all the school hassles, right?"

Lou had promised Miss Hodges she would never, *never* drop out of school. But her future was beckoning. "Right," she said, clicking her glass against Marty's.

He beamed. "Now I can start booking you into week-long engagements, not just weekends, right?"

Suddenly giddy, Lou dropped her glass and spilled it on the table.

"Enough," Gloria said.

"You're sixteen and you're smashed," Marty said. "Happy birthday anyway. Now you can work anytime, anywhere."

"I don't want to miss football practice," Ulysses said.

"I don't want to miss basketball," David chimed in.

"You fellas have to make up your minds whether you're going to be performers or athletes. You've got a head start in the entertainment field. A *very* unusual break, believe me. Has anybody been around offering you sports contracts or scholarships?"

The boys shook their heads.

"Case closed," Marty said, and lit a cigar.

"But I want my high school diploma," Frank said.

His firm resolve shamed and sobered Lou. "Then you should get it, Frank."

"I want my diploma, too," David said. "Besides, *I* won't be sixteen till next year." It was incredible, considering his six-and-a-half-foot height, but it was true.

David seldom looked at books or even at girls; his first passion was basketball. On the court he was known as Dunkin' David for his prodigious leaps and high-scoring slam-dunk shots. A related nickname, Donut, implied that he had more air in his head than brains. But Lou thought he had as much intelligence as the other guys in the group; he was just much younger—in all ways. She feared it would be harder for him to leave school, where he was *already* a star, than for the rest of them.

Marty shrugged. "Oh, well, fellas, it's up to you. I can always round up some other backup singers."

"*Backup* singers?" Frank echoed angrily. "I don't like the way that sounds, man."

"Face it, that's what you are. You think you're all stars? No way. Wake up, fellas, guys like you are a dime a dozen. Lou's the star."

"We're a *group,*" Lou said emphatically. "All for one and one for all. Like a family."

"Don't be a little fool, Lou," Marty told her. "You wrote the hit, you're the lead singer, you're the star."

"That only happened because Jethro died," Lou said softly, tears prompted by champagne and memory running down her cheeks. "The song was for him. And I only started singing to replace him. He was our high tenor."

"Well, never mind how it happened, it happened. You're the star, Lou. I can replace these guys with a couple phone calls."

"Phew," Frank said, wiping his hand across his mouth. "That fish isn't the only thing that smells in here."

"Yeah," David agreed. "I don't like where this guy is coming from. I'd rather stay home, anyway."

"I won't work without them," Lou said. She thrust her face close to Marty's. "And I want *my* high school diploma too."

Gloria calmed the ensuing uproar with one of her magic words. "Tutoring."

Marty threw up his hands. "All right, all right. I must be out of my mind, working with a bunch of children. But I don't want any trouble out of parents; even though I've got the signed contracts in my pocket, I want your folks to be happy about you going on tour. So be sure and tell them you won't be missing any education. I'll get you a tutor, State of New York accredited, and you'll get your diplomas."

"And we'll go on being a group," Lou added. "Nobody in front, nobody in back, everybody equal."

"Sure, sure," he promised. "Whatever you want, Lou."

But it hadn't worked out exactly that way. By now, all four of them were official truants—about to be expelled. They knew this only because Ulysses had made friends with all the black hotel help, and one of the porters had begun giving him their mail instead of letting Marty hold it for them. They'd been in New York a week now, and no tutor had shown up—except for Charles.

Charles had appeared magically, like a genie Marty had conjured out of a bottle, complete with outrageous fringed and embroidered vests, and a bald head sometimes wrapped in a vivid turban. He was as tall and tan and languid and soft-spoken as Marty was short, pink, volatile, and loud, and he did everything *except* teach them the three R's.

Charles was, he said, an Imagist. Lou thought the term had something to do with poetry, her favorite subject in school, but in Charles's very special vocabulary, it had more to do with impressing the public. When they first met, he rattled off a long list of the famous Images he had created, then set to work on Lou's with the thoroughness and intensity of a beaver building a dam. At first she had enjoyed his attentions, but now she was beginning to fear that her real self might get lost under the fantastic structure Charles was building. He fussed over Lou endlessly, applying layers of makeup, teasing her hair, selecting her clothes, setting up her appointments, changing her brisk walk into a glide and her clear speech into a husky murmur. All his ministrations were accompanied by a soothing, meaningless babble, mostly about the celebrities he had known and transformed, and punctuated with "honeys," "loves," and "dears." Also an occasional "naughty" when he saw something he disapproved of—like a pimple.

Suddenly her breakfast sundae seemed revoltingly sweet. Lou hid it under the bed and picked up a hand mirror. She didn't really think she was pretty; her eyes and mouth had always seemed too large for the rest of her face. But Charles insisted she had a unique look. *Piquant,* he called it. And Lou's face *was* forming now, emerging from a blob of baby-fat cuteness into a firm triangle: broad forehead, large eyes tilted by high cheekbones, small pert nose, pointed chin. And, between her wide-set eyebrows, a large pimple glowing like a headlight.

She groaned and leaped out of bed. With magic swiftness she had been granted her first wish—her own bathroom with heaps of soft towels, an inexhaustible supply of hot water, and the largest tub she had ever seen. The hotel also provided a large room with shag rugs, king-sized bed, color TV, and even a kitchen she had never used. The boys had to share an identical room next door, but they were not complaining. Not about the accommodations, anyway.

Scrubbing and steaming with hot towels didn't take the pimple away. It only made the rest of her face just as red. The problem, Lou decided, wasn't sweets anyway. It was the makeup Charles made her wear, gross layers of grease, color, and powder piled on so thickly she didn't recognize herself.

Neither would anyone else, she decided, lolling across the bed in the new red robe that had cost as much as her family's monthly food budget. She felt guilty about that, and worried about all the other expenses, but Marty and Charles insisted that building an Image was an essential investment.

Of course image-building and all their other luxuries had to be paid for out of their earnings. Macro-mé, the Village restaurant where they sang every night, was like paid rehearsing—rather poorly paid rehearsing, at a hundred dollars a night. It had sounded like a lot when Marty first told them about it, but the pay only covered half of their living expenses. Singing in the busy, beautiful restaurant, getting comfortable with performing onstage and getting used to a rude, talkative audience was only a buildup for tonight.

Tonight was the long-awaited concert at the Linden. And they had better steal the show, Marty kept reminding them, or he would lose his shirt. Which one? Lou wondered with a giggle. He owned at least a hundred. "You won't miss one, Marty," she said aloud, and laughed.

Lou stopped laughing as she remembered that any minute now Marty and Charles would be banging on her door to give her her daily pep talk and announce the day's schedule. An interview with so-an-so, whose column in *Blab* or *Rolling Stone* was so important because it was read by so many important people. Be nice to him, dear, Charles would counsel. Don't tell him anything, but make him think you've told him *everything.* Lunch with so and so, who knew somebody who knew somebody in Hollywood. Be sweet to him, love, he can help you. Then rehearsal all afternoon. Then a drink with so and so, who knew someone who could persuade someone really important to come to the concert. Be sweet to him, too. Then, dear, back to your room for your beauty sleep. All the while brushing and polishing her into a parody of herself called her Image. Both the Image and the people it was supposed to impress seemed as phony as the hotel's whipped cream. So did Charles.

Charles would dominate their rehearsal too, for he was their costume designer and choreographer as well as their Imagist. ("I wear many funny hats" was his amusing way of putting it.) But the fellows were not amused by his choreography or his costumes. At least two-thirds of the time, he had them circling around a rear microphone or doing fancy steps in the background while Lou held center stage.

Frank and David complained loudly about this secondary role. As for their costumes, they derided them with one word. Faggoty. Lou was inclined to agree with them. Skin-tight blue satin pants, silver cummerbunds, and ruffled shirts opened to the waist were not exactly manly.

"But this," Charles always pointed out, "is show business."

To which David replied, "One of these nights I'm gonna do that split you keep calling for, and show my behind to the public."

"That's what he's hoping for," Frank had said, none too softly.

Ulysses did the least complaining. "I don't mind wearin' a clown suit, and equal time in the spotlight don't mean nothin' to me. All *I* want is equal pay."

But there hadn't been any pay for any of them yet. Their bill for rooms and meals alone—never mind wardrobes and luxuries—was over $1,200 now. That was more than twice their earnings. Marty waved the bills in their faces whenever anyone mentioned the subject of salaries.

Lou started at the knock on her door, then relaxed when she realized it was not coming from the hall, but from the interconnecting door between her suite and the boys'. She opened the door on her side to Ulysses, who filled the doorway.

"Hey, Lou, how 'bout cookin' us up a home-style breakfast? We're getting tired of this hotel food. I could eat a gallon of grits and a whole ham all by myself."

"I'd love to, 'Lysses, but how would I buy food? I don't have any money."

Ulysses turned to Frank, who had been hidden behind him. "See, I told you. He hasn't paid *her* either. I'd stir up some grits myself, Lou, but I don't have two quarters to rub together. I told those turkeys you didn't have any bread either."

"Of course I'm not getting paid! Did you think I was pulling something on you?"

"Not exactly," Frank said uncomfortably. "It's just that you and Marty and Charles always have your heads together, and we don't have any idea what's going on."

"What's going on is the big show tonight," Lou told them, keeping a tight lid on her emotions, "and that's all I know too. Marty says he'll pay us the first of next month, after the bills are paid."

"You believe him?" Frank asked.

Lou hesitated. "I—yes." She *had* to believe him.

"First of next month is New Year's," Frank said brusquely. "Ask him to come up with something sooner. All of us need some Christmas change."

"I will," she promised. "You guys will just have to rough it with Room Service a little longer."

"Don't get smart with us, Lou," Frank said. "It isn't funny. It's no good never getting to go out and do things on our own. We've been in New York a week, and all we've seen is the inside of this crummy hotel."

"Crummy?" The boys' room had a large living room area with a sofa, two king-sized beds, blue shag rugs, modern paintings, and everything else Lou's had.

"Well," he conceded, "maybe not crummy, but *boring*. I'd even welcome a few roaches. Counting 'em would at least give me something to do."

She knew he was right, but said, "You want to be really bored, you should have to go to some of the phony places I have to go with Charles and Marty."

Frank's anger was showing now. "How come those guys are always taking you places, and we don't get to go nowhere?"

"I don't know," Lou said truthfully. "They've got some idea that getting me seen around town by a lot of people will get us more breaks."

"She looks better in a dress than you do, dummy," Ulysses said, lightly punching Frank's shoulder. "Do you *really* want to go out with Marty and Charles?" He draped a massive arm around Frank's shoulders. "I'm sure all you have to do is ask."

Frank twitched with revulsion. "Aah, get off me, you buffalo. Of course I don't want to go out with them."

"Well, neither does our little sis. Stop picking on her. She's still our true-blue Sister Lou."

"I hope so," Frank said, then turned abruptly, and slammed the door behind himself and Ulysses.

That slam left Lou shaking. From her fortieth-story perch on top of the world she could see a crack that might open wider and plunge her to the bottom. A crack in the unity that had made The Soul Brothers and Sister Lou such a tight-knit group, drawn closer by sharing so many good and bad experiences—the joy of singing together at their clubhouse, the horror of the police shooting their frail friend Jethro, the sadness of Jethro's funeral, the triumph of cutting their first record, "Lament for

Jethro." She thought the bond that held them together was permanent, but now it seemed to be weakening. Mistrust, suspicion, and separation were eating it away like rust attacking steel.

Lou thought of writing to her brother William, then remembered how determined she'd been when they talked. How would she seem if she started complaining after only a week? Exactly the way they saw her at home—like a scared, silly, helpless child. Which was, of course, exactly the way she felt. She wrote a long note to herself instead, to shore up her courage and clear up her thinking, then dressed in her oldest, grubbiest, most comfortable jeans and knocked on the boys' door.

"Let's have a conference, y'all!"

CHAPTER

4

Ulysses opened the door only a few inches. "Wait a minute, Lou. Frank's not decent."

"He never was decent, never will be," continued David over Ulysses's shoulder. "No matter what kind of clothes he puts on, he'll always be a corner boy."

The dreaded knock on her hall door came at that moment. "Rise and shine, lovey mine!" trilled Charles.

"Just a minute!" Lou called, then whispered, "Please let me in, Ulysses. Marty and Charles are out there already. I've got to talk to you guys before they drag me off someplace."

The knocks on her door were getting louder. "Lou, what's the holdup?" Marty called. "Come on, let us in!"

"I'm in the *bathroom*!" she shouted, hoping they'd think the sound of Frank's shower was hers. "Ulysses, *please* . . ."

"OK," he said, and, to David, "Throw the animal a loincloth."

"My tan gabardines will do just fine, thank you," Frank's baritone rumbled from the shower.

"Yes, master. Coming right away," said David in a parody of a valet.

Lou slipped through the other connecting door and locked it behind her gratefully. She looked around for a place to sit down and found none. The mess the boys had made of their room was incredible. Balled socks and underwear, candy wrappers, magazines, comic books, soda cans, and other debris were everywhere. All the ashtrays contained equal amounts of smoked-out joints, cigarette butts, and bubble gum. She picked up one sofa cushion and shook it free of pork rinds, peanut shells, bottle tops, and orange peels to make room for herself. "I feel sorry for your maid," she said.

"Don't. She had a ball with us last night," was Frank's comment as he came in still wet from the shower. He was the shortest guy in the group, and sometimes Lou thought he tried to make up for it with toughness, but at five-six he was still half a foot taller than she. Broad bare shoulders and glistening brown chest tapering to a neat waist. No flab on him anywhere. Beads of water sparkling in his fine 'fro, and a frown that was more attractive than most men's smiles. Lou had never really looked at Frank before. Now she couldn't seem to stop looking.

But Frank's eyes held nothing for her but hostility. "What are you doing here?"

"I need to talk to you guys."

"What for?"

"I just figured out what's happening. Marty's trying to separate us. Get us fighting among ourselves. We can't let that happen."

"How can we stop it?" David asked. "He already said he wants to make you the star and us the backup singers."

"And what did I say to him?" Lou replied.

"He's got it all figured out. You're gonna be flyin' high on a solo star trip, and we're gonna be left down in the street where he found us."

"And what did *I* say?" Lou repeated, staring at Frank.

"She said, 'Everybody equal, nobody in front, nobody in back, all together, side by side,'" Ulysses reminded them.

"But did she *mean* it?" Frank asked.

"Yes," Louretta said, still staring at Frank. "That's why I'm here. So we can decide what we want, all together, and ask for it. I wrote down a few ideas. Let me read them off and see if you agree." She dropped her eyes, finally, to the piece of paper in her lap. "First, the group stays together for the life of the contract."

"Strike that one," Frank said. "I'm about ready to cut out now."

"*Please,* Frank," Lou said. He was being deliberately difficult in a way that reminded her of someone else; exactly who, she couldn't remember. "Second, each of us gets equal solo time, in every number."

"I don't care about that," Ulysses said. "'Sides, it's impossible. Some songs call for a girl singer, some for a guy, some for a group."

"In every *performance,* then," she said, scribbling. "Better?"

"*Sounds* better," Frank said grudgingly.

"Third, everybody gets equal pay."

"Make that number one," Ulysses ordered.

"Okay," she said. "Fourth, we all get spending allowances. *Equal* allowances, starting right now. How much do we want?"

"Ten dollars a week?" ventured David.

Frank snorted. "That'll keep you in bubble gum, junior, but it won't help *me* when *I* go out. This is New York City! The town without pity. Unless you got lots of stuff that's green and pretty."

"That sounds like it could be a good song," Lou said with admiration.

"I know. Somebody already wrote it." Frank hummed the tune of "Town Without Pity." "I want a hundred dollars a week in my pocket. Nothing else makes any sense."

"Right." She wrote it down. "I hope we can get that much. You know how Marty is. Always reminding us of how much we owe him."

"Might as well try," Ulysses said. "I figure nothin' from nothin' leaves nothin'. Anything would be better than the nothin' we're gettin' now."

"Anything else?" Lou inquired.

"Somebody else to work on the routines," David said. "I'm tired of leaping around in satin underwear."

"Why don't you work up your own routines?" Lou suggested.

"Why do we need routines at all?" was Frank's rejoinder. "We're singers, not dancers. Why can't we just stand up there and sing?"

"I don't know why not," she said after a long pause.

"Well, *I* do. They don't want us to have any dignity."

Lou nodded, knowing Frank was right, and that his "us" included all four of them. "No more dance routines," she said, writing it down. This package of demands was going to be harder to negotiate than an international peace treaty.

"Anything else?" she asked.

"We want to see Marty's account books," Ulysses said. "All he ever shows us are the hotel bills. That's not enough."

"Right," Frank said. "I want to know how much we're paying Charles, for instance."

"And what we're paying him *for,*" David added.

"I just thought of one more thing," Lou said. "We were supposed to get a tutor, and we haven't."

Frank said, "Far as I'm concerned, you can let that one slide, Lou."

"I don't want to let it slide!" David cried. "If I get promoted next year, I'll be varsity, and the colleges will be scouting me."

"Wake up, sonny boy," Frank told him. "You're dreaming."

"I am not, man! I was all-county this year, and the second highest scorer in the state, and I was only a freshman. This singing deal might fall through. Do you know what goes along with basketball scholarships? Cars, cash, credit cards, trips—and you don't even have to crack a book! I want to get promoted, man."

"I do, too," Lou said. "I don't know why I forgot about it."

"Because," Frank said, "it isn't important anymore. School is supposed to prepare you for work. We're already working."

"School does more than that," Lou argued. "It makes you a more aware person. We need to know about culture and history, we need to understand what's happening in the world, we need to know how to handle our money . . ."

With a sour smile, Frank turned his empty pockets inside out.

Lou didn't want to voice her fear that this "working" might not ever pay off. Not at the very start of their career. Frank's gesture had been discouraging enough. All she said was, "You really wanted your diploma, Frank. Someday you might want it again." "Yeah, well, I've decided seeing the sights in New York can be just as educational."

"It could be," Ulysses said. "Depends on what sights you want to see."

"All of 'em, man! From the highest to the lowest. The view looking down from the penthouse—and the view looking up from the gutter."

"That could be a song too!" Lou exclaimed. "Frank, you've got a real talent for lyrics."

"All us street niggers do—don't you know that? We grow up shuckin' and jivin', rhymin' and lyin', playin' and signifyin'."

It was true, but she didn't like his sarcasm. She decided to ignore it. "Well, David needs a tutor. And I want one. So I'll add tutoring to the list. Come on, let's go face them together."

"You do it, Lou," David said. "They spend more time with you than us. You can pick the right time to spring it on them."

"But I want us to talk to them together. We can't let them split us up anymore."

"Hoss is right, Lou. You've got the leverage. You're the one they want most," Ulysses said humbly.

"Those feminine wiles," Frank said shyly. "Those daz-zuling smiles."

She decided to ignore that, too. "Does that mean you guys trust me again?"

"We never stopped, Lou," Ulysses said. Dear, strong, solid Ulysses.

"Suppose I can't get us everything we want. Will I still be y'all's sister?"

Frank's look at her was intense in a different way now. Not hostile, but intently focused. Very definitely, purposefully focused. His pupils narrowed; his brown irises widened, moved slightly, then became fixed and bright. A response tingled from Lou's scalp through the rest of her body.

"If that's the way you want it, baby," he said, opening the door for her. Adding in a whisper, his warm breath on her neck, "but if you want it any other way, you got it."

The back of her neck felt all shivery. Frank was definitely going to be a problem. But, she thought with a smile, he might be a nice problem. Now she knew who he reminded her of, with his deep voice, his nervous restlessness, his touchy pride. His slight overbite that gave him a fierce look even when he was smiling. Calvin. Her first love, the temperamental artist who'd been too sensitive to seek her out when her life became busy.

Lou was still smiling when she stepped through her own door to encounter a hysterical Charles and an indignant Marty.

"What are you doing in my room?" she demanded.

"What were *you* doing out of it?" Marty retorted.

"I didn't know," she said icily, "that my contract required me to stay in my room. Or that it gave you permission to walk in whenever you felt like it."

"We were worried about you, Lou. You took so long, we ran downstairs and got the desk clerk to give us a spare key."

"The clerk shouldn't have done that. Next time, use the phone, will you, Marty?"

"She's right," Charles said, his purple turban nodding like a gigantic flower. "A girl needs her privacy."

"What were you doing next door?"

"What is this, the third degree? What am I, a prisoner?"

Charles tried to smooth things over. "Martin! The child was just having some good clean fun. Bathing with the boys."

Marty looked sullen. "I still want to know what she was doing over there."

"Having a wild orgy."

"Oh, goody!" Charles cried, clapping his hands. "Tell us all about it."

"We were having a conference," Lou said. She enjoyed Charles's humor sometimes, but it had a way of wearing thin. "On some things we need to talk to you about."

"Whatever they are, they'll have to wait," Marty said. "We have a lunch date in—" he checked his watch "—forty-five minutes."

"And just look at the child," Charles clucked like a mother hen. "Sloppy. Scruffy. A CARE orphan if I ever saw one." He opened her closet, scanned its contents quickly, and pulled out a jade green dress. "Hop into this, angel, and come back with a towel so I can do your face. No, not the green shoes, the *blue* shoes! Matching things are tacky; how many times do I have to tell you?"

Lou came out of the bathroom wearing a towel over the backless halter dress with its plunging neckline.

"Sit," Charles said, pointing to a stool.

"You don't have to talk to me like a dog," Lou complained. "Marty, the boys and I have to settle some things with you right away."

"Later, later."

"Now, now."

It was difficult to be serious with Charles daubing makeup on her chest as well as her face—it tickled—but Lou managed it. "First, we want equal pay."

"First, you have to earn something over expenses. I hate to even think about how much you owe me. Must I show you all my receipts?"

"Yes," Lou said. "And your account books, too." Before he could object, she added quickly, "We want equal time onstage, too. A solo for everybody at every performance."

"The child's insane," Charles said, dabbing her face with powder. "You've been naughty again, I see. The badness is popping out all over you. You have a hickey here as big as a doorknob."

"A *what?*" Lou began to giggle in spite of herself.

"No, I don't mean a love mark. More's the pity. Love marks are interesting. I know what that word means to your generation, but to my generation, it means a *pimple*. Disgusting! You're only capable of falling in love with chocolate fudge. I call that depraved. Now stop sniggling and hold still so I can cover up this disgrace."

"We can't give equal prominence to everybody in the group, Lou," Marty said. "It won't sell. Somebody has to be the star. —Now this friend of mine, Bill Bland, has very important connections. He's seen your picture in a magazine, and he's interested. I want you to be very very nice to him at lunch today. Very *very* nice."

"I'll be absolutely horrible to him," she said, "unless you give Frank and David and Ulysses as many solos as you give me." She felt a tight pulling at her scalp. "What are you doing to my hair, Charles?"

"Braiding it, love. You'll love it."

"Marty, if you don't let each of the fellows perform at least one solo tonight, I'll order chocolate fudge and vomit it all over your Mister Bland."

Marty groaned. "Yes, you would do something like that. All right. They each get to do a verse, if not a whole song."

"Every performance?"

"Every performance."

It was not what she'd hoped for, but it was a step. She decided to keep pressing. "Oh, Marty, this is no big thing, but we need spending money."

"What do you need money for? The hotel takes care of everything."

"Marty, those guys are my *friends*. They've been cooped up in that room all week without ever getting out. They need a hundred bucks apiece every week. Starting right now."

"Jee-sus! Do you know what this tour is costing me? I'm in debt to my eyeballs already."

"Let's go over the account books. Maybe we can cut down on some of the other expenses."

Marty's face hardened. She could almost see him calculating the preferability of paying them to having them inspect his books. "Twenty-five a week is the best I can do."

"Not enough, Marty. What can anybody do with twenty-five dollars in New York?"

"Fifty is my absolute limit."

"Seventy-five."

"Three hundred a week? You're pushing me to the wall. You're pushing me *through* the wall!"

"Tell you what," Lou offered. "I get to go places, but the boys don't. I'll settle for twenty-five a week if they each get seventy-five."

"The girl's lost her mind," Charles declared. "She wants less money, less stardom, less everything. Tsk. What a pity." He plopped something heavy and itchy on her head.

"My God, what's that?"

"It's your lovely new Luralex wig, sweetie. You earn an extra fifty dollars a day just by wearing it in public. And it's *gorgeous*. Look!"

He spun her stool to face the mirror. A mountainous helmet of shiny orange fibers crowned her head, overpowering her small face.

"I won't wear it."

"You have to wear it. But only in public, love. In private you can take it off."

"Good," Lou said, and pulled the monstrosity off before it could give her a headache.

"Put it back on," Charles ordered. "We're going out."

"You mean I have to wear this thing everywhere I go, not just onstage?"

"Yes, of course. You'll be seen, you'll be getting your picture taken. That's why you're being paid."

"I never agreed to wear a wig."

"Oh, yes, you did. It's in the contract," Marty informed her.

"Pay the guys," Lou said grimly, "and I'll wear it." Why did it have to be *red*—her most hated hair color—and straight, and shiny? No one would ever understand how much her own natural crinkly brown hair meant to her. The day she had refused to let Momma straighten it was the day she began to respect herself.

The whoops and cheers from next door consoled her somewhat; Marty must have given the guys some money.

Charles tried to cheer her up, too. "Frankly, I agree with you, Lou. It's ugly. But it attracts attention, and we've got to get you noticed. Good taste just won't do it at this stage. Good taste is for people who have *arrived* and don't need to be noticed. Besides, wearing the wig pays money, honey. And money is never ugly. You only have to wear this one today. You'll have a dozen others to choose from later."

"I don't care what else a girl wears. If her hair is wrong, *everything* looks wrong," Lou sobbed.

"I know, sweetie, I know," Charles soothed. "But it's only for a little while. When the other money starts flowing in, you can throw the wigs away. Okay?"

"Okay," she said, and took the handkerchief he offered to dab her eyes. "How much did you pay them, Marty?" she inquired when the manager returned.

"What's the matter, don't you trust me?"

"I just asked."

He sighed and nudged her into the elevator. "Fifty dollars apiece."

"You promised seventy-five."

"Lou, you just don't understand the situation. I'm in hock to my Adam's apple with all the expense money I've been laying out for you."

"Well, do you really have to spend so much?" she asked as they left the hotel.

"—For instance," she questioned, stepping into the limousine, "do you really have to rent this? Why can't we just take cabs?"

"You have to *look* successful to be successful," Marty explained.

"I keep telling you," said Charles, "your image is *so* important. Even if you can't afford it. *Especially* if you can't afford it."

But the images of herself in the restaurant were far from reassuring. First there was that grotesque dome of flame-red nylon hair in the mirror. Under their false lashes and spangled lids, her eyes hid from their reflection.

Then there was the clipping from the *National Comet,* passed to her by the stout stranger across the table. A nude Lou with a wild, wet mop of hair, staring with startled eyes at the camera. The towel she clutched covered most of what a swimsuit would, but not all. The recording session, she remembered. The impatient, sneaky photographer at the door of her dressing room.

All of the other diners seemed to be staring at The Wig. Lou suddenly felt as if she had nothing else on. Did people ever really die of shame? She wished she could. Unable to die, she wanted to run from the restaurant or disappear through the floor. But, wedged between Charles and Marty, she could do neither. She could only hold her napkin up to her hot face.

Behind the napkin, she said, "Marty, you promised to get those pictures back!"

"It was a busy day. I had so much on my mind, I forgot," he said. "Besides, what's to get upset about? It's a stunning shot."

"I agree," said Mister Bland, who wore a toupee that made him look in his sixties instead of his fifties. He reached for the clipping with a plump hand on which a diamond pinky ring caught fire, and let his hand rest on hers for several seconds too long. "I think candid photography often captures the real essence of the subject. This, I suspect, is the *real* Sister Lou." He moved his heavy, clammy hand away just as Louretta was deciding to stab a fork into it. But he kept his eyes on her so intently it made her uncomfortable. It was the same kind of look Frank had given her this morning, but this time she didn't welcome it.

"I'm an amateur photographer myself," he continued. "Perhaps Miss Hawkins would consent to pose for me sometime."

Marty spoke for her. "Of course she would."

"I'll need Charles with me," Lou said quickly, "to fix my hair and face and stuff."

"Oh, I don't think that will be necessary," Mr. Bland said.

"Of course it will. Charles is in charge of my Image. Aren't you, Charles?"

Charles kicked her under the table.

Mr. Bland cleared his throat and opened a magazine-sized menu. "Well, what are we having?"

"Turkey," Lou said, looking directly at him instead of the menu.

His face was as wide and white as a whale. Mr. Moby Dick,

she nicknamed him. But his teeth were small and pointed and numerous. No, Mr. Jaws. He had small, squinty eyes swallowed up by fat cheeks. Mr. Piggy.

"Ah, yes," the creature commented, "the breast of turkey en casserole with mushrooms and wine in cream sauce. Excellent choice. And for an appetizer?"

"She'll have *escargots,*" Charles said.

Snails again. Lou made a face.

"Please," Mr. Bland said. "Let the lady choose."

"Do they have any cracklins or chitlins?"

This time Charles's kick on her shin was vicious and painful.

"No," Mr. Bland said. "I regret to say they do not. But I understand your cravings. I'm from Georgia myself, and every now and then I just get a terrible yearning for down-home foods. I had a wonderful colored girl who used to cook for me there, and sometimes I would give *any*thing for a plate of her hog jowls and black-eyed peas. I wonder if you know how to cook those foods?" His accent had thickened like gravy.

"Sure," Lou said, wondering what else the "wonderful colored girl" served up. "I can really deal with the pots, mister. Ham and beans, collard greens and fatback hoppin' john and neck bones, grits and grease—Stop it, Charles."

"Oh, I'd be just delighted if you'd fix me a soul food meal. I'd be *very* appreciative, I can assure you."

"Any time," Lou said, and resisted the temptation to add "Massa." Marty and Charles wanted her to be nice to this blubberball. Well, this was one thing she could do for him without hating herself. "Tell you what. There's a kitchen in my room. I'll fix the food tomorrow and have one of the guys in my group bring it over."

"It would be *so much* nicer if you brought it yourself," said Mr. Bland, smiling slyly. "I know how busy you must be. But here's my card with my private phone number. Just call and I'll send my car around for you. And look what I have in here besides the card!" He poked around in his wallet long enough to reveal several large-denomination bills, and finally produced a piece of red cardboard. "Isn't this wonderful? My front-row ticket for your performance tonight."

Surprise, surprise. Lou smiled woodenly. To her relief, the rest of the conversation was between Mr. Bland and Marty. "I have one property that might have a niche for her. Negotiating for another one that's absolutely *perfect*. I've already signed the screenwriter and the director. If she has the stage presence *and* the voice . . . Well, tonight we'll see, won't we? We'll see."

Lou ignored his stare, picked at her turkey casserole, and worried about that photograph. If Momma or William ever saw it, she could never go back home . . .

Marty's voice intruded on her thoughts. "Bill, Lou would like you to have an autographed copy of her album."

The glossy square presented another shocking image. Lolling on the floor in front of the guys, glassy-eyed, glossy-lipped, with an idiotic open mouth and a fully exposed thigh, she looked exactly like what Momma had called her that night. The words printed on the album cover were even worse:

SISTER LOU and The Soul Brothers
Party All Night
With the Hit Single *Lament for Jethro*

Lou shut her eyes, but the blatant orange letters remained vivid inside her eyelids. Marty and Marcus had changed the group's name around, putting hers first, without letting any of them know. Too numb to react to Mr. Bland and his heavy, roving hands, she took his pen and signed the cover:

With feeling,
Sister Lou

Never mind being specific about what the feeling was.

CHAPTER 5

The theater was frighteningly vast after the small, cozy supper club. It was a huge, drafty building with too many corners and niches to swallow up sounds and catch and bounce echoes. A group called The Bionic Babies, wearing white body suits and bathing caps with attached antennae, had come and gone without leaving any impression of their music. It had been as thin and disposable as white tissue paper, in spite of their ear-splitting amplifiers. Now a group called Primordial Slime was rolling around the stage in plastic snakeskin suits. Slithering about like the inmates of the reptile house in the zoo. Primordial Slime held their instruments aloft—a position not conducive to good playing or even to the imitation of jungle animal sounds.

Lou, in the wings, turned her back on the revolting sight and tuned into her friends.

David was excited. "Man, I rode the subway all day long! Just wanted to see how far I could go. Those trains go everywhere, man! Bet I must have traveled a hundred miles!"

"Dummy! The greatest city in the world out there waiting for you, and you spend the whole day underneath it!" Frank said scornfully. "Me, I spent the day studying all the fine sights on Fifth Avenue. All those fine ladies could be models, and every one was dressed like one. Meantime, you riding the *subway*—but what can I expect from a retarded dummy who just learned how to tie his shoes?"

"You didn't let me finish! The last train I was on took me all the way to the beach. I got to look at *girls* while you were just looking at their clothes."

"Aw," Frank said, "you lyin', man. I don't believe there's no beaches in New York."

"There are too," Ulysses said. "Ain't you never heard of

Coney Island?"

Frank was taken in for a minute, but he bounced back. "Wait a minute. Think you slick, don't you? This is December. And it sure ain't California! Maybe you saw a beach, but you sure didn't see no girls in bathing suits."

"No," David admitted, "but I saw some in jogging suits."

"What'd *you* do today?" Frank asked Ulysses. "Went someplace and stuffed your face, I bet."

"Yep," Ulysses replied calmly. "I was in Harlem with the soul people and the soul food. Smelled some barbecue and went into a little restaurant. And it didn't cost me a dime, 'cause the fine sister who waited on me liked my smile. Said, 'I just love to see a man eat like you, Daddy.' So I decided to make her happy, 'cause I liked her smile, too. Had double helpings of ribs, potato salad, greens, rice and beans and biscuits. I had a fine grease and a fine time, and it didn't cost me a single dime. Still got my money in my pocket. Which is more than you two can say."

Lou was glad for them. But nervous, anticipating the performance and their reaction to the album cover. Her nervousness ebbed as the boys began topping one another, bragging about their exploits of the day.

"I don't know about them, but *I* had a ball! Got my honey and saved my money . . . Barbecue and honey buns too."

"Joggin' on the beach, oh mannnnn, leavin' footprints on the sand . . ."

"Just window-shop and *talk* about pearls . . . and you can pick up *all* the girls!"

"Spare ribs, hot sauce, sweet hot meat . . . Get'em all on One Hundred and Twenty-Fifth Street!"

Lou resisted the temptation to crack, "Oh, I bet you guys just spent the day watching your first X-rated movie." She was getting high on their rapping because it was so exuberant and so inventive. Topping each other with lies . . . improvising innuendos and rhymes. And every line contained the seed of a song. Yet this word-play was the natural street-corner speech in every black community. Every sentence a song, an endless chain of call and response, going back, probably, to Africa. Pride in this natural talent gave her a deep-down good feeling.

The snakeskins slithered off the stage to faint applause, the MC began a new introduction, and a sudden shove from Marty pushed them into the limelight.

Lou almost stumbled in her new high heels, but recovered and skipped as lightly as if they were ballet slippers. Her dress was so tight it felt like a body cast, but she managed to move and bend in it gracefully.

Ensemble, they sang "Lament for Jethro," the song Lou had helped write about the death of their friend:

"Now, Jethro never did nothin' great,
But he was a cat you'd appreciate.
He could laugh and sing and fight and dance,
And he might've done more if he'd had the chance.

But just because he showed no fear
A big cop blew him away from here.
Yes, just because his skin was brown,
A big policeman shot him down.

Lots of people don't know or care,
But if there's a Heaven, I know he's there.
And if he ain't—one thing I know,
It's no place I want to go,
'Cause if they'd keep Jethro out, I fear
Heaven must be just like here!"

The next song, "Hungry Cat Blues," was a solo for Frank:

"You know a hungry cat
Ain't got time for nothin'
But findin' food to eat . . .
He don't want friendly talk
When he visits on your street . . ."

Frank's rumbling baritone voice and his appearance were just right for the song. He had a crouching, tense stance that made

50 him seem about to spring at the audience. He even had a catlike face—sideburns resembling cat whiskers, and slightly bared teeth that made his expression seem menacing.

"You better leave some seafood at my door,
Add a little sirloin to make sure,
Plus a quart of heavy cream—
Or I'll come around and I'll smash your dream!
'Cause I can move real fast,
Jump out in the darkness,
Run and not be seen.
You better treat me right,
Or you'll find out what I mean,
If I can't be rich,
I can sure be mean!"

The applause was thunderous. They joined hands, ran offstage, came back, pranced off again.

The applause continued without abating. They would have to do their encore, "Party All Night." Lou was both elated and terrified.

Do it they did, in the glare and heat of the theater's brightest lights. Went through Charles's complicated dance routines in his absurdly confining costumes. When Ulysses lifted her to his shoulder, she prayed for her strapless top to stay up. When Frank threw her over his back, she prayed for her wig to stay on. When he and the other boys did kicks and splits, she prayed for their pants to stay in one piece. And when they kept her spinning from one to another during the chorus, she forgot about costumes and just prayed no one would fail to catch her and let her crash to the floor in a heap of broken bones. Prayed with a smile pasted on her face. No sign of fatigue or strain. Though her head throbbed and her eyes burned and her throat was sore from the dust and the singing, she was happy. These were her friends, and they were working *together*. Lou knew, for all her inexperience, that she had been right not to let Charles and Marty send her off on a solo star trip from which she could crash alone.

None of the fellows let her fall. And that was just as important as the cheering, foot-stomping, hand-clapping reaction to their encore. Lou felt wrapped in affection and audience approval like a warm fur coat.

They took four bows, and ended with Lou getting a kiss from each of the guys. Frank's was especially long, and almost threw her off balance. She was glad it came at the end.

After the emotional high of the concert came a deep letdown. The trio rode back to their hotel in a moody silence. Marty, who had left earlier, had "deli" waiting for them in his room. Apparently it had been waiting for some time; the boxes were unappetizingly damp and limp—the way Lou and the fellows felt.

But Marty was still excited. "Sens*a*tional, *fab*ulous!" he babbled. "I've never seen such audience reaction to an unknown act! Great press reaction, too. My phone's been ringing ever since we got back. Any comments for the press, kids?"

"No, but I have one for Charles," David said. "Tell him he ought to be designing ladies' underwear. We look like clowns in all those spangles and ruffles. Besides, we can't *move* in those flaky outfits."

"Yeah," Frank chimed in. "Why can't we wear some for-real clothes? I was on Fifth Avenue today, and I saw some mean slacks and blazers."

Marty shrugged. "Costumes are part of show business."

"Lou Rawls wears slacks and sweaters. Ray Charles wears suits. Why do we have to look like chorus girls?"

"Those are big established names. When you're established, you can wear ordinary clothes, too. Right now you're just starting out, and you need all the help you can get to attract attention."

"Do I have to go on eating deli till we get established?" Ulysses asked, unhappily staring at a limp sandwich. "I'm sick of soggy pastrami and coleslaw sandwiches. I need some food for my soul. Some soul food for my strength. Some pot liquor to lubricate my king-sized tonsils."

 "I'll cook up a batch of soul food tomorrow," Lou offered. "I promised somebody else some, anyway."

"Good girl," Marty said with a strange, conspiratorial look.

"You don't even have to go shopping," Ulysses said, and began reaching into the many pockets of his extra-large overcoat. From each tumbled one or more extra-large ham hocks. "I got an uptown sweetie, ooh wee, she looks good and takes good care of me," he rumbled in a blues mode.

Laughing, Lou gathered up the ham hocks in the flimsy spangled tunic she wore on her stage entrance and discarded later in the frenzy of performing. "My costume is too tight, too, Marty," she said. "And I hate dancing in that wig. I worry about it falling off my head all the time."

Marty ignored her and said, "There's this radio guy, Dan Jenkins on KBY, wants to tape an interview with you first thing in the morning, Lou."

"Well, Marty," Lou said with a yawn, "why don't you stay up and think about what we're going to say to him? That's your job. We've done ours, and I'm going to get some sleep."

"Amen," chorused her friends. Marty tried to stimulate them with more excited prattle about interviews and early-edition press reviews, but they foiled him by going to their room. Lou went to hers and kept her word, hopping into bed after a quick shower.

She slept deeply, as if weighted down, until the weight became intolerable and awoke her. A heaviness that was more than fatigue was crushing her. Something was probing, too, touching her in places where no one had touched her before. Horrible, slimy lips were moving across her face like snails, and someone's stagnant breath was stifling her. She let out a yell. It was cut off when the hand moved quickly from her body to her mouth.

"What's the matter, dolly?" a hoarse voice asked. "Why all the racket?"

Suddenly wide-awake and convinced she was not having a nightmare, Lou used her free arm to switch on her bedside lamp. It revealed that a great lump of lard was in bed with her. The shock of the light caused him to pull back momentarily, blinking, naked except for shorts, with a huge, pendant belly. Across the room, the mirror on her closet door showed his back, as wide and white as a refrigerator. His flesh felt as cold and clammy as a refrigerator, too.

"Get off me, you fat ugly hog!" she cried. "Dirty dog! How did you get in my room!"

Mr. Bill Bland looked at her with surprised eyes as if unconscious of having done anything wrong.

"Why, my friend Marty gave me the key. He told me you'd be delighted to receive me this evening. Darlin', I thought you'd be up and expecting me. I brought you flowers and champagne. I was going to be a gallant visitor, go through all the polite preliminaries—" His full lips were pouting like a puzzled child's.

"I'll bet," Lou said, wishing for a knife.

"—but you were asleep, and since I knew you were hot for me at lunch this afternoon, I didn't wait . . . I *couldn't* wait. I'm so excited by you, Miss Hawkins. I can't help myself. Ever since I saw that picture of you. It was so . . . enticing."

Lou tried to stall for time. "Mr. Bland," she said, "I think you've confused your own feelings with mine." His hands were moving to get under the covers again.

Lou tried to calculate her advantages and decided she had none. What use were her hundred pounds against his three hundred? Then she caught a glimpse of herself in the mirror. Plain cloth pajamas brought from home. Thick, little-girl braids, huge startled eyes, a small scared face scrubbed clean of makeup.

"Mister Bland," she said, softly but distinctly, "you could get in a lot of trouble if you don't stop this. I'm only fourteen years old." She didn't have to fake the tremor in her voice. Nor did she have to push his hand away again. He cursed, rolled over with a grunt, and got out of bed with surprising swiftness. "Jeesus. What's wrong with that sonofabitch Ross? They could have me up for statutory rape."

Puffing and blowing, Mr. Bland stepped into his pants and picked up the rest of his clothes from the floor. Studying his own red face and hers in the mirror, he said, "You do look young, little girl. Makeup fools a guy, you know? I just don't understand that crazy Ross, setting me up with a piece of jail-bait. God."

"Marty doesn't know," Lou lied. "He thinks I'm eighteen."

"Please don't hold it against me, sweetheart," he begged. "You can see how I was a victim, too."

"No," she said, "I really can't. I don't think a judge could, either."

His face went from red to ashen. "Now listen, little lady, I didn't mean any harm. Just give me a minute in the bathroom, and I'll be gone."

During that minute and the next, while her intruder was retching and the toilet flushing and the water running, Lou picked up her phone and dialed the number of the room next door. She spoke softly, close to the mouthpiece. "Ulysses? Get the guys up and get them out in the hall quick. I may need some witnesses. A white man broke into my room. I want you to see him leave."

She hung up just before Bland, combed and pale, emerged from her bathroom.

"Girlie, I'm really sorry if I upset you. I'm begging you—please don't make any noise about this. I can't handle it. I'm a respected man with a family. A wealthy man. I have influence, contacts, prestige. . . . So if there's anything I can do for you, anything at all, money, connections, plane tickets, publicity, bookings—"

"There is *one* thing," Lou said softly.

"What's that?"

She yelled at the top of her powerful lungs, "You can get the hell out of my room, and never, *ever* come near me again!"

Her visitor made his departure quickly. But, judging from the noises she heard coming from the hall, Mr. Bland would not have as easy a time getting out of the hotel. She had only asked the boys to be witnesses. But she could not help enjoying the sounds of battle and the pictures they suggested. *Whumpf!* That must be Ulysses, pounding Bland's belly. *Karrump!* That was David kicking his rump. *Yeeee!* A high-pitched squeal. Frank undoubtedly was choking Mr. Piggy with one of his strong, sinewy arms. Good. This was the best moment she'd had in a long time. She enjoyed it for another minute, then picked up her phone and dialed another hotel room.

"Marty, you better get up here. The guys are giving your friend Mr. Bland what he deserves."

"Wha, Lou?" was the sleepy response.

"I said, the guys are beating up on Mr. Bland. You better try and stop them before the hotel detectives do—"

The noises in the hall were softer now. Muffled thumps, cracks, and whimpers.

"—Or before they kill him. After that, I think you and I ought to have a little private talk."

The hall was silent as death after she hung up. When her phone rang, it startled her badly. She was much less in charge of herself and her situation than she had thought.

Frank's voice on the phone was hoarse. "You all right, Lou?"

"I'm fine. Just a little shook up, that's all. How about the, uh, burglar?"

"Fatso? He's headed for the hospital. Our friend the porter took him down in the service elevator. He got to be hurting, sore as my knuckles are. You sure you're okay? Did he mess with you?"

"No," she said firmly, though every part of her but her voice was shaking. "He just gave me a shock."

"Well, we gave him one too."

"Good."

"I picked up a souvenir off the floor for you. One of his front teeth. There'd be enough for a necklace if big ole softhearted Tar Baby hadn't made us turn him loose."

Ulysses, who good-naturedly put up with this nickname only from his closest friends, took the phone. "I had to break it up, Lou. These maniacs were about to kill him. David was choking him to death, elbow in the windpipe, and this other fool was banging away on him like one of those jackhammers they break up the street with."

"Good," Louretta said again.

Frank snatched the phone back. "You *sure* you're all right, Lou? I want to come over and see about you."

"I'm okay."

"You shouldn't be alone in there. Let me come over."

"Not yet," she said. "Give me a little time to pull myself together. I'll call you later on."

"Okay. I'll be waiting. But put the chain on your hall door. I'll go soak my hands. Boy, that was the best fight I ever had!"

Lou smiled into the receiver.

"Listen, Lou, who was that creep, anyway? Did you know him?"

"No," she lied.

"Well, put the chain on your door," he reminded her again.

She kept her promise, but remained close to the door to wait for Marty. He came quickly, bringing a flask for which she was grateful. And a loud, indignant voice, for which she was not.

"Lou, what the hell happened?"

"Shhhh," she said. "I don't want the guys to hear us. Nothing happened. They just taught your friend a lesson, that's all."

Marty collapsed into a chair and exhaled deeply. "You blew it, Lou. That guy was our most valuable contact."

"You had no business giving him the key to my room, Marty."

"Aw, hell, Lou, that was a dumb thing to do without telling you . . . but you ought to know it's all part of the business. When I tell you to be nice to somebody, I just mean be nice. But when I tell you to be very very nice, *that* means . . . Stop giving me that wide-eyed innocent look. Do I have to spell it out for you?" He gulped half his tumbler of Scotch, then rattled the ice cubes irritably.

She took a long cold look at him, slumped in his mauve velour robe over striped pink pajamas. Fat. Frizzy-haired. Unshaven. Now she knew what he reminded her of. A caterpillar. A fat, fuzzy pink worm. "Yes," she said. "I'm afraid you do."

"Christ, Lou, you didn't grow up in a convent. You grew up in the streets."

She put down the drink she had barely touched. "You think every black girl is a prostitute, don't you?"

Marty shrugged. "I think everybody has a price. Color has nothing to do with it; the only color that matters is green. And you don't get anything in this world for free."

She took one of his cigarettes, accepted his light, then blew a cloud of smoke in his face. "Well, I don't want success that bad. Maybe I grew up in the street, but I'm no alley cat. I grew up in a decent family. And I grew up in the *church,* too."

Marty threw his hands up in disgust. "Spare me the religious bit, please. It nauseates me. Sooner or later all my best artists get born again, and all my hard work goes down the drain."

"I think I can understand why," she said. "You're right, Marty, I did spend a lot of time in the streets. I'm not sorry. I learned a few things out there. I learned to fight, I learned to hang tough, and I learned street talk. I *love* street talk. 'Cause it's straight talk—maybe the only kind you understand. So, dig it: I am not going to peddle my behind for you. What I am going to do is give you a chance to save yours. 'Cause you're in big trouble."

"How you figure?"

She sucked on the cigarette without inhaling and blew another cloud in his face. "I read a few papers, catch some of the news on TV. They're cracking down hard on pimps these days." She ground out her first cigarette. "Especially when the girls are *minors.*"

Marty's head was bowed in his hands. "All right, Lou, you've got the screws in. You don't have to tighten them any more. What do you want me to do?"

"Go next door and thank the boys for saving me from that maniac. I know you're too smart to let on you know him, or that you've just been talking to me. Then tell them I didn't know the names would be changed around on the album. I don't care how you explain it, just make them know it's the truth. And promise to change the names back."

"I don't know if I can keep that promise, Lou."

"Try. I'm sure you can think of something."

He stood up. "That's all, I hope."

"One more thing. We want you to get rid of Charles. He's fun to have around, but he's a rotten designer, and he's not helping our image, he's ruining it. All he does is upset everybody."

Marty's eyes were hard and vicious, and his face had that cracked-porcelain look again. "You silly little small-time know-nothing! I should've left you down in the gutter where I found you, instead of trying to make something out of you! And stop giving me that big-eyed innocent stare. Next you'll be trying to tell me you're a virgin."

She was, but she wasn't interested in convincing him.

"Good night, Marty," she said.

"Good night, Miss Untouchable. You're a fraud."

"I already told you what you are. Although, of course, I haven't talked to you."

"Of course not, Miss Impregnable, Miss Inscrutable, Miss Phony. *Good night.*"

She tiptoed to the door he had shut softly behind him, listened until she heard Ulysses admit him next door, then put her chain lock on and got into bed. Too nervous to sleep, she huddled, trembling, under the covers for almost an hour. Finally she dialed the number of the room next door.

Frank must have been lying awake with the phone under his pillow. Before the first ring had finished, he answered softly, "Lou?"

"I'll unlock the door on my side."

"Be right over."

He came in silently as a cat, walking lightly on the balls of his feet, and bent over her. His face seemed strained in the long shadows cast by the dim bedside light. Only his eyes were clearly visible. They were bright and intense—not with desire, but with concern.

He touched her face gently. "Are you sure you're okay, Lou?"

His gentle touch and soft question were enough to make her break down into tears.

Frank touched her hair tentatively. "That guy—what did he do to you?"

"N-nothing," she managed, sniffling. "He just scared me."

Sitting on the edge of her bed, trying very hard not to alarm her, Frank stroked first her hair, then the back of her neck, where tension had caused a soreness more painful than a stab wound. The massage felt good. She let her head droop.

"That's right. Relax."

"I can't," she said, feeling herself begin to tremble again.

Frank put an arm around her. She flinched.

"You scared of me too, Lou?"

"No," she said, a bit uncertainly. Frank was familiar and good to be with, but she was too upset to know exactly how she felt about him. The tears had stopped, though.

"You're shaking." His arm tightened. "You shouldn't stay by yourself tonight."

Both his arms were around her now. His embrace felt warm and safe. But was it? A faint tingle of warning stirred her barely calmed fears.

"Let me stay with you," Frank urged. "I was worried sick about you while I was next door. You shouldn't be alone."

She wanted him with her, but hesitated. She had only one bed, after all. As if he'd read her thoughts, Frank said, "I just want to protect you. Don't worry. Nothing will happen. Okay?"

After hesitating for a few seconds, she said, "Okay."

Frank turned off the light and slipped into bed with her.

At first they lay side by side silently, not touching, stiff as dolls. Then Frank found her hand and held it. "Don't worry. You're safe now," he whispered. They both stirred then, and moved closer, and held one another, and, of course, the snug feeling of safety became affection and then excitement, and then, of course, something did happen.

Afterward, Frank groaned. "I'm sorry, Lou. I didn't mean to do that."

"I know. I let you," she said truthfully.

She didn't feel sorry. She felt wonderful; all her earlier fears and uncertainties gone. Bland and Marty had made her feel cheap—but Frank had made her feel cherished and valuable.

"I hurt you, too. I'm sorry."

"You made me feel better." And that was true, too, except for a new, nagging worry that only time could relieve.

CHAPTER

6

"You ain't my sister no more, Lou. *Unh-unh.* Glad?"

"Mmm-hmm," she said sleepily.

"So am I. I may be a lot of things, but I ain't no insect."

Lou had to laugh at that one.

Frank sighed contentedly, then propped himself on one elbow to give her one of those disturbing stares. His changeling eyes went from brown to amber to brown again, focusing on her so intently she thought they would burn holes in her face.

"You're a funny little character, you know that? Talking so big-mouth and sassy, acting so bad and bold—and here I turn out to be the first one."

For once her voice was very small. "You almost weren't."

"I figured. That's why I put such a hurting on that honky. Ulysses was right; I *would've* killed him. Still sorry I didn't."

She traced the faint growth above his stubborn mouth with a fingertip. "Would last night have been as much fun if you'd spent it in jail?"

"No *indeed,*" he said emphatically. "No, no indeed. Lord, that was nice." He pulled her against his hard chest with a strong-arm hug. "Girl, you are full of surprises. How can you be so much woman? I always thought virgins were supposed to be . . . you know. Scared."

"I already had my big scare for the night, I guess." Wide-awake now, she looked at him seriously. "Frank—I don't know how to say this, but I feel bad about something."

"What's the problem? Tell Doctor Brown. You feel like a bad girl for doing what comes naturally? Did the church put a hurting on your mind about sin and wickedness and going to hell and all that scary stuff?"

There was that, of course. Momma's scoldings, Reverend

Boyd's sermons. Her mother's accusing face flashed on the screen of her mind often, but it was getting smaller and farther away all the time.

"No, not really. Frank, stop tickling me and listen! I think maybe I . . . used you a little."

"Go ahead. Use me up! I love it!" He laughed, white teeth gleaming in his tan face, outstretched brown arms gorgeous against the hotel's white sheets.

"Frank, I'm serious. I had to get rid of the ghost of that other guy. I needed to forget the feel of his hands on me—and the thought of what he almost did to me. I've been wanting you as much as I think you've been wanting me. Maybe more. I just don't think I'd have let it happen so fast if he hadn't made me feel so rotten. I needed you to make me feel good again right away."

"And did I?"

"Yes," she said sincerely.

"Still want me?"

"Yes."

"Then what are you worrying about? You know what I think?" he said, unplaiting her thick, crisp hair. "I think you think too much. Give you a chance, you'll take a beautiful thing and analyze it to pieces till there's nothing left."

"I guess you're right. That's the way I am."

"Ah, but I have a plan. I will keep you too busy for thinking."

She returned his embrace, then stiffened.

"*Now* what's worrying you? I bet I know."

"What?"

"What worries most girls. *You* know."

She nodded. "I just hope everything will be OK. I'll know in"—she counted mentally—"ten days."

"What? Some woman of the world I've got here. Girl, this is serious. You better ask Marty if he has any girl pills in his collection."

"I'd rather not ask Marty."

"No, I guess not. Look—I made some street contacts yesterday. When I go out today, I'll see my partner and pick up some pills. Just promise me you'll take them. One a day keeps the babies away. OK?"

"Okay," she agreed.

"And stop thinking so much, okay? Just relax and let love happen."

She couldn't help thinking what a lovely line that was for a lyric before she said, "We don't know if it's love or not."

"If it is, we'll know when the time comes. Give it time. And stop being so serious."

"I can't help it. I'm a serious person."

"Now that worries *me,*" he said. But he didn't act worried. He began kissing her neck; working his way around from the left side to the hollow of her throat and staying there. Lou knew she'd have a for-real hickey this morning, and that Charles would be sure to notice it.

"Frank, it's nine o'clock. Charles and Marty will be up here soon."

"Make 'em wait."

"I think I hear the guys stirring next door."

"Let 'em stir," was his muffled response.

"Frank, I want to keep this private. Just for us."

"Oh, all right," he said petulantly, pulling back. "I won't talk about it, you know."

"Well, I hope not."

"But if you think you can keep those guys next door from knowing what's going on, you're more innocent than I thought. You're a baby, baby."

"Frank," she said, "what happened last night was very special—"

"Was? *Is,*" he corrected her. "For as long as we both shall groove on it."

"—and I want to keep it just between us."

"Well, I'm not going to tell any tales or details. But love is bound to show, 'cause it gives you that special glow . . ." he sang. "Okay if I use your shower?"

"Sure, if you don't sing in it. Hey," she said mischievously, "let's take a shower together."

"Oh, no," he said emphatically. "Later for that. I can't handle it. We got to wait till I see the medicine man, baby, and get your mojo workin' right."

He disappeared into her bathroom, leaving her with mixed feelings to sort out.

"I see you've been thinking again," he said when he came out. He shook a disapproving finger. "Bad habit."

" 'For as long as we both shall groove on it.' Isn't that what you said?"

"What did you want me to say?" He came closer. "Look, Lou, I'm just not ready for that till-death-do-we-part stuff. Are you?"

"No," she admitted. "Those words always sounded kind of grim to me."

"Me, too. In fact I know a few couples who couldn't wait for natural deaths."

She laughed. "So do I."

"All right, then." He patted her hand. "So—hang loose, baby. Remember—relax and let love happen. Okay?"

She appreciated his honesty, even though it sounded like a business deal. She almost thought he was going to shake her hand. But he planted a long kiss on her mouth instead. It would linger there a long time—far longer than any of Charles's lipstick.

As it turned out, she got to apply her own lipstick—her favorite brownish pink, not Charles's gaudy purple or maroon—and pick out her own bushy hair, and choose her own dress—a loose, lightweight winter-white wool with a pretty lace edging at the neckline. She dressed in luxurious slow motion, humming and singing and adding lines to Frank's impromptu song:

"Love is bound to show,
'Cause it gives you that special glow . . .
Everywhere you go, girl
Folks are sure to know.

So why try to hide?
Don't lock it up inside,
Wear your joy with pride!
Let your beauty glow,
'Cause love is bound to show
Everywhere you go . . ."

We need a piano, she decided as her improvisation was interrupted by the telephone. We make up songs together fast as lightning follows thunder and rain follows lightning. Need to be writing them down, notes, chords, and all.

It was Marty calling her from the boys' suite. Asking her oh so politely if she would mind very much coming over as soon as it was convenient. Lou knew this unusual courtesy was temporary, but she liked it and responded to it promptly.

Frank had been right about the impossibility of concealing anything from his roommates. "Here comes the bride," David sang when she walked in, jabbing Ulysses with his elbow.

"Do something about that retard, will you, please?" Frank growled to Ulysses. "Sit on him or something."

Ulysses happily obliged. His five-foot-wide body obliterated all of David except his head, until their combined weight broke the chair and sent them sprawling to the carpet.

Marty succeeded, with studied effort, in overlooking all this. Lou was glad Charles was not with him. "How *are* you this morning, Lou?" he asked, with feeling and concern throbbing in his voice as if someone had pushed those particular buttons on his electronic organ.

"Fine," she answered.

"I'm *so* glad to hear that," he said with echoes of sobbing violins. He sounded, she thought, like a funeral director consoling the bereaved.

"I was sure you didn't need any more disturbance," he continued carefully, "so I came over here and woke the boys first instead. I waited till ten-thirty to call you."

"Thanks for being so considerate, Marty," she said, watching him narrowly, wondering what trick he was going to pull next. "Why don't you do that every morning?"

"Why, certainly, if you want me to." He was so obliging it was unreal. Only Lou knew why.

"Good way to wake her up fast," David said. "Bring her in here first thing every morning and make her look at four ugly faces."

"Right," Marty agreed absently. "Kids, I have good news for you. Wonderful news!" He sounded like his old excitable self again. "You're booked into Las Vegas for the holidays! After we wind up here, you can start packing your bags. You're headed for the city that never sleeps. Bright lights, big names, big spenders, and pretty palm trees!"

"How did you manage to arrange that?" Frank asked.

Marty was careful to look away from Lou while explaining. "I told you kids when you first signed with me, I have the best connections in the business. Maybe now you'll believe me. I got a call from a friend of mine this morning, a Mr. William Bland. He's basically a New York-based producer, but he has contacts with talent packagers and casino and hotel owners all around the country. After he caught your act at the concert last night, he was so enthusiastic he got right on the phone to Vegas and set the deal up for you."

He did it to keep me quiet, Lou thought, staring at the back of Marty's fluffy head and at his heavy, sagging behind. Men with droopy rear ends were not to be trusted, according to Momma's home wisdom. Still, if it was a decent deal, she wouldn't make any noise. "What kind of a deal is it?" she asked, forcing Marty to turn and look at her.

"Really sensational for a beginning group. Almost unheard-of, really. You'll be working at the Carousel Casino Hotel, one of the top three in Vegas. You'll do three shows a night—7:30, 10:30, and 1:30 AM, Tuesdays through Sundays; you'll have Mondays off. You won't be in the biggest room, you'll be in one of the lounges, but it's the main lounge, the one everybody flocks to. And if the management likes you—you just *might* end up on the big stage with the biggies. You couldn't ask for a better break."

"Never mind all that. What kind of *money,* man?" Ulysses wanted to know.

"Relax. Leave that up to me. I'm still working on getting you the most I can."

The four of them stared at him.

"All right," he sighed. "Two thousand a week, that's eight hundred a week for Lou, four each for the rest of you, minus expenses and my commissions."

"No way! Equal pay!" Lou shouted, setting off a chant, all four of them shouting "No way! Equal pay! No way! Equal pay!" until Marty covered his ears.

"All *right,* already!" he exclaimed. "Any way you want to slice it up is fine with me. Your Vegas contract escalates, by the way. If you get held over after four weeks, you get a thousand-dollar raise."

"Hot pastrami!" Ulysses cried. "Talk that beautiful talk, Mister Manager."

"Yeah," Frank agreed. "Money is honey to my ears."

"Don't spend it till you get it," Marty warned. "Remember, we're up to our belly buttons in debt."

But they were too busy whooping and hollering, slapping hands and pounding shoulders and covering Lou with big sloppy kisses, to pay any attention. They had recovered, at least for a moment, that warm family feeling of sister and brothers. Lou hoped it would last.

"Glad I made you kids happy," Marty said, mopping his face with one of his monogrammed handkerchiefs. He had been sweating heavily all morning, Lou noticed, tempted to suggest he send for Gloria and his extra shirts. "Now," he said, "you've got another concert tonight at the Linden, one next weekend at Madison Square Garden, another three weeks downtown at Macro-mé, and then we leave."

"Hey, wait a minute," David said. "That sounds like we'll be working on *Christmas.*"

"Entertainers don't celebrate Christmas. They help *other* people celebrate it," Marty told him sharply.

"Well, *we* want to go home for Christmas," David insisted.

Marty began pulling at his hair with both hands. "Why am I working with a kiddie act? I must be a masochist. I must be crazy. What is it? You want to see Santa Claus?"

"Unh-unh," Ulysses told him. "We want to *be* Santa Claus. Got a lot of little stockings back home that need filling. So we need to go home with some change in our pockets."

"That's right," Lou agreed, thinking of her little brothers and sisters. She wanted to get frilly dresses for Bernice and Clarice and her niece Cora Lee. A set of racing cars for Andrew, bikes for Gordon and Randolph, a set of trains for them all, and some small, special things to cheer William's heart and, hopefully, thaw Momma's.

"How *much* change?" Marty asked warily.

"Oh, I'll need at least three hundred," she said lightly. "How about the rest of y'all?"

"The same," they responded.

"That is not change you are talking about," Marty informed them gravely. "That is big bucks, and I am not Santa Claus. There *isn't* any Santa Claus, in case nobody's told you yet, and you don't get paid for not working."

"Well, how much have we made so far?" Ulysses wanted to know.

"Less than you owe me," Marty said.

"How *much?*" Frank pressured him.

"You've made a thousand on the concert, a hundred a night in the Village, that's sixteen hundred. Deduct the three hundred I already laid out for your spending money, leaves thirteen hundred—"

"That's enough for our Christmas shopping," Lou interrupted.

"I'm not finished. There's five hundred on my charge accounts for clothes, lunches, miscellaneous promotional expenses; another eleven-fifty for the hotel bill—thank God you'll get free rooms out in Vegas—*that* leaves you owing me three-fifty. Add on Charles's salary and my commissions, you owe me around a thousand. And that's just since we came to New York. Before *that*—"

Marty was interrupted by a barrage of questions.

"What about the album? Isn't it selling?"

"*We* didn't hire Charles. Why are we paying him?"

"How *much* are we paying him?"

"What's all this 'promotional expense,' anyway? What's it for?"

"Has to be done, has to be done," Marty muttered. "As for the album, Lou, we won't get a statement from Jewel till next June. You know that."

Lou didn't know it, really. Twice a year, checks came for her share of their single record, but she had forgotten exactly when they came. She signed them and turned them over to William, that was all. She decided she had not been a very good businesswoman so far. But she thought Marty was not a good businessman, either, to spend money before it was earned.

Yet Ulysses, who was usually so sensible, wanted to do the same thing. Everybody goes crazy at Christmas, she thought.

"You said we'll be making more money in Vegas," Ulysses pointed out. "And we'll be living rent-free. Can't you advance us some Christmas money?"

Marty considered this. "Maybe. But I told you already, you don't get paid for not working. Every store in this town delivers, you know. So work and shop. Shop and send."

"Marty," Lou asked, "how important is that job in the Village, anyhow? If we're moving up to the big time like you say, do we really have to stay there the whole three weeks? Can't we quit after two weeks instead of three, and go home for Christmas?"

Marty averted his head from her look, shrugged, and began what she called his "sit-down dance," a nervous, rapid jiggling of the foot that was crossed over his knee. "I can try to work something out with the owners. If I can arrange it with Jan and

Maribel at Macro-mé, you can go home December 24th and fly out to Vegas December 29th. You *have* to work out there New Year's Eve."

Macro-mé, where they sang every night except Sunday and Monday, was a popular restaurant featuring hanging decorations that looked like spiders' webs and equally insubstantial foods, such as bird-seed pancakes and bean-sprout sandwiches, at very high prices. Marty's admonition, "That's only *if* I can work it out with the management, now. You never know when we might need them again," was drowned out by the boys' cries of jubilation. Marty was bending over so far backward to please her, he was practically looking at her upside down from between his knees, Lou thought. But, in their excitement, none of the fellows seemed to notice.

Then Frank gave her that look of intense interest that always made her tingle with pleasure and for a moment there was a flicker of something else in his eyes, a questioning she hoped she would not have to answer. Just as she hoped their special closeness would not change the family feeling the four of them had just regained.

CHAPTER 7

The group certainly had more family feeling than Lou found at home on Christmas Eve. After a flurry of greetings, her younger brothers and sisters ran off in different directions like mice scared by a cat. Leaving her alone in rooms that seemed empty and musty, as if the house had been vacant for years.

Home was not home anymore. Everything looked smaller. The house on Carlisle Street had always been cramped, but now it had shrunk to doll's-house size. Her treasured room of her own seemed like a stuffy closet in comparison to her hotel room. The Avenue that had seemed a broad highway to adventure was now just another grubby side street. Even her big brother William had lost stature in her eyes. His stooped posture had taken three inches from his height. Worse, he had a ghostly, haunted look as if something had sucked his soul from his body. Louretta did not ask him why. She did not know how to ask. She simply handed him his present, a rolled-up poster with LOVE printed on it in four colors and forty different typefaces, and hoped it would help.

As for Momma, she scarcely spoke to Lou after informing her that she had seen that scandalous hussy picture in that dirty notoriety paper, and she looked at her as if she were a hopelessly hardened sinner. Maybe I am, thought Lou wearily as she put on the demure white dress to wear to Christmas Eve services. She had just endured a stiff meal that was unfamiliar in the root sense of the word, a long silence punctuated only by "Please pass the salt"s and "Please pass the gravy"s like commas, and a chorus of "Excuse me"s like exclamation points at the end. She was going to church tonight to appease her mother, but she doubted very much that she could achieve the only thing that would soften Momma's heart—a genuine possession by the Holy Ghost.

The New Cheerful Baptist Church, where Momma and Jethro's mother, Mrs. Jerutha Jackson, were faithful members, looked smaller too. It had seemed large and grand when the congregation bought it to replace the rented storefront that became William's printing shop and, for a while, the singing group's clubhouse. But now Lou noticed its narrow, sunken steps worn down by many footprints, its small stiff benches in two short rows, its worn red carpet that showed many threads. Behind the gilt altar rail, the choir sang:

"Mary, Mary,
What you gonna name that pretty little baby?"

The deacons and elders sat on a separate bench of honor at one side near the altar, because they were supposed to be closest to the throne of God. As the really lovely singing ended, Lou resolved not to let her mind wander from the sermon.

Unfortunately, the new pastor, Reverend Boyd, was a plump young man who bounced a lot and worked up a sweat as he preached, inevitably reminding her of Marty.

"Ooooooh!" he cried with a great intake of breath. "Oh, Lord Jesus, tonight is the night we have all been waiting for. Tonight is the night you are coming to earth for us. But how many of us will be coming to *you?*

"Who among us is born without sin?" continued Reverend Boyd, mopping his brow. "Only you, Lord! Only you were born perfect and pure of a spotless virgin. But nobody else in this church is free of sin. And every year we stray away from you, no, every *day* we stay away from you, more sins pile up! Now I know some of you are pret'near saints at sixty—and some of you are sinners at sixteen! So old in sin, so steeped in sin, so *deep* in sin your physical forms may be young, but your souls are as old and rotten as a shipwreck covered with rust and barnacles!"

Louretta was almost positive Momma had been talking to the

pastor about her, and that he was now preaching *to* her. She sat stiffly, staring straight ahead, showing no reaction.

"I don't know if any of you've ever seen a shipwreck, but I can tell you it's a terrible sight! All those people pushing and shoving, and crying and panicking, and singing hymns when it's too late! When they're already about to *drown!* Children, don't you be like that! Don't wait till you're going down for the last time! I don't care if none of you ever saw a shipwreck. You don't need to see one to know this life has its stormy seas!"

"Amen!" cried Mrs. Jackson.

"Life isn't all smooth sailing, children. It has its turbulent waves and treacherous currents. You can get swamped and tossed and even thrown overboard if you don't have a lifeline to the Lord!"

"That's right!" endorsed the elders.

"You can drift off your course and get lost in some flimsy little man-made ship if you aren't anchored to the rock of the church!

"You can founder on hidden rocks and sink way, way down to the slimy *bottom* if you don't have a good pilot! Y'know, when you get into foreign waters, the captain's not as important as the pilot! The pilot knows those strange waters best, and the pilot tells the *captain* what to do! Well, the *Laaaawd* is my pilot! When the tempest is raging, and the waves are cresting, and my little ship seems about to founder on the rocks, I cry out to Him, 'Lord Jesus, take over! Guide my hand on this wheel! Steer me to safety!'

"And He answers me *every time! He* takes over and guides me home to port. He speaks to the waves and they obey His will!" Reverend Boyd dropped his voice from a shout to a hushed, dramatic whisper. "He says one word, 'Peace,' and the troubled waters are still."

In the background, softly, the choir sang "Peace, Be Still" while Reverend Boyd continued, "Is Jesus *your* pilot? Is he steering *your* ship?" He held out a welcoming hand and implored, "Come! Come to the place where He is waiting to take your hand and take you over. Come now! Who will come?"

He was staring at Louretta but, though the movement in the little church was contagious she did not budge. All around her, people were rising from their seats and moving toward the altar to accept salvation. Some walked sedately, some danced, some even had fits and fell, and rolled or crawled. Somehow, they found their way there, and as each one made it over to grace, the saved church members thanked the Lord with loud Hallelujahs. Momma nudged Lou several times, but she did not respond.

Then she was jerked out of her immobility, not by the Holy Spirit, but by the sight of her former boyfriend Calvin, advancing in a slow, trancelike wobble to the altar, where he collapsed and was assisted to his feet by two male ushers. It troubled her to see Calvin in this state. And yet she envied it.

"I always knew that was a fine young man," Momma said to Mrs. Jackson. "Serious."

"Maybe too serious," Mrs. Jackson whispered back. "He's been real pitiful since his father died. His dad was all he had in this world."

"What?" Louretta exclaimed.

Mrs. Jackson patted her hand. "I guess no one told you. We buried Calvin's father right after you went away."

"Well, he's not alone now that he's found Jesus," Momma said. "I'm glad he's not worldly like *some* of our young people. This world ain't nothing but the Devil's work of deception."

Louretta knew what was expected of her. But a heavy stone was forming in her heart instead of the lightness of salvation. Though the choir was compelling, she could not feel the spirit moving inside her, could not feel it pushing her toward the altar. Knowing Momma wanted her to be born again only increased her resistance. But that was not all; she simply couldn't feel what the saved ones felt, couldn't even summon up the soulful feelings she had once known singing in a choir like the one up there. She was still too much of a believer to fake a spiritual transformation, but she had moved too far from this small world to return to it again.

The passage from Matthew, "Because strait is the gate, and narrow is the way . . . and few there be that find it," came to her mind.

Those few—they were not so many, after all; maybe seven—were welcomed into the church by the pastor, then taken into a back room for mysterious rites and instructions. The calmed congregation joined the choir in singing Christmas carols while ushers passed out candles. Then each candle was lit in turn from the ones held by the choir as they walked, singing, around the aisles and back to the choir loft.

"Well," Momma said to her as they left, "at least I *got* you here. Maybe you'll be saved someday."

"Maybe," Louretta echoed. She tried to think of something else to say. All she could come up with was, "It was a pretty service."

"Pretty?" Momma said scornfully. "Pretty's a word to use for party dresses and fancy shoes. It ain't a word for a chance to welcome the Lord into your life and give up your life of sin."

"How do you know it's sin, Momma?"

"I know. I knew all along, even before I saw that picture. And now I know for *sure*."

"*What* do you know?"

"I know everything, that's what."

"What?"

"I 'spect it can wait till we get home. I never believed in putting family business in the street, and I'm not about to start now. Good night, Sister Jerutha. May the spirit stay with you."

"The same to you, Sister Rosetta. Though sometimes I think we both need someone *else* to stay with us, too. Merry Christmas!" And Mrs. Jackson, her husband dead five years, her only son two, darted quickly into the little two-story house in which she now lived alone.

Louretta longed to follow her instead of going home with Momma. Mrs. Jackson was eternally young and fun to be with; outrageous remarks like her parting one popped out of her mouth all the time. She was devout, but she didn't seem to see any contradiction between being a Christian and having a good time. And when she was serious, she was an encyclopedia of common-sense wisdom and fascinating information drawn from her years of experience in business and the many books and magazines she kept up with. Momma didn't read anything but the Bible, and lately she seemed to be concentrating strictly on the cruel Old Testament texts about judgment and punishment.

"She's my best friend, and she's saved, but sometimes I think Jerutha Jackson still gives the Devil room to work in her life," Momma declared as she closed the door of their own house behind them. "As for *you,* Miss—I want to know what you're doing with these." She held out the round compact that held Lou's birth-control pills. "Oh, yes, I guess you think your mother's dumb and ignorant, but I know what they are."

Lou was wild with fury at her mother's having snooped in her purse. "I guess you want me to bring home a baby like Arneatha did. Is that what you want? I guess you think that would be the *holy* thing to do!"

"Careful, girl," Momma warned. "What you mean? Remember, I don't allow no blaspheming in this house."

For answer Louretta hummed the tune of "Mary, Mary, What You Gonna Name That Pretty Little Baby?"

"I don't allow signifying, either. *Explain* yourself."

"Well, Mary got Jesus without a husband, didn't she?"

Momma's response was predictable and immediate. After the back-handed blow, she moaned, "Sweet Jesus, help me. This child's gone to the Devil. No hope for her at all."

"You can take your Jesus and give me this world!" Louretta screamed, and ran to her room, her face stinging, her pill compact clutched tightly in her hand.

Later, after she had had her long exhausting cry and slipped downstairs to pile the expensive store-wrapped gifts under the tree, she opened the compact and saw the clipping of herself half naked that Momma had folded and stuffed inside. Saw it through her mother's shocked eyes, and was ashamed. She cried some more, finally fell asleep, and slept late.

Lou awoke to find she had missed the best part of Christmas, the surprise part. The presents had been ravaged long before she was up; ribbons and paper were scattered all around the small living room. She had missed seeing Randolph discover his training-wheel bike and Gordon his five-speed; her six- and fourteen-year-old brothers were already somewhere outdoors with them. William had just left for the shop, muttering something about work to be done even on a holiday. Only twelve-year-old Andrew was in the room, staring as if hypnotized at his electric cars as they whizzed around the tracks. And only one unopened present remained under the tree.

It was for her. A bottle of perfume with a note:

A merry to my cherry Lou! See you at the party at the old clubhouse
tonight. Wish you could wear nothing but this. But I
can wait till

Later,
Frank

Maybe he had misspelled "cherie" or "cheery." Maybe not. Lou quickly crumpled the note and stuffed it into her bra before Momma could see it. Yes, she was a sinner in the eyes of the saved, and she felt guilty and happy all at once. They would have labeled her a sinner even if she had let no one touch her, she realized, and suddenly the guilt was washed away in a flood of excitement.

But she was still hurt by her mother's low opinion of her. There had been no word of thanks for her gifts or the money she'd given her mother, and when she followed her nose to the kitchen and its warm aromas, Momma brusquely refused her offer of help, as if Lou had a contagious disease that might contaminate the family dinner. The meal, unlike last night's, was bounteous, thanks to her contribution, and blessedly noisy because the kids were high with Christmas excitement. William appeared just in time to bless the table and eat swiftly, then excused himself, saying he had to help with preparations for the party. When, automatically, Lou began clearing the table, Momma gave her such a sharply discouraging look she almost dropped the plates.

Lou returned to her room, laid out all the outfits she had brought with her, and finally selected what she thought was a conservative dress: a silky, scarlet one with a flaring skirt that, when she danced, would reveal matching red panties underneath. She opened only the top button, stuck a holly leaf in the buttonhole, dabbed on her new perfume, and came downstairs to meet Momma's accusing glare.

"Come here, hussy. Where do you think you're going in that outfit?"

"What's wrong with it?"

"It's whorish, that's what. That color!"

"It's *Christmas,* Momma. Red is for Christmas."

"Look at those shoes!"

They matched the dress. They had high heels and red laces that went all the way up to her calves. Lou shrugged; there was really no defending those shoes. "Did you like your stole, Momma?"

"My what?"

"Your wrap." Her gift to Momma had been a hand-crocheted wool stole in a lovely shade of morning-glory blue. Next year, she had sworn to herself, it would be mink.

"It's all right," Momma said grudgingly, "but it was bought with the Devil's money.—I asked you before, girl, where are you going?"

To hell, Lou almost said, but for once held her troublesome tongue. "To a Christmas party at William's place." She made her escape quickly.

Her unspoken retort would have been accurate, she thought when she arrived at William's printing shop. The first floor, once their clubhouse, once roomy enough to accommodate two dozen teenagers and all their hopes and dreams, now seemed cramped, shabby, and sad. William had swept the place and pushed his equipment against the wall to make a dance floor.

Someone had put up a skimpily decorated Christmas tree, so old it had shed most of its needles, and a scratchy record was playing on the stereo. But no one was dancing.

Lou's old friends were hanging around the edges of the room, leaning against the walls and looking uncomfortable. She walked up to Sharon, who had two babies now, and Florence, who had one, and Joella, who was very pregnant.

"Hi," she said to each of them.

"Hi," they said reluctantly, as if the response had been dragged out of them. They alternately glared at her with open hostility and averted their eyes as if ashamed.

What was wrong? Louretta wondered. All three were wearing bright new Christmas dresses, but compared to hers with its designer label they were tacky, she realized, ashamed for even thinking Charles's word.

"I like your dress," Joella finally said.

"Thanks. I like yours too," Lou replied. Tall, regal Joella had always looked good in exotic prints like the blazing orange African one she was draped in tonight.

"Would you trade?"

"What?"

"I said, would you trade dresses with me?"

"No," Lou admitted. Joella's was a maternity dress. But that was not the reason, and they both knew it.

"Then don't pull that phony stuff on me, girl. I don't appreciate you grinnin' in my face and low-ratin' me behind my back."

"Yeah," Sharon put in, "You may be up there on top now, but remember, I knew you when you were down here with us."

"You came from the same dirt on the Avenue we did," Florence said viciously, "so don't look at us like we're dirt now."

"I don't look at you like you're dirt. *You* do," she told them, and fled to the darkest corner. A refreshment table had been set up there. Behind William's back, Frank and David were busy emptying pints from various pockets into the punch bowl.

"Have some joy juice, baby?" Frank whispered. "We got to

do something to liven up this lame party."

"Later," she replied, and reached for her brother's hand. "Let's dance, William. Maybe we can get the others started." But they slow-danced the entire record alone.

"It was sweet of you to do this, Brother Bill," she said as he walked her slowly back to the corner. "Only—"

"Only the kids aren't acting like it's a party, right? Don't be blue, Sister Lou. They'll loosen up after a while. I saw your friends tightening up the punch. I just pretended not to see."

"You're wonderful, William. You try so hard to make people happy. I think you're the only friend I've got left here at home. The only family, too. This has been the worst Christmas I ever spent in my life."

"Bound to happen sometime, Lou. Christmas is a big day for kids. The glow kind of gets dimmer when you grow up."

"That's not what I meant."

He knew what she did mean. "Momma is old-fashioned, Lou. Set in her ways. But she loves you."

"I guess so," she said. "You don't look like you have much Christmas spirit yourself. Been seeing Miss Hodges?"

He shook his head. His eyes had that absent look, as if something vital had gone out of them. "Momma invited her over for a little woman-to-woman talk. Told her she ought to look for a man in her own league. A *professional* man." His voice trembled with anger. "And she found one. A dentist. She found him so fast I haven't gotten used to it yet. But I will."

"Momma meddles too much!" Lou cried. "She just wants to hang onto you and your paycheck. You should't stand for it, William! You ought to fight to get Laura back. You're as good as any dentist or any other man. And she loves you. Nobody could *help* loving you."

He shook his head. "Too late, Lou. The dentist was rich, rushed and single. He didn't have to wait for a bunch of kids to grow up. Miss Hodges is now Mrs. Reginald Dorsey. Mrs. *Doctor* Reginald Dorsey. I don't blame her, Lou. Don't you blame her, either."

"I don't. I blame Momma. And I blame you, too, for putting up with her meddling." She turned abruptly, her skirt whirling like a red blossom, and was startled to find an owlish face staring directly into hers. Fess Satterthwaite, once the group genius and militant—in a sober dark suit and tie. No more dungarees and dashikis peppered with Black Power buttons. No trace of the old menace in his manner. He seemed calm, self-assured, and astonishingly grown up.

Lou didn't know how to treat this stranger. "What's happenin', Fess?" she ventured.

"Law school is what's happenin'," he replied. "Call me Phil, please. I transferred to prep school on an Upward Bound scholarship, finished in half a year, and got into an accelerated prelaw program at the University. Got a four-point-oh average and a couple of law professors in my corner already helping me bone up for my LSAT's. Care to dance?"

"Sure," she said, and regretted it. His dancing was jerky and erratic; Fess was all brains and no rhythm. "I'm going to be a corporation lawyer *and* a civil rights lawyer," he confided. "Sort of a legal Robin Hood. Rich clients will pay me high fees so I can afford to participate in the poor people's struggle."

"Great," she said sincerely. "It's really great to run into somebody who knows exactly where he's headed."

"Don't you?"

"Sure," she said with a confidence she did not feel. "Still writing poetry?" Fess had written angry poems and articles, and published them on William's press to stir up their friends and the black community.

"Nope, just term papers. I'll get back to it sometime."

Fess had hated Lou for curbing the kids' anger after he'd gotten them ready to erupt into violence—hated her with a special intensity, she'd found out later, because he was attracted to her. But now he had other preoccupations.

"You own half of two of our songs, you know," she reminded him. "Those are *your* lyrics up there on the top hundred. William's been taking care of business for me, but he's had a lot on his mind lately. Maybe you can ask your law professor friends to help him. Will you, Fess?"

"Phil," he corrected again. "Sure, I'll get them on the case right away. I've heard some bad things about the music industry. Wouldn't want you to get cheated out of anything. Wouldn't want to get cheated myself."

At the end of the record, they stepped apart and shook hands. It was the only way to part company with the cool, businesslike adult her once intensely friendly enemy had become.

Lou retreated to what she thought was a neutral corner to find her first love, Calvin, predictably hiding in the shadows. His jaw was set more stubbornly than ever, and his eyes had a feverish, excited look that reminded her of the portraits of Old Testament prophets.

"I was sorry to hear about your father, Calvin," she said, touching his hand.

He pulled away from her touch as if it burned him. "The Lord giveth and the Lord taketh away," he intoned. "What with working, studying, and serving the Lord, I don't have time to think about my troubles."

"That's good," she said. "This is the Lord's birthday, though, you know. Can't we celebrate a little? For old times' sake?"

"Old times are gone forever, Lou," he said. "You're in the world, and I've decided to leave it behind."

She received this news with less shock than she might have if a new song lyric sparked by William's remarks and fanned by Calvin's had not begun to explode like fireworks in her mind. Something about old rivers and new water, old loves and new loves, and water under a bridge . . . She could already hear the theme.

"I'm glad you're still working with William," she said absently.

"Oh, yes, your brother is going to make me a partner as soon as I've perfected my craft in trade school."

"Are you still painting?"

He shook his head. "Art is one of the Devil's inventions, Lou. It's nothing but vanity. All vanity."

She was horrified and speechless. She was still struggling to frame a reply when Frank grabbed her hand and pulled her forcibly onto the dance floor.

Calvin disappeared like a frightened rabbit.

"Animal," she reproved Frank. "Caveman. You don't have to prove you're stronger than I am."

"I know about you and that dude, baby. I don't want that old torch to get lit again."

"No danger," she said sadly, watching Calvin's stiff back as he left the party. "I think he's a little bit crazy."

"A *little bit* crazy. He's stark raving mad! Afflicted with the worst case of the Gods I ever saw. It's contagious, I hear. I didn't want you to catch it from him."

"No danger of that either," she said ruefully. "The whole church tried last night, and they couldn't get to me."

"Good," he said, pulling her closer. "Girl, I sure will be glad when we get back on the road."

"That makes two of us."

"That makes *four* of us," he said, hands moving sensuously up and down her back as they danced. "I don't know why we were all so crazy to get home for Christmas."

"Neither do I," said Lou, letting her body settle deliciously into his. "I can't wait to get on that plane."

CHAPTER 8

Lou hardly looked out the window of the jumbo jet. There was nothing to see but clouds, anyhow, and she was angrily, intently concentrating on writing the lyrics for one of her new songs. This time she was really leaving home, and the verses were helping her put an emotional distance between her and Carlisle Street, while the smooth-engined, wide-bodied jet took care of the miles. Frank had sat with her for a while, then grown restless and left her to her composing. She put a period at the end of the last verse and looked up at last.

Across the aisle, in one of the six-seat rows, the fellows were studying some books they had bought in the airport. She leaned over and looked at the titles: *Beating the Odds at the Tables, Barney Smith's Basic Blackjack System,* and *Scientific Card-Counting.*

Just then the plane hit an air pocket, making her stomach rise to her chest and fall again. Funny—she'd ridden through two hours of intermittent air pockets, writing steadily in her notebook, and the bumps hadn't bothered her stomach before. But when the stewardess reached her seat, she didn't want any dinner.

She leaned forward and tapped Marty's shoulder beside Charles's in the seat in front of her. "What do you think of this?"

He scanned her notebook quickly and said, "Looks terrific, Lou. Got a tune?"

"Sort of. In my head. When I get to a piano I can work it out."

"I'll have one put in your room."

She held out her hand for the return of her notebook.

"No, Lou, you might lose this," Marty said. "Let me get some copies made and get it copyrighted for you."

She shrugged and rang the stewardess's bell for a pillow and a blanket. The plane's air conditioning was bone-chilling. She had a double seat to herself, and all she wanted to do was get warm and go to sleep—forget the misery at home and the uncertainty ahead.

When she awoke, little chimes were ringing and the NO SMOKING and FASTEN SEAT BELTS sign were on. She sat up, rubbing her eyes, and locked the clasp around her waist. They were descending toward a strange landscape that looked like the moon. Miles and miles of barren sand. Then the plane banked, and she could glimpse an oasis of trees and buildings. Palm trees. Tall buildings. A lake. And, even in the daytime, a rainbow of flashing colored lights. She rubbed her eyes again because it all seemed so unreal.

Frank reached across the aisle and touched her knee. "My sophisticated lady. How blasé can you get? Slept through her first plane ride."

She yawned. "Why not? What's so special about it? It's boring,"

"Blaseé, blaseé!" he teased.

"Besides, I didn't sleep the whole time. I was working for a while."

"We were studying, too."

"I noticed. I hope you guys won't—"

But her comment was cut short by the pilot's voice on the speaker system. "Ladies and gentlemen, we are about to land at Las Vegas on schedule. It is now 5:02 PM, Western Time."

Lou obeyed the rules, but the boys were too excited to stay in their seats. They bopped up and down the aisles, leaning across startled passengers for views from all the windows. The stewardesses either didn't notice them or didn't care. Finally they landed with a surprisingly gentle thump and skidded noisily toward the airport building.

They debarked into the desert and stepped immediately into a van with CAROUSEL CASINO HOTEL lettered colorfully on its sides. The van was air-conditioned, but it dropped them and their luggage off into the warmest air Lou had ever felt in winter. And on the busiest, most dazzling street she had ever seen.

"Looks like Christmas every day out here," Frank remarked, squinting from the glare of neon lights all around him.

"That's right," Marty assented enthusiastically. "This is it, kids! The famous Strip! And this is where you'll be working."

They stared in disbelief at a building that looked like three striped cement circus tents, each as large as an amphitheater, with thirty-foot towers rising from each of the side tents and a neon-lit merry-go-round whirling madly on the low center roof.

"You've only got two hours till showtime," Marty informed them, "so get some rest and do your sight-seeing tomorrow."

"Unh-*unh,*" Frank objected. "We got to see some sights *now.* We got plenty of rest on the plane."

"So did I," said Lou. "Besides," she said as hunger pangs struck, "I'm starving."

"Okay," Marty said. "There's a coffee shop in the hotel, but you can try the Delite up the street. Don't wander off too far, though." He checked his watch. "It's five-thirty, Western Time. Set your watches, and be back in half an hour, forty-five minutes at the outside, for a run-through and your changes. Got to make a good first impression, you know. Pick up your keys at the desk and meet us in the Showplace Theater at six sharp."

Lou felt like Alice in Wonderland. Marty's final shout, "If you're not back on time I'll send the cops after you. I'm your legal guardian, you know!" barely registered on her consciousness. There were too many dazzling distractions.

The four of them were like dwarfs turned loose in a giant-sized world. Everything around them was from ten to fifty times human scale. Giant cut-out forms of showgirls, cowboys, and entertainers loomed brilliantly in the air. Lights advertising *Keno, Slots, Games,* and *Girls* blinked everywhere, blinding them. The sidewalk crowds of pushing, shoving people *did* remind Lou of Christmas Eve; their eyes had the same glazed, frantic expression she had seen on the faces of last-minute shoppers. But none of them carried shopping bags. And there was no snow. After three blocks of the shoving crowds, the glaring lights, and the shimmering heat, Lou said, "Let's go back to that Delite Deli place." She was still wearing the red high-heeled shoes, and her feet hurt.

"There must be some food in here." David said, pushing his way into one of the many doors with neon *Casino* signs.

Inside they found the target of all the frantic people: rows of machines and gaming tables. This is *crazy,* Lou decided, and headed for a side door marked "Salad Bar." It led to a salad bar, all right, as well as a regular bar. She filled her bowl with green leaves, bacon bits, tomato and egg slices, and macaroni. But when she turned back to find a table, she was alone. When she had emptied her bowl, she was still alone.

She sat thoughtfully for several minutes. Then David appeared. "Lou, can you let me have a couple of bucks for a sandwich?"

"Sure," she said, wondering how she had missed the sandwich shop. He disappeared instantly.

In less than a minute he was back. "Lou, can you lend me—?"

"No," she interrupted, beginning to guess what was happening.

"But I'm still growing!" he protested. I can't make it on one sandwich. And that airline food was just what they call it. Full of air!"

He was still holding out his hand. She put nothing in it.

"David," she said, "go on over to the salad bar and help yourself. I'll pay the cashier."

Sheepishly, he obeyed. She thought she knew why he wanted money. Frank and Ulysses were there to confirm her suspicions before David returned with his heaped plate.

"Did you see that old lady next to us take a *bucket* full of dollars out of that slot machine?" Frank asked excitedly.

"Sure," Ulysses said. "But how many buckets did she put into it before we got here?"

"Oh, who cares, man?" Frank said gleefully. "This is the life. This is fun!"

"Your idea of fun," Lou told him, "is my idea of insanity."

"Aw, stop being so serious, Lou. Loosen up. Live a little."

And only five days ago they'd both called *Calvin* crazy. He was, of course, for wanting to kill the artist in himself. But now Frank was enraptured by something almost as suicidal.

As David approached, Ulysses whispered, "The kid thought he had beginners' luck. But it turned on him."

"I heard you. I had more than beginners' luck. I got a hundred silver dollars my third try."

"Yeah, and you gave 'em all back on your next tries. Didn't take long, either, playing five machines at once," Frank said. "Slots are for suckers anyway. The real money is at the blackjack tables. I heard this old guy talking about how he won thirty thousand last night. He was using the same system as my book."

"Frank—there's no system that can beat these places."

"Aw, girl, what do *you* know about it?"

Clearly, he wasn't going to listen to her. If this kept up, she'd have to find somebody he and David *would* listen to.

Ulysses was still acting normal, but the other two seemed to have been turned into zombies. Their eyes had the same glazed, feverish look she had observed on the people in the streets. It scared her. Frank, who could not stop looking at her a few days ago, was too busy explaining the "system" to notice her until he thought of a question: "Baby, you got any bread on you?"

"No," she lied, and stood up. "It's time to get back to the hotel, anyway. We've got a show to do at seven-thirty remember?"

But the Carousel, of course, had gaming tables and slot machines just like the place up the street. It had many more of them, in plusher, more alluring surroundings. And the lounge they worked, the Zodiac Room, was the one everyone had to pass through to enter the bustling casino. It was furnished with blue plush carpeting, large blue lounge chairs, and a blue ceiling decorated with winking replicas of the constellations. Their costumes matched it perfectly—Charles had done a better job of designing than he knew, at least for *this* job—and the people who watched them as they sipped their drinks seemed to enjoy their singing. But after each of their three shows, the boys disappeared and Lou was left alone.

The same thing happened on the next two nights, December 30th and 31st. Ulysses sat with her after their first New Year's Eve show, looking as worried as she felt, but talking about everything but gambling. After the second show, he lumbered off as usual in search of Frank and David after saying, "Hang in there, baby. Got to try and get those guys in line. Got to try one more time."

Lou knew he was having no more success in stopping their gambling than she had. Someone else would have to do it. But she knew no one in Las Vegas, and her tension was so severe she was unable to think of any place to turn or anyone to send for.

Hearing "Auld Lang Syne" swell from the crowded theater upstairs, Lou didn't feel like being alone. As soon as she sat down at a table, a small, dark, fierce-faced man who had been watching her intently while she was onstage came over. He was so sure of himself and of her availability that she couldn't convince him it wasn't his company she wanted. When he moved toward her again after the last show, Lou fled upstairs, locked her door, and slept alone.

Maybe it was the plane ride or the time change or the climate change or the nine shows or the drinks between shows, but she slept later every day, and awoke feeling lost and strange. With neon lights flashing in the daytime and air conditioning in January, this place was unreal.

On New Year's Day, there was a soft whistling outside her door, followed by "Sweet Lou" sung to the tune of "Sweet Sue" in a rich, familiar baritone voice.

"Go away," Lou called.

"Have a heart, lady," Frank pleaded. "I'm a lonely stranger in this town."

She opened the door only partway. "You won't get any sympathy from me," she told him. "I had to spend New Year's Eve in that bar by myself, without even a good-luck kiss. I had to fend off a sex-starved Sicilian without any help from you."

"Gee, hon, I'm sorry," he said contritely. "I was so busy, I guess I forgot it was New Year's Eve."

"Sure. You were with another lady."

"Who told you that?" he asked so indignantly she became suspicious.

"I meant Lady Luck."

"Lady Luck is no lady," he responded. "But I think I've got her figured out now. See, you count the cards, and you don't bet unless every hand around the table is showing higher than four. Then you can beat the odds."

She didn't understand it. "I don't want to hear about it."

"I won big the first two nights, enough to bankroll my boy David *and* keep myself rolling. I didn't lose at all until late last night. I was hoping you could lend me a few bills to build my stake up again."

"Frank, I'm fresh out of cash. But if I *had* any I wouldn't give it to you for that!"

"Did I say 'give'? I said *'lend'!*" He paced the hall angrily. "Where's Marty, anyway? Have you seen him? We're supposed to get paid the first of the month. That's today."

Lou shrugged. "Go look for him, if you're so anxious to give your pay back where it comes from."

"Hey, you're looking at a *winner,* baby. I can't lose."

He did look like a winner in his sharp silk shirt and matching woven slacks, just a shade deeper brown than his skin, which was set off richly by a gold neck chain. But then, so did most of the well-dressed people who came through the casino's doors. They couldn't all be winners, or the place wouldn't stay in business.

That thought made her call him. "Say, Frank, you know

something?"

He stopped pacing and came in. "What?"

"I haven't seen any black people here except us. Have you?"

"Not yet. I hear a charter bus of Elks was here last weekend, and a busload of frat men and their wives is due in this weekend. But so far, I've seen no guests. Just help. Porters, waiters, and maids. And one of the dealers, a real fox. I'm going to stick at her table tonight."

"I hope she cleans you out," Lou said in a fit of jealous anger that chased him from her room.

Marty, who'd been missing ever since their arrival, never appeared that day either. Charles showed up instead to help them work on their act. He explained that their agent had flown to the West Coast on business.

"You're not his only clients, you know, chickens. Besides, he's lining up something big for you out in Hollywood."

"Well, when will he get back?" Frank demanded.

"We want our paychecks *now!*" Ulysses shouted.

"Oh, my, how it roars," Charles said, mockingly picking up a chair to fend Ulysses off. "Back, back to your corner. Martin didn't say anything about paychecks. He only authorized me to give you your allowances. And let you run a tab in the hotel, of course."

They sang badly that night, unable, somehow, to get their timing right. Afterward Charles gave them a vicious talking-to. "Atrocious. My ears have never been so insulted. You sound like a cat fight. Do you realize how lucky you are to be here? Do you realize you won't last out the week if you don't improve?"

"We sing better when we get paid," Ulysses told him.

Charles's answer to this was, "They pay the dishwashers here a dollar above minimum wage. Maybe you'd better go see if the kitchen is hiring."

To escape his sarcasm, Lou followed the fellows into the casino. It was a huge, mirrored room reflecting brilliant lights from every corner. Even its columns were mirrored. Lou, seeing a hundred dizzying reflections of herself, imagined how easy it might be to get lost in here and never find your way out. Probably that was the decorator's intention. She could not count the crowd with its many reflections, but they seemed like millions, all glittering, gorgeous, and glassy-eyed with lack of sleep and gambling fever. Near her, David was shaking a slot machine as if he could tilt it like a pinball game. A few yards away, Frank was seated at a fifty-dollar blackjack table with three other players. Behind it stood the most stunning black woman Lou had ever seen. She winked at Lou and said, "Hi! I'm Tina."

"I'm Lou," Lou answered sullenly, and dropped her eyes to the table. Slap, slap, slap went the cards in Tina's long, skilled fingers. In came the chips at the end of each deal. Everyone was losing except the house. A small, desperate-looking white man motioned to his wife, who opened her handbag and handed him a wad of money. It was quickly gone. Lou did not care about them. She cared about Frank. He had been broke that morning, and yet he was playing steadily, and, steadily, losing. How could he afford to go on?

She turned her back on this mystery and headed for one of the several small restaurants that surrounded the casino. There she found Ulysses with a sandwich in each hand.

"Halfies," she demanded, climbing up on the stool beside him. "It's crazy in that casino. I sure am glad *you're* not gambling."

He gave her a ham sandwich and patted his rotund stomach. "I like to put my money where I can *see* it."

Frank, looking glum, joined them. "I haven't given up yet," he declared. "Just taking a little break."

"Have some nutrition," Ulysses offered. "Take a steak break."

Frank shook his head. "I couldn't eat, man. Nerves too jumpy."

"Well," Ulysses told him, "you better be ready to jump up on that stage in twenty minutes."

"I will, don't worry," Frank said, and rushed back into the

gambling arena. His graceful, catlike stride had been replaced by a jerky, nervous trot, Lou noticed.

"I'm worried about him," she said between bites of her sandwich. "David, too."

"Lou," Ulysses replied philosophically. "I've tried, and I've learned there's nothin' you can do with hard heads but let 'em take their knocks and learn the hard way."

CHAPTER 9

At the end of Lou's strange, lonely week Marty arrived and called the four of them into his room. He appeared unusually solemn.

When they brought up the subject of salaries, Marty said nothing for a moment. Then he told them: "The accountant and I have gone over your books. Here they are; you can look them over yourselves. You owe me five thousand dollars for advanced expenses: twelve hundred for your Christmas advances; fourteen hundred for train and plane fares; a thousand from New York; and fourteen hundred I had to spend getting you *ready* for New York. That would have been paid back in three more weeks. After that you would have begun to draw full salaries."

"What do you mena we *would* have begun to draw salaries?" Ulysses demanded.

"I mean you would have been paid if you hadn't gambled. You owe the casino twenty-seven thousand dollars."

Lou gasped.

"I don't know what idiot gave the okay for you kids to run up a gambling tab, but that's your debt, and it has to be paid. I've cut off your line of credit now, but the damage is done."

Tina, Lou thought suspiciously, looking at Frank.

"What makes me feel so bad," Marty continued, "is I lined up a motion picture deal for you out on the Coast. But now you have to stay on here another fourteen weeks just to work off your debts." He paused to let this sink in.

"Three weeks plus fourteen—*seventeen* more weeks in this place! *Maaaannn,*" David groaned for them all.

"Or you can sign on for another year with me. They'll take my IOU's here. Then you can leave after three more weeks, and come back and work off your debt *after* we do the picture."

"What if we don't want to do either?" Frank asked truculently.

"You can buy yourselves out of your contract with me for thirty-five thousand. That's the twenty-seven you owe the casino, plus the five you owe me, plus three thousand for my time and effort, which, by the way, is worth much more. Do you have thirty-five thousand dollars?"

"Of course not, man," Frank grumbled, his head bowed in his hands.

"Frankly, I wish you did," Marty said, "You kids have potential, but I don't like the direction it's taking."

"It's not fair," Ulysses protested. "Lou didn't gamble. Neither did I."

"You told me," Marty stated slowly and deliberately, "that you wanted equal shares for everybody. Equal shares in the good times *and* the bad. Isn't that what you said?"

"Yes," Lou said, looking sadly at Frank.

"Still want it that way?"

"Yes," she said, looking levelly at Marty. "We're like a family."

"It's not fair," Ulysses repeated.

"You ought to cut me loose, Lou," Frank said with a heavy sigh. "That big bill we owe is all my fault."

"Mine, too," David said. "I'm sorry."

"Sorry is what you *both* are," Ulysses said with unusual anger. "A pair of sorry, trifling, no-good niggers."

"Don't blame David," Frank said. "He just fed the slots a little chump change I gave him. *I* was the big gambler, the big loser. But "—he looked up wide-eyed—"I figured I had to win sometime. Eventually I just had to come out on top."

"That's what gamblers always think," Marty said. "That's why the house always has an edge—the losers' stupidity."

"Yeah," Ulysses said. "I thought you were supposed to be so street-smart."

"This ain't the street, man. This place is Oz. Nothing here

works by the rules I know. This town is as full of tricks as a fun house . . . that casino with all its mirrors. . . . Ahhh, there's no excuse for what I did. Marty's right. You ought to drop me, Lou."

"I don't want to drop you"—she paused for a beat—"professionally." That cut deep, she saw.

"Too bad," Marty said. "I could get *you* into picture work right away, Lou. A property with parts for all four of you was a lot harder to find, and, frankly, it's a grade-B production. But at least it's a beginning." He sighed.

"I'll wait," she said.

"You'll have to," Marty told her, "You really don't have any choice. There is one good thing that's come out of this mess. The management here is pretty understanding. They want to give you a chance to get out of the red faster, so you're getting a shot at the big room this weekend. You'll help warm the crowd up for the big-name act—Miss Dora Lee Lynn."

Lou groaned. Miss Dora Lee Lynn was a middle-aged white singer with a pseudo-black style and enormous popularity—with white audiences.

"Now," Marty continued, "let me tell you about being a warm-up act. You've got to be good, but not *too* good. Miss Dora Lee Lynn doesn't want anybody to steal her thunder. None of the big names do, but she's especially touchy about young acts getting more applause than she does. And, frankly, she doesn't like to work with black performers."

"I know why," Lou said. "Isn't she the one who stole all of Carmen McRae's arrangements?"

"I don't know if that's true or not," Marty replied, "but if you repeat that remark outside of this room and can't prove it, you're dead in this business. Help get the people ready for Miss Dora Lee Lynn, don't draw too much attention to yourselves, and your salaries will be doubled."

"It's an ill wind that blows no good," quoted Ulysses.

"But," Marty reminded him, "you won't see a dime of it till your debts are paid off. If you can hack it on the big stage,

maybe you can cut your stay here in half. We'll see. Play it mellow and low-key, with no showing off. Understand?"

"Yassuh," Frank said. "We just be happy darkies moaning in the background for Missy."

"I don't need any smart mouth from *you,* kid. Your gambling days are over. All four of you are barred from the casino. Oh, and by the way, they fired your friend Tina. You'll find her back out on the street where she started."

"But that's not fair! She has three kids and a mother to support!" Frank cried.

"You're breaking my heart," Marty said. "She should've thought of that when she was advancing you credit and not even checking your ages. Now sign this producer's papers, and I'll see if I can get you off the hook here in time to make his movie."

"We want to think about it," was Lou's instinctive response.

"Think? There's absolutely nothing to think about. You're in no position to think. I'll do the thinking for you."

They signed.

"Okay," Marty said, taking the papers back. "Now be good kiddies, go to your rooms, and stay there and play Old Maids or something."

"Like animals in cages," Frank grumbled, tagging behind the others to walk Lou back to her room.

"*You* ran up the big bill," she reminded him. "You and Tina."

"I know what I did. And I know what you're thinking. But, believe me, Tina wasn't anything but a friend."

"She wasn't your friend."

"Yes, she was. Can I talk to you about her?"

"Later," Lou said, about to close her door in his face.

"Now," he said, putting a forceful arm around her. She let him push his way into her room, then dropped into a chair and stared at him as if he were a stranger. Which he was, after casually dropping her for an entire week. At least one good thing had happened that week; she'd found out she wasn't pregnant.

"Don't take too long," she said. "I've got to change."

"That's cold. But I don't blame you, baby. I don't expect things to be the same between us—at least, not right away."

The nerve, she thought. How could he expect things to be the same *ever?* But she said nothing, just stared at him silently.

"I know what you think about Tina and me. You're wrong. It wasn't that important, but it's standing between us, and I want to get it out of the way. Sure, I was attracted, but not all that much. She's twice my ge. Hell, she has a *kid* my age. It was the cards that fascinated me.

"And she *was* my friend, Lou. She didn't want to let me gamble, even though she had this letter saying we had a line of credit. But I insisted, and once I was winning big, she said I might as well stay with it. The minute I started losing, on New Year's Eve, Tina tried to make me stop playing. She wouldn't even deal me in at her table. But her sharky-looking boss came over, and then she *had* to let me play. Understand?"

"Yes."

"We haven't taken out any ownership papers on each other, have we?"

"Not that I know of."

"Well, all right then. But I still want to set the record straight. It wasn't Tina that attracted me, it was the way she dealt those cards. You believe me?"

"I want to," she said.

"You should have gone with us over to her house the other night. In West Las Vegas, where the blacks live. It's Southside all over again, Lou. Southside with grass and trees, but everything else is the same. Boarded-up houses, vacant lots, rats and roaches, trash and garbage, the whole tired scene. Tina's house is no bigger than yours or mine back home.

"She ran it all down to us, how it is out here. She remembers when even the top black stars had to stay over in West Vegas where she lives. Now they can stay in these hotels, but otherwise nothing's changed. Nothing is happening on the job scene for blacks out here. A few groaners and hoofers like us passing through, a few blacks in decent jobs like hers, lots of porters and maids, and a lot more people on welfare. Only way to make it here is welfare, hustling, and hooking. Tina had to sleep with her boss to get her job. I wasn't all that turned on by her to begin with, but, believe me, *that* turned me off in a hurry."

"I believe you," Lou said.

"Good. You still mad at me, baby?"

She watched his eyes change color and waited for her reaction. It didn't come. "I don't know. I think I'm mad at everybody. You, Marty, the whole world."

"Well, at least we got Tina out of the way. I wish you'd get to know her. You'd have to like her, she's so honest. Doesn't believe in lying, says she had to feed her kids somehow, sees no point in being guilty about how she does it. She fed us a good home-cooked meal, barbecued chicken wings and macaroni. We helped her clean up and put the kids to bed, and that was that."

"I already said I believe you," Lou said.

"I know you're sick of hearing about Tina. But I've got a reason for talking about her so much. After she ran it all down to us, I got to thinking. Niggers ain't got no power in Vegas. Nowhere else, for that matter, but they *especially* pitiful here. So how come she got fired?"

"I don't follow you."

"I think they fired her cause they needed a scapegoat to blame for letting us gamble. Lou, I know I was a jackass to keep on playing when I was losing so heavy. But the point is, *who let me do it?* And why?"

Lou spoke the first name that came to her mind. "Marty?"

"Uh-huh. Now your mind's in the same groove as mine, baby. I think Marty and some of his buddies out here fixed up that credit for us. Now, why would he do a thing like that?"

"I don't know."

"So he could have us tied up all nice and tight. The way we are now. Like turkeys trussed up for Thanksgiving, ready to be plucked and roasted."

"It makes sense," she said. "We were pushing Marty pretty hard, getting things all our way—"

"And now," Frank interrupted, "he's turned it around and got it all *his* way. We have to go along with his program. We can't make a move on our own, practically have to beg his permission to *breathe*. All on account of my damn fool blackjack fever."

Sensitive to his self-blame, Lou tried to be encouraging. "Four months goes by fast, Frank. We'll be out of the hole soon."

"By then he'll have thought up something else to get us in deeper. You watch and see. Marty owns us, and he means to keep it that way. We ain't nothin' but slaves in star-spangled costumes."

Louretta shivered and moved close to him. "You scare me, Frank."

"I mean to. I scare myself. Now I got to go scare the other guys." He gave her a brief, reassuring squeeze. "See you later, satin doll."

"Later," she echoed hollowly, and put the chain lock on her door. Then she sat down at her dressing table. Her face was what Momma would call *peaked*—wan and washed-out. She needed Charles and his magic box of paints, Marty and his magic pocket of pills. But she needed time away from both of them more. Carefully she painted on a glamorous mask, getting ready for her debut on the Carousel's biggest stage.

CHAPTER

10

Sweating, pinched by her costume, weighed down by her long red wig, Sister Lou smiled in the burning rays of twenty spotlights and talked in a intimate voice to a crowd of two thousand strangers as if she were alone with only one.

"Now," she said with a wink, "we're gonna get *down,* real low-down."

The gown, as low-cut as possible in conformity with the law, felt as if it were slipping to a low-down level, too. She touched its bodice for reassurance and went on:

"I just hope this song don't make nobody mad, 'cause it sounds like we're playin' the dozens, and where I come from, that can get you killed in two seconds."

Laughter, the sure-fire laughter they could always count on, that of black folks responding to one of their own inside jokes, came from a newly arrived busload of blacks in the audience. The white majority, persuaded that they had heard something funny, followed a beat later.

"Y'all know what I mean: *yeah,*" Lou said, playing to the black patch in the white audience. She was apprehensive about their reaction to her new song. This was the first time the group had performed it. "But we ain't playin' the dozens or any other game, we're serious. So we hope you'll keep your cool and dig on our message while we sing this new song called 'Talkin' 'Bout Yo' Mama.' "

A low growl (anger? appreciation?) came from the audience as the band up-tempoed its funky beat and The Soul Brothers and Sister Lou went into their precisely choreographed movements.

The silvered platform sandals she wore to augment her height felt awkward as stilts. The wig weighed about ten pounds, felt like fifty, and itched. And the dress, the star-spangled blue satin dress, was too tight for breathing, let alone dancing.

Yet in this straitjacket she was required to kick left, kick right, grind her pelvis, flap her arms like an angry chicken, fling back her head and arms with abandon (she always expected to lose the wig at this point, but so far, it had stayed on), point an accusing finger at the audience, then bump hips with each of the fellows in turn.

Bump left, bump right—she silently cursed Charles, who had created both these steps and this skimpy dress—bump left, bump right, until Ulysses, the last in line, gave her the extra bump that signaled "playtime's over," and the boys circled their own microphone and left her alone at hers.

She knew their costumes, of matching spangled blue satin, were no more comfortable than her dress, but their voices sounded mellow and relaxed.

"Son, always love your mother.
You will never have another."

Time to begin the silly slide-wiggle-slide that would bring her in place in front of them while they sang:

"Not your father or your brother
Can love you like your mother."

David gave her the little jab in the ribs that meant "hit it," and, once again, the miracle happened. Though her own mother would not have recognized her, though Lou hardly recognized herself in the mirror, her voice, her strong, dependable voice, was the same: earthy, rich, a magnet for listeners' attention:

"Mama does the best she knows,
But Mama don't always know best.
If you ain't so sure she's right.
Just try this little test.
Ask Papa what he thinks sometime,
And if Papa ain't around,

Just ask yo' Mama why.
That ought to make you wonder—"

Ulysses's deep bass rumble joined her contralto to underscore the shock of:

"Do yo' Mama ever lie?"

After a scattered barrage of screams, whether of pleasure or rage, she could not tell, they repeated the chorus. Then each sang a solo verse in turn, followed by a chorus. Ulysses's verse was:

"Mama said, when I grew up
I could be President.
Now I'm boss of the garbage men.
Could that be what she meant?"

And David's:

"Mama said, 'Son, go to church,
And things will be real cool.'
I only read the Good Book,
So I flunked out of school."

Then Frank sang:

"Mama said, 'If you leave home
You'll fall on evil times.'
So I stay home with Mama
And support myself with crimes."

And Louretta concluded with:

"Mama said, 'Girl, don't go there,
There's sin behind that door.'
So I asked her how come she knew—
Had she been there before?"

Together, the four of them recapped the chorus:

"Always love your mother,
You will never have another.

Not your sister, not your brother,
Can love you like your mother.
Always love your mother,
You will never have another . . ."

As their voices faded out on schedule in the middle of the last chorus the band took over, only to be drowned out by applause. The people liked it, then. Lou didn't know whether to be glad or sorry. It was an angry song, and she had plenty to be angry about these days, though by now she had vented the anger at Momma that had prompted her to write it. Too much had happened since, and she was much madder at other people now.

Ignoring Charles's and Marty's orders to, "keep it fast, keep it peppy, keep it moving," Lou decided to insert a little conversational bridge between songs. Why go through all this, the tormenting costumes, the silly dance steps, the withheld pay, if she couldn't use her position in the limelight to talk about the little she knew?

"If you dug it," she said, "and I know you did from the way you applauded, we weren't playing the dozens. 'Cause the dozens ain't nothing to play with. See, the dozens got started back in slavery times, when the young, strapping healthy blacks like Ulysses, here"—she had to pause for audience laughter—"were sold one at a time. But the old, weak sickly ones were sold in dozen lots. Like cases of dented sardine cans, you hear me? Or boxes of reject shoes. So when you talk about somebody's mama or grandmama, all you sayin' is maybe she wasn't a prize slave, and maybe *yours* was."

The audience response to this was a vast, chilly silence. The orchestra quickly filled it with a loud intro to an unscheduled number. The act called for Lou to say a few gentle words of tribute to her own mother and slide tenderly into "My Mother's Eyes," a slow, sweet ballad that would soften the impact of the previous song and also give The Soul Brothers and Sister Lou a chance to catch their breaths.

Instead, the orchestra was jamming on a frantic arrangement of "Dance, Dance, Dance," a no-holds-barred disco number that called for the wildest possible acrobatics and some that, in these costumes, were not possible. All of them disliked singing disco arrangements anyway, but this surprise substitution was too much.

Lou, rebelliousness popping out of her just as she was popping out of her costume, stood stark still, fists clenched, mouth tightly closed, in spite of David's jabs to prod her into action. The orchestra was finally forced to cut out raggedly, one instrument at a time. Only after there was total silence did she speak.

"I guess I ain't nothin' but a prize slave, too, y'all, 'cause I was bought with a piece of paper called a contract, and the Massa who owns me tells me what to sing and when to sing it. But nothin' in that contract says he got the right to change our act without notice. And I intend to sing this next song to tell you how I feel about my own momma." She gestured to the bandleader in the pit. "'My Mother's Eyes,' please."

This time the orchestra cooperated, and the group was able to smooth over the shock of Lou's statement with the lovely ballad. It drew warm applause. But an angry Charles was waiting for them backstage.

"I am very angry," he said pompously. "Mr. Ross is very angry. Miss Dora Lee Lynn is very angry. And the management is very, *very* angry. You interrupted the entertainment to deliver a boring *lecture*. And you took attention away from the *star*."

"Couldn't have been all that boring, if it got attention," was David's acute comment.

"If she's such a big star, she shouldn't mind," Lou added.

"She minded enough to cancel her engagement. It is an absolute scandal. You will have to fill in for her until the management gets someone else."

"In these costumes?"

"In this wig?"

"Yes, in those costumes and in that wig. You will get star billing, of course."

Ulysses, always practical, asked, "What about star *pay*?"

"Yes, of course, that too."

"If this is punishment, I want more of it!" Lou exclaimed, tossing her wig into the air.

"Your pay will simply go toward canceling out your unfortunate debts," Charles reminded them. "And, by the way, cut out the vulgar race jokes in the future, please. In case you haven't noticed, this place attracts a class audience."

"You mean a *white* audience," Frank said bluntly.

Charles shrugged.

"Yeah, that's what he means," Ulysses said. "If that tour bus full of bloods hadn't come in today, we wouldn't have got over."

"Phew," Frank said to Charles. "You are one weird character. "You don't even know if you're black or white."

"I'm mixed," Charles said.

"That's for sure," Ulysses agreed.

Charles elaborated haughtily, "My mother was a Martiniquan of good family who married a Creole from New Orleans. My grandfather on my father's side was a free man of color from Pennsylvania married to a German woman. My maternal grandfather was—"

"Hold it," Frank interrupted. "Hey, y'all, what d'you call an American dude descended from a free man of color, a sister from Martinique, a Pennsylvania Dutchwoman, and a light black dude from N'awlins?"

David scratched his head for a minute in mock stupidity, then looked up with sudden illumination. "A nigger?" he asked innocently.

"*Kee*-rect," Frank said. "A black, a blood, a splib, a spade."

"You got it," said Ulysses.

"Thank you for clearing that up, David," said Lou.

Charles, a hand covering one ear, the other glued to the phone that had rung at the beginning of this byplay, pretended not to hear any of it. But he could not repress a lopsided grin when he hung up. "Congratulations," he told them. "You have just set the world's record for rapid promotion and demotion. Fifteen minutes."

"What's that supposed to mean?" Ulysses asked.

"I have just been informed," Charles told him, "that Miss Dora Lee Lynn has consented to continue at the Carousel on one condition."

"What's that?" asked Lou.

Now Charles's sneer was evident. "That she never, *ever,* even for one minute, have to work on the same stage as you. So it's back downstairs for you kids—with instructions to keep your act short. Management wants the people gambling, not sitting around and listening."

Wondering what made Miss Dora Lee Lynn so desirable a performer, Lou sat in on her first show the next night. There on stage was a corpulent white woman, draped in so much white satin she was like a blinding snowbank, playing a white guitar and singing, "What Did I Do to Be So Black and Blue?"

"If she wants to be black and blue so bad, I'm ready to help her," Lou muttered with clenched fists. And went downstairs to her secondary place and her reduced pay which wasn't hers anyway.

Tina, spectacular in blue satin with a slit skirt that showed off her long brown legs, was seated at the bar in the Zodiac Room. Lou walked up to her and said softly, "I'm sorry you lost your job." She wondered why she had ever been jealous of this woman who had tired dark circles under her sad eyes.

"Wasn't your fault," Tina replied, expertly blowing smoke over Louretta's head. "It's just the way things go around here. Besides, I still have a job.—Hi, Carlo!" she called with a wave of long garnet fingertips at a tall man with crisp dark hair. "I'm still working for him, and so are you. Even if it's one rung down for both of us, it's a living."

"Who is he?"

"Girl, don't you know *any*thing? That is Mr. Carl D. Sipp, Vice-President and General Manager of Carousel Enterprises. And a few other enterprises he doesn't talk about." Under her long lashes, Tina's eyes swept the bar to take in the crowd of men who were either staring at the two of them or trying hard not to stare. "Looks like business will be good in here tonight. Miss Whitefolks upstairs ain't the hot attraction she thinks she is. The way things are shaping up, I'll make my quota of tricks long before midnight and turn in early. I'm in 402. Maybe you can stop by after your last show for a little girl talk."

"Thanks. I'd like that," Louretta said.

"You're welcome. You *need* it," Tina informed her. "Look, Carlo never pays any attention to his employees unless he thinks they're doing something wrong—like not working hard enough. So you get up there and sing your little head off to stir up the action for me—know what I mean? See you later." She turned her back abruptly, cutting off the conversation to flash a brilliant smile at one of the men at the bar.

Lou, understanding the situation now, told the bandleader to change the numbers. She sang "Light My Fire, "Fever," "Temptation," and "You Got What It Takes" with a deliberately sexy come-on. Her voice attracted the men's attention, which Tina caught like a skilled outfielder, getting up from her bar stool to dance expertly, her long legs kicking high, the blue satin falling away, the electricity generated by Lou's singing diverted to her dancing. After the group's first set, Tina disappeared with one of the men. After the second, she whispered in passing, "Keep that up, girl, and maybe I'll be able to run home at ten-thirty and kiss my kids goodnight."

But it didn't work out that way. Mr. Carl D. Sipp returned to the lounge, and when Tina came back from her third disappearance wearing a mink stole, he took it from her shoulders and escorted her to the bar. He snapped his fingers, and a glass of champagne appeared for Tina. It was all done so smoothly, no one would suspect it to be anything but the behavior of a perfect gentleman. Except Lou, who was sure he was ordering Tina to stay at her post.

Everything about Mr. Sipp was perfect: his lean figure, his close-cropped dark hair, his deeply tanned, clean-shaven face, his soft voice, his quiet shirt and tie. *Too* perfect; scarily perfect.

There must be a factory somewhere, Louretta thought, that turned out hundreds of these clones. Stamped them out of pink plastic with cookie cutters and gave them deliberately forgettable names like Carl D. Sipp and Bill Bland. Carl D. Sipp apparently had no vices; he didn't smoke, didn't raise his voice, didn't drink anything but club soda. She did not want to know anything else about him, but he gave her a long appraising look over his glass, and with it the frightening feeling that she might not have any choice.

The group finished its last set with a fast number, "Party All Night," and Tina joined them onstage to do a spectacular solo dance with flips and kicks that showed not only her legs but her red satin bikini pants. It seemed a perfectly natural finale, as if it had been a planned part of the show. But Mr. Sipp frowned slightly and said a few words to Tina when she left the stage. Louretta could lip-read the ugly street phrase Tina tossed back at him as she returned to the bar, where she was immediately surrounded by admirers.

"That was some dance, huh?" Frank said appreciatively. "You're not still jealous, are you, baby?"

She shook her head. "Unh-unh. We working girls have to stick together."

"I hope you know she doesn't turn me on. *You* do," he persisted. "I'll knock on your door three times tonight, okay?"

His certainty that she was available annoyed her. "Sorry. I've got another date."

"Who with?" he said angrily.

"Tina," she said, laughing mischievously.

"You two gonna sit around all night and talk about *me?*"

There's got to be something bigger than the male ego, Lou thought, but I don't know what. The continent of Africa, maybe. "Do you really think you are the only thing we have to talk about?"

She immediately regretted her words. An icy, remote expression in his eyes glazed over the warm one that was usually reserved for her, and his mouth turned down stubbornly. She began to think of lyrics for her new song even as she tried to make amends. "Listen, Frank, I'm sorry. I have to talk to Tina. She's going to tell me how this operation works. Knock on my door around three, okay?"—she gave his arm a squeeze, but it was hard and unresponsive—"or don't if you don't want to anymore, but keep an eye on that man in the beige suit over there."

Frank's eyes followed hers. "That's the shark who wouldn't let Tina deal me out of the game."

"His name is Carl D. Sipp. He owns this place. If we're not careful he'll own *us*. Are you stopping by later?"

His look and his voice were distant. "Maybe. Why don't you just wait and see?"

Which, she thought ruefully as she headed for Tina's floor, was probably exactly what she would do.

"Welcome to the life," Tina said, opening the door of her room, which was decorated exactly like Louretta's but was only half its size. It had only one bed and was strewn with exotic clothes and jewelry. "Sit down if you can find a space. Want a drink?"

"No, thanks." Louretta wanted to keep her head clear. She knew she had a lot to learn.

"Coke, then?"

"Fine," Louretta said. She was puzzled when Tina offered her a doll's-house-size china sugar bowl containing some white stuff and a doll-sized spoon.

Tina laughed huskily and took the bowl back. "I just wanted to see if you were as innocent as I thought. There's some straight Coke on the bar over there. Help yourself while I indulge." Louretta poured herself a soft drink and watched Tina snort a spoonful of the white stuff up each nostril, then lie back on the bed with her eyes closed. At last she opened them.

"Aaah. The best. Mr. Carl D. Sipp is very considerate of his employees. How old are you. honey?"

Louretta decided not to lie to this woman, whose eyes were penetratingly honest. "Sixteen."

"Same age as my oldest daughter." Tina opened her purse and her wallet. "That's her picture."

Louretta looked at the picture of a pretty girl in a ruffled white dress.

"Do you know what this stuff is?" Tina asked, pointing to the bowl.

Louretta shook her head.

"It's cocaine, sugar. Derived from opium. A hard, addictive drug. It makes you feel wonderful. For a little while. And if I ever catch you using it, I'll beat you the same way I would Cynthia. That's the only reason I work so hard, to keep my kids from getting turned out like I was. Why isn't your mother with you?"

"She doesn't approve of me being in show business."

"She's right," Tina said with one of her hard, level looks. "I wasn't kidding when I said 'welcome to the life.' Do you know what 'the life' means?"

Louretta nodded.

"Say it."

Louretta gulped and swallowed the word.

"I said, *say* it!" Tina slapped her sharply.

Oddly, Louretta did not mind the stinging slap; it was like one of her mother's, and meant that Tina was treating her like one of her children. "Prostitution," she managed.

"That's right, sugar. I don't mean you have to jump in bed with every guy who comes along. Only the dumb ones do that. I mean sooner or later the right guy will come along, and you'll have to give in to him whether you like it or not. I don't mean your romantic Mr. Right. I mean the guy with the right connections who can help you get over. A producer, a promoter, an A & R man, somebody like that. There will be a *lot* of somebodies like that, if you want to make it as a girl performer."

"It's already happened. Almost." Louretta said. She told her about the episode with Mr. Bill Bland.

"You were lucky that time. Incredibly lucky. You won't be that lucky again. Oh, no, not the way you look and the way you move and the way you sound. Next time, you'll have to follow through. I used to be a professional dancer. I *know*."

"You're still a very good dancer," Lou complimented her.

"That by itself won't pay for my Dr. Scholl's supplies. But my performance here"—she patted the bed—"is putting my kids through private school. I made better money as a dealer, and I guess I could've made it as a hoofer. But I was one of the dumb ones. I made it with the wrong guys; the ones I liked, not the ones my manager tried to fix me up with." Tina picked up the little bowl and raised the spoon to her nostril again.

"Do you really have to do that?" Louretta asked.

"Yes," Tina answered. "Yes to both questions. You have to sleep with who they tell you, and you have to use something like this so you don't mind it so much. It's a good high. It doesn't leave any marks on the body. That's important. Got to keep the body looking good as long as possible. And it doesn't kill you fast, only be degrees. I only want to live long enough to see my kids safe." She completed her drug ritual, then asked Lou suddenly, "How old do you think I am?"

Lou hesitated, calculated, then guessed, "Thirty-two?"

Tina did not confirm or deny this. Instead she began stripping off her makeup with cold cream. As the fake lashes, mascara, lipstick, and foundation came off, a worn face emerged. Then the wig came off, and hair liberally sprinkled with gray became visible. "Add ten more years and you'd be about right. But this life ages you a lot quicker. I think I look about fifty. Don't you?"

Lou hesitated.

Tina raised her hand. "Tell the truth, girl!"

"You look about fifty."

Tina nodded, satisfied. "Take my advice, little girl. I'm talking to you like a mother, that's why I won't stand for any lying from you. Get rid of that manager of yours. He's no good. Get rid of him and run home to your mama as fast as you can."

"We can't," Louretta said. "We owe him a fortune. Thirty-five thousand dollars.

"I know how that happened." Tina said. "I tried to warn your friend Frank, but he wouldn't listen. Then Carlo interfered, and I had to let Frank lose after I'd been letting him win."

Lou was shocked. "You mean the games are rigged?"

"Well, no, most of them are straight—but every dealer knows how to build up a player or bust him. Those were my orders from Carlo after he told me to give your friends all the chips they wanted: "Build 'em up, make 'em confident, then bust 'em.' And then he busted *me* so I could get blamed for it! He's real cute, that Carlo. A real sweetheart." Tina laughed herself hoarse. "Pay no attention to me, child. This stuff I use makes me crazy and silly sometimes, especially when I'm tired. I think it's the only time I ever laugh."

Lou believed her.

"Anyway, your problem could be worse. Thirty-five thousand is *nothing* compared to what most performers owe out here. Don't you have any money saved up, or any friends who can bail you out?"

Lou shook her head. "I've got about four thousand in the bank from our first record, that's all. I don't know about the guys."

"Scrape up every cent you can. Borrow the rest. Borrow it from anybody except Carlo and his friends.—Can't do it?"

Louretta was shaking her head. She had no idea of how to raise a sum that large.

"Try," Tina advised. "If you can't, well, it's like I said—welcome to the life. I never had much faith in that dealer job, anyhow. The Equal Opportunity people were leaning on the casinos, so Carlo sent me to school and stuck me in there to get them off his back for a while. I was pretty sure it wouldn't last forever. So now I'm hooking again. And hooked again. Lord, have mercy." Her throaty laughter filled the room, then cut itself short. "Not that I didn't expect it to happen. Mr. Carl D. Sipp has many ways of getting people in debt to him. Gambling's one, drugs are another. I don't use much, but my weekly supply costs more than most people spend a year on prescription

medicine. Then, when you're broke, Carlo lends you money. You're always in debt to him, and you never get paid up."

"It sounds like sharecropping on the old plantations," Lou observed.

"Exactly," Tina said. "The company store keeps you hooked. And don't think the big ones get away." Tina laughed. "Maybe I should've been a comedian. I could name you some names, big names, who are sharecropping out here." And she did, famous names, big stars whom Louretta had revered most of her life.

"Do you think those people work out here so much because they *like* it? No—they work here because they *have* to. You'd be surprised to know how many of them are broke or in debt to Mr. Sipp and his friends.

"If they refuse to work, what happens?"

Tina made a throat-cutting gesture. "This business is cold, honey, *cold*. And a pretty girl like you doesn't even get to pick her own bed-warmers."

Louretta thought of Frank. "I'm going to be different," she declared. "I know it, I've got talent."

"Sure you do, honey. That's what they all say. Do me a favor. If you won't leave, write your mama and tell her to come out here and look after you. Do it tonight!"

Louretta shook her head, thinking of Momma's strictness. She would never fit into this world that broke all of her rules.

"Then get out of here, you hard-headed little heifer. Get out and let Tina get her rest. I got nothing more to say to you!"

To emphasize her point, Tina flung a shoe at the door. Its noise was answered by a knock from the other side.

"Come in!" Tina shouted.

"Ladies," Carl D. Sipp said, bowing, "please keep your discussions polite. We mustn't disturb our guests."

"Sure, Carlo. I know you're very big on politeness. How long you been listening outside my door?"

He didn't answer Tina directly. He turned his back on her and looked Louretta over thoroughly, a look that went slowly from her head to her feet, from appraisal to approval. Under his moist stare, she felt naked and clammy.

"You know," he said, "I'm inclined to agree with Tina. You ought to leave the Carousel as soon as possible. I'd be happy to see you leave, myself. You're too young, all of you. That causes problems." He paused. "—But there *is* the matter of the money you owe us."

His soft voice was more disturbing than screaming could ever be. "I might be inclined to cancel your debt if you would pay me a visit tonight. I'll be expecting you in the Manager's Suite."

Tina yelled, "Don't go, Lou!"

"Don't interfere, Tina," he said without looking away from Lou. "You know, I've been waiting a long time for you to bring your daughter to meet me."

Tina went ashy in the face, but defied him. "Come here a minute, Lou." She whispered in her ear, "Stay away from him. He's slime, he's filth. He likes young girls."

"This one, or your daughter, Tina?" Carl D. Sipp asked gently. "Have you decided?"

"Neither, you nasty little boy! He looks like a man, Lou, but that's all he is—a nasty little boy who can only feel like a man with young girls. Let me handle Carlo. I have a business idea that'll excite him more than you do. Run along and do what I told you. Don't worry about my daughter. He'll never lay eyes on her, even if I have to work hard enough to send her to *Switzerland!*"

Lou fled down the corridor to the elevator and took it up her floor, but went to the boys' room instead of her own, to ask the guys if they had any money saved or knew where to borrow some. In the hall outside, she could hear maniacal laughter. She knocked and called, but no one came to the door. It was unlocked, though. She opened it on a weird scene. Under a flashing strobe light, to the background of a pulsating record, Frank and Ulysses were laughing and playing an inane word game. In rapid-fire voices, they exchanged words:

"Cabbage."

"Garbage."

"Manure."

"Dirt."

"Filth."

"Bugs."

"Lice."

"Worms."

"Maggots."

"Germs."

Each word apparently seemed more hilarious than the next to them, since each was followed by whooping laughter. Lou thought they sounded like three year olds. No one could tell what David thought. He sat on the floor, staring into space in a frightening sort of trance.

"Germs."

"Rats."

"Flies."

"Fleas."

"Fallout."

"Your funky drawers."

"Your mama's drawers."

And off they went into another fit of laughter while David continued to stare at nothing.

Only Charles, coiled gracefully on the couch, seemed sane. He uncoiled himself and said, "I was just leaving." On a gold chain around his neck, Lou noticed he wore a miniature spoon like Tina's.

"David?" she cried. There was no response. She tried shaking him, slapping him, pinching him. He was limp and passive as a wet sponge.

"David! Hey, you guys, he's out of it. Help me wake him up. Put him in the shower."

"Shower."

"Flower."

"Tower!"

"Power!"

They slapped five, palms echoing like pistol shots, and collapsed on the floor laughing.

"What," Lou asked, "have you guys been taking?"

"Goodies," Frank said, rolling his eyes at her. "Free goodies from the hotel. Chocolate cherries, frosted strawberries—"

"And sweet snowberries," Ulysses completed before he rolled on his back like a beached whale and began snoring.

Clearly, nothing could be done till morning. Babbling a fervent prayer, *ohsweetjesuspleasehelpus,* Lou ran to her room. She locked herself in, flung herself on the bed, and scribbled a long despairing letter to William.

Then the urgency of her situation made itself felt in her rapidly pounding heartbeat. She picked up the phone and sent a telegram instead.

CHAPTER 11

In the morning, the sun shone as if everything was perfectly normal. Lou was encouraged when the collect wire she had asked for arrived with her breakfast.

CAN'T LEAVE HOME. MRS. JERUTHA JACKSON COMING TODAY ON AIR WEST FLIGHT 438. LOVE, WILLIAM.

Lou was delighted. Jolly little Mrs. Jackson was a good member of the Cheerful Baptist Church, but she was cheerful without the capital C, too. After Jethro died, she had come out of mourning dancing, as if she intended to live life fully enough for both of them. She would probably be able to help them straighten out their finances, too. She had kept a beauty shop and then a dress shop going through good times and bad. William had made a wise decision.

"I love you, too, William," Lou whispered, and kissed the telegram. Her breakfast looked delicious. She started to dig into it, then remembered last night and looked, horrified, at the egg on her fork. Maybe she was going crazy, but she was afraid of what might have been scrambled into it.

She had to see about the boys! Throwing on her robe, she ran to their room and banged hard. A sleepy Ulysses opened the door in a cherry-red robe that matched his eyes.

"Damn, Lou why'd you wake me up so early?"

"Are you guys all right?"

He rubbed his eyes. "I dunno. I guess so. Never been so tired in my life."

"Well, get some more sleep then. Just don't eat any more of the hotel food. I'll cook this morning. Mrs. Jackson will cook for us when she gets here."

"You mean Jethro's mom? Why's she coming?"

"Because we need her, that's why. We can't trust anybody in this place. What happened last night?"

Ulysses let his bulk cave into the sofa. "Aw, Lou, no lectures, please. Not this morning. We just got a little high 'cause we were bored. Nothing else to do."

"What'd you get high on?"

Ulysses shrugged. "Who knows? My head feels like it got hit with a wrecking ball. I know David smoked some hash, and Frank and I did some coke, but there was something else first, something in the candy the hotel sent up. It made us feel real good, you know? Real up. We worked on some new arrangements—"

He walked over the to the piano, tinkled a few notes, then gave up. "We had some good sounds going last night. But now it's all gone. Maybe when we feel better it'll come back."

"When I stopped in, you and Frank were stark raving mad. Laughing like lunatics. And David was like a statue. How's he doing now?"

"See for yourself," Ulysses said, pointing.

David was still on the floor in the same place he'd been last night. Only now his eyes were closed and he was snoring gently.

"David?" Lou called, gently shaking him. "David?"

"Wha? Wha?" was the sleepy response.

"David, do you know me?"

"Aw, go 'way and lemme sleep, Lou."

Lou was relieved and glad to oblige him. But she was angry with the others. "He isn't even sixteen yet. You two are older, you ought to look out for him. He really had me scared last night. Are you guys gonna do dope again?"

Ulysses shrugged. "Who knows? It makes us feel good, it makes the creative juices flow, it's free . . ."

"*Nothing* in this place is free," she corrected him. "Don't let them fool you."

"Well, it does help us produce. You should have heard the new song Frank wrote last night. Just for you. It's called 'Lou

120 in the Limelight'"

"I'd love to hear it. Think he'll remember it?"

"Maybe, when he wakes up. Right now . . . who knows? Look, Lou, we're wasted. Come back a little later." He yawned massively, exposing a cavernous throat. "About noon, maybe. OK?"

By noon Lou had dressed, found a grocery store and some pans, and was busy stirring sausage and eggs on the stove in her room.

Frank's special triple knock announced his presence at her door.

"Smells great," he said, stolling barefoot into her room as if he owned it. Wearing a striped bathrobe, he was as arrogant and graceful as a tiger. He stretched out on her bed as if it were his and furrowed his brow in mock puzzlement. "But there's one thing I never can get straight. Is sex bad for you before you eat, or after?"

"I hear you wrote a song for me last night," Lou said coolly.

"I did?" he said in astonishment. "Oh, yeah, I did. 'S hard to remember anything I did last night."

"How about running through it for me now?"

"Sure, as soon as I taste some of those good grits. I'm starving."

"No, first you have to sing for your supper—I mean, your breakfast."

"Women are a pain," Frank said with a sigh. He went to the piano, played a few chords, then slumped on the keys, head and all, producing a hideous dissonance. "I can't remember any of it, Lou. It was good, believe me. But it's all gone."

"I figured it would be." She brought him a plate. "You gonna do dope again tonight?"

"No. That was stupid. Blowing all the fuses in my brain. But you got to understand, baby. Wasn't anything else to do. Can't gamble anymore. Nothing else to do in this town *but* gamble. Can't even look out the windows 'cause there's nothing out there but concrete walls." He banged the table with his fist. "This place is my idea of hell."

"Well, we won't get away from it till we pay them off. I came over last night to ask if you guys had any money saved."

Frank shook his head. "Not me. I blew my first check in a week, so my mom made me sign the others over to her."

"What about the other guys?"

"I'll ask them. I doubt if they've got two dimes to rub together, though."

She sighed, figuring he was probably right. "Look, Frank, Tina schooled me last night. We can't take any more favors from the hotel. The more we take, the more we owe. Nothing in this place is free."

"Except the drinks."

"That's only for the gamblers. We pay for *everything* except our rooms. The bigger our bill, the longer we have to work here. That's one reason I cooked this morning. The other is, I don't trust the food after what happened to you guys last night."

"So—no more gambling, no more dope, no more drinks, no nothing."

"Right. We just work out our time."

"Yep. Like jail."

Frank groaned. "But if we can't drink, gamble, or use, what else is there to do?"

Suddenly, mischievously, she let her robe slip off and ran naked into the shower. "Use your imagination!" she cried.

"That's the meanest trick I ever had played on me," he complained when she came out of the locked bathroom ten minutes later, nude except for a towel turban. But she soon convinced him it had not been a trick.

Later, while their legs were still tangled, she said, "See? The only way to do time is use your imagination. You wrote a good song last night and lost it. So—write another one. How'd you get that stuff last night?"

"Dunno where it came from. The first sample was on the dresser when we walked in. In a fancy bowl with one of those engraved cards that says 'Compliments of Carousel.' Then

Charles brought us some more."

"You gonna use it again?"

He hesitated, then said, "No."

"Took you a long time to answer me."

"That's 'cause you've never tried it, baby. You're asking me to give up the greatest feeling in the world.

"—Hey, what'd I say *now?*" he complained as she pulled herself free with a sharp elbow jab to his chest, leaped up, and began pulling on her clothes.

"You figure it out," she said. "Maybe you can put it in a love song. I've got a great title for you. 'Sweet Cocaine.' I have a plane to meet now. If you want to do something for me, you can call me a cab. Then bring the guys over here for their breakfast. And make 'em do the dishes!"

"Why don't you use the hotel's limo?"

"How can I get *through* to you guys? The more independent we are, the sooner we can cut this place loose. I don't want any more favors from this hotel, or from Charles and Marty either. That's why I'm paying for my own cab."

"Is Jethro's mom going to stay here with you, in this room?"

"That's right. We can't run up an extra room bill."

"Baby, that'll be a drag. I mean—it'll be like you having a chaperone. How can we ever be along together?"

"You'll think of something," Lou said, zipping up her yellow terrycloth running suit and darting toward the door. "And if you don't—well, it shouldn't matter much. I don't give you the greatest feeling in the world anyway."

The big blue-and-white plane landed smoothly, and in less than five minutes, Louretta was hugging a tiny, energetic woman who could never be described as old. Lou's greeting was so desperately affectionate she knocked off Mrs. Jackson's hat, a strange little feathered affair like a bird sitting on its nest. A playful breeze caught it and sent it flying down the street like a live dove.

Louretta ran to get it. "Here's your pet. I mean—your hat."

"Don't you laugh at me, young lady," Mrs. Jackson said, and put the feathered creation back on. But, in spite of herself, Louretta did laugh. It looked like a pigeon perched on Mrs. Jackson's head. Soon they were both laughing.

"Shush. People will think we're a pair of fools. But what could I do? Stores don't sell hatpins anymore. And I got myself together so fast, I couldn't find any of my old ones."

Louretta pictured Mrs. Jackson's house, a tiny place she loved, crammed with antique furniture, bric-a-brac, odd pieces of mismatched china, photographs, postcards, jewelry, tracts, and magazines, and wondered how she ever managed to find anything. "Never mind," she said. "Big Bird won't leave the nest anymore. Got any luggage?"

"Just this." Mrs. Jackson picked up the large suitcase she had lugged off the plane. "They didn't want me to carry it on, but I said with all those planes going to different places I didn't trust it to get here with me. And I said I don't take up as much space as most people, so I thought I ought to be allowed to keep my grip. And they let me."

"I never expected you to get here so fast."

"That telegram sounded like some fast action was called for. That's why I wore my wings." While Louretta giggled, Mrs. Jackson looked down at herself. "Mercy! I dressed in the dark, and look!" She had on one brown shoe and one black.

"Don't worry about it," Louretta said, picking up the heavy suitcase. "The mates are in here, aren't they?"

"I hope so. When your brother called me, I just hauled this up out of the cellar and started throwing things in. No telling *what* might be in there."

"Well you're here, that's the main thing. I'm *so* glad."

"I could tell that from the way you hugged the breath our of me and sent Bertha flying."

"Bertha?"

"My hat. She's insulted 'cause you called her Big Bird. That telegram sounded like you needed some looking after."

"I think we *all* need looking after," Louretta said.

124 "Well, of course you do. You're children. What are you doing?" she asked as Louretta stepped to the curb.

"Getting us a cab."

"Isn't there a bus?"

Louretta was uncertain. "I don't know. I guess so. But I've never used it. All the people out here take cabs."

Mrs. Jackson nodded toward a group of people, mostly black, standing across the street at a Bus Stop sign. "Are you saying those aren't people? Save that taxi money, child. It might come in handy sometime."

Louretta thought, Mrs. Jackson is exactly what we need, and followed her aboard the bus. It was full of working folks, but they found a seat and room for the suitcase in the aisle.

"What church do you attend out here?" Mrs. Jackson asked.

"We don't," Lou said. "I don't believe there's a church in the whole town."

"Let's find out." Mrs. Jackson tapped the broad shoulder of a woman in front of them. "Excuse me, ma'am, but we're new in town. We're wondering where the Baptist churches are."

The woman turned and gave them a smile that lit her broad brown face like the sun. My church is Thankful Baptist, on the West Side. We have a small congregation, but it's growing. And we have a wonderful pastor. We'd be pleased to see you and your daughter there this Sunday. My name is Anita Lawson, and here's my phone number."

"Jerutha Jackson," Mrs. Jackson replied, taking the scrap of paper. "Very pleased to meet you, Mrs. Lawson. This is my godchild Louretta. I'll bring her, too."

"Just call me for directions. I'd be pleased to have you over for dinner after services."

"Thank you so much, ma'am. We'll be there."

"See you Sunday!" Mrs. Jackson called as their new friend got off the bus waving and beaming.

"You see? she said, turning to Louretta. "Your mother told me this was a sinful town. But I told her you can find sin anywhere if you're looking for it. And you can find good decent people anywhere, too. You've lost your way a little, so far from home. Right?

Louretta nodded, amazed at how quickly Mrs. Jackson was making *herself* at home.

"Haven't even been on a bus to see the plain people like the people you came from," her friend went on, paying no attention to the advertised stars; the gaudy signs and buildings, or the glamorous people. "They're ordinary friendly people out here, just like the folks back home.—How do, ma'am," she said politely to an older lady leaving the bus, and, to the boy who was with her, "Nice to see a young man dressed up so respectable. I like your haircut, too." Then to Lou, she continued, "See? All you have to do is get out and mingle and friendly. But I guess you been flyin' high ever since you got on that plane. Don't forget who you are and where you come from, Louretta, no matter how high you rise."

"That sounds an awful lot like Momma," Lou said, frowning.

"No. I didn't say, 'Don't rise.' I just said, 'Don't forget who you are.' There's a difference."

An important difference, Lou realized, thinking it over. She was, however, eager to change the subject. "Say, where did you get the money to come? I was planning to send you a ticket."

"Now, don't you worry about that, Lou. I had a little something left over from Jethro's insurance. And I held onto it, waiting to see what the Lord wanted me to use it for. Oh, I could've given it to the church, but I thought, No, Jerutha, wait, something else may come along. And I was right. When your brother got that telegram, I thought, what better use could I have for that money than to go see about my other children?"

So Jethro's insurance money had brought his mother here. Louretta tried not to cry, thinking of how her friend had been killed, and how their song about him had become a hit and led them to this strange, dangerous life. Now his death benefit had paid his mother's way out here. Jethro was still a part of the group. The tears welled up anyway. She averted her eyes and noticed some landmarks. "Hey, this is where we get off."

"Mighty fancy," Mrs. Jackson said, but with appreciation, not disapproval. "The Carousel Hotel. My, my. I might take a few rides on that merry-go-round myself."

Louretta didn't have the heart to tell her the merry-go-round was only a display.

"Well," Mrs. Jackson continued as they trudged into the dazzling lobby. "I got nothing against comfortable living. The Lord didn't put us here to be singy and mean with ourselves. He said, 'Have life more *abundantly.*' Now, you just take me on up to your room and finish your crying, and then you can tell me all about everything.

"—No thank you, young man, I can carry my own bag. But here's a dime for you anyway," Mrs. Jackson said to a porter. "Good afternoon, young lady," she said to a maid on Lou's floor."—Well, I have a general idea of what's been going on. You'll have to fill me in on the details, of course, but I don't think you can shock me. I've seen a lot of things in this old world."

"This must be the most expensive room in the place," Mrs. Jackson said, after she had seen the extra double bed, the large kitchenette, the lavish bathroom, and the huge closet.

"I don't think so," Louretta said uncertainly. "Anyway, it's free because we work here. There are some smaller ones, though, I know because I have a friend downstairs. I want you to meet her," she added impulsively. "A lot of people might say she's a bad woman, but I think she's a good person. She's tried to help us." Since Mrs. Jackson had remarked that decency could always be found in wicked places, Lou thought she would be able to see Tina's goodness.

"Nice kitchen," was Mrs. Jackson's only comment. "You can save by doing your own cooking. Do you?"

"Yes. Uh—well, I just started," Louretta admitted.

"Fine. We'll keep it up. My, my!" Mrs. Jackson had just opened the closet and seen Louretta's extensive wardrobe. "All these outfits, and all of them will fit me! Can I wear one to your show tonight?"

"You're going to watch our show?" Louretta asked incredulously.

"Certainly. And I want to be dressed for the occasion. I haven't completely left this world behind yet. Not ready to, either. You mind if I have a look through your things?"

"Help yourself." Louretta thought this was going to be fun. And it was. Over twenty-five years apart in age, they were identical sizes. Louretta had forgotten how petite she was until she saw tiny Mrs. Jackson take out an armful of her clothes and try them on. She studied herself in the mirror in scarlet knit, in magenta wool, in purple jersey, in gold satin with fringe at the hem. All of them, as she had predicted, fit her perfectly.

"I think I like this one best," Mrs. Jackson announced. Louretta stifled a giggle as Mrs. Jackson, wearing Lou's blue stage costume, looked down at her chest. "But where's the rest of it?"

Wordlessly, Lou handed her the sheer spangled jacket that covered the dress at the start of her act and came off shortly thereafter.

"Fits just fine. But why are you laughing? What's wrong with it? Do I look silly?"

"No, you look wonderful. It's my stage costume, that's all."

"Well, what d'you know? I must have some show-off in my soul. I see you have a piano. Play me a tune. I used to be able to ball the jack a little." Louretta obligingly tinkled out a rag, and Mrs. Jackson did a neat little performance, twirling and kicking around the room three times; finally landing, laughing, on the bed. She leaped up instantly.

"What am I thinking of? I mustn't muss this. I'll press it for you if I have. You don't mind me messing in your things?"

"Of course not. I love it," Louretta said. "Wear anything you want except that one."

"Good. I'll wear the purple one tonight. Why should I buy new clothes when we both wear the same size?"

Standing in her underwear, Mrs. Jackson hung up the costume neatly. "No, I think I'll wear the red one. I don't see anything wrong with wearing bright colors. That church of ours is a little too strict, if you ask me. They look at you like you're a scarlet woman if you wear anything besides gray and navy. I'm tired of being a drab old gray hen."

"Mrs. Jackson, you could never be drab or old. And I wish I could lend you my costume. I'm sick of it."

"Yes, I'm going to wear bright red. Scarlet," Mrs. Jackson said with satisfaction. She patted the bed. "Now, you just come over here and tell me why you're sick of a dress that helps you earn such a good living."

"But I'm *not* earning a living!" Louretta cried. And went on to explain tearfully that they were thousands of dollars in debt to Marty and the hotel. And that there seemed no way out of the hole they were in, because the boys had picked up expensive habits and she wasn't sure they would drop them.

"You make it sound like it's all the boys' fault. Are *you* so perfect, Miss?"

Louretta dropped her eyes.

"Your momma told me what she found in your purse. I told her, 'Rosetta Hawkins, you're twice a fool. Once for snooping, and twice for fussing at your girl. At least she isn't planning on making extra mouths for you to feed at home.' So I know what's happening, Miss Lou. Same thing that's been going on in this old world since Adam met Eve. Who is it? Not some white man, I hope?"

Louretta shook her head. "No. They've been after me, but I've escaped them so far. It's Frank Brown."

Mrs. Jackson cocked her head to one side for a moment, considering, then nodded her approval. "That's nice. He's the most serious one. The smartest one, too. Are the two of you serious?"

"I don't know."

"Well, is it still going on?"

Louretta started to say "I don't know" again, realized how stupid that would sound, and said instead, "I think so. We go by how we feel."

"Well," Mrs. Jackson said, "looks like you don't know much of anything, doesn't it? But if you feel like having company, just let me know and I'll be out of this room till you say to come back."

Louretta looked at her in amazement.

"Did I shock you? You think I was brought up in a convent? You think I got Jetro out of a stork's bill? What young people do now wasn't done so much in my day, and I wouldn't have encouraged you to start—but then, you didn't ask me, did you? Now you've started, I wouldn't try to stop you. I don't believe in trying to stop nature once it gets started. It only makes worse things happen.—Oh, I brought you some messages, but I guess you won't be interested in them now."

Mrs. Jackson opened her gigantic, worn black purse and pulled out a bundle of colorful papers. They were a collection of original greetings from Calvin, hand-decorated with doves and hearts and cartoons and flowers. The troubling ones were less well drawn and had crosses and crude portraits of Jesus.

Lou looked through them quickly and said, "No, I guess not." But she put them away carefully in her night-table drawer.

"He didn't know where to mail them, so he sent them by me. That boy was getting too churchified for his own good. But he's coming out of it now. I believe you've got to be balanced—not too holy, not too worldly. And you know I'll soon have me plenty of friends out here, so if you and Frank want to be alone for a few hours, just tell me. So that's that." She stood up and brushed herself off briskly. "Now. What time do you start work tonight?"

Louretta liked the way she put it. *Work*. A sensible word for what she was doing, instead of a glamorous one. "Seven-thirty."

"That's plenty of time," Mrs. Jackson said, putting on her traveling dress and her mismated shoes. "I'm going to find a grocery store and cook dinner for you-all. Then, at dinner, I'll look the boys over and find out how they're doing. And *then*—"

"Yes?"

"I think I'd better meet your Mister Marty Ross."

CHAPTER

12

"Call me Aunt Jerutha," Mrs. Jackson said, after everyone had been served from the platters of smothered chicken and rice-and-beans and okra-and-tomatoes she had conjured up like a magician. "As far as I'm concerned, I'm your mama away from home."

"Yes ma'am," Ulysses said respectfully. "Please pass me some more gravy."

"Certainly, son."

"Thank you, Aunt Jerutha."

"You like to eat. That's good, boy. I think I'm going to have the least trouble out of you. What's wrong with that one over there?"

David was nodding over his plate like a drooping flower.

"Looks like he's sleepy, ma'am," Frank said.

"Tell me the truth like you would your own mama."

Frank could not evade her unblinking stare. "He had something last night that made him sleepy. I think he had some more this afternoon.",

"But you two, *you're* not sleepy."

"No, we're wide awake."

"Mm-hmm. So wide awake you can hardly sit still. How come?"

"We had some stuff that makes us wide awake."

"I think I want to hear some more about this stuff. It's not vitamins, is it?"

Frank shifted uneasily. "You might call it that. It gives you energy."

Lou's memory flashed back uneasily to that recording session back home and all the pills Marty had made available.

“This food’ll give you energy, too,” Aunt Jerutha continued relentlessly. “Is that what you had? Food?”

“No, ma’am.”

“Well, what, then?”

“*Tell* her, Frank.”

“Aw, Lou, she won’t even know what I’m talking about.”

“I know more than you think,” Aunt Jerutha informed him. “There are two kinds of drugs—uppers and lowers. David had lowers—that’s why he’s sleepy. You two had uppers—that’s why you’re fidgety. I want to know two things. How much did they cost you, and will you be able to work tonight?”

Aunt Jerutha had drugs and dentures a little mixed up as far as terminology went, but her basic understanding was accurate.

“They were free, ma’am. As far as working’s concerned, I can only speak for myself. I’m in fine shape.” Frank pushed his plate aside and went to the piano. “I’m even in a mood for composing now. What I took helps musicians.” He played a rapid series of glissandos that did not cover the lack of melody in his composition.

“Sounds pretty. Like fancy icing on a cake. Only there’s no cake underneath it,” Aunt Jerutha commented. “Speaking of cake, you boys want some?”

While Frank and Ulysses were happily devouring the yellow cake with chocolate icing and babbling excitedly and erratically about all the great new songs they were going to write, David jerked awake, then nodded toward his plate, jerked upright again, nodded almost until his face was in his plate, jerked up again, and began his slow descent. He repeated this movement interminably while Ulysses drummed on the table with his fingertips and Frank hummed a snatch of a tune and Ulysses said, “Yeah, man, that one’s really got it!” and Frank responded, “Mmmm, yeah, it’s got that freaky outer-space sound!” Mrs. Jackson observed all this in patient silence.

Then she lowered the boom on them. “There will be no show tonight. I won’t have you shaming yourselves. You are in no condition to show yourselves to the public.”

"We're fine! Fine as wine!" Ulysses cried.

"Yeah!" said Frank. "Who does she think she is, coming out here bossing us?"

"You and Ulysses are crazier than squirrels drunk on fermented grapes," she told him. "And David can't even stay awake. I think we'll just have to sit here quietly in this room and pray to see what we should do next."

"She's right," Louretta said. "Marty won't like it, but she's right."

"I need to see your Mister Ross. I do believe, if you don't appear downstairs in that barroom or whatever it is, he'll show up here pretty soon."

Right again, Lou thought.

Aunt Jerutha's eyes were closed. "Lord, give us the wisdom to know what we should do, the strength to carry it out, and Your presence always to walk with us and help us up when we fall."

Louretta went to the piano and played, softly, "Sweet Hour of Prayer." After a few bars, Mrs. Jackson began singing in her soft, pure soprano. Surprisingly, Ulysses's rumbling bass and Frank's baritone soon accompanied her. David's only contribution was a steadily rolling snore.

They were subdued and quiet for a full twenty minutes after that. Every now and then, Mrs. Jackson would hum a snatch of a hymn, and Louretta would pick it up softly at the piano. Sometimes one or more of them would sing or hum, sometimes not. Mostly there was silence.

"I feel grace," Mrs. Jackson declared suddenly. "I feel grace and peace descending on this evening. And I feel joy. I feel love and joy. Oh, thank you, Jesus!"

Louretta played an up-tempo version of "Love Lifted Me," and Mrs. Jackson, still in her mismatched shoes, moved with the spirit all over the room, then returned sedately to her chair. "Thank you for that moment of renewal, Lord. Thank you for strengthening our faith. For the Devil is everywhere, and even now approaches to test us."

Aunt Jerutha was right for the third time. Marty's impatient knocking, like the rat-tat-tat of a trap drum, beat on their ears, followed by a barrage of angry language. "What the friggin' hell is going on up here? You were due downstairs ten minutes ago! The management is ready to kill me! You little brats get the lead out your butts, or I'll put my boot up—"

Louretta opened the door very quietly.

"This is Mr. Ross, Aunt Jerutha. Mr. Ross, meet Mrs. Jackson. She's come out to look after us."

"Pleased, Mr. Ross," Aunt Jerutha said with great dignity. "We just finished supper, but there's plenty left over. Won't you have some?"

"No time, no time," Marty said frantically. "Got to get these kids into their costumes. Got to get them downstairs to sing."

"Oh, we've all the time in the world," Aunt Jerutha said serenely. "You might as well sit down and take your time, too, Mr. Ross. We have a lot to talk about."

"Who are you? Who sent for you?" Marty demanded.

"These children's parents sent me here to look after them," Aunt Jerutha said. "And I do believe the Lord sent me here to look out for them, too. Do you like light meat or dark meat?"

"I can't eat," Marty said. "I'm too nervous. These kids have to go on right away."

Aunt Jerutha calmly went on pouring gravy onto his plate. "Now you know, I decided not to let these children perform tonight. They've had some strange medicine, and their heads are just not *right*."

"We're right as rain, feelin' no pain!"

"We're right as might; we've seen the light!"

Frank and Ulysses, sparring with one another, and David, with open eyes that saw nothing, were testimony to her statement.

"That SOB Carlo! Excuse me, ma'am. He's up to his old tricks," Marty said.

"And who is Carlo?" asked Aunt Jerutha.

"The owner of this place. The stuff came from the hotel,

didn't it?"

Frank and Ulysses nodded.

"You see?" Marty said to Aunt Jerutha. "He wants an excuse to fire them. If they don't go on, he can say they broke their contract."

"Marty," Lou volunteered, "I didn't do any drugs. Suppose I go on by myself tonight. Would that satisfy him?"

His eyes brightened almost too eagerly. "Would you, Lou? Could you?"

"Yes. Just this once, though."

"Sure. Just this once."

Aunt Jerutha nodded approval. "That sounds acceptable to me. Mr. Ross, I would like you to stay with the young men. Make sure they do not take any more harmful medicine. Now, my niece and I will be changing to go downstairs. So, if you'll excuse us . . . you can take your plate with you."

Marty rose. "Come on, guys. I'll never forget this favor, Lou."

Aunt Jerutha firmly closed the door in his face. Louretta slipped into her costume while Aunt Jerutha put on her scarlet dress. Arm in arm, dressed like ladies of the evening but walking like a queen and a princess, they took the elevator down to the Zodiac Lounge. A loudmouthed comedian was onstage, making corny jokes to fill in for them.

"Oh, here she is now—Sister Lou without her brothers. Looks like she brought her mother instead. Let's have a big hand for the little girl with the big voice!"

Under cover of the applause, Lou whispered, "That's Carlo over there at the bar. And that's my friend Tina next to him."

"Just do your work, child, and forget about everyone else. I'll be fine." Mrs. Jackson sat at the table nearest Tina's bar stool and watched as Lou performed "Lament for Jethro" and then announced, "Ladies and gentlemen, I'd like to dedicate this next song to Jethro's mother, my Aunt Jerutha Jackson, who is here with me tonight." Instructing the musicians to follow her and pick up the tempo more with each verse, she sang:

"He's got the whole world,
In His hands,
He's got the whole world
In His hands . . ."

At an almost invisible signal from Carl D. Sipp, the comedian took the mike away from Lou and cut in with his inane patter. "Well, now, that was a nice encouraging song for all you high-rollers out there. It won't hurt to have a little hlp from the Man Upstairs when you're at the tables. I know Sister Lou wanted to give you some extra inspiration to get in there and win."

While he was babbling, Aunt Jerutha came up to Lou and said, "I appreciate what you were trying to do, child, but I don't believe the Lord's music belongs in a worldly place like this. Besides, I would like to hear something I could *dance* to. And I think the other people would, too."

A strong downbeat was struck, and Lou hit the second bar hard with:

"Can you move your body?
Does the beat come through?
Watch me move my body!
Can you do it too?
Oh dance, dance, dance,
Dance the night away!
Dance, dance, dance,
We've only got today!"

As she sang and gyrated, microphone in hand, she became aware of two amazing things in rapid succession: Her unaccustomed freedom and lightness of movement were due to the absence of the wig on her head. And, flanking her onstage, in place of the boys, were Tina and Aunt Jerutha, apparently engaged in a contest as to who could kick the higher. As far as Lou could tell, Aunt Jerutha was winning.

"These are my Las Vegas sister and my adopted mother from back home, y'all! I won't tell you our ages but they add up to almost 100! *'We can move our bodies/ Can you do it too?/ On your feet now, people! See what you can do!'"*

The usually languid patrons of the Zodiac Lounge were suddenly up and moving frantically to the beat. What had been a resting place between stressful bouts of gambling had become an instant discotheque. Lou thought she saw an edge of teeth showing between Carl D. Sipp's thin lips. It was not encouraging. Thinking quickly, she shouted, "Now, one more chorus, y'all, then have one of those nice long cool drinks, and get all rested and ready to go in there and *Win!* Oh, yeah, I feel a lucky streak coming on! I feel that luck so close to me I can *taste* it! I feel like I just might make a *million* tonight!

I can win big money,
Can you do it, too?
I can beat the odds, now,
Can you do it, too?
Luck is ridin' with me,
Make her ride with you!
Get on in there, people,
See what you can do!"

Carl D. Sipp broke into the first smile she had ever seen on his face as she and Tina and Aunt Jerutha, arms around one another's waists, wiggled their way offstage. It was an unpleasant smile, and Lou felt sick inside. There were, she felt, more kinds of prostitution than one.

Wordlessly, when she came offstage, he handed her a cupful of twenty-five dollar chips. Compliments of the house. Like the other things that had gotten them in so much trouble.

"I guess I have to go through with this," she said dubiously to Aunt Jerutha.

"Well, if you have to, you have to. Some folks say gambling's sinful, but I say let's give it a try. What they got in here anyway?" she asked as they headed toward the CASINO sign.

It should read ABANDON HOPE, ALL YE WHO ENTER HERE, Lou thought. "Slot machines, roulette, baccarat—whatever that is—crap tables, and blackjack," she recited. "And no windows, and millions of mirrors, and all the liquor you want. I don't know how to play anything."

"Blackjack's easy," Aunt Jerutha said. "All you have to know is how to count to twenty-one. You can use your fingers, your toes, and your nose. Come on."

They found their way to a table and stacked up their chips. Aunt Jerutha lost on each of her first six hands but Lou, to her amazement, kept winning. When she had twenty, the dealer had eighteen; when she had twenty-one, the dealer had twenty, and none of the other players could beat her cards. Whispering, "You've got the luck," Aunt Jerutha turned her remaining chips over to Lou. In less than twenty minutes she had won ten thousand dollars.

But on each of the next five deals, she lost a hundred.

"Time to quit," Aunt Jerutha said firmly, sweeping Lou's remaining chips into her large black handbag and pulling her away from the table. "See, I think that man back there, that Mr. Sippio, wanted you to win, but not too much."

Aunt Jerutha was right. All the dealers knew how to build players up and then bust them, Lou remembered from her talk with Tina.

"This'll pay off all your bills and then some, won't it?"

"No, but it'll help."

"You mean you owe more than what you won?"

"Yes," Lou admitted sadly.

"We'll see about that later," Aunt Jerutha said with tightened lips.

Lou cashed in her chips, received $9,500, and, guided by Aunt Jerutha's firm hand on her elbow, headed straight for her room. Carl D. Sipp was waiting at the elevator.

"Don't you want to settle some of your debts now?"

Aunt Jerutha's pressure on her elbow tightened. "I'd rather wait till we confer with our manager, if you don't mind," Lou said. "That is, if you trust me."

He bowed in acquiescence. "Of course. You impress me as a very responsible young lady. You know, I enjoyed you and this lady and the other one—what's her name?—when you performed together tonight. What *is* her name?" He snapped his fingers to prod his memory.

It was ridiculous. He knew Tina's name perfectly well. "Tina Williams," Lou supplied.

"Ah, yes. Tina. The three of you went over very well tonight. I think you and two other young women would have excellent potential as an all-girl act. Just what the Carousel needs. You know, my dear, it's a proven fact that young men mature more slowly than girls. Until they do grow up, boys tend to create more problems. At this stage, I feel they can only be a handicap to you. I'm sure Mr. Ross would be amenable to my idea. Why don't you consider it?"

"I'll do that," Lou said, grateful for the elevator door closing on his sharklike smile. Once she and Aunt Jerutha were alone, she said, "Everybody's been trying to do that ever since we signed with Marty. Separate me from the boys, I mean. Make me the star. Marty's even tried to turn them against me. I don't like it, Aunt Jerutha."

"Then don't do it," was the comforting response. She sighed. "It's the same old same old. White folks always trying to put us black women up front and leave our men by the wayside. We got to work hard to try not to let it happen. We got to do a lot of work on those Soul Brothers, though. And they got to do a lot of work on *themselves*."

Louretta changed into a soft robe, but Aunt Jerutha kept her brilliant dress on. They headed for the room where Marty was presumably watching over the boys.

They seemed better. David was alert and awake, and Frank and Ulysses were calmer, though they kept sniffling as if they had caught colds. The latter two were fooling around at the piano with chords that actually sounded like the core of a song.

"There's some cake there. Cake that'll stand up," Aunt Jerutha commented, perching like a cardinal on the arm of a chair.

Marty seemed the most nervous of them all, pacing and biting his fingernails. He'd spilled gravy on his shirt and hadn't even noticed. "How'd it go, Lou?" he asked.

"Okay, I guess. Mr. Sipp liked it very much, he said. But I missed the guys. I'm hoping they'll be downstairs with me for the 10:30 show." All at once the fatigue of the long day and the realization that she had two more shows to do before she could rest overwhelmed her. She headed back to her room for a nap, but Frank followed her.

"C'mon over here, baby," he called from the piano. "I got something nice for you." Dragging her feet, she walked over and sank to the piano bench beside him. He played and sang softly:

"Look at her up there tonight,
I'm so glad she's mine.
Smile so gorgeous, eyes so bright
She deserves to shine.
Lou in the limelight
Stirs up my desire,
Lou in the twilight
ights my little fire."

"Nice, Frank. Really nice," she complimented him in a weak voice.

Frank played a few aimless chords. "Tired, baby?"

"Bushed."

"Try this. You'll feel better right away."

She shook her head as he offered the little spoon. "I don't want my head messed up. I just want some rest."

"Trust me, baby. It'll help you make it through the night."

The night stretched unbearably long ahead of her. If anything would help her get through it, Lou wanted some.

At first she felt nothing. Then she felt as if the top of her head had been blown away. And then a surge of power and strength enough to last her through a hundred nights. "Gorgeous," she said. "Oh, gorgeous. Beautiful."

Thinking she meant his song, Frank continued:

"Lou in the limelight

Makes the people rave;
Lou in the twilight
Warms our little cave—"

Oh, wonderful. Wonderful feeling of renewal and strength. She held out her hand again for the spoon.

"Not so fast, baby. Take your time. Let the first glow wear off before you go for another."

"Nice, Frank. Ohhh but that's nice."

"You like the song?"

"Yeah. That too. Hey!" She grabbed his hand. "Let's run through it for the group!"

Back in the boys' room again, she climbed on top of the piano, swung her legs, and sang:

"Frank in the limelight
Makes the girls feel good.
Frank in the twilight
Does just what he should!

—Oh wee! He can really T—C—B! That means Takin' Care of Business, y'all! Let me tell you, now:

Frank in the limelight
Makes you shake and sweat.
Frank in the twilight—
What you see is what I get! Yeah!"

Exulting in the rush of synthetic excitement, she began to dance around the room with explicit movements punctuated by shouts of "All right!" and "Yeah!" and another half-verse:

"I mean to tell you all cats
Ain't alike in the dark,
Frank in the twilight
Really fans my little spark!

—Up the tempo, baby, up the tempo, I think we're on to something!"

"I think *she's* on something," David remarked from the sofa where he had been quietly observing.

"Louretta, go to your room and take a nap," Aunt Jerutha ordered.

What? Lou couldn't believe what she had heard. It had sounded like Momma giving an order to an eight year old. "I can't. I'm too excited," she said.

"Well, go lie down anyway. Save some of that energy for work."

"This *is* work, Aunt Jerutha. We're working on a song. You don't understand."

"I understand more than you think. You've been doping too. You can go back in there with her if you want to, Frank. Nothing natural offends me. But please leave your little dope package here, because that is *not* natural."

Reluctantly, he took the package from his pocket and put it in her hand.

"Thank you. I will take care of this. Where is the toilet?"

After David pointed the way, she went to the boys' bathroom and flushed.

Ulysses groaned. "Five hundred dollars' worth of joy down the drain."

Aunt Jerutha was back quickly enough to hear him. "Your lives are going down the drain, young man, but you're too young to see it. As for you, Mr. Marty Rosynose or whatever your name is, you should have watched these youngsters more carefully."

"I never took my eyes off them."

"Well, you should have made them empty their pockets."

"I guess I should have. They've emptied mine," he said disgustedly.

"Well, perhaps you've been a bit wasteful with money. Just look at the size of this room. It's an *apartment!*"

"The rooms are free, Mrs. Jackson, as long as they perform to management's satisfaction."

"But Lou tells me they're deeply in debt. Exactly how was that allowed to happen?"

Marty's eyes were wary. "They used other things in the hotel that aren't free."

"If they'd been properly supervised, that wouldn't have happened, would it?"

"Mrs. Jackson, I'm not a baby-sitter. I'm a manager."

"And I intend to find out just how good a manager you are, Mr. Rosiness. I haven't had time yet, but I intend to go over your books very carefully."

Marty bristled. "Why should I let you do that? Who are you, anyway?"

"I am these children's legal guardian, not you—appointed by their parents, not you. The papers putting me in charge of them are on their way right now."

"Well, you don't get to see my books until I see those papers," Marty told her. "Right now I have a more urgent problem—getting them in shape to go on at ten-thirty."

"Go take a nap, Lou," Aunt Jerutha ordered again.

"I told you, I'm too excited to sleep."

"What Lou needs is a good slug of brandy to bring her down from that high," Marty declared.

Mrs. Jackson's lips tightened as Marty produced a flask. "I don't want her to get started on another harmful habit."

"Believe me, Mrs. Jackson, I've had this experience with performers before. I know what works."

Aunt Jerutha kept shaking her head.

"One shot of liquor never turned anybody into a drunk," Marty declared.

"Just give me a tranquilizer, Marty. One of the blue ones—no, two of the yellow ones."

Aunt Jerutha made the decision according to one of her ground rules. "Liquor is more natural than pills. Take the drink, Lou. Then go and lie down. —That was a nice song she was singing, wasn't it? Why don't you fellow run through it for me?"

CHAPTER

13

"Seems like these children write a song a day," Aunt Jerutha said the next morning. "Songs just come out of them naturally like leaves come out on trees. Now, who owns the copyrights to these songs?"

Marty cleared his throat. "Excuse me, Mrs. Jackson, but why don't you just relax and enjoy your visit here and leave the technical details to me?"

"I intended to do just that, Mr. Ross. I was trying to. That's why I invited you to have breakfast with us, to relax and be sociable. But I turned my little transistor on just now, and I heard that new song of Lou's, 'Talkin' 'Bout Yo' Mama.' Only, it wasn't Lou singing. Listen for yourself. It's still playing."

Marty fiddled with the radio. "I don't hear it."

"You must have changed the station." Aunt Jerutha reached over and moved the dial. "There. Children! Who's that singing?"

"It's my song!" Louretta cried in shock.

"I know that," Aunt Jerutha replied. "But it's not you singing."

"They sound like those freaks we worked with in New York," Frank observed. "The ones with the bathing caps and phony antennas on their heads."

"The Bionic Babies!" Lou supplied.

"Mr. Ross," Aunt Jerutha queried, "who manages The Bionic Babies?"

"I don't know."

"Then I'll come back to my first question. Who owns the copyrights to these children's songs?"

Marty looked up at the ceiling, ahead at the wall, down at

his plate, everywhere but at her.

"Are they copyrighted at all?" Aunt Jerutha persisted.

"Oh, yes. Yes, indeed."

"In whose name?"

"Mine."

"First thing I do when I go out," Aunt Jerutha told Lou in a none-too-soft whisper, "is find us a good lawyer."

"Mrs. Jackson," Marty told her, "I *am* a lawyer."

"That so?" she said skeptically.

"Yes. I have a contract to represent these young people, and I am looking out for their interests."

"That so?" Aunt Jerutha repeated.

"Yes. I was hoping you and I could work together with these kids."

"So was I," Aunt Jerutha said. She removed Marty's coffee cup and refilled everyone else's.

Marty stood up. "Look after them, will you? They barely limped through their shows last night. I have a good relationship with the management here, but only if I deliver what I promise."

Aunt Jerutha told him tartly, "Maybe you should tell the management to stop delivering dope to their rooms."

"I don't believe that happened, Mrs. Jackson. Maybe that's what they told you, but I believe they got hold of it on their own. Why should the hotel want its entertainers too zonked to perform?"

While she pondered this, Marty stood up. "I've set up a rehearsal for them at three this afternoon, in the Starlight Theater upstairs. All four of them had better be there. And none of them had better be stoned." He slammed the door behind him.

"Now I wonder," Aunt Jerutha said, taking a delicate sip of her coffee, "why that man is so upset this morning?" She winked, and Louretta laughed.

"I wonder what he's promised to deliver to the management," Frank said sourly. "Our singing—or our souls?"

"Both, probably," Lou said. Thinking over the events of the past eleven days, she began to fear that Marty and the casino people might be after even more than that—though she could not imagine what else there could be. She thought a moment, then said, "Aunt Jerutha, Tina would know what's going on better than anyone. Have you had a chance to talk to her yet?"

Mrs. Jackson shook her head. "Every time I tried, she was disappearing out the room with some man."

David snickered.

Aunt Jerutha put him in his place immediately. "That's enough, youngster. You know what she was doing, and so do I, so there's no need to go into the details.—To tell the truth, Lou, a woman like that is somebody I'm a little shy about getting to know."

"Shy? *You?*" Lou and Frank chorused. Lou added, "You even *danced* with her the other night—remember?"

"That was before she began her little disappearing acts," Aunt Jerutha explained. "Now, all of you know I've nothing against having a good time, within reasonable limits. But I never went in for hanging around with sporting folks. And your friend Tina seems a little too worldly for me."

"Maybe so, but she understands this crazy world out here better than anybody else we've met. I wish you'd talk to her," Lou urged.

"She's moving in the wrong direction," Aunt Jerutha argued. "How can she possibly steer you right?"

"Because she *wants* to. She doesn't want me to end up like her, Aunt Jerutha. She's the one who suggested I send for somebody from home."

Aunt Jerutha was silent, thinking this over. Finally she said, "Does anyone have Tina's phone number?"

While Frank was searching for it, Lou said, "Tina told me we should scrape up every dollar we can to pay our bill and get away from Marty. I know Frank's broke, but what about you, David? Do you have any money saved up?"

David shook his head. "I signed my checks over to my dad to

fix the roof and get us a new furnace."

"How 'bout you, Ulysses?" She didn't expect a more encouraging answer from him than from the others, because Ulysses was the oldest of nine children, all with appetities as large as his. But to her surprise, he replied, "I've got about two thousand in the bank, Lou. There ought to be some interest on it by now, too—I just never got around to having them put it in the book."

Lou was amazed. Ulysses had managed to save most, if not all, of his money! She didn't know exactly what the fellows had earned from their first record, but she knew her checks were larger, because she was paid for composing as well as for singing.

"That's great, Ulysses. I have four thousand saved, plus the money I won in the casino. That adds up to almost half of what we owe Marty. Aunt Jerutha, do you think a bank would lend us the other half?"

Their adopted mother shook her head. "A person has to have a good credit history to get a bank loan. All of you are too young to have built up any credit—or to apply for any. But before we start paying anybody *any*thing, I think I ought to go over Mr. Ross's books and see if his figures are correct."

"Here's Tina's phone number," Frank said, handing it to Mrs. Jackson. "Sorry I don't have anything else in my pockets."

Aunt Jerutha looked at the slip of paper uncertainly until Lou took it from her and said, "*I'll* call her." Sitting on the floor on the far side of the bed most distant from the kitchen area, she dialed and talked softly for several minutes, then announced, "She wants us to meet her for lunch." She stifled a yawn; she was still tired from the night before. "At a place in West Vegas called The Chili Bowl. You guys coming?"

"Not me," Frank said. "I've got to cop some Zs. We've got a heavy rehearsal this afternoon."

"I could use a nap, too," Ulysses said with a cavernous yawn. David's yawn followed his by less than a second.

After the threesome had left for their room and their naps, Lou said a few more words into the phone, hung up, and stood

up, stretching. "Well, Aunt Jerutha, I guess you and I are the
only ones going."

"You're tired, too, girl. You worked with too much strong medicine in your system last night. You sure going out to see this woman makes sense?"

"Yes, because nothing that's happened to us in this hotel makes sense, and she's the only person who might be able to help us figure it out."

Aunt Jerutha reached tentatively for her sweater. "You know, I didn't like the way that Mr. Carl Sipp was looking at you last night. He reminded me of a tomcat staring at a piece of liver."

"He always looks at me like that," Lou told her. "I don't like it either. Neither does Tina. He offered me a way to get our bill canceled, but she talked me out of it."

Aunt Jerutha already had her sweater on. "What did he want you to do?"

"Spend the night with him," Lou said, putting on her shoes. "Tina stopped him from bothering me—but she can't stop him from looking, I guess."

When she looked up, Aunt Jerutha had Bertha on her head, her purse in her hand, and a fierce, impatient look in her eyes.

The Chili Bowl in West Las Vegas, a bombed-out, boarded-up, neighborhood hidden by a freeway from the glittering gamblers' Strip, was not a glamorous place or a "nice" place, but something in between—what they would call at home a "decent" place. It did not have tablecloths or flower vases, and it did have a bar. But the bar was a completely separate room from the restaurant. There, good behavior seemed to be enforced and women could feel comfortable and safe.

Tina, in a black sweater and slacks and sunglasses, was waiting for them in a booth. She looked better by daylight, Lou decided, with her gray natural exposed and practically no makeup. Like The Chili Bowl with its unadorned tables and worn linoleum, she looked *real*.

Standing, Tina gave Lou a handshake as firm as a man's and said, "I'm glad you took my advice, Lou, even if you *have* been scared to introduce me to your mama."

"She's not my momma, Tina. This is my mother's best friend, Mrs. Jackson."

"Pleased to meet you, Mrs. Jackson," Tina said, and extended her hand again. After a brief hesitation, Aunt Jerutha shook hands, then sat down stiffly on the very edge of the bench as if poised for immediate flight.

"She's like a mother to us, though," Lou said. "We call her Aunt Jerutha."

"That's nice. But I can tell what she'd call me. And she'd be right," Tina said, taking off her sunglasses to give Aunt Jerutha one of her penetrating looks.

"Seems to me," Aunt Jerutha said, looking off somewhere past Tina's earlobe, "a determined person can always find decent work."

"Not in this town," Tina said, lighting a cigarette. "This is the most depressed black community in America—in a town where people throw money away like Kleenex. Our unemployment rate is the highest in the country, and our poverty level is nearly the lowest. It's crazy. It's ridiculous." She laughed. "I tried to earn an honest living once. I tried doing hair, but the natural style and the do-it-yourself perm kits ran me out of business. Not that my customers could afford to pay me anyway. Most of them were on welfare. I can't work as a dealer anymore; once you're fired by one casino, you're blackballed in all of them. I don't feel I have to apologize for myself, Mrs. Jackson. I do what I have to do to take care of my children. And I don't like to see *any* of our children abused."

Aunt Jerutha unbent a little. "Lou tells me you've been a good friend to her out here. That why?"

"Sure. I don't want to see anybody her age pushed into a life like mine. But she was so hard-headed when I talked to her, I never thought she'd pay any attention to me. What changed your mind, Lou?"

Lou bit her lip. She didn't want to mention her experiment with cocaine. "Uh—a couple of things scared me."

Tina turned her intense stare on Lou. "Your act wasn't up to the usual mark last night. It was almost like you and your friends were singing different songs. What went wrong?"

"We were tired, I guess."

Tina raised her hand. "Told you what I'd do if you ever lied to me, girl."

Lou flinched instinctively. "I tried some of that stuff you use."

Tina's mouth worked itself into an ugly expression. "I thought so. You were bipping and bopping off-key half the time, and the other half you were jumping around off the beat like a puppy with fleas." She shifted her gaze to Mrs. Jackson. "I promised her I'd give her a good beating if she ever messed with drugs. You want to do it for me, or do I have your permission to go ahead?"

"No beatings today, please. We just want your advice."

"—Order the chef's salad, it's the only decent thing on the menu," Tina said, for a waitress had appeared. Lou and Aunt Jerutha nodded. "Three chef's salads," Tina told the waitress, and waited till she was out of earshot before saying, "Want my advice? Get them out of that hotel right away. Get them all the way out of Vegas if you can. But if you can't, at least move them out of the Carousel before something else happens."

"But the rooms are free there, I understand," Aunt Jerutha objected.

"You end up paying a high price for them, Mrs. Jackson. You need to move them away from the slots and the tables and the hard stuff and all the other temptations. I know a place in this part of town that's clean and decent." She handed Mrs. Jackson a card. "It's no palace, but it's not as dangerous as the Carousel. Tell them I sent you; you might get a better deal."

"Tell the truth, I don't like the looks of that Mr. Sippio," Aunt Jerutha confided. "He acts like he wants to get his hands on Lou."

 "Believe me, if she stays there another week, he will."

Lou got the cold, clammy feeling she always experienced when Carl D. Sipp paid attention to her. It was like standing in front of an opened tomb. "But I thought you said you could make him leave me alone, Tina!"

"I did talk him into leaving you along—for a little while. He backed off when I promised to cut him in on my retirement plan. But I can't guarantee he'll back off forever."

"What was your retirement plan? Why'd you give it up for me?" Lou's curiosity prompted her to ask.

"Not just for you, brat. For my daughter. He's stopped asking about Cynthia since I promised to introduce him to a certain party."

"Who?" Lou wanted to know.

"Don't be so nosy, child," Aunt Jerutha reproved her. "We didn't come here to pry into Miss Tina's business."

"It's all right. I think I want to tell you about it," Tina said. "See-one of my friends is a merchant seaman. He can bring things into the country when he comes back from his trips. I was going to go into business selling the things for him."

"What sort of things?" Aunt Jerutha wanted.

"Things people want . . . binoculars, cameras, radios, watches, souvenirs."

"Oh, I see," Aunt Jerutha said.

"No, you don't see. All those things would have hollow spaces in them to hold *other* things people want—like heroin and cocaine. That's why Carlo was interested in meeting my sailor friend. Do I shock you?"

"No," Aunt Jerutha said, and proceeded to choke on her first forkful of salad.

"Sorry. I know I didn't have to spell it out for you, but I like to be up front with people I like. Especially when I think I need to scare them."

"I appreciate your honesty," Aunt Jerutha said when she had finished coughing. "But Lou and the boys have to work at the Carousel for another fifteen weeks."

"Try to cut the engagement short if you can. There is no way for those kids to stay at the Carousel that long without becoming junkies or drunks or—well, low-lifes like me."

"I don't think you should call yourself names like that, Tina," Lou said.

Tina shrugged. "That was a polite one. I've been called worse names, and they didn't hurt me. Mrs. Jackson, I guarantee you, if those children stay at the Carousel another week, Lou will be another one of Carlo's playthings. He only keeps his promises to his cronies. His promises to people like us don't mean anything. And he has as many tricks as a double-run hand of pinochle."

Aunt Jerutha fished in her purse for money to pay for their lunches, which Tina refused by snatching the check with one hand and pushing Aunt Jerutha's hand away with the other.

"Well," Mrs. Jackson said, stirring, "we better be getting back. Lou has to rehearse, and I have to see about some mail I'm expecting. If it comes, I'll be able to go over Mr. Ross's books."

"They'll be padded, don't worry," Tina told her. "Marty Ross has no principles. He's known for pulling shady deals out here. He works hand in hand with Carl Sipp—you know that, don't you?"

Both of them shook their heads.

"Sure," Tina said, expertly blowing smoke above their heads. "They're a team. Marty is small fry, but he'll do anything Carlo asks him because he wants to feel big and important. Carlo gives him a big line of credit in the hotel in exchange for favors. He told my pit boss to let Lou and her friends tap into that line of credit, because he wants them in debt to him. Marty may not have agreed to it—he was out of town when it happened—but he can't say anything about it, because Carlo owns *him*."

Lou felt sick and scared. Like she'd stepped into a nest of poisonous snakes and couldn't even tell where one ended and the other began. "What do you think Carlo and Marty are after?" she asked.

Tina shrugged. "Who knows? You're good-looking, but so are thousands of other girls out here. What's different about you is your talent. You and your friends are extremely talented—you sing, you dance, you write, you compose. Talent isn't as common as people think. There are a lot of no-talent groups around."

Aunt Jerutha asked suddenly, "Have you ever heard of a group called The Bionic Babies?"

Tina chuckled. "They're playing right down the street from you, in a smaller casino called the Valencia. And they have about as much talent as a cageful of chimpanzees."

Aunt Jerutha rose, her face set grimly. "Thank you, Miss Tina. Thank you very much."

"One more thing. You'd never be able to prove it, it's done through dummy corporations, but Carlo and his associates own the Valencia."

"Didn't I say this morning we needed a lawyer?" Aunt Jerutha said to Lou.

Tina scribbled a name on a napkin and handed it to Aunt Jerutha. "This is the best one in town, if you can get to see him. Don't mention my name."

This time Mrs. Jackson was the first to extend her hand. "Miss Tina, you are a very kind and generous lady."

Lou saw Tina blink from the sudden moisture in her eyes before she concealed it with the oversized sunglasses. "Thank you. Hope you can help the kids keep their noses clean. As for you—she raised a menacing hand to Lou—"you'd better have your head straight when I see you tonight, or I'll knock it off your shoulders. And you'd better introduce me to Mrs. Jackson as if we'd never had a conversation."

Lou promised to obey both of Tina's injunctions. As they left the restaurant, Aunt Jerutha said, "You were right, Lou. She's a good person—stuck in a bad life." As they boarded the bus, she clutched her stomach. "I think I've got indigestion."

"From the lunch?" Lou asked solicitously.

"No—from taking in so much other garbage."

The group spent many hours rehearsing in the Carousel's Starlight Theater, mainly because the bandleader had such strong ideas about the public's taste. A very short man named Toledo, he wanted to turn every song in their repertoire, from blues to ballads, into a disco arrangement. And Marty, who was trying to set up a new record album, agreed with him.

"Disco is what sells today," Marty said. "People want the beat that moves their feet."

"People in this business have no imaginations," Lou retorted. "They keep pushing the same old thing on the public just because the public bought it last year. Me, I'm tired of disco. How 'bout you guys?"

"*Been* tired," was Frank's reply. "My feet wore out about three years ago."

"My arches fell around the same time," David said.

"Disco puts me to sleep," Ulysses said. "I mean it. It's so monotonous, I just turn on the disco station at bedtime, and I conk right out."

"You four are not exactly a valid sample of the buying public," Joe Toledo told them. "*I* keep my finger on the public pulse, I follow all the record polls, and I tell you disco is the craze. Disco, disco, disco, day and night."

"Craze? He's crazy. Disco is dead," Frank whispered as the band struck up, for the fourth time, an absurd disco rendition of "Let Your Love Show."

"That's not how it goes!" Lou cried, waving her arms to emphasize the rhythm. "Slower, slower, slooowerrr . . ."

"You are not the conductor of this orchestra, Miss. *I* am."

"True," Frank conceded. "But I agree with her, and *I'm* the composer of the song."

"I don't care if you're Paganini, you *will* follow the tempo I give you!"

"Did you hear that German accent?" David observed. "He sounds like Hitler."

"It's not his nationality, it's his chin," said Aunt Jerutha, who had come in late. "If you notice, people with big chins are always bossy."

"What about big noses?" Lou whispered. "He has one of them, too."

"Yes, big noses tend to be bossy. Also, Mr. Toledo is a dwarf. People that tiny always try to boss everybody."

"You and I are short, Aunt J. Are we bossy too?" Lou wondered.

"Certainly," her proxy mother said. "You can tell a lot about people from the way they're shaped. Marty, there is round and soft like a marshmallow. He can be pushed around easily. But Ben Carroll, the lawyer I saw for you today, has a big log-shaped head. That means he's smart and strong. He knows what he wants, and you can't sway him easy. He's like a big strong tree."

Lou enjoyed Aunt Jerutha's lesson in black phrenology, though it was the sort of thing she had been hearing all her life and not believing. But she was surprised by her bold mention of the lawyer's name, which turned Marty white as a marshmallow, when before he had only been soft as one. A nervous silence descended.

It was broken by the bandleader, impatiently tapping his baton on his music stand. "Let's get on with this rehearsal! I only have thirty more minutes to waste with you. Gentlemen to the rear, please."

"How many times do I have to tell you? They're not backup singers!" Lou exclaimed.

They were beginning to wear Toledo down. "All right, stand in a row, stand on your heads, do anything, I don't care. Just don't blame me if you bomb. An act only gets one chance to bomb at the Carousel."

By the end of the rehearsal they had compromised on singing most of their numbers the way he wanted them sung, but keeping a few of the arrangements their way. One was "Lament for Jethro," which had become almost a sacred song to them.

Another was Lou's new song which, she and Frank agreed, needed a calypso rhythm.

"Calypso? What's that? A town in Idaho?" the little bandleader scoffed.

"Toledo? What's that? A town in Ohio?" David echoed.

"Nobody's listened to calypso since the forties," the conductor objected. But, after much argument, Lou and Frank prevailed.

And that night in the Zodiac Lounge, they joined hands and sang:

"Love is a river,
Love is a river.

You never see the same water,
Whatever the river's name,
The river never changes
But the water's never the same.

I loved a fellow,
So fine and mellow
Before I loved what's-his-name."

Lou ogled Frank archly after singing that line, and audience laughter held them back for several beats.

"The river never changes,
But the water's never the same."

Lou felt a glow like love showing during that performance and the next. She sensed good vibes beaming back at her from the audience and a good feeling flowing between her and Frank like the warm currents of her song. Aching to be alone with him, she felt frustrated when Aunt Jerutha disappeared shortly after the second show, presumably to go to sleep in Lou's room.

Tina came over and congratulated her on her calm, clear head. Lou didn't tell her she'd achieved the calm with the help of a vial of Valium from Marty.

Then Tina warned her in a whisper, "I don't think your

friends are gonna stay cool, though. I saw that snake Charles slip them something out in the hall."

"That Charles is nothing but trouble!" Lou fumed. "What good is he to us, anyway? He wasn't even at our rehearsal."

"Easy, girl," Tina warned. "The walls have ears around here, you know. And I could be wrong."

Lou ran out into the corridor that circled the casino like the rim of a wheel and into first one and then another of the lounges that occupied the spokes. An organist was playing in the third one she entered, and Frank was singing along with him.

She tiptoed up behind him and put her arms around his waist. "Baby," she whispered in his ear, "why are you working on your break?"

"My train's on the fast track," he sang, "and I can't slow it down."

"Can I come along for the ride?" she teased.

"No," he said, detaching her hands from his waist. "This is the uptown express. You board that old slow-moving local on some other track."

"I think you've gone off your rails," she told him, but managed to coax him into a booth. "Come on, sit down. Have a drink with me. *Be* with me."

But Frank didn't want a drink. And he didn't want to be with anybody. His eyes looked at her without seeing her, as if he were thinking of her as "What's her-name." She couldn't even hold one of the restless hands that were drumming tattoos all over the table.

"Oh, Frank, who does this have to happen? Why can't we be nice and close and happy like before?"

"Shhhhh," he said, finger to his lips. "I've got an inspiration for a song."

"Ah babee,
Ah babee,
Ah babee . . ."

He seemed stuck for a long, dreadful interval. Then he continued:

"Ah babee, ah babee,
Please don't drag me down.
Put on your wings and fly with me,
Or stay down on the ground."

"Where do I get wings?" she asked.

"In fairyland, of course," he said with a laugh, nodding toward the table where Charles was sitting with some friends.

Lou wanted to be close to Frank so badly she was tempted for a moment. "I'll smoke some grass with you if you want," she offered timidly.

"Grass is for playgrounds, little girl," Frank informed her.

Angrily, abruptly, Lou changed her mind. Maybe her frayed nerves were turning her into a pillhead and even, possibly, a liquor-head, but she didn't want to smoke herb or try any of the stronger illicit drugs again. Drugs wouldn't bring her any closer to Frank; all they did was separate people and lock them in solitary-confinement cells.

She got up and left him singing a love song to himself.

Their last show was a near disaster. The current between her and Frank had been short-circuited, of course, and so had the one between them and the audience. He was still singing to himself.

David was so far gone, he had forgotten most of the lyrics and had to substitute doo-wahs and ooblie-dees.

Only Lou and Uylysses had the words and the tunes and the rhythms all together—in effect, they were a duo performing for the audience and trying to drown out two soloists who seemed to have wandered onstage by mistake.

Afterward, Lou didn't hang around to wait for the reaction. She caught the nearest elevator, unlocked her door quietly, and tiptoed in to keep from waking Aunt Jerutha.

But her friend was wide awake, poring over a thick ledger book with reading glasses on the tip of her nose.

CHAPTER 14

"Aun Jerutha," Lou asked the next morning, "what did the lawyer say?"

"He said there's nothing you can do about the songs Mr. Ross has already copyrighted, because your contracts gave him the privilege to put them in his name. From now on you are to bring all your new songs to Mr. Carroll, though, and he'll put them in *your* names. And he said there's a chance you can get out of your contracts with Mr. Ross if you want to, because you're all minors—but it won't be easy, because your manager was smart enough to get adult relatives to sign for each of you. But if that's what you want to do, and you have just cause, there's a way to break the contracts, he says."

Lou digested this. They had just cause to break their ties with Marty if anyone ever did. Because she and Mrs. Jackson both distrusted him so deeply, she wondered, "Why did you let Marty know you'd been to see Mr. Carroll?"

"My legal guardian papers hadn't come, and I wanted to scare him into letting me look at his books anyway. It worked." A vertical frown creased Aunt Jerutha's forehead.

"What's the matter, Aunt J?"

"His books seem to be in order, except for one two thousand-dollar item I can't account for. I was hoping to get you all away from here fast. But you really *do* owe him all that money."

Lou searched her mind for possible escape hatches. "Marty did tell us," she said, "he would pay the hotel bill for us if we went to California to make a movie. We'd have to pay him back later, of course."

Aunt Jerutha didn't seem exactly thrilled by the prospect. "That would get you away from here," she conceded, "but you'd still be tied to Mr. Ross, and if his friends out there are anything like his friends here . . ." She sighed. "I'd better stop crossing bridges before I get to them. Go round up your friends, Louretta. It's time we had a talk with Mr. Ross."

Ulysses was in the corridor outside his room, practicing kung fu moves in an extra-large kimono. For all his bulk, he was graceful and coordinated. When he checked and reported that his roommates couldn't be aroused, Lou wasn't surprised.

"I rolled 'em over, Lou. I picked 'em up and dropped 'em back on their beds. Then I hollered loud enough to make 'em open their eyes. They said 'yes' when I asked was it okay for me to speak for all of us. But I'm not sure they heard what I said."

Lou shrugged. "If their heads are still twisted, they wouldn't be able to think straight anyway. Come on, Bruce Lee. You look nice in your kimono."

"It's called a *ghi,*" he corrected her.

"Whatever you call it, it's nice to see *somebody* trying to stay in shape," Lou said.

"Mr. Ross is expecting all five of us. Where are the other two?" Aunt Jerutha asked sharply when Lou and Ulysses showed up.

"Sleeping," Ulysses told her.

"Stoned," Louretta corrected.

Aunt Jerutha's mouth tightened. "That settles it," she said, moving briskly ahead of them.

Lou and Ulysses looked at each other, wondering what was settled. Charles and Marty were having a late Continental breakfast in Marty's room when the three of them walked in.

"Well, Mr. Ross," Aunt Jerutha said pleasantly, "I've gone over your books carefully, and there's been a lot of waste, but you haven't been cheating these children—no more than most people would cheat."

Marty almost choked on his croissant. "Mrs. Jackson, please. How can you say a thing like that?"

"Because it's true. There's only a few honest people in this world, and you ain't one of them. But that don't make you especially bad. Just ordinary. There wasn't no reason for all of those limousines and lunches in New York City. Those hotel rooms back there were much too high. There's no way I can check on the other back expenses, except to ask about this item here."

Marty looked at the line her finger indicated. "Oh," he said. "That's Charles's salary."

"What exactly is his function? I've been meanin' to ask."

Haughtily, Charles handed Aunt Jerutha a card.

"'Charles Astral, Imagist to the Stars,'" she read aloud. "That don't tell me anything."

"I take care of their clothing, their makeup, promotion and publicity, costumes and choreography," Charles informed her. "I have fifteen years of expertise in all those fields."

"How come," Ulysses wanted to know, "we didn't have the benefit of your exper-*tise* at our rehearsal yesterday?"

"I was called away," Charles said evasively.

"Yes, and I bet I know where you were. Out getting that junk you gave Frank and David! He's a dope pusher, Aunt Jerutha! He's been supplying the guys with that stuff," Lou exclaimed.

"Is this true, Charles?" Marty asked. No one could tell if his surprise were real or feigned.

"Of course not," Charles said. "My job is to make them look good in the public eye. I've spent weeks trying to groom these awkward teenagers into professionals; why would I suddenly want to turn them into zombies?"

"How can you sit there and deny it, man?" Ulysses asked hotly. "I was right there when you were passing out the free samples and showing us how to use them."

"And Frank told me you supplied him last night," Lou added.

"You even got high with us that first night. You *did,* man," Ulysses insisted.

"Well?" Marty demanded, his eyes glaring.

"My little weaknesses," Charles said sullenly, "are my own affair."

How much do *you* owe the hotel?" Marty asked.

Charles did not answer this directly. "Look, you know yourself, nobody says 'no' to Carlo. He told me to turn them on."

"Never mind, never mind," Marty said hastily. His face was tomato red.

"I knew it," Aunt Jerutha said. "This Room Service bill—three thousand dollars in three days—that can't be nothin' but dope."

Lou had that horrid, slimy feeling of stepping into a serpents' nest again.

"Like I said, Mr. Ross," Aunt Jerutha went on, "you haven't exactly been cheating these children. What's happened is, they've been allowed to cheat themselves. —Children, you've got about nine thousand dollars in earnings here and about fourteen thousand in legitimate expenses. —Or illegitimate expenses, it doesn't matter. But you've got another twenty-seven thousand in gambling debts. And, like I said, three thousand for dope."

"And forty percent interest a week on that thirty thou," Marty interjected.

"Mr. Ross, you must agree this is not a healthy environment for these young people. Do you think there is any possible way we might get them out of it?"

Shrewd Aunt Jerutha. She was treating Marty like an ally, Lou noticed, and he was giving her earnest, respectful attention.

"What about the film we were supposed to make, Marty?" Lou asked. "You told us you'd pay the hotel bill for us if we went out to California to work on a film."

"Do you want to do that?" he asked Lou.

She looked at Ulysses before answering Marty. "I say yes," Ulysses said. "You got to be strong to stand up to this place, and we ain't strong."

"I say yes, too," Lou said. "I figure, if we stay here, we'll just get deeper and deeper in debt. Maybe out in California we can get a fresh start and make enough money to pay off our bills."

"When can we start packing, Mr. Ross?" Aunt Jerutha asked.

Marty told her, "Let's see if I can still arrange it first. He began dialing numbers and jabbering with increasing impatience on the telephone. "Right, Al. Oh, Jesus, Al, can't you do anything better for me than that? —All right, I'll call this other guy, see what he says." Marty made several other calls, his words spilling more rapidly and the pitch in his voice growing higher with each conversation.

The upset in his face was visible when he finally gave them the news.

"Look, the film, the film they wanted you to work in, the film has been held up for budgetary reasons. One backer pulled out, and another is shilly-shallying, so they're fishing for other investors. But not to worry. Quite a few big parties are interested in the property, so the money's bound to come through eventually. In the meantime I've got you work in another film right here in Vegas. Not the kind of vehicle I'd hoped to see you in, but a job is a job. Treat it like that, and you'll do fine. I've lined up some club work for you on your day off, too."

"What's the name of the film?" Aunt Jerutha asked.

"*Disco Delights,* ma'am. It all takes place in one of those new dance clubs. Shooting starts at eight in the morning."

"Who's producing it?" Charles wanted to know.

Marty shot him a stern look of warning, then said, "Rog Marcos."

"Ah, old Rog is still at it," Charles said with a snigger. "Take my advice, ducks. Don't use your real names. Call yourselves Starry Night and the Flips or something like that."

"Why?" Louretta wondered.

"Because we are grooming you to go to the top," Marty told her, "and we only want your name associated with top-notch productions. I've done the best I can for you right now. I'll keep trying. Something better may turn up any minute. In the meantime, you'll be picking up extra money here in Vegas, and that'll set you free a lot sooner."

"But I want to leave *now!*" Lou cried.

" I know you do," Marty said. "But you can't. Look—maybe

it'll make you feel better if Charles and I take you and Mrs. Jackson out to dinner."

Aunt Jerutha drew herself up. "I am not," she stated, "in the habit of keeping company with the Devil."

"You want me to escort that—that dusky *duenna?*" Charles exclaimed.

"Imagist is nothing but an alias for Lucifer!" Aunt Jerutha retorted.

"Quit it, you two, please. We've got enough troubles without the two of you arguing," Marty said. "And I blame most of the recent troubles on you, Charles. Considering your behavior lately, you're lucky I'm not firing you. As it is, I'm cutting your pay in half, starting right now."

Charles jumped to his feet. "What? You expect me to subsist on a measly $150 a week?"

"I'm taking a pay cut, too," Marty said gloomily. "Venus Productions doesn't exactly have Columbia's budget, you know. Now apologize to the lady. You just insulted her."

"Why do we have to have her along, anyway? What is *her* function?"

"I have some papers here that came in the mail this morning," Aunt Jerutha said, producing a document from her capacious purse. Marty inspected it quickly, nodded, and handed it back to her.

"She has legal guardianship over these youngsters," he informed Charles. "She can't be dispensed with. But *you* can."

Charles underwent an instant transformation from sullenness to sparkling good humor. He bowed deeply, took Aunt Jerutha's hand, and to her astonishment, kissed it. "Dear, gracious lady, please forgive me for being such a boor. I beg you, please try to understand that I have been agitated lately. From now on, I promise to treat you with all the esteem you deserve."

"Well," Aunt Jerutha said, trying to rub the kiss off on her skirt, "I know my faith is strong enough to stand up against all conditions and associations."

Dinner was at a candlelit place a block or so away called The

Valencia. Lou suspected it was kept dark so customers couldn't see the dirt. But they ate, and enjoyed, paella, rice with chicken, and every imaginable kind of seafood, and drank the red wine punch called sangria. A rather disappointing flamenco act—one elderly guitarist, one middle-aged dancer—entertained them half-heartedly.

When the table had been cleared and the sangria pitcher was being refilled, Marty brought up business. "About that club date, Lou. There's just one little concession you'll have to make. The club owner wants you to work with some new musicians. He's got a special interest in them, they're his nephews or something, and he wants to give them a break."

Louretta's eyes narrowed. "Does he want me to work with them instead of with my guys?"

Marty's eyes dropped. "Well, he'd prefer that, yes. Look at it this way, Lou. It means you've arrived. That's real star status, when you can help boost another group."

"It's a white group. Right?"

Marty nodded.

"What's the name of the group?" Aunt Jerutha asked.

"I forget," Marty said. "You know how these kids are, always making up all kinds of crazy names. The Unbalanced Wheels, or something."

Louretta was furious. "I say, no way. What do you say, Aunt Jerutha?"

"I think we ought to sleep on it," her proxy mother said.

"But we were going to take you there now," Marty protested. "Let her look the place over, meet the owner, and run through a couple of numbers with these kids."

"We can do all of that," Aunt Jerutha said serenely, "and still sleep on it. As long as nobody signs anything."

Marty came down hard in response to that. "In case you've forgotten, they've *already* signed a one-year contract with me to work wherever I send them."

The Club Valenciana turned out to be very conveniently located. Right downstairs, in fact. It had lots of candles in red glass holders and wooden kegs against curved plaster walls to give it a cave look.

"He's a slick one, all right," Aunt Jerutha whispered in her ear. Just play along with him until I can think up a way to out-slick him."

But Lou was in no mood to play along. The Club Valenciana was not open yet, but onstage, a group of scruffy young white men with hair that reminded her of Aunt Jerutha's bird hat were banging on drums, fiddling with amplifier knobs, and twanging guitars. On the drums were the initials BB.

"Hi, Marty," the guitarist said. "When'd you make it out here?"

"This morning," was Marty's curt answer. "And I'm suffering from jet lag, so don't bug me."

"Hey, Marty, don't be such a sourpuss. You're supposed to be the world's sweetest manager. Lay back and listen to us run through these new changes."

They hit a few cacophonous chords, then went raggedly into the first chorus of "Talkin' 'Bout Yo' Mama." The biggest one threw back his sheepdog locks and began howling Lou's lyrics into the microphone.

Marty made a sharp gesture to cut off the sound. "Where's Larry? I brought these ladies over to meet him."

"Oh, his usual place. Over there," was the answer.

At the dimly lit bar, poring over a large ledger with his face six inches from the page, sat a plump man whose feet did not reach the floor. He had a large, smiling, expressive face and held out an equally large hand which was disappointingly limp when Lou shook it. "Larry Gabriel," he introduced himself. "Charmed to meet you ladies. You are the angels who are going to save me from ruin. Those kids out there"—he shrugged despairingly—"well, what can I say? Last night the audience threw *trash* at them."

"Well, tonight they'll be throwing bouquets. Right, Lou?"

"*Tonight?* I thought we just came here to talk."

"Louretta is tired," Aunt Jerutha stated. Also, there are some details that need to be cleared up before she comes to work here."

"You didn't tell me the mother was traveling with her." The short man, Larry, was still smiling, but his smile looked stretched and painful. "Mothers mean trouble."

"She just arrived," Marty informed him. "But she's very easy to get along with. Right, Aunt Jerutha?"

"Call me Mrs. Jackson," Aunt Jerutha said. "From now on, our relations will have to be strictly business. You are managing this other group too—is that right, Mr. Ross?"

Marty was evasive. "Every manager handles more than one talent package. I don't see anything wrong with that."

"Not unless there is a conflict of interest," Aunt Jerutha informed him.

Lou, who had been containing her feelings very well, suddenly erupted. "Aunt Jerutha, I know them!" She pointed to the men onstage. "They're The Bionic Babies! I know because they went on before us the night we played that theater in New York. I didn't recognize them at first because they had on such crazy costumes then."

"Uh-huh," Aunt Jerutha acknowledged calmly. "And they made that record of your song I heard on the radio."

"Auntie," said Larry, "believe me, the record was a flop."

"I'm not surprised," Aunt Jerutha said. "They have no talent. And now you want Lou to step out in front and save your little boys from failure. By the way, I am not *your* aunt, either."

"Lady, give me a break," the club owner pleaded. "That big one, Jeff, is my son-in-law. He's absolutely useless. He has a law degree and won't practice law; won't practice anything but guitar. I have thirty thousand dollars' worth of tuition tied up in him."

"Well, I don't have a law degree," Aunt Jerutha told him, "but Lou's not going to work here until I find her someone who does."

"Lou works when and where I tell her to," Marty stated.

"Haven't you heard? The Emancipation Proclamation was

over a hundred years ago," Lou retorted. "Slavery is *over.*"

"Don't be so extreme," Marty said, with a touch on her shoulder from which she flinched. "We have a binding legal agreement, that's all."

"Well, maybe you can force me to work under that agreement. But you can't force me to work *well.* I can choke, croak, shriek, screech, even lose my voice entirely. What you gonna do about *that,* Massa?"

"Nothing," he admitted. "I know you're capable of all those things."

"Besides," Aunt Jerutha said, "I believe you said Lou has to report for film work early tomorrow. Let her get her rest tonight. No need for an argument, gentlemen," she said to the duet of raised voices. "We'll just work things out in a calm, businesslike way. Tomorrow."

"Hey, wasn't that Sister Lou?" cried one of The Bionic Babies.

"It was. She just blew," the club owner said.

"And you guys probably just blew your whole future," Marty added. "Why, for Chrissake, did you have to tell them I was your manager?"

After screaming that sentence, he ran in vain after the two petite figures who had already left the club.

CHAPTER

15

Lou came in so quietly Aunt Jerutha never noticed her presence until she looked up from the Bible she had been reading.

"Why are you home so early? I thought you'd be working all day on that movie."

"They sent us home. They weren't quite ready for us, I guess," Lou lied.

Aunt Jerutha scrutinized her sharply over her reading glasses.

Aware that she couldn't meet the older woman's searching look, but unwilling to go into the details of the dreadful experience she'd just been through, Louretta wailed, "I'm so dumb, Aunt Jerutha! *So* dumb! I don't know *any*thing!"

"Ignorance has nothing to do with intelligence," Aunt Jerutha stated. "It has to do with inexperience. Now, just what are you crying about?"

"It's Frank," Lou said, still holding back the main cause of her grief. "I stopped by to see him last night, and he acted like he didn't care if I was there or not."

"Had he been taking that funny stuff again?"

Lou nodded. "I think so. He seemed all—far away." Frank hadn't been rude or mean to her, just withdrawn and abstracted, as if something far more important than Lou were absorbing his attention.

"Well, then, Frank wasn't himself last night. What he does or doesn't do when he's been doping shouldn't make you go all to pieces like this."

"No," Louretta sobbed. "I hoped he'd be glad to see me, but—"

"He probably will be, when we get him away from these dope

peddlers. And we *will*. What else is bothering you?"

Lou couldn't keep it in any longer. "That movie! I can't work in it. I walked off the set."

"Where are the boys?"

"I don't know. They walked off, too. Aunt Jerutha, they took me on this set, and it was nothing but a motel bedroom with bright lights, and a strange man came in and took off all his clothes. And they told me I was supposed to take off all my clothes too, and—they would take pictures of us doing—you know. And when I wouldn't, they said I could start by doing a scene with one of my friends instead. They said I'd get used to it. It was just acting, they said. Acting! They wanted me to do five separate takes, one with each of the boys, and one with this strange guy I never saw before. And then they wanted to do another one with me and *all* of them—" Louretta's crying became uncontrollable.

"Where was your friend, Mr. Ross?" Aunt Jerutha asked tartly.

"He showed up after I kept saying no. Reminded me that it was a job that paid good money. Said to shut my eyes and pretend I was somewhere else, and I wouldn't mind it, and nobody would know. But *I* would know, Aunt Jerutha! I just couldn't do it!" Anger helped dry up her tears. "When I left the producer was teasing him about hiring high-school virgins. And Marty was actually *apologizing* for me and the guys!"

"How far did you go along with it, Louretta?"

"I didn't go along with it at all! They didn't even get an inch of film. I told them I wasn't that kind of actress. And I ran out and told the guys what was going on, and they said they wouldn't go along with it either. So we all left. But Frank took off with the other guys and left me alone." Louretta held back a new rush of tears.

"I'm proud of you, child," Aunt Jerutha said quietly.

"I don't see why. I'm so dumb, thinking they would give a nobody like me a part in a regular movie. And never even suspecting it might be a porn movie instead."

"You are not a nobody. You are somebody," Aunt Jerutha lectured her. "You just proved it today. You had a good upbringing, and it shows.— Go wash the tears off your face, now, while I make a quick phone call."

When Lou came out of the bathroom, Aunt Jerutha said, "You look fine." She patted Lou's bush into a neat shape. "Hold your head up, now, and act like you're doing just fine. Because you are. Come on, let's go see the lawyer."

On the way, Aunt Jerutha told her, "You and the boys can work at that other club on Mondays without being worried with any test-tube babies. The lawyer said Mr. Ross was already in enough trouble for letting them record your song. He's a tough lawyer. Ane he's high connected."

Aunt Jerutha wasn't kidding, Lou thought when they reached their destination. She stared with awe at the letters chiseled over the door of the building:

UNITED STATES DEPARTMENT OF JUSTICE

"Aunt Jerutha," she finally asked, "are you sure this is the right place?"

"You bet," said her cheerful companion. "When I go looking for professional advice, I don't go half-stepping."

The elevator whisked them up twenty-six stories to a frosted door labeled BENJAMIN CARROLL, UNITED STATES ATTORNEY. And then, rising to meet them was a large, square-faced man whose complexion, matched his mahogany desk.

"Ladies," he said, indicating two chairs. "Miss Hawkins, Mrs. Jackson has told me there have been some new developments. The film work you were offered was not what you had been led to expect. Am I correct?"

Louretta nodded and felt herself blushing.

"Were you shocked?"

"Yes."

"I'm not," he told her. "I used to represent a lot of performers out here, and I'm familiar with all of their problems. There's no easy road to fame and success, as I'm sure you've learned,

young lady. But no one can force you to do anything distasteful
or illegal if you and I work together. Do you understand me?"

Lou was impressed with the power and force of his manner. "I think so," she said. "I'm just wondering if we can afford you."

"You can't," Ben Carroll informed her bluntly. "That is beside the point. You are, hard as it may be to believe, in a position to help *me*. I am *so* tired of seeing our talented people robbed and corrupted and shackled and destroyed by these parasites! I have been building my case against certain key crime figures in the entertainment industry, patiently, brick by brick, for years. But the keystone has always been missing. You, young lady, are that keystone. You and your friends are a godsend to me because you are all minors. I can't represent you—I already represent the U.S. government—but I need you as witnesses. There are Federal laws against drug-trafficking, loan-sharking, and other activities with which you have become all too familiar. But the courts tend to be too lax with offenders against these laws. *Except* where minors are concerned. There are very strict statues against transporting minors across state lines and corrupting them. Do you follow me?"

"I think so. You have a cause that's more important to you than money."

"Astutely interpreted, young lady." His face was a taut mask of determination. "I want to put some of these unscrupulous people you have met behind bars before I die. I want to see at least some of our taleneted people exercise their talents freely without being robbed and shackled by these bloodsuckers. Slavery is supposed to be over."

"What I always say," Louretta echoed.

"Amen," Aunt Jerutha intoned.

"But it will never be over unless we join hands and fight!" In a surprising gesture, the lawyer caught both of Louretta's hands in his fists and raised them high above their heads. "Are you with me?"

"Yes!"

"Good." The lawyer released her hands as suddenly as he had grabbed them. "Give me any new songs you have so I can have one of my former partners copyright them. Then, before you leave, I want you to give a deposition to my secretary, describing everything that has taken place since you signed up with your manager, including that filming session this morning.—Don't worry, my secretary's as unshockable as I am. I want your friends to come in and give depositions too, as soon as possible. I am very interested in the operations of the Carousel in Las Vegas. Especially as they involve loan-sharking and drugs in connection with performers. Okay?"

Louretta was not sure. "If I give out all that information, won't I be in danger?"

The lawyer's face was grave. "Are you safe now?"

Louretta took a minute to think that one over.

"Let me put it to you another way. Was Rosa Parks safe when she sat down on that bus? Were the Southern voters safe when they went to courthouses to register? Is any one of us safe in America as long as other blacks are in danger?"

"You've convinced me, sir," Lou said, thinking how formidable this man must be in a courtroom.

"Fine. Your deposition will remain locked in my files for the time being. I won't release any of it without your permission."

"I trust you," Lou said.

"'Bout time you started trusting the right people," Aunt Jerutha observed.

"But," Ben Carroll said with an upraised finger of warning, "I may ask your permission to use that information very soon. For your own safety, if for no other reason. I want the young men's statements today, too. You'll be hearing from me shortly, probably sooner than you expect. Don't be disturbed by the form my communication takes. Just consider the way your life has been going lately, and be open to an alternative."

He stood, looming over them like a black colossus, signaling that the interview was over.

"What did he mean by that?" Lou asked as they were going

down in the elevator.

"'Speck you'll find out soon," Aunt Jerutha said.

"He's something else, that lawyer. He scares me."

"He does better than that. He scares the Devil. And that's going some."

"I think we'd better not let him down," Louretta said soberly.

"You'll be letting yourselves down if you do."

Back at the hotel, Aunt Jerutha lingered in the lobby to say a word to Tina while Lou proceeded directly upstairs.

Frank, his eyes at last clear and focused on her, was lounging against the door of her room. "Where you been, baby?"

Why should you care, she thought. "Taking care of business," she told him. "Would you please move and let me in my room?"

"Not unless I'm goin' in there with you."

"Frank, I'm tired. "Tired of the casino scene, tired of problems, tired of Frank and his on-again, off-again attentions.

He grabbed her around the waist with his right arm and used his left hand to pull her face forcibly up to his.

With a firm shove against his chest, she was free. "Frank, you know I don't like caveman stuff in public."

"Well, how about in private?"

He was too pushy, too arrogant. "Not there, either."

"Why are you so unavailable all of a sudden?"

"Because you've been unavailable to me for days," she said, inserting her key into the lock.

"I was busy," he said, his eyes going far away again.

Oh, sure, she thought. Busy sitting in a chair and staring into space. "Well, now *I'm* busy. I'm not a faucet you can turn off and on, you know. You've got to prime my pump every day if you want my love to keep flowing."

"What's going on, Aunt Jerutha?" she heard Frank ask as she turned her back on him and opened her door. He sounded bewildered and pathetic.

"Life, son. Life's goin' on. Be thankful for that, and be patient. Main thing is, I've found you all a good lawyer. I want you to get down to his office with the other boys right now. Take your songs with you so he can copyright them in your names. Here's his card."

"Is he white or black?"

"If Mr. Ben Carroll were white, I think he'd be President. As it is, I think he's about as powerful as a black man can get to be in this country," was Aunt Jerutha's answer. "Get some rest, Lou," she added. "I'm going grocery shopping."

Lou closed her door and locked it from the inside. She wanted to be alone to daydream about the past, which seemed safer and simpler than the situation she found herself in now. Sure, there had been bad times, even dangerous times—gang wars, police raids, even Jethro's death. But there had been fun, too. The four of them and their friends had known their way around and found ways to exert some control over their lives. Here in this strange place they were powerless, and back home suddenly seemed a better place to be. She must have daydreamed for more than an hour before she took out the beautifully hand-drawn greetings that were tucked into the top flap of her suitcase. She leafed through them thoughtfully, then spread them on the bed around her, smiling at the scripted "Calvin" on the bottom of each one. He was even more temperamental than Frank, and his religion had become extreme, but Aunt Jerutha had said he was getting over that. She took out her notebook and began to write a romantic letter to the past.

But before she finished the first page, she fell asleep. The sky was navy blue outside when Aunt Jerutha came in with Frank right behind her. Apparently misunderstanding and assuming they wanted to be alone, Jethro's mother withdrew before Lou could call her back.

"What's all this?" Frank demanded, pointing to the illustrations scattered on her bed and the letter she'd quickly covered with her hand.

"It's private."

She hadn't covered the letter quickly enough.

"Dear Calvin," he read aloud, "I'm sorry if it seems like I've forgotten about you. But though you may have every reason to think so, it's not true. In my heart, I've never stopped caring about you. And the way things are going out here, I miss you more and more every day . . ."

With a howl of outrage, Frank balled up the letter and threw it on the floor.

Lou's howl was even louder. "Give that back! You've got no right touching my private papers!"

Frank stood stubbornly at the foot of her bed. "Why are you writing to that Jesus freak? He can't help you now."

"Because he's gentle, he's kind, he knows how to treat a woman. Which is more than I can say for some caveman types I know."

"Don't play with me, baby. I'm past the game stage with you."

After his recent indifference, his seriousness surprised her.

"Do you feel the same way?"

"I don't know," she said. "The thing is, Frank, your feelings change with the weather—or whatever junk you're on."

"I'm through with junk," he said with such determination she believed him. "After talking to that lawyer, I'm afraid to take an aspirin. Are you ready to be serious with me?"

She searched her feelings. "I don't know. . . ."

"I want you to wear this."

It was too big to be a real diamond, but it looked real.

Frank swept Calvin's drawings to the floor to make a space for himself. "You know, baby, I like your new song, but I don't like the message. It's like that saying the old folks have: 'Men are like trolley cars, you can always catch another one.' "

"The song isn't about us, Frank. I wrote it about something that was happening to my brother William."

"What's happening *now,*" he said, forcing her chin up to make her look directly into his eyes, "is we're in a serious situation, maybe a dangerous situation. You'd better forget about that creep Calvin. When the flak hits the propeller, I think you'll be glad to have this tough old corner boy in your corner."

"I am already," she said, shivering with a premonition. She didn't know when the "flak" would hit, but she had a feeling amounting to a certainty that it wouldn't take long. Annoyed by Frank's pushiness, but afraid of the future and grateful for his presence, she didn't resist when he pressed her down. She didn't cooperate—she simply didn't resist. What was worse, he didn't seem to notice the difference.

"We're clicking, baby!" he exulted. She had no such feeling after their lovemaking; only an empty desolation.

"At least," she said wryly, "there's no movie camera clicking behind us."

Frank's mouth turned down instantly. "Boy, was that a bummer."

"Did you tell Ben Carroll about it?"

"Sure. We told him everything. He seemed very interested. I have a feeling he works for the FBI or something like that."

"I know he's building a case against the Carousel people," Lou told Frank. "If we go along with everything he wants, we might get free."

"And we might get dead," Frank said soberly.

"When it comes right down to it, isn't that always the choice?" she asked softly.

"The bottom line," Frank agreed, and sang:

"And before I'd be a slave,
I'd be buried in my grave . . ."

Frank's baritone had a heroic resonance that vibrated throughout her body. That, and the way he was holding her hand, thrilled her more than his impetuous lovemaking, and convinced her to keep his ring—for a while.

Their show went well, so well that Marty invited them to join him for a snack in the room he shared with Charles. None of them wanted to go, but Aunt Jerutha pulled them aside and talked them into it.

"Any of you happy staying in this place?" she asked.

They all shook their heads.

"Well, then, let's go to his room. We got to talk to Mr. Ross about moving to another hotel."

But none of them had a chance to bring up the subject. They were just getting their first helping of assorted cheeses and crackers when the "flak" arrived in the form of a small, nondescript man in a rumpled gray suit. When Marty let him in, the little man produced four envelopes from his inside coat pocket.

"Louretta Hawkins, David Weldon, Frank Brown, Ulysses McCracken?"

They looked at each other, then nodded.

"Sign here."

They complied.

"It's from *Washington!*" Lou cried, staring at her envelope.

Frank tore his open. "You are hereby subpoenaed," he intoned, "by the Attorney General of the United States to testify at a grand jury hearing in U.S. District Court." He ran off the place, the time, and the date. Next week!

"Where the devil did those come from?" Marty cried.

"The lawyer we hooked up with, Ben Carroll. He's *on the case,*" Frank told him.

"We goin' to jail, man? What we done?" Ulysses cried.

"No, ignoramus. We're going to serve our country."

"I wish I *had* joined the Army," Ulysses groaned.

"Do we have to go?" David asked plaintively.

"You are the lawyer, Mr. Ross," Aunt Jerutha said, "but I believe it is not wise to ignore a subpoena."

"They can't ignore it. But what I want to know is, why did they have to pick a lawyer who would blow their whole deal? Why a lousy Fed lawyer? *Why?*"

"Because," Aunt Jerutha said, "he is in the best position to protect them."

Marty was sweating. "Look, kids, you have to show up at that grand jury hearing. But you don't have to say anything. Keep your mouths shut, or—" He made a throat-cutting gesture.

"You don't know anything. You don't understand the questions. If you have to, you take the Fifth Amendment when they ask you something uncomfortable."

"But we haven't done anything criminal," Lou protested. "The Fifth Amendment is, 'I refuse to testify on the grounds that it might tend to incriminate me.' And we haven't committed any crimes!"

"Stop quoting from your schoolbooks, little girl. This is real life. You guys show her what to do. Make like the three wise monkeys. You know what I mean?" He pointed to Ulysses. "See no evil."

Ulysses put his hands over his eyes.

Marty pointed to David. "Hear no evil."

David covered his ears.

"That's fine," Marty said, and pointed to Frank. "Speak no evil."

Frank simply stared back at him without covering his mouth.

"Stubborn, huh? Why do you want to get me into trouble? I'm just a guy who tries to help people. I got too much feeling, that's my problem, I got a big heart and I'm too generous for my own good. Gloria keeps telling me that. But I can't resist helping young people, especially underprivileged young people." He wiped a tear from one eye. "I got you all your breaks, went into debt for you, risked my reputation for you. Is this the thanks I get? Trouble with the government, after all I've done for you?"

He really believes it, Lou saw with amazement. The tears were genuine. Marty really believed he was a kind, generous person.

Charles articulated her thoughts. "Martin really thinks he's a good person. That's why he's so dangerous. That's why all liberals are dangerous; they aren't aware of their own motives. I'm not worried, though. I know none of you would say anything to incriminate me. I'm one of your own. A man of color. A brother."

"Brother," Frank echoed in disgust.

"But I *am* a brother. What's more, I can manage you better than Martin. I can groom you for real stardom instead of the tacky hack jobs he's gotten you. And I know my way around. I can steer you around all the pitfalls."

"Yeah, sure—like giving us drug habits to help support yours," Ulysses said.

Marty said angrily, "Some friend you turned out to be. Trying to steal my talent right out from under my nose. Well, you can't do it. They're under contract to me, not you."

Charles stood up. "You won't be seeing me anymore, any of you. One advantage I have over Martin—I can always disappear into the ghetto."

"You?" Marty said scornfully. "You'd stand out like a gardenia in a row of collard greens."

"You think so? All I need is a wine-stained T-shirt, a pair of ragged dungarees, and a bit of the local *patois*." Charles pulled a crumpled cap from his pocket and pulled it down over his eyes. "Hey, man, where duh action? Nemmind what kind of action, any kind suit me fine." Along with this went a limp, sagging posture as if Charles's bones had suddenly dissolved.

"You're a great actor!" Lou cried in admiration.

"A great survivor, darling. Acting is just part of it. Charles Astral will disappear and be reborn with a new identity. Last time it was Buddy or Booty, I forget which. This time, Bobo or Bubba. Whatever. It doesn't matter. No one has real names in the ghetto. My names are legion and so are my counterparts. We have no surnames and no addresses, and we are not counted in any census. *Au revoir,* children. Hang tough. By which I mean, *survive!*"

They watched in amazement as Charles ambled out of the room with a brand-new walk that was as old as memory, a wino's slow shuffle and slide.

"Excuse me," Marty said. "I got to talk things over with somebody. Help yourselves to what's here, and if you want anything else, order it from Room Service on my bill. Don't anybody leave, now. I'll be right back."

He was radiant when he returned ten minutes later. "Kids, I have great news. The management wants you to take your time and think things over. In the meantime, they're giving you a big break. Tomorrow night you move up to the Starlight Theater."

Marty's news met with silence.

"What's the matter with you kids? Big-time billing in the big room, with doubled salaries. Who could ask for a better deal than that?"

"Well," Lou said slowly, "I don't see anything wrong with singing in the theater."

Aunt Jerutha was shaking her head, but before she or anyone else could say anything, Marty said hastily, "Good. It's settled then." He glanced at his watch. "Oops! Only five minutes till showtime, kids."

Back downstairs in the lounge, Frank chose their first number. It was a resounding rendition of "Tell the Truth."

CHAPTER 16

After their last show, Aunt Jerutha kept all of them up an extra hour, trying to talk them out of performing in the big theater.

"It just doesn't *feel* right," she kept saying. "The Devil has a way of looking good, children, but when you're dealing with him, you'll know in your hearts it's wrong. And, I tell you, this plan just doesn't feel right to me."

"But we haven't promised them anything, Aunt Jerutha," Lou assured her. "Just because we're singing in the theater doesn't mean we aren't going to testify."

Both Frank and Ulysses wanted to do it for the extra money. So Aunt Jerutha was overruled, and they spent most of the day rehearsing.

And that night the four of them skipped out onto the Starlight Theater's stage and opened their act with Lou's new song:

"Life is a river,
Life is a river.
Monongahela,
Susquehanna,
Ohio,
Delaware—
Old rivers flow forever,
Old water stays nowhere.
Life is a river,
Love is a river.

I loved Anita,
Then I loved Rita,
Before I loved What's-her-name."

Clowning, Frank struck his head as if to awaken his memory and pointed to Lou, who made a face back at him, drawing laughter from the audience.

"The river flows forever,
But the water's never the same.

Chattahoochee,
Mississippi,
Zambezi,
Niger,
Nile—
Old rivers flow forever,
New water stays but a while.

Life is a river,
Love is a river,
Life is a river,
Love is a river . . ."

The applause was generous, booming so loudly as they bowed Lou did did not hear the first popping sounds. But then there was a scream in the audience.

"Jump, baby!" Frank urged her. "Jump!"

Lou just stood there, numb and confused. Something like a giant mosquito whined past her ear. Jump where? Jump why? she wondered.

Frank didn't wait for her to figure it all out. He grabbed her waist, pushed her, and jumped beside her into the orchestra pit. They landed on Joe Toledo, toppling him from his podium; bounced off him and rolled under the trumpeters' chairs, while David and Ulysses took a crash dive into the kettledrums. Over their heads, the pinging continued. The screams were louder now.

Ulysses, a large piece of drumhead around his neck like a ragged clown collar, crawled over to them. "Everybody okay here?"

"Yeah," Frank said, having checked Lou over. "Just a few

bruises."

David, wriggling wormlike on his belly Army-style, joined them. "Man," he cracked. "I didn't think our singing was *that* bad."

"When you bomb at the Carousel, you *really* bomb," Frank said.

"Frank," Lou said, shivering, "I'm scared. D'you think they were really shooting at us?"

The gunfire seemed to have stopped, but no one could be sure because of the ear-splitting wail of an ambulance approaching the casino. Frank stood up and peered cautiously over the edge of the orchestra pit. "Not sure, Lou. Everybody's running for the exits. Somebody's hurt out there."

"So are you! Your leg's bleeding!" she cried.

He looked down in astonishment at his blood-soaked pants leg. "I didn't even feel it."

"Ladies and gentlemen," someone was saying over the microphone they had abandoned, "please remain in your seats and do not panic. The emergency is over. I repeat, the emergency is over. The disturbance has been quelled. Please, do not panic. There is absolutely no danger. The show will go on in a few moments."

"Later for that show-must-go-on jive," Frank growled. "Let's move out, troops."

"I wish I *had* joined the Army," Ulysses complained. "At least I'd have a weapon."

Limping, one hand on Ulysses's shoulder for support, the other holding Lou's tightly for reassurance, Frank led them through a little door under the stage and and a maze of backstage corridors to the elevators and their rooms, leaving a vivid trail of blood behind him.

He collapsed on one of the beds and, as Aunt Jerutha approached with her sewing scissors, cried "No! Save my good gabardines!"

"You better be thinking 'bout your leg, not your pants, you banty peacock," Aunt Jerutha informed him. But she gently rolled up the pants instead of cutting them. Washed the wound and proclaimed that it wasn't as terrible as it looked. The rest of her first aid included peroxide for disinfecting, sugar for quick clotting and healing, a torn piece of sheet for a bandage, a pile of blankets, and a glass of whiskey for shock and pain. Then she declared that he probably wouldn't need a doctor, but that she intended to make the hotel send one up anyway.

Frank said no thanks, she was all the doctor he wanted. Lou, squatting on the floor beside him, clutching his hand to reassure both of them, asked him softly for a nerve pill. "Hey," he said sleepily as he put one into her hand, "you take too many of these, you know that?"

"Yo!" cried David, who had disappeared and returned without their noticing. "A couple of guys got killed out there! Maybe they weren't shooting at us, after all."

Frank, who had been drowsing, woke up then. He pointed to his leg. "They were *definitely* shooting at us."

"Maybe they were shooting at some other people, too. Sort of a two-birds-with-one stone operation." Ulysses stood up. "I think I'll go check out the scene."

"You are not going anywhere, Ulysses," Aunt Jerutha said firmly. "Lock that door and come back here. And stay in here, all of you." Aunt Jerutha took up her familiar humming of what might have been any of a dozen hymns. After ten minutes of that calming influence she said, "Let us join hands and bow our heads. We thank you, Lord, for delivering us from death and danger. We pray for the souls of the slain and the peace of their families. And we pray for the souls of our enemies too, Lord. Help us love them and forgive them so that we may be forgiven."

"Excuse me, Aunt Jerutha," Frank said, "but that's the part I can never go along with."

"Me neither," Lou said. "How can you love somebody who's just tried to kill you?"

"It's hard, child. It's the hardest part of being a Christian. If you can't go that far yet, just be thankful you were all spared.

Amen and praise Jesus."

"Amen," they chorused. They all felt better. Aunt Jerutha took up her soft humming again. This time it sounded like "Amazing Grace." Lou joined in with the words and so, soon, did Ulysses. Around the beginning of the third verse, the part about "dangers, toils, and snares," a slow, heavy series of knocks resounded at the door like impending doom.

"Who is there?" Aunt Jerutha called out.

"Ben Carroll," came the deep-voiced answer.

"Just a minute, sir," Aunt Jerutha called. She moved to a chair facing the door. "Ulysses, wait and let him in when I tell you to. I will sit over here, just in case." She reached into an outside flap on her purse and took out a small but serious handgun.

"I don't believe it!" Lou cried.

"Why not? I believe in being prepared," Aunt Jerutha said, checking her weapon and cocking it. "Someone shot my son. Someone else robbed my house. Then someone attempted to snatch my purse on the Avenue. This is a troublesome world. I have never used my little friend here, but I know how. You may open the door now, Ulysses. But be careful."

"If you're going to shoot, holler 'Duck!' " he said, and obeyed.

But it was only the lawyer, after all—large, grave-faced, and alone.

"She's got you covered, Mr. Carroll," Ulysses informed him.

"Please put that away, Mrs. Jackson," Ben Carroll said. "There's been too much shooting tonight already. Although I must admit I, too, am armed." He opened his well-tailored jacket to reveal a shoulder holster. "I come in contact with a lot of desperate people. In fact, it is my job to make them desperate. So I try to be prepared."

"Nothing wrong with that, Mr. Carroll. That's what I was just saying." Aunt Jerutha put her gun back into its neat little pouch. "A man has to protect himself. Especially an important man like you. The people need you."

"Thank you," the lawyer said. "My wife needs me, too. Or so she says. What took place out there in the theater tonight was not target practice. It was an example of desperation—a desperate attempt to silence you young people before the hearing. And it was also, I think, an attempt to silence others who might also be tempted to tell what they know to the grand jury. That's why there was shooting in the audience. The rats are afraid of being flushed from their hiding places, and they were trying to frighten everyone who might blow their cover. Unfortunatley they were so nervous they aimed badly. Two people are dead, five injured. All innocent, uninvolved patrons." He grimaced. "I asked for a change of venue to protect you until the hearing. My request was denied. *This* had to happen before it was granted. Now the hearing has been moved to Washington, D.C. Are you ready for it?"

David shrugged. "After tonight we ought to be ready for anything."

"Are you willing to testify to everything I have in your depositions?"

Lou said, "I'm scared, but I will."

The others declared their willingness, and Aunt Jerutha approved. "Sometimes evil gets so big, you got to try and slay it like David did Goliath. As long as you got faith, you can overcome. Look what he did with a puny little slingshot."

There was a flourish of raps at the door. They all started, even though it was familiar.

"One of the rats," Frank said. "Our manager."

"A toothless one, I think," Ben Carroll said. "You can let him in."

Marty came in, shaking, holding a hotel tumbler which he kept refilling from a bottle of Scotch in his other hand. "Hey, there was a stampede out there. People got hurt in the crush. You kids were supposed to go on singing, keep the audience from going into panic."

"Would you have sent flowers?" Lou asked.

Marty sat down, mopped his brow, and refilled his glass. "All right, it's a crazy world. These things happen. But, like they say, the show must go on."

"*You* go on," Frank told him, pointing to his leg. "Go entertain the people, clown. I'm in the shop for repairs."

"Oh, my God. You got hit?"

"You do, of course, carry medical insurance on these young people," Ben Carroll interposed.

"Yes, of course. No. I don't know. Who the hell are you?"

"I am a U.S. attorney, Ben Carroll. And you, I suppose, are Marty Ross." The lawyer did not offer his hand. "I think you might as well stay to hear the rest of what I have to say to them." He turned his back on Marty and spoke directly to them.

"Let me refresh your memories as to your testimony. Item One: Pandering, resulting in Item Two, attempted rape. Item Three: Solicitation to gambling and facilitation of gambling, leading to Item Four: loan-sharking. Item Five: Falsely assigned copyrights to original creative works. Item Six: Misappropriation of said creative works and withholding of royalties therefrom. Item Seven: Introduction to prohibited drugs. Item Eight: Misrepresented work assignments. Item Nine: Attempted coercion to perform in pornographic productions. Item Ten: Willful abuse of minors, including transportation of minors across state lines for said abuse. Are you still willing to testify to all of that? Are you ready to supply names, dates, places, everything?"

"We are," Frank said.

"You're crazy!" Marty screamed. He jumped to his feet. "I had a recording date all lined up for you in Philly. Studio booked for day after tomorrow. You go along with this guy, you can forget about your next album, your next club date, your next everything."

"And if we don't go along with him," Frank said, "we can forget about breathing."

Lawyer Carroll was impartial. He simply looked at the foursome and said, "Well?"

Lou was still nervous and shaking. "Give me a nerve pill, Marty, please," she requested.

Unthinkingly, he reached into his inside pocket and came out with a rainbow handful. "The yellow ones work best, Lou. Especially if you take two and have a shot with them. Here, have a shot," he offered.

"Let me see those pills, please, Miss Hawkins," their lawyer requested. He studied them in his big brown palm. "Do you have prescriptions for these, Mr. Ross?"

"Sure," Marty said.

"Who is your doctor?"

"I travel a lot. I got doctors all over."

"Well, if that's so, one of them should have attended to this young man's wound. This is a major tranquilizer, Miss Hawkins. One now and then isn't harmful. But this man is no doctor, and he has no business passing them out to you like candy. They are prescription drugs and have been found to be addictive."

"She doesn' need it," Frank declared. "She just had one half an hour ago."

"I do too need it, Frank!" Lou cried, and snatched both pills from Ben Carroll before he could close his giant fist around them, and swallowed them with a glass of water. "No booze, though, Marty. I never mix pills and booze."

"I'm still waiting for my answer," the lawyer said, observing her thoughtfully.

"We . . . we will testify, Mr. Carroll," Lou answered. Her voice was shaky, but inside, she was firmly resolved.

Marty went into a fit of temper that began with a sort of dance, kicking at the furniture, and ended in a small snowstorm as he tore their contract into bits and threw the pieces in the air above his head. "All right. I cut you loose! From now on, you're on your own. I'm dead in this business if I go on handling you. I'm dead if I'm even *seen* with you!"

"What about the money we're supposed to owe you?" Lou asked in wonderment.

"Forget it. It's not worth my life. You never heard of me. If you say so, I'll say I don't know you. You *or* your smart-aleck nigger lawyer. He's going to get you killed, don't you know that? How many bullets have to whiz past your heads before you understand?"

Ignoring Marty's language and his dramatics, Ben Carroll asked suavely, "You are terminating your contract with this group as of now?"

Marty jumped up and down like an enraged infant. "Yes! I'm through with them. I've had it!"

Lawyer Carroll opened his briefcase. "Fine. But just in case you have other copies of that contract, which I'm sure you do, and just in case you change your mind—would you sign this little document, please? It waives all their debts to you and any claims by you against their future earnings."

"Gladly," Marty said, and signed.

"Is that your real name?" Ben asked.

Marty hesitated. "No, but it'll do. It's the one I'm known by."

"Sign your legal name, too, please. And any other aliases."

Marty wrote for what seemed an interminable time. Then, brushing himself off as if getting rid of cobwebs, he stalked out of their room and out of their lives, leaving a great silence behind him.

Ben Carroll broke it by noting that he had also left his liquor. "The man does drink good Scotch. That's about the only good thing I can say for him." He poured himself two fingers. "No point in wasting it. One for you, Mrs. Jackson?"

"I wouldn't mind," she said.

"And one for our wounded hero. *Only* because he is wounded." The lawyer carried a glass over to Frank. "The rest of you will have to abstain till you reach legal drinking age, at least when you're around me." He raised his glass. "To freedom!"

"To freedom!" they chorused, still unable to believe they were really free of Marty.

"What *is* his real name?" Lou asked.

Ben Carroll chuckled. "Which one? He signed seven."

How did you know to have that form ready?" David wondered.

"Good question. I told you I believe in being prepared. I

expected a performance like that from your manager. I was going to send for him tonight if he hadn't shown up so conveniently. Once the gangsters showed their hand in the theater, and you agreed to testify, tearing up your contract was the only way he could save his skin. I wanted that form signed to protect you from any further exploitation. He was just trying to scare you to save himself from his associates, by the way. I believe the worst danger to you is over. If you don't testify, then the temptation to silence you by force would continue to be overwhelming. But once you've told the grand jury all you know, what point would there be in harming you?"

"I don't know, man," Frank said dubiously. "It sounds logical. But I heard these guys go in for revenge."

"Only against each other, when one of them breaks their code of secrecy. No, it *is* logical. They shot at you to keep you from testifying. Nothing is guaranteed, but I know them, and I think they'll leave you alone after you testify."

"I'm just worried about getting from here to there," Ulysses said.

"I've taken a few precautions," their lawyer said. "I have some armed men in the corridor. They will escort you to the service entrance of the hotel when it's time to leave. A car will be brought around to meet you there and take you to a private airfield about twenty minutes from here. A plane is waiting there to fly you to Washington."

"He's thought of everything," Lou said admiringly.

David was excited. "Wow! It's like a TV serial. Or a spy movie."

"Yeah," Frank said sourly, and touched his bloodstained bandage. "Only this one is *really* in living color."

CHAPTER

17

At the hearing, which lasted three days, Lou and the others learned that Ben Carroll was not merely a U.S. Attorney; that he was, under the Attorney General, the head of the West Coast Organized Crime Strike Force—a large Federal investigative team. They also learned that Carl D. Sipp, who opposed Ben like a statue on a pyramid of equal height, was not merely the manager of the Carousel Casino, but an important assistant to the invisible head of a giant octopus of crime that reached its tentacles into almost everything illegal—drugs, gambling, loan-sharking, prostitution, and pornography. The octopus used the money it sucked from crime in the community to purchase business interests, including nightclubs, casinos, jukeboxes, record companies, and the management and booking of performers. It bought allies in government, too, and had made the mistake of approaching an honest Congressman, which was how this investigation had begun.

The octopus sought to own everything it touched and to suck the blood out of everything and everyone it owned, until nothing was left but a lifeless shell to be tossed on a trash heap. It had happened to many famous performers. It had almost happened to The Soul Brothers and Sister Lou.

With the help of their testimony, Carl D. Sipp and two other tentacles were indicted. But the Departmentof Justice would not be able to chop off the monster's head. Marty, it turned out, was too insignificant to interest the government. He was not even a tentacle; he was just a sort of jellyfish scavenging around the edges of one.

Lou and the boys had to stay in Washington in a heavily guarded apartment for two more weeks until the trial, at which

Sipp and the other men were sentenced. "So now you see how the ugly thing works," Ben told them when it was all over. "They sell junk and numbers to our people, they sell our young girls on the streets, and then they take the profits and make records to sell to them, too. It's a vicious circle. Thanks for helping us break part of it."

"Thanks for helping us break *out* of it," Lou said fervently.

"You have your freedom now. And, though I think you're safe, you have my help any time you need it."

"We need a lawyer to take care of our song copyrights," Frank said.

"And our other legal stuff," Lou added. "In case—in case things get complicated again."

"You've got one," Ben assured them. He gave them the address of his partner in Nevada, and told them to expect free services in return for their help.

Lou reflected that they were probably the least important clients Ben Carroll would ever work for. But he didn't treat them that way. He thanked them again, congratulated them on their freedom, and put them on the train for home.

While the train ride lasted the four of them had a euphoric feeling of accomplishment. But when they stepped out of the train station onto the familiar, battered streets where spring was struggling to break through cracks in the concrete, depression quickly set in. Lou looked at Ulysses, Ulysses looked at Frank, and David said for all of them, "What next?"

"Something will be next, don't you worry," Aunt Jerutha counseled. "Just give yourselves time to calm down from all that excitement. And don't spend your money."

They headed dolefully for their respective homes. When Lou arrived at the little house on Carlisle Street, William had the good grace not to say, "I told you so." Which was more than could be said for Momma, who went around declaring that she knew Lou's career would come to a bad end and that all her dire warnings had been vindicated. She seemed to think Lou's appearance before Congress made her a criminal—not a heroine. Momma took such lip-smacking satisfaction in these statements that Lou decided to move out of the house immediately and move in with Aunt Jerutha. Before she left, though, she had a talk with her brother.

He came in from work and read her face immediately. "Feeling blue, Sister Lou?"

"Over the hill, Brother Bill."

"Over the hill at *sixteen?* Come on, now. What happened to all your spunk and spirit?"

"I don't know. I feel like I've lived ten years in five months. You were right, William. Show business is rough. I had no idea *how* rough."

"Tell me about it. I heard snatches on the news, and you called me, but I still haven't pieced it all together. What happened to my little sis?"

"William, I've been through so much, I don't even feel like thinking about it, let alone talking about it."

But gradually, with gentle persistence, he drew it out of her. She knew better than to tell him about the men who had tried to abuse her. But she told him about the gambling debts, the stolen songs, the drugs, the movie that never got made, and the lawyer who had subpoenaed them to Washington and set them free—in limbo.

"He's a wonderful man, William. A *great* man. He's fighting crime because crime hurts black people, and he's winning."

William listened patiently, with no interruptions, until she had talked herself out. Then he said, still rhyming to lighten the discussion, "Now what you wanta do, Sister Lou?"

She shrugged. "Guess I'll have to give it all up. I'm washed up at sixteen." Her laugh was bitter. "Guess I'll just hang around the streets, lay around with boys, and get myself pregnant like all the other girls around here do. Like I'm *supposed* to do."

"Don't sound like you, Sister Lou," he rhymed. Alarm was in his eyes, if not in his voice. "All you need is a little time, a little rest, and a little boost from some people in your corner.

Then you'll be headed straight for the top again."

"I don't even want that anymore, William," she said wearily. "There's nothing at the top but loneliness and scary stuff. You go trying to climb a mountain, all you find up there is ice and snow and holes to fall into and bears waiting in the holes to chew you up."

"Well, how about aiming for someplace in the middle?"

"I don't know where that is," she said in puzzlement.

"It's located somewhere above the bottom. Which is where I definitely don't want you to be."

"It's where *Momma* wants to be," Lou said with anger, the first emotion she had shown in this entire conversation. "I tried to talk to her about getting a better house for the family. Said I might have enough money to help with the down payment. She said she wasn't interested in moving, and even if she was, she wouldn't move with the Devil's money. William, Momma wants to *stay* down!"

"I know," he said, his face taut with frustration. "I've been there already. I found a better property for us back in March, nothing fabulous, you understand, but bigger and clean and nice and something I thought I could afford. She wouldn't even go look at it."

"You should have bought it for yourself, William."

"Can you keep a secret?"

"Sure."

"I did. I mean, I made a down payment. Once the mortgage money comes through, I'm moving out of here. Momma and the kids can come with me, or they can stay here and live on welfare, I don't care. I have a right to live, too. I think the boys will come with me, anyway. And there's a new lady in my life who will be glad to have me *and* them."

"Good for you, William!" she exclaimed, thrilled at his sudden independence. "It's about time."

"I know. You keep your money for yourself, Lou. You'll find a good use for it someday."

"Well, I know one thing. I can't stay here either. Momma

bugs me too much. She won't like it, but I'm going to move in with Aunt Jerutha for a while."

"Fine," he approved. "You need to be comfortable. And I've got an idea. You remember my friend Lucas, the one I told you used to be in show business?"

She nodded.

"Well, I have to go run off some printing jobs now, but after that, around nine, I want to take you and your group over to his house to meet him and some other friends of mine."

"What for?"

"To help you find the middle."

"Can we bring Aunt J?"

"Sure," he said after a moment's hesitation. "Aunt J and the Soul Brothers.. But nobody else. Lucas is still a little gun-shy."

"I know the feeling," Louretta said.

Louretta tried to explain her reasons for moving to her mother, met with an angry barrage about her selfishness and ingratitude, and finally gave up trying to talk to Momma. She shrugged, picked up her suitcase, and trudged the four blocks to Aunt Jerutha's house. There, after an hour of phone conversation, Aunt Jerutha was able to convince Momma that the move was for the best.

"Rosetta, you hush now, and listen to me. The child is weary. She needs peace. She'll be perfectly safe here with me, and you know it. It's just your pride interfering. . . . No, I'm not sending her home. She came to me, and I won't turn her away. . . . No, she won't be any trouble. I'll be glad to have the company. . . . No, I already said I'm not sending her home now. I'll send her home as soon as the two of you can talk sense to each other, whenever that is. . . . Of course I'll watch out for her, and you know where she is. Just around the corner. Not all the way on the other side of the country, where she's been. . . . Of course you love her. I know that. She knows it too. And she loves you. That seems to be why the two of you can't get along. . . . No, I wouldn't dream of coming between mother and daughter. She'll always be your child, Rosetta, no matter where she is. . . . Yes, of course, pray for her. And I'll do the same for you."

"Pheww," was how Aunt Jerutha expressed her exhaustion after she hung up. "Dealing with your mother is harder than dealing with all those trips and Sipps. But I've got her settled down now, I think. I've made up Jethro's bed for you in the little back room upstairs. Why don't you go take a nap? We'll eat when you wake up."

"What time is it?" Lou asked.

Aunt Jerutha opened her beautiful, old-fashioned neck chain watch. "Two-thirty. Why?"

"William's invited us somewhere at nine."

"Oh? Where are we going?"

"To find the middle, he said," she said drowsily. Realizing that she *was* tired, she took Aunt Jerutha's suggestion and fell across what had once been Jethro's bed. She cried for her friend, dead so young, and for herself and all her other friends, with hopes dead so young they might as well be buried along with him. But her heart beat sturdily, pointlessly on. And soon she slept.

At Lucas's house they were welcomed by music, wonderful music. Lucas, a broad, barrel-chested man with a pronounced limp, seated himself at the piano and played as if his hands were melting into the keys. A tall friend of his called, for obvious reasons, Hands, walked his long fingers up and down the bass fiddle in tantalizing rhythms. Another middle-aged man nicknamed Tomcat did amazing things with a battered acoustic guitar, moving from strong chords to wild runs executed with brass picks worn like rings on his fingers. And a dapper, gray-haired gentleman called Sam, much older than the others and much more formally dressed, in a snow-white shirt with a jacket and tie, brushed lightly on the trap drums, tapped the cymbals, and kicked the big bass drum right on time. A seemingly endless supply of barbecue and beer was produced from the kitchen by Lucas's wife, Ruby, a plump, pretty woman who also contributed occasional snatches of song.

"Shake a hand, shake a hand," she sang in welcome. *"Shake a hand every day."*

Then she proceeded to do just that with all the newcomers. Besides Aunt Jerutha and the group, there was William's new girl friend, Gloria, whose broad smile proclaimed clearly that she loved life and William. Warmed by it, Louretta was happy for him.

The music vibrated through her very bones and through her skull into her memory. This was not disco or rock or pop or any of the current fads; this was the ancestor of all of them, blues and early jazz and ragtime, and, like any other ancestor, it commanded her reverence.

"Sing 'Sun Gonna Shine in My Backyard Someday,' Ruby," Hands requested.

"No. Do 'Good Morning, Blues,'" was Tomcat's demand.

"Just sing any old blues you feel like singing, honey," Lucas told his wife. "After all, you at home."

"I expect these youngsters have had enough of the blues for a while," Ruby replied.

"We *never* get enough," Lou said. Because the magic of the blues worked this way: it started by meshing with your lowest mood, and ended by resolving your problem and cheering you up, even making you laugh about it, as the singer did the same thing for himself. Blues was art and blues was therapy: it took gloomy situations and worked on them, turned them around and inside out and upside down until you could live with them and even laugh at them.

"Well," Ruby said, "I got to see to my pots first." When she came back, she declared that she was too hot and tired to sing, and sat down beside Lou to fan herself and sip a cold beer while William's musician friends tinkled and tickled a ballad into a rag.

"Brings back old memories," Ruby confided. "Lucas and me and these old boys, we were on the road for years. We played mostly black clubs and theaters. What they called the 'Chitlin Circuit' in those days."

"Was it rough?" Lou asked.

"What you think, girl? Is red pepper hot? We gave it up,

didn't we? I'm settin' in this house now and glad to be here; ain't goin' nowhere for *no*body. But we were young then, and it was fun. After a while, you kind of forget the bad times and just remember the good times. And you even find ways of turning the bad times into fun."

Just like the blues, Louretta thought.

"Except," Ruby said softly, "for one bad time Lucas can't forget. His leg won't let him."

"I heard about that," Lou said softly. "You know, Frank got shot in the leg, too."

"I hope he gets over it. Lucas never did." Ruby's eyes looked remote for a moment, then returned to focus on the present. "This is shaping up like a patrty. Let's talk about the good times. —Hey, Sam!" she called to the dignified-looking old man on the drums, "you remember that time the bus broke down outside of Natchez and we had to end up sleeping in somebody's barn?"

"I surely do," he answered without missing a beat. "I'm still picking straw out my hair."

Ruby laughed heartily. "That ain't straw, fool. That's gray. You remember that old car we used to have? It had two temperatures. Red hot and froze up."

"And two gears," Hands added. "Slow and Stop."

Ruby laughed again and said to Lou, "It's funny to think back on those old days. We always got to the next stop somehow. But we had some narrow escapes from those peckerwoods down South. If we hadn't gotten past 'em, guess our memories wouldn't be so funny. Shoot, we wouldn't even be here to *have* memories."

"*You* caused the most trouble," her husband stated from the piano.

"That man's ears are so sharp they might cut somebody," Ruby complained. "He's just talking about that time in my home town when the whifolks wouldn't let my relatives come hear us in their hall. So we played out in a big old field instead. And caught the next train out of town. Our people are always on the run from something. Maybe that's why there's so many old songs about trains—"

"Like 'Midnight Special,'" Lou interrupted eagerly.

"And 'Ticket Agent, Ease Your Window Down,'" said Ruby.

"And 'Glory Train' and 'Get On Board, Little Children,'" Lou added.

"Those are holy songs," Aunt Jerutha told her.

"They're *slavery* songs," Ruby said. "I've heard old folks say, when the slaves sang those railroad hymns, they were pretending to be singing about going to Heaven, but they were really making plans to get on the Underground Railroad and run away to the North. We been running a long time, girl. A *long* time."

"The North isn't Heaven, though," Lou said.

"That's the truth, child."

"No place on earth is," Aunt Jerutha said.

"And that's the truth too, lady. We just got to do the best we can wherever we are. Hey!" Ruby shouted suddenly to the musicians. "When you dried-up old stage hogs gonna invite these young folks to join in?"

"Well, what they wanta sing?" Lucas asked.

"Some blues," Louretta said. "We never get a chance to sing the blues the whole time we were touring."

"Of course not," Sam said, turning his brushes and drumsticks over to William and approaching Lou. "You were playing mainly to white audiences, and they only want our music after it's been put through a strainer, mashed up, creamed, and sugared till all the grit is gone out of the grits and all the chip is gone out of the chocolate. Can't stand the real thing. Can't stand the raw pure-dee truth in it."

"You know, you're right. Our arrangements kept getting stranger and soupier all the time. Watered down with violins and hopped up with disco. Half the time we didn't even recognize our own songs," Frank said.

"What you gonna sing, little girl?" Lucas asked again.

"Just play blues in B. We'll think of something."

But after four bars, she realized with a shock that she'd forgotten all the blues she ever knew, including the ones her first teacher, Blind Eddie Bell, had taught her.

"Cat got your voice, Lou?" William asked.

"No! They done stolen my blues from me!" she shouted angrily.

"Well, sing about that then," Lucas encouraged.

"They done stolen, done stolen, done stolen my blues from me,"

she improvised.

"They done stolen, done stolen, done stolen my blues from me,
Took 'em and shook 'em and changed 'em to a money tree.

They done took away the songs that satisfied my soul,
I say, they took away the songs that satisfied my soul,
And where my blues was hummin' is a great big empty hole."

"That's all right," Sam said appreciatively.

"Say on," Lucas encouraged.

"They took everything I got,
My gravy and my pot,
And left me on my own
Without a song to call my own!"

Frank nudged her aside and took over:

'I'd go out lookin' for a rope and a hangin' tree,
Yes, I'd go out lookin' for a rope and a hangin' tree,
But hangin's too good for the man who stole my blues from me!

Gonna get me a shotgun, shoot him full of holes.
Get me a shotgun, shoot him full of holes,
And get back the songs that satisfy my soul!

'Cause I got to put a hurtin' on that man,
Yes, I got to put a hurtin' on that man,
Till he turns loose my blues and gives 'em back to me again!"

"You ain't lost your blues, children," Lucas said with a chuckle. "You just misplaced them for a little while. How 'bout letting us hear one of your own songs?"

They looked at one another indecisively, then agreed on the shocking "Talkin' 'Bout Yo' Mama," which, Lou explained first, had been stolen from her, too. It sounded better in that little living room, with those old-time professional musicians, who picked up the tune and the beat perfectly in something like thirty seconds, than it had ever sounded on a stage after many hours of rehearsal. William, who liked to beat the drums ferociously, wound up the song with a long, emphatic fusillade.

"Your mamas wouldn't like that song," Ruby said. "But *I* do."

"So do I," said Sam. "Maybe they stole a few songs from you, but they didn't steal your talent. I been wondering how to ask you something. Let me put it this way. You want to go on using that talent, sharing it with people who will really appreciate it?"

Ulysses shrugged. "Ain't got nothing else to do."

William crashed down hard on the cymbal. "What about finishing school?"

"I don't think we can go back now, William," Louretta said. "The term's half over. They'd make us wait till September."

"You sure?" he asked suspiciously.

"No," Lou admitted. "but—"

"Nobody's interested in school anyway," Frank interrupted.

"Speak for yourself, Frank," she told him.

"I think she's right," Aunt Jerutha said. "My Jethro was sick once from Christmas till March, and he'd missed so much work he had to wait till September and repeat half a year. You better go to the school and check on it, though, Lou."

"Me?" Lou was troubled. She didn't like being a dropout, but she didn't want to face her teachers again.

"I'll go, Lou," William volunteered. He understood. "Maybe your friend Too-Tall will go with me."

David, who was indeed too tall for his age, said, "Sure. I don't care much either way, though. Basketball's over till fall." Then he focused his attention on Sam. "What did you have in mind, sir?" he asked respectfully.

"Sam Banks, here, used to be our manager in the old days. He's single and spry and thinks he's still young, and *I* think he's itching to get back on the road again," Ruby explained.

"I ain't goin' *nowhere,* woman!" Lucas bellowed from the piano, with a wild arpeggio for emphasis.

"Course you ain't, fool," Ruby said. "I got you hog-tied and satisfied. Your sharp ears tricked you that time, honey. Nobody asked you to go anywhere."

"Oh," Lucas said, mollified, and went back to playing gentle, pensive chords and runs.

"I can't promise you nothing like what you been used to," Sam said humbly to the young singers, "but I think I can get you some good audiences in the places where I'm still well known."

"Where are they?" Lou asked.

"Down South."

"Oh." That syllable and the silence that followed it betrayed their feelings. All of them were scared to death of going Down South.

Sam read their thoughts. "It ain't as bad as it used to be," he said. "Nowadays they treat you nice. You can stay anywhere you want and eat anywhere, too, long as you got the money."

"That's the only problem," Ruby interjected. "Sam doesn't have any money." She laughed. "Last time he ever saw a Roosevelt *dime* was when Roosevelt was President."

"*Which* Roosevelt?" David clowned.

"I don't know," Ruby said. "But I can tell you one thing—Sam's honest. That's *why* he's poor."

Sam bowed his head slightly. Lou could see his bald spot as well as the shininess of his suit. And his carefully polished shoes had a hole in one sole. She felt sorry for him. But she needn't have; he was an eternal optimist.

"Yeah, she's right, times have been tough lately. But since I heard you sing, I have a feeling things are gonna turn around." His smile was broad and full of hope. "'Course, I can't promise you the kind of money I *used* to make. I used to be in the big time. There used to be a lot of big showcases for race talent in the North—the Cotton Club in Harlem, the Earle in Philly, the Harlem in Atlantic City."

"Used to be don't eat for free," Ruby commented tartly.

Sam ignored her. "But those places are mostly closed now," he continued, "and those new people you ran up against are in charge of just about all the entertainment up North. But they haven't taken over the South yet. 'Cause, say what you want about the Southern cracker, he likes those people even less than he likes us. He wants to tell us, 'You stay over *there,* and I'll stay over *here.*' But he won't give those new people an inch of room *any*where."

Those 'new people' being, of course, the ones they had just testified against . . . the ones who had shot Lucas's leg and Frank's too.

"You know the people I mean? Just got off the boat and breakin' laws left and right because this isn't their country, so they don't respect its laws? Stealin' everything in sight because back home where they come from, a big thief is somebody to admire?"

"Yeah," Frank said sourly. "We know 'em."

"We just helped put some of 'em in jail," David boasted.

"Good for you, son. Makes me sick the way they steal from us, when this country is rightfully ours."

"How you figure that, Mr. Sam?" Ulysses asked.

"'Cause we slaved for it for 350 years! That's enough back wages to buy up the whole USA! I keep dreaming about the day when those wages will be paid back with interest. 'Course that would break the government budget, so it's just an old man's dream. But there's other things besides money. If you want to make some money—told you I can't premise you a lot—and have a good time singin' for people who really appreciate what you do, I'll take you on."

"Where we going?" Ulysses wanted to know.

"Well, down the East Coast is best. You don't want to go too far inland 'cause there's still Kluxers running around, and a lot more people with the Klux mentality, and the little towns are run by white sheriffs and black preachers, and neither one is too friendly to popular entertainers. So I say our first stop is Richmond, Virginia. Petersburg, Virginia after that. Then Greensboro and Raleigh, North Carolina. Wilmington, North Carolina too, maybe . . . it's nice, it's on the seashore. Then right on down the coast to Charleston and Beaufort, South Carolina. Stops in Savannah, Darien, and Brunswick, Georgia, and wind up our tour in Jacksonville, Florida, unless you're so famous by then they want you in Miami." He considered this a moment, then shook his head. "No, not Miami, no matter *how* bad they want you. We don't go near those big-time resort places anymore. Those new people play too rough. I do know of a record company on one of the Georgia Sea Islands that don't have nothing to do with gangsters, though. Maybe they'll be ready for you when we get there.

"Comin' back," he went on, "we'll hit Valdosta, Georgia, and then Albany and Augusta—there's big colleges in both those towns; Columbus and that big Army base, Fort Benning; Macon; then head east to the Atlanta University colleges and go on up to Greenville, South Carolina, and Greensboro, North Carolina. We'll do a big loop, see"—he traced it with his finger in the air—"straight down and then a little over to the left and back, and then straight up home. I'll call up people I know, and there'll be articles in the papers and posters on trees in all those towns before we get there. And there'll be musicians waiting for you all along the route—old boys I used to work with, like these here."

If sounded exciting to the boys, Lou could tell—but to her, just hearing him describe the trip was exhausting. And Marty had caused them so much trouble she was wary of all managers—even if they were William's friends.

"If we decide to go," she said, "our lawyer should draw up the contracts."

Sam looked pained, but said, "Certainly, young lady. Lawyers don't frighten me because I wouldn't cheat you anyway."

"No offense meant, Mr. Banks," Ulysses said. "We had a lot of hassles with our last manager. I think Lou's right. We ought to be more careful from now on."

"Aw, Man," Frank said impatiently, "can't you see this is a different situation? Mr. Banks ain't no slickster."

"Nobody said I was, son," Sam said. "I'll work along with your lawyer if it'll help you feel easier in your minds. All I'm looking for is ten percent of the profits. I hope we never get to fighting over money—there probably won't be much money to fight over, anyway, cause our people aren't rich like those other people. But I think they'll appreciate you, and if we don't make more than our expenses in the big towns, we can stop at the little ones in between. I know people in most of them, and I know they'll turn out to hear you, help you make a little extra."

Ruby commented, "Yeah, they'll turn out all right. In some of those little Southern towns, the biggest thing happens all year is a funeral. Work enough of those one-night stops and it might be yours."

"Stop scaring them, Ruby," Sam said. "They're young and strong; they can take it. And I'm old and tough."

The Soul Brothers and Sister Lou looked at one another, weighing these plans that had suddenly been made for them.

Frank made the decision. "When do we leave?"

"Soon as I can get in touch with some people down there and get some repairs done to my station wagon. I figure it'll carry the five of us easy over those roads, with room for two to be sleeping anytime. Can any of you boys drive?"

All three of them could, they said—even David, who was too young to have a license. But he would be old enough for his learner's permit in a few days.

"That's good, that's good," Sam said happily. "Now I really hate to ask you this one, but I have to. Can any of you advance me the money for car repairs?"

"What's wrong with your car?" Frank asked suspiciously.

Sam put as delicately as he could. "See, the people here in this city, they don't fix the potholes in the steets. So—well, it's the axle. But she's a good old car."

Lou didn't know an axle from a cotter pin, but, from the way Frank winced, she could tell a broken one was pretty serious. She turned to Aunt Jerutha and said, "Remember that night we were in the casino? I have lots of money, don't I, Aunt Jerutha?"

"Yes, but I'm hoping you'll keep it for a little while. That high-interest bank certificate we bought for you won't mature till you're eighteen."

"Then I couldn't have bought Momma a house anyway, could I?" she said.

"You could have—you can always cash that certificate in—but I'd like to see you let it sit and draw some interest. You have your own future to think about."

"But I still have the money William saved for me."

"That you do."

After a quick huddled conference, the four of them agreed to advance Sam the money to fix his car.

"You was a good ole wagon,
Daddy, but you done broke down."

Ruby sang meaningfully.

It didn't seem like a promising beginning. But it was better, they agreed, than hanging around home and doing nothing at all.

CHAPTER

18

William Davids and Lou went to the high school the morning after the party at Lucas's. Lou was relieved to find out she'd been right; that it was too late in the term for her and the boys to re-enroll. For all of its dangers, her show business life had been so exciting that high school now seemed confining and drab, like a dress she'd outgrown.

So that objection to the tour was removed. She expected worse ones from Momma—but, suprisingly, they were not forthcoming. When Lou asked her if it would be all right to go, her mother simply shrugged and said, "You cut me loose last year, girl. Why bother to ask my permission now?" Somehow, that hurt more than if Momma had raised a fuss.

Three weeks and six hundred dollars later, the car was ready. While they waited, Frank kept a calm front, but Lou and David and Ulysses admitted to each other that they were scared to death. The South! All their lives they had heard scary tales about it; about lynchings and shootings and cruelty and hooded terrorists and burning crosses. Sam could not reassure them, Momma didn't evey try, and Aunt Jerutha's reminder that they had already faced every imaginable danger did nothing to diminish their fear of going South.

But there were their bags, all packed; and there was the station wagon, repainted bright yellow with THE SOUL BROTHERS AND SISTER LOU on its sides, in black letters on a black treble clef. And there was Sam at the wheel in a dapper new straw hat, tooting the horn at Aunt Jerutha's door.

She and Momma were both there to see Lou off. Lou was glad she wasn't leaving from her own house, with six crying, clinging children to say good-bye to her. Momma's tears and worries were enough.

"You see, your mother *does* love you, Louretta." Aunt J said. "She loves you so much she worries herself sick about you.—Rosetta, stop all that carrying on. She'll be all right. If I didn't think so, I'd be going on the trip with her. But she's going with a good man this time."

"How you know a good man from a bad one?" Momma asked, sniffling through her soaked handkerchief. "There's no such thing as a good man, anyway."

"That's a terrible thing to say, Rosetta, and what's more it's untrue. Your husband was a good man. So was mine. So is your son William. And so is that Mister Sam Banks there. I've checked him out, and he's a very fine gentleman."

Momma looked at Aunt J suspiciously. "Sister Jackson, you got any special reasons for checking him out besides these children?"

"Well, Rosetta, I just might. I have been widowed a long time, you know, but I never got used to it. Somehow it just doesn't come naturally to me. I've been thinking, when they get back from that trip, I might offer Mr. Banks a nice soft chair and a place to rest his feet, and a cool drink and a good cigar. And maybe a little shoulder rub with Jockey Club Cologne in case his arms are sore from driving."

"You got it all planned out, huh?"

"Matter of fact, we have discussed it," Aunt Jerutha said with great dignity. Then, her girlish side taking over, she skipped down her front steps. "My, doesn't Mr. Banks look fine in his new automobile and his new straw hat? And that neat little mustache. I always did admire a man with a mustache. Don't you, Rosetta?"

"He looks all right," Momma conceded grudgingly, and turned a wet cheek for Lou to kiss good-bye. "Keep your dress down and your legs crossed," was her last admonition. Lou had heard that one a few times before, as well as the ones about always wearing clean underwear in case of an accident and remembering to send a postcard from every town.

"Don't the boys look fine in those suits?"

Lou agreed that they did.

Aunt Jerutha leaned into the car. "We have confidence in you, Mr. Banks. We know you are going to take care of these children just like they were your own."

Sam tipped his hat and said, "That I will, Mrs. Jackson. You have my word. I'll be in touch regular. And, if I may, I'll be ringing your doorbell as soon as we get back in town."

"I'll be pleased, I'm sure," Aunt Jerutha said, and withdrew her head from the car. It was all so proper and formal on the surface, Lou had to smother a laugh. And then, because her mother was standing stiffly at a distance from the car, she thought somberly that Aunt Jerutha had become more of a real mother to her than her own Momma.

And then they were off on the highway, and she felt as if she had left her stomach behind her at Aunt J's safe, cozy house. They were going down South, to the scary place where the worst things happened; where all the white people hated blacks and treated them badly.

Sam Banks drove smoothly around Baltimore and Washington, then got out and turned the wheel over to Ulysses. Sitting between them because it felt safer that way, she asked Sam fearfully, "When do we cross the Mason and Dixon Line?"

"We crossed it hours ago, little girl. Just outside Philadelphia. Didn't they teach you any geography in school?"

"Oh," she said, and felt stupid. She had always thought "down South" was very far away from home. Maybe it was because her elders had always made it sound so far away in the past that she thought it was a long distance in miles. Somehow, she had expected the sky to turn red with flame or gray with ash the moment they crossed that line and entered Dixie, but it had remained a serene, brilliant blue. "You mean *Washington* is in the South?" What a shock—she had already been South and didn't know it!

"You better believe it, Miss Lou! I can remember when the only place any of us could eat was in the train station, if we wanted to eat with the white folks. I was never that interested in eating with the white folks, anyway, but one time my friends took me to the Washington, D.C., train station for my birthday so we could have a real fancy meal. You see, that was a place of interstate travel, and it had just been integrated by the Federal government. Now that was long after World War II, but we still couldn't eat at any lunch counters or soda fountains; couldn't even try on clothes in any department stores. 'Course, it's all different now; we can go anyplace we can afford. But I remember when D.C. was as bad as Jackson, Mi'sippi. Worse in some ways. I remember when . . ."

Sam's long I-remember-when ramble put Lou to sleep while Ulysses drove steadily down Interstate 95 to Richmond. When they stopped on the outskirts of the city for gas, she rubbed her eyes and was almost disappointed to find it a large city like any Northern city. Factories on the edges, office buildings and shopping malls and tract houses further in, and poor people's rundown houses right next to a shiny, sky-high downtown. That was where their hotel was located—not in the shiny downtown, but in the slums next to it, on one of the neat, clean streets found in all black slums, a street where people might be poor but had pride. Just a dingy, double-sized row house with DUNBAR HOTEL painted on it in faded gold letters, and above it three stories of windows with plain white shades. It was named, no doubt, for Paul Laurence Dunbar, one of the great black poets Miss Hodges had introduced her to in school. Lou thought indignantly that he deserved a better monument than this.

Sam saw her disappointment and explained, "I go to the places I *know,* Lou. Maybe it looks old-fashioned, but I know the people here will make us comfortable, and, besides, we'll save money."

He was right about that. For half of an entire floor, three bedrooms and a shared bath, they paid only forty-five dollars. And, once they were inside, the Dunbar Hotel turned out to be a lot cleaner than it looked. The rooms were plain, with open coil springs under striped mattresses and old dark furniture on plain linoleum floors. But there were no bugs; everything was scrupulously clean, with the pleasant scent of lemon scrub water everywhere. The decorations consisted of holy pictures and funny, hand-lettered signs: "No Gambling," "No Noise after Ten," "No Whiskey or Beer," "No Profane Language," and "No Company." Momma would approve, Lou thought, and copied the signs for her first postcard home.

Next door was an equally clean restaurant, open twenty-four hours every day. But it was definitely not a deli. You picked your dinner from the soul food menu—Lou ordered fried fish; Ulysses, of course, had ham hocks—and got a big helping of every vegetable with it. Corn, string beans, red beans, rice, macaroni, and collard greens were heaped on her large plate along with her mullet. No matter what you ordered, the price was the same. Three dollars. They stuffed themselves while listening to Big Maybelle and Johnny Ace and Laverne Baker and some other good oldies on a jukebox that seemed to have been unchanged for thirty years.

After dinner, Sam quickly whisked them off to the Musicians' Union Hall to find them some accompanists. There they rehearsed for two hours with a guitarist, a pianist, and a drummer they'd never seen before. The first hour was spent just getting the musicians, who apparently hadn't seen each other before either, tuned up and coordinated. The second hour was spent going over their songs. This was to be their routine at each stop, Sam explained; find good cheap shelter, eat a good cheap meal, and then get the musicians together, without wasting money or time.

The turnout at the hall where they were to perform was disappointing. It was a large building owned by the local Prince Hall Masons, with an auditorium built to hold at least 500 people. But less than a hundred of the seats were filled, and the audience was scattered—some up front, some in the back, some in the middle. The applause was scattered too—a few polite claps here and there, and a vast emptiness in between.

Their harmony was off, their tempo was lame; they were suffering from the lack of warm audience response that nourishes a good performance. Trying to heat things up, the fellows called for "Dance, Dance, Dance" and tried to perform some of the ambitious acrobatics Charles had taught them. David slipped on the well-waxed stage. The audience tittered while he got up painfully and brushed off the seat of his slacks.

"You don't have to do that anymore," Lou whispered fiercely. "You don't have to wear monkey suits—why are you jumping around like monkeys?" They looked at her sheepishly; they had forgotten. Pulling them close to the apron of the stage, she called out into the auditorium, "Why's everybody so far away? Come on up close, y'all, so we can get to know each other!" The People remained in their seats. Lou was inspired to sing the spiritual, "Move on Up a Little Higher." The fellows joined her, *a cappella,* clapping their hands to keep rhythm, and soon a patter of hand-clapping came from the audience and grew stronger, like first drops of rain becoming a sudden shower. Some of the people began to sing with them. And all of the people moved up into the front rows.

When they were all settled, Lou said, "That's good. That's real good. Richmond people, I want you to meet my road brothers—Frank Brown, Ulysses McCracken, and David Weldon. I'm just here by accident. An accident that happened to another of our brothers, Jethro Jackson. Well, maybe it was an accident and maybe it wasn't. I hope Richmond is different from our town. Up our way, they call the police the gang that can't shoot straight."

"Same thing here, sister. Same thing everyplace."

"That's right."

"Amen."

"Sorry to hear that," Lou continued." Cause our friend died, and we wrote this song about him, and I took his place in the group, and that's what started it all". They sang "Lament for Jethro" to an attentive audience, then sang one chorus of "Talkin' 'Bout Yo' Mama," with a tantalizing "Don't go anywhere, anybody! We'll be right back to finish it," at the end.

During the fifteen-minute intermission all of them, including

Sam, ran out in the streets and gave away free tickets. They came back breathless, and had a late second curtain. But when it rose, a hundred more seats were filled, and the audience was eager to hear the rest of Lou's song. They performed it with spirit, strengthened by the vibes of appreciation out there, and went on to "My Mother's Eyes" and "Let Your Love Show," slow selections that gave them a chance to get back their breaths. They concluded with another hymn, "God Be With You Till We Meet Again" and, by beckoning encouragement, actually managed to get most of the audience to join in.

"That's good, that's good," Sam said to the crowd while they were still singing softly. "I can tell there are a lot of you good church people out there. So, let me say along with these young people, 'God Be With You Till We Meet Again,' and may that meeting be soon. Come back tomorrow night, everybody, and bring your friends!"

"That was some salesmanship, young lady," Sam complimented her after the performance. "Salesmanship *and* showmanship. You really know how to win the people over."

"But I meant it. I meant every word of it," Lou protested.

Sam was quickly diplomatic. "Sure you did. I know you did. I didn't mean to imply you were faking. Just thinking fast. You know what was the smartest thing you did?"

"What?"

"Singing those hymns. Everybody down South goes to church, believe me, and they'll warm up to church music even if everything else leaves them cold. From now on, I want you to sing a couple of hymns every time you go on."

Louretta had some misgivings about that remark too—she'd never thought of hymns as crowd-pleasers, just as spiritual songs she loved. Sam, who seemed able to tune in to her thoughts like a psychic, reassured her, "Nothin' wrong with praisin' the Lord and gettin' paid for it. Ain't that what preachers do?"

She had to admit that he was right. But, somehow, it didn't *feel* right.

Sam said, "The house was so bad tonight, I was going to push straight on to Petersburg. But now I got a feeling in my bones that tomorrow night they're gonna pack the hall. And my bones are never wrong. They're tellin' me something else, too. Tellin' me to get some rest. You all do the same."

Sam and his bones were right. After a good night's sleep at the hotel, on clean sheets that were comfortable the way only old, worn-soft sheets could be, and breakfast at the Dunbar Restaurant (one dollar, grits and hot biscuits complimentary with eggs and one strip of bacon), and another rehearsal, they played to a packed hall. Sam's last word to the audience were, "See you in church tomorrow morning!"

But fifteen minutes later, in the restaurant, he told the group, "Pack in the grits, kids, and then go pack your bags. My bones tell me it's time to move on." He explained that they had lost money the first night, but Saturday night's success had saved them. They had cleared $1,800 after paying for the hall and the musicians. He had hoped to do better.

"But," he explained, "this big city is too close to the North. They get a lot of big-name acts, and three of them were in town this weekend. It'll be better when we get further south, where there's less competition. You'll see."

"I thought we were going to church tomorrow," Lou said.

"I thought you were a seasoned performer," he shot back. "We all got to do a little acting now and then to make the people happy."

So they pushed on further south.

In Raleigh, North Carolina, they had a good crowd, made up mainly of students from the nearby colleges. The students clapped and cheered through every number and blew out so much marijuana smoke the group got a contact high. Afterward Lou was disgusted. They had given their best, but they could have sung badly, and the students would have been too stoned to know the difference. Instead of going to bed or accepting the students' invitation to party with them, the foursome followed Sam to the Boilermakers' Hall, a practice they'd begun in

Petersburg, Virginia, and made a habit of since.

All the after-hours halls in all the cities had different names but common features: they and their bars were open all night long; live music, usually the best in town, was played in them continuously; and the atmosphere was convivial and democratic for both the unemployed craftsmen and musicians who were hanging around hoping for work and the working ones who dropped in for a drink after work and ended up staying for several drinks and sitting in for several numbers. Once you got into the after-hours habit, it was a hard one to break. Everyone meant to get to bed early, but everyone kept staying around for just one more drink, just one more tune, just one more song. As usual, they got back to their boardinghouse and fell into bed as the sun was coming up—only to have Sam wake them an hour later to say it was time to move on. The Masons who owned the hall they'd played had been even more disgusted with the pot-smokers than Lou, and they had refused to rent it to them for a second performance.

At Goldsboro, North Carolina, where they played at a black VFW post, they only broke even. "Still too much up North. Still too big-city," Sam grumbled. "Got to hit some small towns now."

So, with Sam telephoning ahead to get stories printed and plugs on the radio, they began to stop at the small towns. The crawling fear of being down South was still curled like a worm at the pit of Lou's stomach, but she was beginning to feel something else too, a relaxing sense of the familiar. In Pittsboro, North Carolina, they stayed with a woman who fried okra with bacon just like Momma did. Only her bacon was thicker, and the okra had come out of her garden, not out of a can. She also used an expression, "Honey, *hush,*" meaning emphatic agreement, that sounded like a familiar refrain to Lou, though she could not remember who had said it before. Maybe it had been her father, who had left home when she was only ten-going-on-eleven.

As the landscape rolled by their road-specked windows, she

often had a haunting feeling of *déjà vu,* of having been there before. She discussed it with the boys and found they all felt the same thing. They found, too, that they could always tell the black sections of towns from the white ones, and not only on the obvious basis of who had the most income. Poor or not, the black homes had something different about them—collard greens growing out front instead of or along with flowers, paint in unusual color combinations, or even one crooked window shade instead of the perfection for which whites and Northern blacks strove.

Half-dead with weariness after singing all night at a rough roadhouse near Smithfield, North Carolina, they tumbled into the station wagon and rolled on down the highway. Lou wanted to stop at one of the first-class motels for a nap and a bath, but Sam was watching their budget very carefully.

"I got friends in Fayetteville," he said. "They'll put us up free."

When she kept pressing him, repeating like an overtired child, "But I want to stop *now!*" Sam admitted that he wasn't so sure the Old South had changed all that much to a New South, and that he didn't feel comfortable stopping at places he didn't know.

Sam's Fayetteville friends were the fairest-skinned blacks Lou had ever seen, but they cooked hush puppies and said "Honey, hush" just like everybody else. And at their house, just as at every other house where they stayed, there was one woman who was especially fond of Sam. The last one had been brown-eyed, and this one was green-eyed, but that was the only difference. That and her sweet urging that the group stay on the several days and sing at her church on Sunday. After a crowded concert at the Fort Bragg Non-Commissioned Officers Club, Lou wanted to stay, to sleep late and go for long walks around the beautiful old town with azaleas bright as lipstick on green lawns, but Sam and the boys reminded her firmly that they couldn't earn a living from church collections.

So they headed east for the coast and Jacksonville, North

Carolina, where Camp LeJeune's Marines were waiting for them as hungrily as if they hadn't seen live entertainment or a woman in years. The Marines whistled and cheered at Lou and threw money at her for encores, keeping them singing all night. The sun was coming up when they left the base, so Sam suggested they save room expenses by not pausing to sleep and heading on down I–17.

The coastal towns went by in a beautiful blur. At Wilmington, North Carolina, they rested at last in the spotless home of one of Sam's many lady friends, where the boys slept on a screened porch, Lou slept on the living room sofa, and no one dared ask where Sam slept. Aunt Jerutha really had her work cut out for her if she wanted to tie this man down, Lou thought.

In Wilmington, they sang for a crowd of teenagers at a church recreation center, mingling and dancing to records between sets. Frank danced with every girl but Lou, but she was too tired to care. They had earned only a hundred dollars, so immediately after the dance they headed east on I–76 to I–95, turned south, and stopped at the world's largest and gaudiest souvenir stand, to eat tacos and buy postcards and wonder why the Chicanos hadn't blown the place up with some of its own fireworks.

There were no Chicanos in South Carolina, that was why. There didn't seem to be much of anything in South Carolina. After the lush beauty of the other Southern states, it seemed ugly and barren. When Lou saw the dreaded triple K painted on a barn, she felt fear crawl under her skin like a colony of worms, but kept the sight a secret. Then David pointed out the same symbol scrawled on a fence, and she began to shake. This was the South she had always heard about: the dirt-poor, red-eyed, mad-at-everybody Deep South.

And here, in the middle of a desolate stretch of highway, was where Sam's station wagon began to complain. Its engine began to ping in perfect pitch, E above high C. Its rear end developed a thunk and grind that they nervously nicknamed the "fender bass." Then its temperature needle shot way over into the *hot* zone, and they sat in tense silence while Frank took the first exit ramp and drove grimly in search of a gas station. He found one, an unfamiliar brand name with only one pump, and pulled in just as the engine began to boil over.

"Stay here in the car. Let me handle this," Sam told them. He needn't have; they were all too drained to move. Then Lou, heat and thirst overcoming her fear, decided to get a soda from the station's machine. She liked the sweet Southern cola, bought another, and overheard Sam's conversation with the evilly grinning, gap-toothed mechanic whose skin looked like red alligator hide.

"He's convincing that man we're all Southerners!" she reported back to the boys. "He said, 'No, sir, not a single Northerner in our group, no matter what those license plates say'. Said we'd been up North working, didn't like it, and came back home. Said all of us were good Southern children, and we all loved South Carolina and never wanted to leave it again. Can you believe it?"

"I guess," Frank finally said, "it's what you have to do down here. They're still fighting their damn dumb war."

The mechanic ambled over and looked under the hood for what seemed like hours. "Waall," he finally said to Sam, "I can't do nothing about her today. My partner's gone, and she's got to cool off before we can work on her, anyway. You-all just take yourselves over to the Beau Regard Motel over there, tell them Merle sent you, and we'll see what we can do tomorrow."

The motel rooms were expensive—twenty-four dollars per person per night, and not very clean or comfortable. But Sam explained that if they wanted the man to fix the car, they had to stay there; the mechanic wouldn't have sent them to the motel if he didn't have a kick-back arrangement with the place. Of course they were being overcharged, but they were at Merle's mercy.

"Where in hell are we, anyway?" Frank asked.

"Somewhere around Florence, South Carolina," Sam replied. "I don't think it has a name."

They hung around No-name for three days, trying to sleep with air conditioners that didn't work and forcing down greasy food, while the mechanics worked on the wagon and Sam scurried around in a rented car trying to line up appearances for them.

They did an interview on the Florence radio station and a free performance at South Caroline State College, which sent a van to pick them up, but found no paying audiences except the congregation of the First Macedonia Baptist Church, which took up a collection for them. It was only a pittance, but Lou thought it was their best experience down South so far. The church people were warm, appreciative, and intensely responsive to their gospel songs and hymns. Applause was taboo, of course, but the congregation urged them on with perfectly timed "All right"s and "Amen"s, and, when Lou sang "How Great Thou Art," with a silence that showed even more profound appreciation.

Afterward, the women of the congregation fed them a rich home-cooked meal in the church annex. Lou watched Frank disappear outside with one of the young girls who had been serving, but she was too happy to care. She shrugged and went on eating her dessert, gingerbread with real whipped cream.

At the end of their third day in No-name, the station wagon was ready, and Sam was handed two bills: seven hundred dollars for repairs, including a new rear end, ball joints, motor mounts, water pump, radiator, and other things Lou didn't understand except for "Parts and Labor." That, plus their rooms and meals, added up to more than half their earnings on the entire tour. They weren't broke yet, Sam reminded them. But they were getting perilously close to it.

Sam said, with his broad, hopeful, childlike smile, "We've got a lot of stops to make yet, children. And look. We've practically got us a brand-new car." He put his straw hat on at a cocky angle, eased behind the wheel, and proudly started the engine. Lou was beginning to suspect that he cared more about driving that car around his old familiar haunts than about managing a singing group.

"No way I'd have paid that bill," Frank said angrily. "I'd have left the car with him and caught the bus."

"Oh no, youngun. You don't want to do a thing like that down here. You got to realize they don't like us, and another thing, this ain't the big city. So they got nothing much else to do but look for us. Our descriptions would go out on the local police radio, the state police radio, and all the CB radios. A lot of bad things could happen. Let's just mention the least bad thing. Let's just say you don't want to spend any time in a South Carolina jail."

"I don't want to spend any more time in South Carolina, *period,*" Lou declared.

"You don't have to, darlin'," Sam said. He was in a good mood, whistling and singing, happy to be behind the wheel of his car again. "Beaufort's nice, but I'll call up and cancel it out if you want to. My bones tell me this state is no good for us."

Sam seldom drove more than two hours before turning over the wheel to one of the young men, but tonight, for some reason, he kept on for nearly four hours until he suddenly decided to stop for coffee and turned off at an exit. He made his turn too sharply, bounced over the curb, and went up on the shoulder of the highway. With a sudden, sickening thud, the car came to a stop.

"What happened?" Lou cried, jolted awake in the dark.

"I just hope it ain't what I think it was," Sam said and got out with a flashlight. "I got to get out and get under. I bet none of you ever heard that song, 'Get Out and Get Under.' It dates back to the first days of the automobile."

"So does this car," David muttered.

Sam sang a few bars before he slid under the wagon, but his cheerfulness sounded false. When he came out, he had stopped singing. "It was what I thought it was," he said dolefully. "The axle went again."

"Oh, no," Ulysses said with a groan. "I started to ask you to let me take over at least a hundred miles back there, Sam, but you were doing so fine, I never said a word. I just kept quiet and let you go on."

"Yeah, one of us should have spelled him," David said.

"It's my fault," Sam said. I was so glad to get my car back, I just got road-happy, and stubborn, and wouldn't turn over the wheel even though I knew I was tired."

"What do we do now?" Frank wanted to know.

"Well," Sam said sadly, "I guess I know when to fold a bad hand. We catch the Dog, that's what." He patted the hood of the station wagon fondly, said, "Farewell, old lady," and turned his back on half their earnings, stuck on the shoulder of the road.

"How old was that car, anyway?" Frank asked. Lou could tell he was angry.

"Older than you," was Sam's only answer. "We been through a lot of things together, that ole wagon and me. I remember when. . ."

Frank was moved to curse, softly but viciously.

Lou was inspired to sing a eulogy for Sam's car:

"You was a good ole wagon,
Daddy, but you done broke down."

"Honey, hush!" Sam cried in alarm, meaning it literally for once. "Rest your voice. It's cracking just like that old axle."

So, silently she sat down on the luggage beside the others and waited with them in the strange Southern night to flag down a Greyhound bus.

CHAPTER

19

"We used to *have* to sit on that seat back there," Sam confided as they hauled themselves wearily aboard the bus. "If there wasn't any seats at all, we had to stand. But if we sat anyplace at all, it was back there. By *law*. And that seat is *hard*, children. We used to call it 'the nigger-killer.' But now we can sit anywhere we find a space."

The boys were not thrilled by this news, and Lou, totally indifferent to it, stretched out on the hated "nigger-killer" and fell asleep in the frigid air conditioning.

When Ulysses shook her awake to tell her it was time to get off, she had a painfully sore throat.

"Where's the throat spray?" she whispered, unable to talk in the sudden change from air conditioning to oppressive Georgia heat.

Sam, no pill-peddler, shrugged. "Kerosene and sugar mixed together is the only remedy I know. With a spoonful of honey after to help it stay down." He made the taxi driver stop at a store so he could buy the concoction.

But there was no time for Lou to swallow the honey. All the home cure did for Lou was to make her throw up violently. "Please, somebody," she croaked, doubled over with stomach cramps. "Please go to the drugstore for some throat spray."

After the taxi took them to their boardinghouse, a beautiful gingerbread mansion in the section of Savannah called West Broad, where poor blacks were restoring and renting historic houses with, the black driver explained proudly, U.S. government money, Ulysses went out and came back with some mild cherry-flavored cough syrup. Standing over her bed worriedly with Frank beside him, he said, "This was all they would sell me, Lou. They're real tough about prescriptions here in Georgia."

"I have a pocket *full* of prescriptions, man," Frank said.

"Yeah, but they won't fill 'em unless they're from a Georgia doctor," Ulysses informed him.

"Sleeping pill, please, Frank," Lou said weakly.

"Pills are all gone, babe," he told her. "You took them all. You were popping them all the way down."

She moaned. Talking was painful, but finally she managed to say, "Ask Sam—ask Sam to find me a doctor."

They caught Sam on his way out to make his rounds and find his musician friends. He came into Lou's room, took a good look at her, and was visibly upset by what he saw. Perspiration popped out on his forehead, and his perky mustache drooped downward along with the corners of his mouth. It was the first time Lou had seen him look worried.

Before she could say, "Don't worry," he was gone. He came back in half an hour with a doctor who sprayed Lou's throat and gave her an injection that miraculously restored her energy.

Frank, meanwhile, was out making street contacts, something he was very good at in any city. He returned an hour after the doctor left with his pill pockets replenished and a bottle of turpin hydrate cough syrup with codeine. Lou dosed herself liberally with downers and cough syrup and went to sleep in the high-ceilinged white room with the big fan blades whirling above her head. Had a confused dream in which a New York hotel served her sundaes with real whipped cream and then they were riding in a station wagon down South with a sheriff's car bearing down on them. "Faster, faster!" she was screaming, but the old station wagon would not speed up, could not; and the police car got so close she could see the driver—who looked like Merle, the mechanic who had fixed Sam's car—and his partner, who looked like the rookie cop who had shot their friend Jethro, and who was aiming his revolver squarely at her.

She woke up still screaming. And trembling, and alone. Where was Frank? Where was everyone? Most importantly, where was she?

She turned on the light in this latest of many strange bedrooms, this time large and lovely but white like a hospital room, and remembered. Savannah. They had ridden in a taxi through streets that smelled of the sea, past aisles of giant gray-bearded oaks like grandfathers, past mansions that had the grandeur of another century, and none of it had made her feel better. She was staying in one of those mansions, and the sea air was still coming through her white-curtained window, but it was not reviving her. She needed something—a shot, a pill, an arm to lean on—to help settle her nerves and strengthen her for the rehearsal and the concert to come. She almost needed help just to get out of bed.

She accomplished that on her own, though, and looked at herself in the old-fashioned armoire mirror. She seemed to have lost weight. After she put on her worn costume, she was convinced she had. The costume was baggy as well as threadbare. She wished momentarily for Aunt Jerutha to help her take it in, then shrugged—the costume was too tacky to bother with—and changed to a dress with a belt she could cinch in. Inspecting her face, she saw that her cheeks were unusually red. Good. She needed no makeup except lipstick and eye stuff, especially light stuff under her eyes where the dark circles were. She felt hot. But this was Savannah in May. Or June. She'd lost track of the calendar, but it was *supposed* to be hot. She was fine.

She walked into the hall, lost her balance, and, luckily, fell against Ulysses, who was just coming out of his room.

"Hey, Lou, what's the matter?" he asked, holding her up. "You're shaking. You don't look so good. Maybe you ought to go back to bed. Want me to carry you?"

She shook her head, though he was, in fact, supporting all her weight.

"You should get some rest. We can cancel the show. No big thing."

She shook her head again. She was no quitter. "Where's Frank?" she asked.

Ulysses looked uncomfortable; like Lou, he was no good at lying. "Well, he went somewhere . . . I'm not sure . . . I think he . . ."

Lou found her voice and pounded her friend's chest. "Where *is* he?" she demanded.

"Hey, take it easy, Lou." Ulysses picked her up as if she were a feather pillow and deposited her lightly on her bed. "You just lay here awhile longer and cool out. We got plenty of time."

"Where's Frank?" she repeated, staring hot-eyed at Ulysses.

"Say, that fan feels good," he said. "Wish we had one in our room. I'm going to let it blow on me for a while. Think that little old ruffle-skirt rocker will hold me?"

She continued to stare at him with eyeballs that felt dry and hot while he lowered himself gingerly into the rocker and sighed a fake sigh of contentment.

"He's got another girl. Right?"

Ulysses paused, then nodded sadly. "I didn't know how to tell you, Lou. I still don't know if I ought to. Frank's my ace. But since you already guessed—Look, he had one girl back in Smithfield, and another one in Wilmington, and one in Florence, too. My man moves *fast* whenever we hit a new town. I don't see how it took you so long to notice. You were too busy, I guess. But those girls, they probably don't mean anything."

Lou was silent. Frank had tried to ration her pills at first, but somewhere between Fayetteville and Jacksonville he had given up and started letting her help herself from his rainbow-filled pockets. Soon she was taking green or white pills to pep her up before each performance and yellow and red ones with liquor to get her to sleep. He had complained more than once that she was too tired and sleepy at night for love. She had ignored his complaints. So he had gone out and found love elsewhere.

"You're the only one he really cares about, Lou. I know you are," Ulysses said, clearly miserable about having betrayed his buddy.

"All *I* care about is the medicine he's holding for me," she snapped back. "Don't worry—you haven't told me anything I didn't already know. If he wants to play, let him play. I don't care about his playmates. Just help me find him. He's got my medicine."

She didn't mention that it was not prescription medicine, and Ulysses didn't question her. "He ought to be over at the Savannah State gym by now. They're having a sort of reception for us there, and then that's where we're rehearsing. Want to go over there? It's not far."

"Sure," Lou said, aware that she was leaning too heavily on Ulysses's arm, grateful to him for not mentioning it.

The reception was crowded with attractive students, and the most attractive of them all was hanging on Frank's arm. She was a tall, slender beauty with perfect legs shown off by the high slit in a white dress and a perfect complexion made dazzling by its color. And, of course, perfect health. Miss Savannah State, as Lou named her, didn't have to work all night and travel without sleep. All she had to do was go to school on her rich daddy's money and be beautiful.

"Funny thing I've noticed," Ulysses whispered, guiding her to a chair, "all of Frank's foxes have been tall."

"Who cares?" Lou said lightly, though she was burning with anger as well as fever. She was miserably conscious that she was unusually short. She remembered Aunt Jerutha's talk about dwarves. Frank was short, too. It probably made him feel important to have a six-foot fox on his arm.

He detached himself from the campus queen as soon as he saw Lou. "What's happenin', baby?" he asked easily.

"Nothin's happenin' between you and me," she told him.

His hair-trigger temper flared. "Well, what am I supposed to do, stay home all the time and watch you sleep? That can get pretty boring, you know. You're always asleep or getting ready to fall asleep."

"Lou's been sick," Ulysses reminded him.

"Yeah, yeah, I know she was sick. Feelin' any better?" he asked her.

"No. I need some medicine."

"Sure," Frank said, and took a handful of pills from his pocket. "Help yourself. You look all shot out."

"Thanks a lot," she said tartly.

"Want some punch to wash it down with? It started out tame and lame, but it's tightened up now and righteous."

Lou nodded.

When he came back with the brimming paper cup, after pausing to speak to the tall beauty, Frank said, "I really like this school, Lou. They're militant. The sister was telling me, they're the last black college to hold out against integration. They marched on Atlanta last year to stop it, and they won. Here's your juice. Be careful. I hear some chem student spiked it with methyl alcohol. I mean, I *really* like this school. I wish you and I could go here."

"You and I aren't going anywhere," Lou told him, taking the drink from him.

"Hey, don't be so hard on me, baby. I didn't mean to hurt your feelings. But you do look kinda worn out. Anything else I can do for you?"

"Just hand me the candy when I ask for it."

At the word 'candy,' Frank started a little.

"So that's her name," Lou guessed—accurately, from his angry, narrow-eyed reaction. "This seems to be a 'C' year. Candy, Cheryl, Christy, Carol, Cocaine," she improvised.

"Next year," she went on dreamily, "will be a 'D' year. Diane, Dolores, Deborah, Denise and . . . Divorcées. That means I only have to wait ten years for you."

"Now , wait a minute, Lou. You haven't been taking care of yourself. I care, I really do. Let me take care of you and help you get better."

"I can take care of myself," she said and nodded her head toward the refreshment table. "Candy's waiting."

He hesitated, then said, "I'll be right back."

But he didn't come right back, of course. Lou washed down a pep pill with a swig of codeine syrup, then walked over and got another cup of punch from the refreshment table. She chatted brightly with some of the students without remembering a word she said. The young men were mannerly and soft-spoken, and at least six of them were attractive, but she couldn't remember any of their names. Finally she had to excuse herself, walk outside, and lean against a wall.

But that night, the combination of pills and liquor allowed her to walk over to musty theater that had been dark for six months and light it up with electric energy.

Ironically, they opened the performance with Frank's song, "Lou in the Limelight," looking daggers at one another instead of love. Using her anger to strengthen her performance, Lou sang "Love Is a River" with a vicious, growling emphasis that excited the audience. They began to talk back to her. You could always tell when a black audience liked your performance, because it talked back.

"Tell us 'bout it, sister!"

"We hear you, we hear you!"

"That's right. That's how it is."

"Do it one more time!"

Exhilarated by the reception, Lou flung herself with abandon into "Dance, Dance, Dance."

"I can move my body,
Let the beat come through."

"Faster, faster!" she exhorted the musicians, though they were already jamming sixteen beats to the bar.

"Watch me move my body,
Can you do it too?"

"Faster, faster! Up the tempo!" she cried. And whirled and spun and lost her balance and collapsed into Frank's arms for a moment, then straightened up and stood on her own two feet, held up by sheer pride.

"This is crazy, Lou," he told her. "This is insane. Time for something slow."

And, signaling the musicians for silence, he took the microphone away from her and sang a moving rendition of "Deep River," *a cappella* all the way through once, then again with the musicians after they caught up with him. It was eerily beautiful, as if Paul Robeson had been reborn. The audience went wild and gave Frank the biggest ovation of the evening. Lou wasn't jealous of *that*. He deserved it. She joined in the applause.

Remembering Sam's advice, they sang two gospel songs, "Grace" and "Sign Me Up for the Christian Jubilee." Then after their obligatory performance of "Lament for Jethro," they sang the Black National Anthem, "Lift Every Voice and Sing," in a gospel mode and tempo. And down here—unlike the integrated North—the audience knew all the words and sang along with thrilling unity.

After their bows and the descent of the curtain, the boys gathered around her anxiously. "How you feel now, Lou? You okay?"

"Fine," she said irritably, "if you turkeys would just back off and give me some air. I really feel fine. I feel like partying all night."

Which she proceeded to do with the Savannah State summer school students she had met earlier, who treated her with deference—even though they were all older and she had not even finished high school. But sweet wine and sweet music dissolved all the differences, and after dancing and laughing for three hours, Lou felt completely at home with the college crowd, though none of them stood out distinctly in her wine-clouded mind.

"We're coming back tomorrow and bring the whole school!" they promised as they dropped her at her boardinghouse door.

The students kept their word. The theater was jammed that night, and their original weekend engagement was extended for another week. It was good news. Better still, they realized that they were back to their original, natural singing style, basic soul and gospel, instead of the whiteface, phony arrangements they had contorted themselves to fit up North. They could relax and sing the way they wanted instead of the way they were told. They could wear comfortable clothes instead of costumes and wigs. And a record company further South wanted them to do an album!

Sam was jubilant. "I told you so! You have to come down here, where your roots are, to be appreciated."

"But our roots are up North," David objected.

"No such thing as a Northern black," Sam growled. "Where's your daddy from?"

"North Carolina," David admitted.

"Where's your mama from?"

"Baltimore."

"Where's *her* mama from?"

"Georgia."

"See what I mean, children? You may be from the city, but you can't put down no roots in cement. Y'all's roots are down *here,* whether your folks told you about it or not. And these folks appreciate your music because they're your home folks and it's *their* music, too. —What's the matter, Lou? Aren't you happy?"

"Sure," she said from the porch swing where she was fanning herself languidly and dosing herself with gin-spiked lemonade. "It's just this miserable heat."

"Well, you got a fan in your room. Why don't you go in there and lie down?"

She did as he suggested, trying not to drag her feet and reveal her fatigue. She lay with her eyes open thinking about what Sam had said—"No such thing as a Northern black; roots don't grow in cement"—and wondering if that explained the vague but unmistakable familiarity of most of the places they'd been. Then she heard cries of welcome, and saw Candy's long legs twinkle past her window in a pair of red shorts.

She turned over, beat her pillow in anger, and finally fell asleep in a furious, feverish state. Once again she had the nightmare and woke up alone. She had lived through it before, she told herself, reaching for the gin. She could live through it again.

Now that she and Frank had cooled toward one another, Lou was not the only one who was suffering. The entire foursome had lost some of its closeness. Lou had worried about the effect her affair with Frank would have on the group's unity. But she had never thought about the possible effect of their breaking up, which was inevitable and much worse. Everyone was loyal, but there were too many awkward moments, and the tight unit they had been was creaking and cracking like Sam's old station wagon, threatening to fall apart at any moment.

After that first night's disaster with "Lou in the Limelight," Lou suggested, as coolly and professionally as she could, that they drop the romantic ballads. The guys agreed, and from then on they stuck to theme songs, gospel songs, and rhythm and blues numbers. It left a hollow place in their repertoire, but that was better than a hollow space in the theater, which continued to be filled for three nights.

On the sixth night, though, the theater was less than half full. Apparently Savannah had grown tired of them. After he had finished going over the night's receipts and paying the musicians, Sam announced, "We lost money tonight. I'm no gambler. I leave that to the casino people. Let's quit before we lose more, and move on."

He got no arguments because they had no complaints. It had been a good stay in a beautiful, hospitable city, and they had made several thousand dollars and had a good time besides.

Lou's new found college friends were at the bus station to see her off. She was glad to see them even though she didn't remember any of their names, because they helped make up for Candy's prolonged, effusive farewell to Frank and Lou's sudden isolation from the group. Somehow, without her knowing how it had happened, the Soul Brothers and Sister Lou had regrouped into The Soul Brothers and Sam and closed ranks with male solidarity, leaving one scared, sick girl feeling shut out and alone.

She *was* sick. There was no longer any possibility of kidding herself about it, though she tried to hide it from the men. Somehow she dragged herself aboard the southbound bus and stretched out again on the "nigger killer," this time with Sam's raincoat for a blanket. She tried to go to sleep; she didn't want to hear any more of their deep laughter and lies and dirty jokes, but her sleeping pills weren't working anymore. So she feigned sleep and listened.

"Boys, you just wait till we get to Darien," Sam boasted. "I got me a lady friend there whose biscuits would make you call on the Lord. But when I'm in town, she saves all her biscuits and jelly roll for me."

David said, "That was some nice long barbecued rib Frank had in Savannah, wasn't it?"

"Hush your mouths," Ulysses said.

"It doesn't matter. She's asleep anyway," Frank said callously.

"And that one in Fayetteville was *fine,* Frank," David pressed on. "Remember the build on her?"

"Truthfully, I don't," Frank replied, and hummed a few bars of "Love Is a River." "I don't even remember her name. She was just a little down-home country girl. Sweet but ignorant. Those college girls have it all over the rest. They are cool and sophisticated and *aware,* man. Just right for me."

"I like older women, myself," David said. "They can teach you a lot of things. And they don't tell, and they don't get caught."

"Neither do the college girls. They're too smart."

Right then, shivering under her borrowed blanket, Lou made up her mind to be a college girl. Someday, somewhere, somehow.

"Maybe so," David teased, "but why would college girls be interested in a grade-school dropout type like you?"

"Class, boy. Chemistry and class," Frank boasted. "I got that magical something the ladies can't resist, that's all. When you got it, you got it."

That and a broom will get you a job sweeping streets, Lou thought bitterly. And I hope I'm home when you're picking up trash at my front door.

She had lost so much weight, the engagement ring he'd given her back in Vegas slipped wasily off her finger. She stumbled up the aisle and stuffed it into his hand.

"You got it, all right," she said.

She didn't know how she would manage to get off that bus without help, but she was determined, and she made it. She didn't know how she would perform tonight without Frank's pills, either, but she would, because she was equally determined never to ask him for another thing.

Air conditioning into heat again—that was Darien, Georgia. A fishing town where boats came came in with wriggling hauls on their decks, and black workers cleaned fish and headed shrimp with hands that flew like gulls.

The owner of the Cocoa Club and two of the fishing boats picked them up in his Ford station wagon and drove them to two hot, stuffy cabins behind his large, octagonal entertainment center. The paint was peeling from all of his buildings, but Ham—that really seemed to be his name—blamed it on the salt air. Ham and Sam, old friends from Sam's I-remember-when days, got off on a long discussion about the superiority of Fords, which seemed to date back to their fathers' I-remember-when days, when Ford was the only auto-maker that hired black workers. Lou fell asleep on this discussion in the back seat of Ham's wagon, but was uncomfortably awake for three hours in her airless cabin.

Then it was time to head from its heat into the club, a big drafty room ventilated by powerful fans. Lou coughed and sneezed until water ran from her eyes and she had to redo the makeup that hid the hollows and pouches beneath them. One fan blew directly onstage. She put on a sweater and climbed onto a stool someone brought her from the bar. She would sing her way through this show and save the dancing and wiggling for another time.

But her voice was simply not there when she needed it. The fellows covered for her, singing all the verses of "Lament for Jethro" while she merely moved her lips. But the time came when she had to perform a solo. The first six bars were raspy and hoarse. The next ten she did in a whisper.

Frank passed her the cough syrup. She had no choice but to take it. There in front of that crowd of working folks in their print dresses and sports clothes, she tilted back her head and emptied the bottle, then belted out a dynamic beginning of "Dance, Dance, Dance." While she sang, the fellows and the audience got up and began dancing. She remained safely on her stool.

Something was making Lou drowsy, though. It must be the heat of all these people in here, she thought. She tried to remember the words of the second verse, but found she had forgotten them. Trying to recall them while she repeated the first verse, she closed her eyes for a fatal moment. She never felt herself slipping from the stool.

This time the nightmare, the police car and the sirens and the flashing red lights, was real. Only Lou was *in* the car, lying in the back seat with her head in Sam's lap, and they were taking her somewhere she didn't want to go.

CHAPTER 20

At first Lou thought the all-white room was the same one she'd had in Savannah. But it was smaller and plainer, with no ruffled curtains or furniture. She asked the inevitable question, "Where am I?"

"Glynn-Brunswick Hospital, Brunswick, Georgia," Sam replied. "They didn't have a hospital in Darien. So we brought you here."

"Why? There's nothing wrong with me!" she said, sitting up indignantly, almost jerking the tubes from her nose. The tubes scared her into submission. She made no protest when, with the politeness that made him so different from Marty, Sam gently pressed her shoulder back to the pillow. "Lay quiet, girl, please. You passed out in the middle of the show last night. They worked on you two hours after we got you here. I been sitting here all night, just waiting for you to open your eyes."

"But I'm OK now," Lou said, but softly, with doubt in her voice. She had just noticed the other tube running from a bottle over her head into a vein in her wrist.

"Let's wait on your doctor and see what he says." Sam looked tired, troubled, and terribly old.

For a moment Lou panicked, wondering if her underwear had been neat and clean last night. Then she smiled at the absurdity of her concern. No matter what Momma believed, doctors did not specialize in underwear. Eyes, ears, throats, hearts, yes—but not underwear.

"They found too much junk in your blood, Lou. And they had to pump some of it out of your stomach." Sam bowed his head in his hands. "I feel like an old fool for going back on the road with a group of young people after twenty-five years. I should have had the sense to stay home. I promised your mother and Miss Jerutha I'd look after you, and I never really paid any attention. I was having such a good time getting back with my old friends in my old hangouts, I just let you look after yourselves."

"It's not your fault, Sam," Lou said. "It's mine."

"I can't let myself off the hook that easy, little girl. No, I should have seen to it you got your proper rest instead of rushing you all over like I did. And I should have paid attention to what you were taking to keep you going." He shuffled his feet nervously.

Lou could not console him; a nurse had stuck a thermometer in her mouth and was taking her blood pressure. When the thermometer was removed, she said, "Sam, why don't you go eat and get some sleep? You look terrible."

"So do you," he said bluntly. "I mean, you don't look exactly like yourself. Excuse me, Lou, for the way I put that. After they finish building you up in here, I know you'll look just fine. Here comes your breakfast now." He got up wearily. "Eat it all and go back to sleep. I'll be back later. Who else do you want to see?"

She did not hesitate. "Ulysses and David. And nobody else but *you*."

The effort of all that talking was enough to make her doze off immediately. When she awoke, she was annoyed to discover that the fellows had pulled a switch on her. Ulysses was standing at the foot of her bed. Fine. But Frank was standing beside him, holding a bunch of wilting flowers.

"What am I supposed to do with these?" he asked.

"I could give you a suggestion," she snapped back, "but you wouldn't like it."

He laid the flowers awkwardly on the dresser and came over to her bedside. Knelt there, head buried in her covers. "Forgive me, baby," his muffled voice said. "I didn't mean to neglect you. I was just having a good time. I should have taken better care of you."

It sounded like Sam's speech all over again. Tentatively, she moved her hand toward his head, touched the crisp hair briefly with her fingertips, then withdrew them.

"It's all right, Frank. What we had was nice for a while—but it wasn't supposed to last forever, I guess."

Frank began to sob, his broad shoulders heaving in spasms. "I want to make it up to you. I want to do something for you. What can I do? Tell me, Lou."

"It's all right," she repeated, feeling her anger rise. Here she was, sick in a hospital bed, yet trying to console this flighty dude. "We weren't married or anything. And I'm not dying. So will you please get up and stop soaking my bed?"

"Get out of the way and let her eat, man," Ulysses said. "She hasn't even touched her breakfast."

"I'm not hungry," Lou told him.

But Frank sat up on the edge of her bed and proceeded to feed her lukewarm soft-boiled eggs by the spoonful until she had gotten them all down. "Now a sip of juice," he said. "Now a bite of toast. Now, more juice. Now, more toast," until she protested that she had had more than enough.

"What else can I do for you, baby?"

"Is there a mirror over there?"

He brought it and she looked with thoughtful, detached horror at the wreck she had become. Great, glassy staring eyes with pouches beneath them, pinched red cheeks, hollow throat, wild hair in peaks like a field of weeds. No wonder Frank had sought out and found other foxes. It was all over between them, but no one was ever going to see her looking like this again.

"You all," she told him and Ulysses, "can get me a makeup kit. And some hair grease, and a pick, and some lemony cologne. And a decent nightgown, and some slippers. Size seven for both." Then she remembered how much weight she'd lost. "Better make it size five for the gown."

Her doctor came in then. Lou immediately fell in love with him. He was slim and good-looking, with warm brown eyes behind gold-rimmed glasses, a sexy touch of gray in his mus-

'tache and his sideburns, and, of course, one of those white coats that looked so good against brown skin.

"Get me a white gown if you can," she told the boys. "If you can't, get any solid color, as long as it doesn't have tacky little flowers all over it. D'you need money?"

They shook their heads.

"Then what are you waiting for?"

They took the hint and left her alone with her doctor. He bent over her close enough for her to read his name tag: *Doctor Burnette.* Close enough for her to smell his Old Spice cologne. I like Old Spice men, she decided. I can't stand Pierre Cardin men. Frank was always fragrant with fancy French cologne. She was glad she still had a nice round chest for Doctor Burnette to rest his stethoscope and then his ear against.

But then he said, "Turn around, please," so he could listen to her back as well as her front, and she was miserable because she had on one of those ugly, rough-dried, tied-in-back hospital gowns.

"Well," she asked when he had finished knocking and listening, "what's wrong with me, Doctor?"

"Basically," he said, "dehydration, malnutrition, and exhaustion. "I've never seen a young woman so run down. You're anemic, of course, and you're running a slight temperature. I've ordered megadoses of vitamins and antibiotics to try to build up some iron in your blood and get rid of the infection. You have fluid in your lungs, too, young lady. That worries me. But something else worries me even more."

"What's that?" she asked in a small voice, frightened into a seriousness that matched his.

His tone of voice was angry. "You damn near OD'd last night on more junk than I ever found in a person's system. Barbiturates, hypnotics, amphetamines, tranquilizers, alcohol—where do you young people *get* this stuff?"

"It's all over the place," she said. "Anybody can buy it on the street."

"But why do you *do* it to yourselves?" he scolded.

"I don't know why other people do it," she said. "Maybe because they don't have anything else to do. *I* did it so I could keep on working."

"Well, you almost stopped working last night. Heart, lungs, *everything* almost stopped working."

"I won't take any more," she promised.

"Have I scared you?"

She nodded.

"Good," Doctor Burnette said, studying her chart. "Has your blood pressure always been this low?"

She thought about it and remembered. "Yes. I went to give blood for a friend once, and that was why they wouldn't take mine. Can I leave the hospital today?"

"No," he said. "I told you there's fluid in your lungs. After we get you X-rayed, I want you on complete bed rest." His voice was gentler now. He pointed to the tube that ran into her wrist. "This is flushing the junk out of your bloodstream."

"You have to flush me just like a toilet," she said in shame.

"Exactly," Doctor Burnette said. "But you're not a toilet, you're a person. Treat yourself like one, and we'll get you well faster. Promise?"

"I promise," she said weakly. "No more junk."

"It may be rough," he warned. "I don't know how long you've been taking mood drugs or how much you've been taking. But I'd rather not sedate you until your blood is clean. OK?"

Louretta nodded.

"And *this* tube—he touched the one in her nose—"is supplying you with extra oxygen. That means no smoking in here. So—no sedation if we can help it. No overexertion. Visitors only twice a day, 11 to 11:30 in the morning and 6 to 6:30 at night. Only two visitors at a time, and not too much talking, and no smoking. Because"—he brought his thumb and forefinger almost together—"you came this close to suffering brain damage. Understand?"

Lou fell back on her pillow as the doctor disappeared. Brain damage! She had almost lost part of her brain, the most valuable part of her, in the strenuous effort to exploit her voice. Her teacher's, Miss Hodges's, words came back to her: "You have a good mind, Louretta. Don't let it go to waste," as they stuck a needle in her wrist to drip things in and another into a finger to take blood out.

It went on like that for three or four days. Lou drowsed while nurses and attendants came in and out, taking her temperature, sticking needles into her, even putting a catheter into her so she wouldn't have to get up and go to the bathroom. When she was awake, she thought mostly about Miss Hodges's words. And about the desperate, crazy ambition that had landed her in this hospital instead of in college, the way she and her teacher had planned. About the pressures that had turned her into a pill-head and very nearly an empty-head. She had been tired for so long she had forgotten what it meant to rest. She had been tired, she realized now, when they left home to start this tour, a thousand miles away and what seemed like a thousand years ago.

Across the room her gown and toiletries sat, useless, on the dresser. I must look, she thought, like an Egyptian mummy, wrinkled and dried up and dead. But the important thing was not how she looked. It was whether she could still think. When she wasn't sleeping, she recited verses of Langston Hughes and Longfellow and Wordsworth and James Weldon Johnson to make sure her brain was still intact. Each time she remembered a verse, she felt surer. And the seed of a quieter ambition took nourishment and grew. She didn't want to be a singing star anymore. She wanted to go back to school and—somehow—to college.

On the fifth morning, Doctor Burnette came in and gave a nod to the attendants. They removed the tubes.

He picked up her wrist and asked, "How do you feel?"

"Better" she said cautiously.

"You look better," he said, leaning over to listen to her chest. After a long careful session of rapping and listening, he said, "Your lungs sound clear. We'll take an X ray to make sure. Think you can walk down to X ray and have it done?"

"Sure," she said, though she was not sure at all. She went to the X-ray Department on her own tottery legs, though, clinging when necessary to the walls. When she got back to her room, she took a shower and put on her new white gown at last. Then she climbed back into bed, made up her face, and combed her hair. It needed washing, but she was afraid of having a wet head after pneumonia. Her thick hair took too long to dry.

"You don't need any more oxygen therapy," her doctor announced that afternoon. "What you need now is collard greens therapy."

"Sounds good," Lou said. "Where do I get it?"

"Allow me to present Mrs. Braxton," her doctor said, and brought a short, round-faced black woman into the room. "Mrs. Braxton works here sometimes when we need her. And sometimes she takes patients home when they need up, like you. She's not just a nurse. She's a specialist in collard greens therapy, a nature doctor, and probably a witch doctor, too."

Mrs. Braxton smiled broadly. "That's right," she said, and winked. "You like this doctor?"

"Very much," Lou said.

"So do I. 'Cause he's got sense enough to know there's a lot of medicine they didn't teach him in school. You trust him enough to come home with me?"

Lou nodded yes.

"All right. I run a strict house, now. You have to eat everything I fix you, and do everything I say. You agree to that?"

Lou nodded again.

"Let's go, then," the little woman said joyously, as if there were nothing she enjoyed more than nursing run-down teenagers back to health. She pushed Lou's wheelchair through the hospital door, where a surprise was waiting.

Sam had the station wagon back! It was fixed, freshly shined, and had a fancy new horn that played a five-note blues riff.

"I called Triple A from Darien and had 'em tow it back to Merle," he confessed, pronouncing it 'merrily.' " Then a couple days ago, Hambone ran me up there to get it. Didn't cost too much this time. We can't deal without wheels, Lou."

Lou was happy for him and said so. She didn't want to spoil his pleasure by saying she was through with singing. Then she covered her face with a handkerchief, for Brunswick had pungent, marshy air that was hard to breathe, though it also had the grandfather trees with mossy beards and palms growing everywhere and a semitropical heat. Mrs. Braxton's house was naturally cool, though, with thick walls of "tabby" clay, and as clean as the hospital. Lou's room was bright pink with red roses on its wallpaper. She was so happy to be there, she wouldn't have minded black wallpaper.

Her first nourishment was a cup of strange, sharp-tasting tea. "Drink it," Mrs. Braxton ordered when Lou made a face at its taste.

"What is it?"

"It's a tonic for your nerves and your blood. Made with some herbs and roots I get in the woods. You'll get used to it. You have to drink it four times a day."

After the tea she ate ox-tail soup, a rich broth with barley in it. And that night they had a spendid stew, with more ox tails and barley, plus carrots and tripe and another sweet, fat meat that Lou devoured greedily. "What was that?" she asked when she had eaten her last piece.

"Possum."

"Ugh," Lou said, and covered her mouth.

"Don't make a face over my good possum. It tasted good, didn't it?"

"Yes'm."

"You ate it all, didn't you?"

"Yes'm."

"Well, then, what's the problem? Only thing upsetting you is the name. I had somebody kill that possum specially for you. But from now on, I won't tell you what you're eating. I'll just fix it and make you eat it."

But Lou recognized the thick, dark soup she had for lunch the next day. It was turtle soup, she knew, because she'd eaten it in New York. This time it seemed less disagreeable. In time she might even learn to like it. And, under Mrs. Braxton's watchful eyes, she ate it all.

Sam and the boys came to see her every night for a short visit. Afterward Sam would stay on, chatting with Mrs. Braxton, while the fellows sat on the porch outside and sang her to sleep. No one said anything about the next concert or the tour. No one seemed to have performing on their minds. So Lou didn't have to break any unpleasant news to them.

Lou's doctor visited every day and spent more time with her than her traveling companions did. She was improving rapidly, he said, and gave all the credit to Mrs. Braxton. "She's a miracle worker," he declared. "She comes from the country, and she used to be the only doctor people in the country had. She knows all about natural medicine. Indian medicine and African medicine."

"And collard greens," Lou added.

"Yes," the doctor said laughing. "She grows them herself out back."

After a week, in which she learned to like fricasseed squirrel, roasted coon, and even stewed conch, Lou decided she felt like going outside and looking at that garden. Mrs. Braxton helped her wash her hair first. She sat on a weathered cypress bench, drying her hair in the sun, then went to pick that evening's greens from the proud-looking row that stood thigh-high and full of broad leaves.

"One little walk outside, and I'm worn out!" she complained when she came back in the house. "How will I ever get well?"

"Remember, you went out in the sun in the hottest part of the day," Mrs. Braxton reminded her. "We never do that down here. But you were so anxious to go outside, I wouldn't keep you in. Don't worry, you're getting better. Your cheeks have plumped out, your color is back, and you've put on some pounds. See?"

Lou was pleased at what she saw in the mirror.

Mrs. Braxton, who usually was too busy stirring about to pause for conversation, did an unusual thing. She pulled up a chair and studied Lou's face long and hard. "You know," she said finally, "now you've plumped out and started looking like yourself instead of some wild razorback hog, you put me in mind of some people I know around here. I don't know any Hawkinses, though, so they can't be your father's people. Where was your mother from?"

"Georgia," Lou said after a pause, surprised that she remembered the name of the state. Most of the time, she had only been told that her mother was from "down South." "I don't know the name of the town, though. She never wanted to talk about it much. But I think it was near the ocean."

"The ocean," Mrs. Braxton informed her, "is less than a mile from here. You know that smell out there that takes your breath away till you get used to it? That's the marshes. The marshes of Glynn."

"I know that poem!" Louretta cried.

"I expect you do," her hostess said. "You been reciting poetry all the time in your sleep. First I thought, 'Lord, the child's out of her head.' But then I realized the words had rhyme and sense to them. What was your mother's name? I mean, her maiden name."

"Church. Rosetta Lee Church."

Mrs. Braxton's smooth, plump skin made her seem younger than she was. But there was no doubt that she was over sixty when she wrinkled up her face in thought. Then the wrinkles were erased by a broad smile. "I remember her!" she cried. "She left here a long time ago, when she was about your age. Child, you have people around here. This place is *crawling* with your relatives. There's a bunch of Churches on Bartow Street, another over on G street, a bunch out in the woods, and a Miss Church on Albany Street. And you look like *all* of them!"

"Just because I look like some people doesn't mean they're my relatives," Lou objected.

Mrs. Braxton ignored her skepticism. "I won't tell any of them. Once the word gets out, they'll all be over here to meet you. Too many visitors could tire you out."

That was fine with Louretta. She was in no hurry to meet these so-called ralatives anyway. They might turn out to be false cousins and she might be disappointed. Or, worse, they might be real relatives and she might not like them. She did, however, want very much to know more about her mother. She followed Mrs. Braxton into her kitchen and began tearing and washing the greens she had picked.

"What was my mother like when she was young?"

"Pretty as a picture—and I shouldn't say this, but she was wild. All the boys were crazy for her, I remember. She had a way of switching up the street that had them all following her."

"*My* mother?" Louretta said, picturing Momma with her Bible and her roomy apron.

"You asked, so I'm telling you. If Rosetta Church was your mother, she was wild before she even reached your age. Dropped out of school to have that Bangs boy's baby, and left it right here with her mother and father. Always said she was coming back for her, but never did. —Wash those greens in three waters, now. You're not supposed to be working around here, but if you must, do it *right*."

Louretta's hands had been immobilized by her thoughts. She set them to work again, but her mind was elsewhere. It made sense. Why would her mother be so easy on Arneatha for leaving a baby at home if she hadn't done the same thing herself? It made perfect sense. Then she realized with a shock that she had a sister she didn't even know.

"Why did she leave?" she asked. "Was it because of the baby?"

"I imagine so," Mrs. Braxton said. "Rosetta was proud; the Churches are all proud, too stiff-necked for their own good. And people around here don't accept things like that too easily. It's different up North, I hear, but this is a small town. Girls who have babies usually leave, especially if they're from respectable families. I think your mother might've had another reason for leaving, though. I remember she loved clothes. Wore 'em well, and had a different new outfit every week."

Just like my sister Arneatha, Louretta thought.

"Rosetta was always willing to work for what she wanted, though," Mrs. Braxton continued. "Had her a job from the time she was thirteen over at the McFadden place. The McFaddens used to be the richest white folks in town. They liked Rosetta over there, paid her well, and gave her a lot of things. Mrs. McFadden cast off clothes fast as she bought 'em, and your mother always caught 'em. I remember one time Mrs. McFadden gave her this brand-new outfit. —Sit down, child, and let me deal with those greens."

"But," Louretta protested, "you've been doing all the work, and I haven't paid you or helped you."

"I love to work, and I love to nurse people back to health," Mrs. Braxton told her. "I'd do it for free anytime. But the county pays me, child. I'm what they call an out-care facility. Isn't that some mouthful? —Anyway, what I was saying was, one time Mrs. McFadden gave Rosetta an outfit she hadn't even worn. Said she'd changed her mind and didn't like it, and it was just too hot for her to go down to the store and return it. It was a blue suit, I remember, with a silver silk lining and a blouse to match. My, it was fine! And Rosetta looked fine it it. She put it on right away and forgot the price tags were still on it. Then she went in town and walked right into the same store where Mrs. McFadden had bought it. She just wanted to look at more clothes, I guess. Rosetta never got tired of looking at clothes in those days. When she had looked at everything in the store, she walked out, and old man Golub hollered, "Stop, thief!" He had her arrested for shoplifting because the tags were still on that suit. But I always maintained he knew she hadn't stolen it; he just couldn't stand for one of us to be looking that fine."

"Did she go to jail?" Lou asked in wonderment.

"Yes, they had her locked up for two nights, until her white folds heard about it and came down and got her out. Her family shunned her for a while. Getting pregnant was bad enough, but going to jail is the one thing Churches just don't accept. I was living out in the country then, and they sent her to stay with me until the baby came. I don't think Rosetta was ever the same after that. She said she'd never want anything showy anymore, never want anything she couldn't afford. Got religion all of a sudden and said fine clothes were just worldly vanity anyway. From then on she just wore cotton housedresses, old flour sacks, anything. —Girl, this is a terrible thing I'm doing, talking about your mama."

"No, it's a good thing. It helps me understand her." No wonder Momma didn't want to rise. No wonder she was afraid for her children to rise, too. "Poor Momma," she said aloud. "She still doesn't want anything."

Mrs. Braxton made no comment. Instead she came up with a cheerful suggestion. "Now you've cropped and washed all those greens, and I've got a hunk of deer meat in the oven, why don't we ask your friends over for dinner? They've been staying at Rowena Bangs's boardinghouse, and she's a good cook, but still, they might like a change."

That evening Sam, looking tired, sat at the head of the table to say the blessing His face, puckered with concern, smoothed out when he got a good look at Lou.

"You're looking well, girl," he said.

"I *am* well," she replied with conviction.

"Thank you, Jesus!" Sam cried, and went off into a long prayer of praise for the food and thankfulness for good health and their many other blessings.

"Thank you, Jesus, for stopping that man before the food got cold," Mrs. Braxton said tartly. "Mr. Banks, don't you know these young people are starving?"

"We already ate over to Miss Bangs's, ma'am" Sam said. "But we're pleased to take a little bite with you, too."

"A little bite! Mr. Banks, surely you must know these are-healthy, growing young people. They can put down two big meals in one night with no trouble at all."

And, indeed, David and Ulysses were already holding out their plates for second helpings of everything.

Sam looked crestfallen. "That's what I've been telling myself for two weeks. "Sam, you old fool, you had no business taking four youngsters out on the road. You don't know how to look after young people. You don't know what they heed in the way of supervision and nourishment and rest. And when this little girl here got sick, she had me so scared"—he put his hand over his heart—"I thought I would die."

"Well, nobody's dying around here tonight," their hostess said. "I don't allow people to die when they're eating my cooking."

"Say, what kind of meat is this?" Frank inquired.

"Deer meat. You like it?"

All three of the young men held their forks in the air and stared at them in horror.

Mrs. Braxton only laughed. "That's the same way *she* looked when I told her she'd been eating possum. She was licking her fingers when I told her, too. Filled her out some, though, didn't it?"

"Boys, you don't know what good eating is," Sam said. "Fresh game from the woods—why, most city people can't get it at all, and those who can pay a fortune for it. I'll have another piece. Fine food like this doesn't come my way every day."

The boys were still staring at their plates.

"When you get back to baloney sandwiches, and then mayonnaise sandwiches, and then air sandwiches, you'll wish you'd filled your bellies tonight," Sam advised them. "Speaking of air sandwiches, you know, we haven't worked in two weeks. Folks around here tell me they have a fine hall called Selden Park. And there's an affair there this weekend that could use some entertainment. What do you say, kids?"

Lou turned her face away from his eager, expectant look. "I don't feel like performing anymore. Let the guys go on by themselves."

"You mean you don't feel like it right now," Sam said hopefully.

She didn't want to let him down yet. "Let the guys try it without me. I think they'll go over just fine. You can play the drums, Sam. Call yourselves the Soul Brothers and Sam; that's a good name."

Sam drummed a paradiddle on the table. "Sounds like you're

thinking about giving up singing for good, Lou. What else do you have in mind?"

Mrs. Braxton spoke up. "Don't push the child. I've been letting her get up and around a bit the last couple of days, but I'm pretty sure she can't do much more. Takes time to get over these chest ailments, you know."

"We know," Frank said, pacing restlessly, "but it's a drag, sitting and waiting around this dumb town."

"Excuse *me,*" Mrs. Braxton said with exaggerated offense. "We kind of like our town. Sorry you think it's dumb."

"Haven't you found any playmates to keep you company?" Lou asked.

"No. I've been too worried about you to even look at anybody else."

"Well, you can stop worrying and start looking," she told him. "And if you don't see anything you like, I'll lend you the fare to catch a train and ride."

"Children, children!" Mrs. Braxton exclaimed at this outburst. "I thought you were all close friends."

"Some of us," David muttered darkly, "got *too* close."

"I see," Mrs. Braxton said. "Well, then, I suggest that you gentlemen go out and enjoy the breeze on the front porch. I'll join you as soon as I've finished clearing the table. It's time Louretta was in bed."

CHAPTER

21

Doctor Burnette agreed emphatically with Mrs. Braxton. "Visitors, yes. An hour a day. Activity, same thing. Short walks or visits, helping around the house and garden, an hour or so a day. But no more. And no concerts for a long, long time. We don't want to have to put her back in the hospital and repeat the whole process.

Tactfully, Sam and the boys stayed away for several days, and kept busy rehearsing for their performance. In their place, cautiously, like cats sniffing around a mouse hole, the relatives began to arrive to look Lou over.

The first one to come was an uncle. Uncle Randolph Church, her mother's brother. He had her mother's tilted eyes, pushed into a slant by high cheekbones—"Indian blood," they stated matter-of-factly down here, without the pride or shame that would have accompanied such a statement up North—and her mother's heaviness, carried above his waist with the help of stern discipline or a girdle or both. He also had a wife, Aunt Cordelia, who was plump, plainly half his age, and beaming with well-being. Louretta thought she was beautiful. And they had two pretty daughters—her first cousins!—one in college and the other in her last year of high school.

Uncle Randolph played hymns at the piano Mrs. Braxton kept under a camouflage of lace tablecloths, photographs, china figurines, and souvenirs. Both his daughters, Leslie and Kim, sang sweetly, though not exceptionally. Lou listened quietly and watched, trying to decide if these pretty, privileged girls were really her cousins and, if so, whether she liked them.

"Music runs in the family," Uncle Randolph said after a rippling version of "Love Lifted Me" that sounded suspiciously like ragtime. "But none of us ever thought of earning a living by it." He implied clearly that earning a living as a musician was not respectable, and that Churches did not do that sort of thing.

"Except Julia," his wife reminded him.

"Oh, yes, of course, Julia. I forgot. My niece Julia"—Uncle Randolph cleared his throat and blew his nose—"your *cousin* Julia is the church organist and the music teacher at the high school, and I believe she has a few private pupils. That's different. Besides, *Julia* is different. She has always been a law unto herself."

Lou was immediately intrigued by the 'different' Cousin Julia, but thought it would be tactful not to ask direct questions about her right away, and to ask about someone else instead. "I heard I have a sister here," she said.

Uncle Randolph looked blank. Behind his back, his daughters covered their mouths to hide giggles.

"Someone told me," Louretta explained, "that my mother had a child before she left here. A girl."

"We don't want to tire you," Uncle Randolph said, rising swiftly from the piano stool. "We'd better go now. When you get stronger, we'll take you out for a day at the beach, and we'll talk more about the family."

They all left swiftly after giving her warm hugs, and Lou decided that she liked them even if she had made a terrible mistake by bringing up a taboo subject.

"He don't want to discuss things like that in front of his daughters," Mrs. Braxton explained afterward. "That man is as jealous of his girls as a mother cat with her kittens. Don't want them to grow up, when any fool can see they're already grown. Don't want any kind of scandal talk to reach their ears. Done his best to spoil them, he has. But I think they'll turn out all right in spite of him. And I think they *been* knowing everything he tries to hide from them."

Mrs. Braxton was right. After dinner, the phone rang. It was the older cousin, Kim. "Louretta, your sister lives over on L

252 Street. Daddy don't want us to visit her, but we can sneak out at night and take you there. Tonight?"

"Fine," Louretta answered, in spite of doctor's orders.

Kim and Leslie tapped lightly on her window late that night, the agreed-upon signal, and Lou climbed out to follow them through a maze of dark streets and bearded trees to a very small house with only one light, the pale blue one of a TV set.

"Who out there bangin' at my door?" came a rough voice.

"Your cousins Kim and Leslie, and your sister from up North."

"My *what*" Ella Mae Church stood in the doorway, a small, fierce figure, fists on her hips, eyes glaring murder at the intruders. "I ain't got no sister up North. I just got myself and these children." Around her legs, five small, beady heads clung and stared with large frightened eyes.

"This is your sister Lou from up North, Ella Mae," Kim said. "She wanted to meet you."

"What for? I don't want to meet her."

Kim and Leslie giggled. Leslie said to Lou, "Well, we brought you here; that was all we promised. We got to go now. Daddy be checking up on us at eleven." As they disappeared into the night, Lou decided she didn't like these cousins so much after all.

"You don't have to let me in," she said, "but my mother is Rosetta Church Hawkins. She has eight other kids besides you, and she thinks I'm the no-good one. Everybody down here says we're related. I just wanted to see your face to see if it's true."

"Come in, then," Ella Mae said reluctantly. She was, Lou guessed, around twenty-six or twenty-seven, but looked older because of the deep circles under her eyes and the tired sag of her body. "I ain't got anything to offer you, unless you want a beer."

"I don't want anything," Lou said, standing awkwardly in the middle of the sparsely furnished, bare-floored little room. "I mean, I don't want anything to drink. I just want to get to know my family."

"This oldest one here is James Lee", Ella Mae said, abruptly detaching the tallest head from her skirt and presenting him. "And these others, who ought to be in bed, are William, Gordon, Andrew, and Randolph. Couldn't manage to have me even one daughter."

"But those are my brothers' names!" Lou said excitedly. "You have brothers named William, Gordon, Andrew, and Randolph up North."

"They're family names. Our grandfather was James Lee Church. His sons were William, Gordon, Andrew, and Randolph. —It don't matter what you name 'em, they're nothing but trouble. Shoo!" she cried, and clapped her hands sharply, as if chasing a pack of puppies. The small ones scattered, but not very far, and gradually they began edging closer again.

That phrase, ('our grandfather,') was like a golden clasp linking Lou to a chain of relatives. She stared at the woman in front of her and was reminded of her older sister. "Arneatha!" she cried. "Put some long false hair and high-heeled shoes on you, you'd look just like Arneatha."

"Then you *must* by my sister," Ella Mae said. "Can't be two Arneathas in this world—least, I never heard the name but once. Momma wrote me about her. Her and William. Those were the only ones I ever heard about. After that, she stopped writing."

"I came next," Lou explained.

"You want to have a beer with me, Sis? Or you too seditty for that?"

"I'm not too seditty for anything," Lou told her. "I'm just too sick. I just got out of the hospital. But—yes, I will, Sis."

While the TV set babbled softly, and the children fell asleep on the floor around them, Lou and Ella sat and sipped beer and talked. About their strange, hard-nosed mother, who had been Grandpa Jim's spoiled only daughter. About Ella's two come-and-gone husbands and her struggles to bring up five kids alone, and Lou's come-and-gone career and her struggle to regain her health here in Brunswick.

"I been buked, scorned, spited, backbited, everything but mourned, since I was borned," was Ella's poetic summing up. "And I'm only twenty-seven."

"I've had my skinny butt kicked across the country and back, been robbed, cheated, and almost raped, and just got a monkey off my back in the hospital. And I'm only sixteen."

"We'll make it," Ella Mae said, lifting her glass. "We Churches have *got* to be tough."

"Uncle Randolph seems kind of seditty to me," Lou said, trying out the tongue-twisting pleasure of the new word.

Ella Mae had another one for her. "He just got asteperious since he got a wife and had to settle down, her being good family and all, and him being a much older man. He used to be an old rip and he thinks everybody else is just like him. He's bringing up those girls like they was born in plastic bags."

"I know," Lou said, and finally got around to asking about the relative that intrigued her most. "What about Cousin Julia?"

"That's Uncle Gordon's daughter. His only child. He's dead now, but he left her well off. She's educated and has her own funny ways, but they're *her* ways, and I say she's got a right to them. Lots of folks say she puts on airs, but I like her. She got me a job at the school cafeteria so I could stop working nights at the laundry. Now I come home same time the children do, and it's a lot easier. People can say what they want to say, but I think Cousin Julia is one fine lady, and regular, too—in her own way. She does *everything* her own way. That's what some people can't stand. But she helped me, and that's something none of these low, back-biting people who talk about her would do. You go see her. Maybe—maybe she can help you, too." Ella Mae stood up. It was late. "Where you staying?"

"Mrs. Braxton's. You know her?"

"That your landlady? Then you must be sick, girl. She don't take in no well people. You get on home. Fog rolling in from the marshes gets thick and nasty here at night. Get home. I don't want to meet my sister one day and have her up and die on me the next. Sunday, maybe, I'll drop by to see you after church."

"You do that, Sis."

They embraced, and Lou had that unmistakable feeling of family, like William's wiry hair, like Clarice's soft neck, like Momma's rough hands, that made her know, impossible as it seemed, that she had found a sister. Carefully following Ella's directions, she snaked her way back through the foggy streets, climbed back into her bedroom, and slept late, long past time for breakfast.

Mrs. Braxton brought lunch into her room on a tray. "I would say," she said, "that somebody had been out late last night, but I know better, because I know *they* know better." She raised the shade to let more light in. "What are those pink spots on your ckeeks? Rouge?"

She popped a thermometer into Lou's mouth before she could answer.

"You've got a temp, young lady. Ninety-nine. Not too bad. But not good , either. I'll have to tell your cousin Julia to wait till tomorrow."

"Oh, no *please,*" Lou begged. "I promise I'll stay in tonight. I'll stay in *all week* if you'll just let me see her."

But Mrs. Braxton was firm. "Your cousin Julia left this for you to look at," she said, putting a thick album on Lou's bed," and said she hopes you'll be well enough to visit her on Thursday."

Lou groaned and fell back on the pillows. This was Monday; how could she stand to wait that long? But finally, resignedly, she ate her soup and took her medicine and, eventually, reached for the album.

Cousin Julia's album was full of clippings about her father, Uncle Gordon, who had been a vaudeville dancer and singer—so much for Uncle Randolph's denial—and clippings and programs from her own career as a concert pianist. By Thursday, restless from too much resting, her temperature long since normal, Lou knew every word of every clipping by heart.

Cousin Julia's house on Albany Street, set back behind a pair of giant oaks and half a dozen Latania palms with brown fringe on their trunks, had a veranda and two tiers of balconies. It looked like a steamboat about to set sail on the Mississippi. Cousin Julia rose from a fanback wicker chair on the ground-floor veranda to greet Lou with outstretched hands. Those hands, with short, unpolished nails and long fingers that caught Lou's in a powerful grip, were the only undecorated part of Cousin Julia's person. She was not tall, Lou realized when her cousin did not have to bend to kiss her cheek; she merely carried herself in a way that made her *seem* tall. And though she wore no rings or bracelets or nail polish or makeup, long ivory carvings dangled from her ear and two necklaces, ivory and amethyst, decorated her neck. She wore a strange, spicy perfume and weird, wonderful clothes: a lacy purple shawl over a hand-embroidered ivory cotton blouse over a tiered skirt in three shades of blue. And she wore ivory stockings that were more daring than bare legs, with little clock designs running up their sides; and black shoes with thick high heels like a gypsy dancer's. Altogether, it was like a gypsy costume, but it became her. All that was lacking was a fan.

As if reading Lou's thoughts, Cousin Julia produced one—a folding fan carved out of ivory, which she unfolded and proceeded to fan herself with as they talked. This made Lou notice her strong, plain hands again, and her face, which needed no makeup—it was round and smooth and ruddy brown like a Macintosh apple.

"Tell me," she said, staring deeply into Lou's eyes, "all about yourself."

"I want to hear about *you,*" Lou said, and began babbling almost incoherently about the clippings in the album. "Your wonderful life—all those concerts—it must have been wonderful."

Cousin Julia sighed. "I suppose so. But my father would never let me go on the popular stage, you understand. That had been *his* life, and he didn't want it for me. But there were opportunities—and sometimes I still wonder what I missed."

Lou proceeded to tell her exactly what she had missed. Near-murder, near-rape, drug addiction, theft, and all the rest of it.

Cousin Julia listened unflinchingly as Lou told her tale of horrors. "Then I suppose," she said when it was over, "I have had a good life after all. I have just wished, sometimes, that I had chosen it instead of having it chosen for me." She took Lou's hand in her surprisingly strong grip. "Come inside now, where it is cooler."

Cousin Julia lived alone, but not alone. Her large living room was full of company—books, record albums, portraits, plants, and a bewildering array of musical instruments. Before Lou could ask about them, her cousin impaled her with a piercing black gaze and subjected her to a barrage of questions.

"What about your studies, child? Did you give up your studies?"

"Yes," Lou admitted. "I got stars in my eyes."

"Every young girl does, these days. When I was growing up, we weren't permitted to look at anything that might put them there. I'm not sure it was such a bad system, now. When you were in school, were you a good student? How were your grades? What was your favorite subject?"

"English," Lou said, remembering last year as if it were five years ago. "I really liked poetry. I used to memorize a poem every day."

Cousin Julia bent forward eagerly. "Do you remember any of those poems? Do you know Shakespeare? 'Shall I compare thee to a summer's day?/Thou are more lovely and more temperate.'" "'Rough winds do shake the darling buds of May/And summer's lease hath all too short a date,' Lou completed. "I know a lot of poems by heart, Cousin Julia. That's how I kept myself from going crazy in the hospital, by reciting poetry to myself. I even know a poem called by my name. 'Sister Lou.'"

Cousin Julia nodded. "Sterling Brown. One of our greatest poets. I know him. Do you know any James Weldon Johnson?"

Lou recited "The Creation" without pausing, from beginning

 to end. When she finished, Cousin Julia was smiling, but she had tears in her eyes. "Child, I didn't think there were any youngsters like you left in this world. Why on earth did you drop out of school?"

"One thing led to another, I guess. I began writing poetry, and so did some of my friends, and pretty soon I was setting the poems to music—and then we sang them, and they asked us to make a record, and suddenly I was part of a singing group." She shrugged. "You know the rest."

"Play me one of your compositions," Cousin Julia commanded.

Lou was embarrassed. "No, please, Let me hear *you* play first."

Cousin Julia threw off her shawl, walked to the piano, and again seemed twice her real size, producing chords that shook the room and vibrated long after she had finished the short piece. "Chopin. *Prelude in C Minor,*" she said. "Now it's your turn."

Hesitantly, Lou approached the piano and began, softly, the introduction to "Love Is a River." Then, growing more confident, she began to sing for the first time in weeks.

"Oh, I wish I could do that!" her cousin cried, applauding. "It's so free. So spontaneous."

"I wish I could do what *you* just did," Lou said.

"Oh, but you can. And you will. I'm going to teach you."

Lou looked around the room, at its assortment of instruments—everything from a harp to an African xylophone, and others she could not name, until Cousin Julia informed her that the wooden flutes were recorders and that the miniature piano was called a virginal. She also introduced her to the lute and the African guitar, the banjor. "From which, of course, our ancestors created the banjo." She pointed to a painting on the wall, a darkly rich rendering of an old black man teaching a boy to play the banjo. "That's *The Banjo Lesson,* by Henry O. Tanner. It's the only reproduction I would hang in my house. Even if I could afford the original, it's in a museum. He was one of our greatest painters. I knew him."

Louretta was thrilled. "I could live here forever and be happy!" she cried.

"Then why don't you?" Cousin Julia asked.

Louretta couldn't believe what she had heard. "H-how? why?" she stammered.

"I'm alone. I was too busy studying in my youth to go out courting. I'm not lonely, you understand, but I would appreciate the company of someone with similar interests. And there's no one like you in this town. *No one.*"

"Why not?"

"They all left," Cousin Julia said simply. Her face looked tired and sad. "We—my friends and I—did our best to prepare them, and they all left for that great Promised Land up North."

"It doesn't always keep its promises," Lou said.

"I know."

"Did you know my mother?" Lou asked.

"Yes. Rosetta was a bright girl. Bright, ambitious and—difficult. She thought she could rise by mating with a pretty-faced boy with long curly hair. But there was nothing behind that face or under that hair; *nothing!* I won't encourage you to go on the blocks, the honky-tonk streets, but you can see Ella Mae's father there anytime. Still looking like an angel; still staring into space and seeing nothing. Pretty faces count for nothing without potential and persistence. *Passionate* persistence. I think you have those qualities. What do you intend to do with them?"

Lou had been thinking about her future for weeks. Now that someone who cared was making inquiries, her answer came fluently. "I haven't exactly told anybody yet, Cousin Julia, but I don't want to be a pop singer anymore. I like singing, but I don't like the things that go along with it—wearing silly costumes, getting involved with crooked people, taking pills to keep myself going. Those things kept me from feeling good about myself. I made up my mind in the hospital to quit singing and go back to school. I have to get well first, of course, but then I want to finish high school and go on to college."

“What would you major in?” Cousin Julia asked.

“Music or English. Maybe both, if they’ll let me. But that’s a long way off in the future. It won’t be easy. My family can’t afford to help me.”

“I’m part of your family, and I want to help you,” Cousin Julia said, “if you’re sure that’s what you want to do.”

“I’m sure,” Lou said with conviction.

“Well, then, I want you to move in with me and learn harmony from me right in this room. And then I want to send you to the same school I attended. Savannah State.”

Lou was excited, remembering the students at Savannah State and how much she’d liked them. Remembering, too, that grim night on the bus when she’d made up her mind to be one of the college girls Frank admired there.

“But, Cousin Julia,” she objected, “you just met me. “Are you sure I can do all that?”

“To the trained eye, it only takes a moment to distinguish gold from brass. I have a trained eye, child. Don’t worry about ways and means. I have some income, and no one but myself to provide for.”

“I have some money saved up myself,” Lou said.

“You’re independent. Good. I like that. I don’t want to push you into anything.”

“You’re only pushing me in the direction I want to go,” Lou told her.

“Well, then,” Cousin Julia said decisively, “it’s all settled.” Lou looked more closely at her cousin. She was youthful in her enthusiasm, but there were many fine lines around her eyes and mouth, and gray hairs pulled into her bun along with black ones.

Cousin Julia seemed to read her mind. “Yes, I’m older than you thought. Even if I were to marry one of these eager gentlemen who keep coming around, I’m too old to have children. Therefore,” she declared peremptorily, “I’m adopting you.”

Lou had a few half-hearted objections. “But,” she said, “I don’t know how to tell my friends in the group. And besides, I dropped out of high school.”

Cousin Julia had moved to the harp and was playing something angelic. Her voice was equally sweet, but commanding.

"You drop back in as soon as you have recovered," she said. "The superintendent of schools here happens to be one of my friends. He'll send a tutor over here for you. If you have the intelligence I think you have, you'll have your G.E.D. certificate in a few weeks. Then—Savannah State! The music department there is superb. But don't be like me; don't spend all your time in the classrooms and practice studios. Meet people. Meet the young man who is right for you."

"Wasn't there—ever a young man who was right for you?" Lou asked daringly.

"Not according to my father," Julia said, agitating the harp. "He would have found something wrong with the emperor of Ethiopia. —Pardon me, Saint-Saëns," she apologized to the composer, and resumed her smooth playing.

"I don't understand," Lou said, "why you want to do all this for me." Though, through her bewilderment, she was beginning to get a glimmer.

"Because I never had a child . . . Because I've searched all my life for someone to share special things with. You are different. You are special. I claim you!"

Cousin Julia had a flair for the dramatic, flinging her shawl around Lou's shoulders and drawing the ends tightly toward her after that statement. But she was sincere. Lou could feel it. She thought she knew why Cousin Julia wanted her so badly: she had missed a large part of her life, and wanted Lou to live it for her.

"I—I just hope I don't disappoint you," Lou said, intimidated by her cousin's intensity.

"I hope not, too," Cousin Julia said gravely.

"Do you really think we could get along?"

"If we don't, then this old house is big enough for us to hide from each other for weeks!" Cousin Julia laughed, and Lou saw what a beauty she must have once been. Her teeth were white, her skin was smooth, her back was ramrod-straight. Her impressive profile, with its large nose, was balanced by the heap of long hair piled on her head. She wore dramatic clothes, but the effect was artistic, not showy.

Cousin Julia's expression and attitude softened. "This big old house does get lonely sometimes. Please say you'll come and live with me." She caught Lou's hands tightly. "I know we can be friends. I know it!"

Her appeal was irresistible. Before Lou could answer, a Bavarian wall clock chimed five times. A little cherub with a harp came out with each chime.

"It's five o'clock. I have to be home for supper."

"*This* is home," Cousin Julia informed her. "But I'll take you over to Marian Braxton's right away."

Cousin Julia even drove an unusual car, a stubby, homely black one with a stick shift. Questioned about it, she said, "This is my old Morris Minor. I picked it up on my last trip to Europe. It has a bad temper"—Lou could believe it, as she heard the snarl of the engine—" but it gets me everywhere. Over dirt roads in the woods when they've turned to mud; even along the beach like a dune buggy."

"You've been to *Europe?*" Louretta asked in wonderment.

"Certainly, child. A dozen times. Most of my trips were concert tours, of course, but the last two were strictly for pleasure. The next time, we'll go together. We'll see Paris, Rome, and Athens. All the Mediterranean countries are heaven, even in the winter. And when it gets too cold for us, we'll go on to Africa. Egypt, Tunisia, Morocco, Ghana, Nigeria, Senegal. . . . We'll see the Pyramids and the other ancient wonders. You are hungry for culture; I can tell. And no one else I know is." Cousin Julia downshifted viciously, spun around a corner, and stopped neatly in front of Mrs. Braxton's house. "No one else in this family; hardly anyone in this entire town. They think culture is a church concert with a bad soloist. That's why I want you."

You've got me, Lou thought. But did not say it aloud; said only "Thank you" and gave Cousin Julia a kiss on her soft, creased cheek before she ran into Mrs. Braxton's for supper.

“What’s that running?” Mrs. Braxton said, looking up disapprovingly from her paper. “Slow down, miss. Sit down and let me take your temperature.”

Lou was excited, and her face felt hot. But her temperature was normal.

“Did you have a good time at your Cousin Julia’s?”

“A *wonderful* time!” burst from Lou.

“Hmmmmm,” Mrs. Braxton said, pouring Lou’s compulsory cup of the terrible tea. “She’s different from most folks around here.”

“Yes! Wonderfully different!” Lou exclaimed.

“Different, even, from her family,” Mrs. Braxton went on calmly. ”Folks say she’s stuck up, but I don’t go along with them. She just likes different things. People try to talk about her because she never married, but nobody can say anything low or mean about her unless they’re so low and mean themselves they make up lies. ’Course, a lot of people are just jealous because Julia has money. But she isn’t stingy like they say she is; just strange. I happen to know she made the biggest contribution toward the new church organ herself, even if she did make the church buy it.”

“How’d she do that?” Lou asked.

“Drink all that tea. She said if she was going to be our organist, she was going to play a decent instrument or they could get somebody else.”

Lou smiled. It sounded like something Cousin Julia would do. “What did the people say?”

Mrs. Braxton shrugged. “There wasn’t anybody else. Your cousin Julia Church is the finest musicianer in Glynn County, maybe in Georgia. The congregation fussed a little bit, but pretty soon they got busy and raised the rest of the money. And my, that’s a fine organ. Pipes all around the back of the altar, all the way to the ceiling.”

“She wants me to stay with her,” Louretta blurted out. “She wants to send me to college.”

“And what do you want to do?” When serious matters came

up, Mrs. Braxton had a way of asking questions instead of giving answers.

"Everything she wants me to do!" Louretta cried. "Study music with her, get my high school diploma, go to Savannah State and study music. Write and compose and teach, and live and travel with her."

"And be an old maid like her?"

"Oh, Mrs. Braxton," Lou said patronizingly, "nobody gets married anymore. I think Cousin Julia was way ahead of her time, that's all. And besides, she wants me to get married someday. And besides, I have years and years to think about it. I'm only sixteen."

"That's true."

"I could get married at *thirty* and still have children."

"True. What about the boyfriend you've got now?"

"He's not my boyfriend anymore, Mrs. Braxton. He's too interested in other girls. I gave him back his ring."

"What about your other friends? What about the concert tour?"

Lou frowned and was silent. This was going to be the most painful part. "I don't know how to tell them, Mrs. Braxton. I hate being the one to break up the group. And I hate to disappoint Sam. He tried so hard. But I don't want to be a performer anymore. It almost killed me."

"If your friends can't accept *that* reason," Mrs. Braxton said, "they're not really your friends, Lou. Just tell them the truth. Tell them exactly how you feel. Maybe it won't be as hard as you think."

Lou had her chance to break the news that night. Frank, David, and Ulysses showed up at suppertime with Sam to devour Mrs. Braxton's good cooking.

"Um," she began, as they helped themselves to ham, black-eyed peas, okra, and rice, "how do you guys like working as a trio?"

"It's all right," Ulysses said, his mouth full of corn bread.

"Works out fine," David said. "I had to reach for some of the high notes at first, but now Sam's changed the arrangements."

"That's good," Lou said, "because I've decided to quit singing."

The fellows seemed about to choke on their food. Even Ulysses stopped eating.

Sam was the first to speak. "I think you are making the right decision, Lou. You are still a child. I forgot that when I brought you on this road tour. I didn't look after you properly."

"I'm not a child," Lou said, thinking of the things she'd been through. "I don't think I ever was one."

"No offense meant, young lady," Sam said.

"When I got sick," she continued, carefully avoiding Frank's eyes, "the doctor said I'd almost suffered brain damage. That was enough to convince me singing wasn't good for me. I decided I wanted to *use* my brain—not lose it. So I hope"—and now she looked straight at Frank—"that you guys will be able to get along without me."

It was an emotional moment. Ulysses got through it by picking up his fork. "No problem," he said through a mouthful of peas and rice.

"Excuse me," Frank said suddenly, and left the table.

Only Sam seemed calm. "It would help," he said, "if you would go on writing songs for us, Lou. Your songs would help keep the group alive. We're not big-time yet, but exclusive rights to record your songs would give us a big boost."

"Sure," she said quickly, glad of this opportunity to do something for the guys. "I'll write Ben Carroll's partner right away and tell him nobody gets to sing or record my songs but The Soul Brothers. I just hope I get inspired to write some new ones."

"We can wait," Sam said.

Frank was back, looking flushed and upset. "Lou, if you're not going to sing with us anymore—what *are* you going to do?"

"Go to school," she told him. "I made up my mind in the hospital to finish high school and go on to college. I didn't know how I'd manage college then, but now I've found a cousin here who wants to help me."

"I didn't know you had any relatives in this town," Frank growled.

"I didn't either. Mrs. Braxton found them for me. And one of them, my cousin Miss Julia Church, is a great musician. She wants me to live with her for a while and study music. And then she wants to send me to Savannah State."

"Go for it, girl," Ulysses encouraged.

"Yeah—if you've got a break like that, I say jump *on* it," David added.

Lou was surprised and pleased by their support. Only Frank was stubborn and contrary.

"They use drugs in college, too," he warned. "Remember that concert back in Raleigh? We played to a college crowd, and everybody in the audience was stoned."

"Frank, you must not think I have any sense," she told him angrily. "If I picked up those habits again—in college or anyplace else—I'd *deserve* brain damage."

"Aw, man, *you* sound like the one with brain damage," David told Frank. "Let Lou go ahead and do what she wants. It beats banging around the country in Sam's station wagon. Do you want to see her get sick again?"

"No, of course not," Frank said. "But I'll miss her."

"You should've thought of that when you were cutting out on her," Ulysses said.

"That was then. Now, I'm sorry."

"Yeah, you're sorry," Ulysses informed him. "Sorry and trifling. Your act is so raggedy, you've got the sisters mad at all three of us. Ain't that right, Dave?"

"Yeah," David confirmed. "I can't rap to any of the girls down here because they've all heard about Fast Frank. You've made so many swift moves on this tour, our rep gets to a town before we do. And the ladies shy away from us 'cause they've heard The Soul Brothers are slick and swift."

"Sorry to hear it," Frank said with a hint of a tomcat grin.

"I already told you how sorry you are," Ulysses said. "Lou's cleaned up her bad habits. You need to leave her alone and clean up your own Casanova act."

"Hey, how come everybody's picking on me?" Frank complained.

"'Cause you deserve it, man," Ulysses said. "Lou's decided to change direction and she's found somebody to help her. You've got no right trying to stop her, when you know you ain't got a thing to offer her but a hard time. You're as jive as a counterfeit five, and you know it."

Lou was beginning to feel sorry for Frank. "Aren't you being a little too hard on him, U?"

"No!" Ulysses shouted. His eyes bulged in his round face. "Don't you let yourself get softhearted with him, either. You can't afford to. Let him talk you into staying with us, you'll be sorry later. Cause he'll forget you soon as he sees comebody else he likes. And you'll have let somebody talk you out of an education."

"Nobody can talk me out of *that,*" Lou said fervently.

"Good," Sam said. "I really think, if you have this opportunity to lead a normal life and advance yourself, you should take it, Lou."

"That's right," Ulysses agreed. "Go on with your fine self and get that ed-u-mucation."

"Yeah. Keep on steppin' and don't look back—and don't worry about us hard-faces. We got muscles and mustaches, we can take care of ourselves."

Lou looked at David and saw he was speaking the truth. He had always been tall, but now the inside of him had caught up with the outside. The skinny, big-eyed baby of the group had filled out, grown a mustache, and become a strong young man. He had a deeper voice, too. No wonder he suddenly had to strain for the high notes. Observing this made her feel better about letting the guys go on without her. They were all grown now. They would be able to fend for themselves.

"Won't you miss your family?" Mrs. Braxton inquired. "Your mother, and your brothers and sisters?"

Lou's mouth was full. It gave her time to think about the folks at home—William, Momma, Aunt Jerutha, Bernice and

Clarice and the rest—before she answered. "I'll miss William and Aunt Jerutha most," she said, "but they'll be fine without me. I'm going to write them and Momma tonight and tell them I've found a new family here. I'll say it's all your fault, Mrs. Braxton, for helping me find them."

"Child, you've just begun to find them! Now they're finding *you*. While you were out today, the phone kept jumping off the hook. The L Street Churches want to visit you tomorrow. The other Churches over on Wolf Street wanted to visit you tomorrow too, but I told them you still had to take things slow."

Taking things slow seemed natural in this town with its tropical summer heat, but everyone seemed to be hustling and bustling all week long. Her cousins Kim and Leslie were free on Friday, though, and they took her to the most beautiful beach she had ever seen, an island beach with tall dunes held fast by massive oaks. The warm sand and sun made her feel like she was in Paradise. Cousin Julia's house made her feel that way, too. But then there was Ella Mae and her poverty, and the L Street Churches who were even worse off, working on the docks heading shrimp for a nickel a pound, to offset that feeling.

No matter what they did all day, her cousins made it a habit to drop by after work and sit on Mrs. Braxton's porch to wait for Lou to wake up from her nap. They swung in the porch swing, and rocked in the porch rockers, and told funny tales about woods animals and swamp creatures, and even funnier jokes about humans that were not meant for her ears—right under the window where she was supposedly asleep. The old retired men sat the longest and told the funniest jokes. Uncle William, called Cooch, and Uncle Andrew, called Tick—everyone down here had a nickname that bore no relationship to his given name—never came inside, because Mrs. Braxton didn't allow whiskey in her house, and the porch was outdoors. Sam usually sat up late with them. He was a temperate man, but he liked to have a drink or two late at night.

Though Frank seemed to have disappeared, Ulysses and David continued to show up with Sam at suppertime. Each meal had an undertone of sadness, as if it might be the last one they would share, but no one mentioned the imminent parting. The boys did mention that they might have a surprise for her on Saturday night, if her doctor would allow her to go out for several hours.

She went to Doctor Burnette's office on Thursday and found he would allow her to do whatever she wanted.

"You gave me a scare, girl," he told her. "But you're fine now."

"Thanks to you."

"No. Thank Mrs. Braxton and her collard greens therapy. Your blood tests look good. I take it you've given up psychotropic drugs?"

Lou was puzzled. "What are they?"

"Mood pills, narcotics, pep pills, tranquilizers . . ."

Lou laughed. "I haven't even thought about them in weeks. Besides, I haven't seen my connection lately."

"Whoever he is, don't see him anymore," the doctor warned her.

Never see Frank again? Impossible.

"I want to see you again in four weeks." So the word was around town. If her doctor assumed she was here to say, no doubt everyone else did, too. Probably Dr. Burnette was part of Cousin Julia's circle.

"Now, go be a model teenager, whatever that is," wer her doctor's final instructions.

A model teenager? That, too, was impossible. On the beach last week, she had felt ten years older than her carefree, frolicking cousins. Being a teenager was a phase of life she had skipped over, like an arc of electricity between two live wires. Being a model woman would have to be her goal. At least she had someone now to pattern herself on.

On Saturday night, The Soul Brothers made their debut as a trio. They sang without her at Selden Park, a large community hall in the center of a recreational park. Seated at a table with Mrs. Braxton and Sam Banks, Lou listened proudly. Those were her guys up there, and they were good—not great yet, but good. They would make their way without her.

"They sound fine, Sam," Lou told their manager between numbers.

"Thanks. I'm pretty proud of them, myself. We may have to find another replacement, though. You seem to have inspired young Weldon. He's talking about going back to high school in September."

"I think he planned to do that all along," Lou said.

"Well, I won't try to persuade him to stay with us, so we may have to look for another tenor. Perhaps your cousin can help us. There might be someone in her choir—"

"I'll ask her," Lou promised.

The fellows called her up on the stage for their finale, "God Be With You Until We Meet Again." By now that hymn had so many meanings for Lou, she had to have a good cry in the ladies' room before she could return to her table.

And even that was not the final good-bye. That was reserved for the great farewell dinner at Cousin Julia's home—now Lou's home, too—on Sunday. First they attended church services, where Cousin Julia alternately soothed the congregation with Bach chorales and excited them with rocking spirituals. Her perfectly blended, well-rehearsed choir of two dozen people sounded like two hundred. Without any warning, Cousin Julia then announced that "her daughter" would sing a solo for the congregation. At that moment, Lou could have cheerfully killed her. She foresaw that life with Cousin Julia was not going to be as heavenly as she had imagined.

But she climbed into the choir loft and sang "How Great Thou Art" without stumbling or missing a note. Then all four of them joined the choir to sing "God Be With You Until We Meet Again," accompanied by the thunderous organ. Cousin Julia had made it the closing hymn.

"That was a terrible thing to do to me," Lou complained in the passenger seat of the funny little car.

"It was a measure of my confidence in you," Cousin Julia said, driving serenely. "It was not, I am happy to say, misplaced."

Cousin Julia flung open the doors of her house and put a red

Chinese silk kimono over her conservative dress for "receiving." Unlike Mrs. Braxton's, hers was not a dry house. The first thing she did was open her well-stocked cellarette for the men who were beginning to arrive. Then she set out trays of liver paté, caviar, and smoked oysters, noting with approval that Lou did not shrink from any of her appetizers. Of course not; she had tasted them all in New York with Marty and Charles.

Sam and the boys were there with Mrs. Braxton, of course, and so were the numerous Churches—imperious Uncle Randolph, beaming Aunt Cordelia, pretty, confident Kim and Leslie, plain Ella Mae and her scrubbed-for-church children. The dock-worker Churches were there too, with *their* four children, and so were the drinking, joking old uncles.

Cousin Julia treated them all with equal graciousness. She seated them all around a long table with two large chafing dishes of shrimp creole she had cooked the night before, two huge bowls of green salad with croutons, French bread, and French wine, which Sam uncorked for her.

"To the future!" she toasted, her arm around Louretta's shoulder. "Here it is at last, right under my roof!"

"But not forever," Lou murmured and slipped out of Julia's embrace. No one, not even her captivating cousin was ever going to own her again.

She ran over the The Soul Brothers, who were looking with raised eyebrows at one another. "She's not phony," Lou hastened to explain. "She's just dramatic. I think she's lived alone too long. But I'll fix that."

Frank looked at her earnestly and said, "This is the best thing that could have happened to you, Lou. Better than anything I could have ever offered you. I wish—"

"Yes?" she asked softly.

He hesitated, cleared his throat, then said, "I wish you the best of luck."

Lou gave him a quick kiss, then looked away from his wet, shining eyes to her newfound relatives, the poor Churches and the comfortable ones, the plain ones and the pretty ones, and the unique one at the piano, playing a baroque improvisation so full of runs and counterpoint it took Lou five minutes to recognize her own composition, "Love Is a River."

"We head up toward home after we leave here," Ulysses whispered to her. "Soon as we get there, we'll tell your folks you're in good hands down here."

"Thanks Ulysses. I've written to Momma and William and Aunt Jerutha, and I'm going to call them tonight, but they'll feel better if you talk to them, too."

Lou looked around her again. These were her folks, too. She would probably quarrel and make up with some of them. Some of them probably did not like each other. That was the way families were. But they were her family—no question about that. The music sparkled.

Love is a river,
Life is a river.

Frank was right. This was the best thing that could have happened to her.

The river never changes,
But the water's never the same.

She had traveled thousands of miles, from East to West, from North to South, only to find herself—of all places—*home.*